Praise for Di...

'Deliciously dark and suspens...
Alex Mich...

'Pacy, twisty and full of shocks, all the way
to the jaw-dropping finale'
S.E. Lynes

'A scorchingly good thriller'
Lisa Hall

'Brimming with tension, riddled with doubt and
suspicion, insidious and compelling with a terrifying
ending that had me catching my breath'
Sue Fortin

'A tense, gripping domestic noir that shows just how fast the
dream of a new life can turn into your worst nightmare'
T.M. Logan

'With twists and turns that will wrong-foot you all the way, a
dash of dark humour and a strong emotional punch'
S.J.I. Holliday

'A thought-provoking and gripping read'
Roz Watkins

'Superb . . . Maps the complex territory of female friendship
with great insight, and kept me gripped from the very start'
Kate Rhodes

'Heartbreaking and nuanced – with a clever twist but so much
more than a thriller . . . beautifully written and gripping'
Catherine Cooper

'An intriguing concept and an addictive read'
Annabel Kantaria

'A thoughtful drama exploring an unlikely friendship'
John Marrs

DIANE JEFFREY is a *USA Today* bestselling author. She grew up in North Devon, in the United Kingdom. She now lives in Lyon, France, with her husband and their three children, Labrador and cat. *The Crime Writer* is her seventh book.

Diane is an English teacher. When she's not working or writing, she likes swimming, running and reading. She loves chocolate, beer and holidays. Above all, she enjoys spending time with her family and friends.

Readers can find out more about Diane and her books on her website: https://www.dianejeffrey.com/

Also by Diane Jeffrey

Those Who Lie
He Will Find You
The Guilty Mother
The Silent Friend
The Couple at Causeway Cottage
The Other Couple

THE CRIME WRITER

DIANE JEFFREY

ONE PLACE. MANY STORIES

HQ
An imprint of HarperCollins*Publishers* Ltd
1 London Bridge Street
London SE1 9GF

www.harpercollins.co.uk

HarperCollins*Publishers*
Macken House, 39/40 Mayor Street Upper,
Dublin 1, D01 C9W8, Ireland
This edition 2025

1

First published in Great Britain by HQ,
an imprint of HarperCollins*Publishers* Ltd 2025

Copyright © Diane Jeffrey 2025

Diane Jeffrey asserts the moral right to be identified as the author of this work.
A catalogue record for this book is available from the British Library.

ISBN: 9780008735579

This novel is entirely a work of fiction. The names, characters and incidents
portrayed in it are the work of the author's imagination. Any resemblance to
actual persons, living or dead, events or localities is entirely coincidental.

All rights reserved. No part of this publication may be reproduced, stored
in a retrieval system, or transmitted, in any form or by any means,
electronic, mechanical, photocopying, recording or otherwise,
without the prior permission of the publishers.

Without limiting the author's and publisher's exclusive rights, any unauthorized
use of this publication to train generative artificial intelligence (AI) technologies
is expressly prohibited. HarperCollins also exercise their rights under Article
4(3) of the Digital Single Market Directive 2019/790 and expressly reserve this
publication from the text and data mining exception.

Printed and bound in the UK using 100% Renewable
Electricity by CPI Group (UK) Ltd

This book contains FSC™ certified paper and other controlled sources
to ensure responsible forest management.

For more information visit: www.harpercollins.co.uk/green

*For Emmeline & Maëlys,
my sleeping angels.
17th April 2005*

Missing, Presumed Murdered
A True Crime Podcast
Hosted by Gabriela Conti
2024

This eight-part series, hosted by North Devon Echo *journalist Gabriela Conti, examines the case of Leona Walsh – the thirty-four-year-old mother of two whose husband, Matthew Walsh, reported her missing on 1st December 2019. She was last seen the previous evening, jogging with her dog along the footpath around Wistlandpound Reservoir on the edge of Exmoor.*

Despite the extensive search conducted in the surrounding area throughout the month of December, no trace of Leona was found, and to this day, five years later, the disappearance remains shrouded in mystery.

The case received unprecedented media and public attention. Everyone had a theory and social media was rife with wild speculations. As every member of the British public will know by now, a recent turn of events has brought this mystery back to the fore and reignited an investigation that had grown cold. It may soon be possible to finally shed some light on what really happened to Leona Walsh.

Featuring interviews with family members, police officers and potential witnesses, Gabriela Conti's investigative podcast, a Spotify exclusive, dives deep to uncover the truth about the disappearance of Leona Walsh. Packed to the hilt with shocking revelations and unsettling truths, **Missing, Presumed Murdered** *is a must-listen for all true crime aficionados.*

Chapter 1

Sunday, 1st December 2019: Day One

By the time Matt rang the police, at about eleven a.m., no one had seen Leona since the previous evening. He'd rung round everyone he could think of, although many of his calls had gone unanswered – people having a lie-in on a Sunday morning, he supposed, or perhaps they hadn't turned on their mobiles yet. He hadn't slept a wink and Trixie had been up since the crack of dawn.

Scarlett wasn't back yet, either. She'd gone to her best friend's house yesterday for a birthday party and stayed over. Just as well. She'd missed some of the drama. Her friend's mother was on her way over to drop Scarlett home. With Leona absent, Matt desperately wanted Scarlett and Trixie with him. He needed to know that his daughters, at least, were safe.

But when the doorbell went, it wasn't Scarlett or the police. It was Roxanne. Through the frosted glass in the front door, he could make out her large frame. He should have known his sister-in-law would be round here like a shot the second he called to ask if Leona was at her place. He swore under his breath and Sydney, his Australian shepherd, growled as Matt opened the door. Roxanne erupted into the hallway, accompanied by a cold blast of wind. Her shoulder-length black hair, messy at the best of times, had gone uncontrollably frizzy in the humid air.

'Have you rung 999?' she demanded.

Behind Roxanne, through the open door, Matt glimpsed low, dark clouds laden with rain, or more likely snow, hanging intimidatingly over the hills. He and Leona had bought Blackmoor Manor for many reasons – size, tranquillity, charm, nearby schools. Perched on the top of the hill, the Georgian building dominated the small village and surrounding countryside. It was the end of May when the estate agent had first shown them around the house and fragrant lilac clusters of wisteria mottled the grey stone façade, intoxicating them with its fragrance. But the real clincher had been the view from inside, through the white-latticed window panes, looking out over green hills, undulating as far as the horizon. Today, the snow-capped hills were barely visible and the house's secluded location on the rugged edges of Exmoor might have struck them as more of a drawback than a selling point.

Roxanne handed him her coat and repeated her question.

'The police are on their way,' he answered. He didn't admit he'd rung them only a few minutes ago.

He was about to close the door behind Roxanne when a car pulled into the driveway. Scarlett leapt out and rushed to him, throwing herself into his arms. He held her tightly and bent his head to breathe in the fruity smell of her hair.

Her friend's mother also got out of the car and came to the front door. 'Any news?' she said.

He was going to get this question a lot, he could tell. 'Afraid not.'

'Please let me know if there's anything I can do.'

'That's very kind of you. Thank you.'

Trixie, who must have heard voices from her bedroom, came down the stairs as he was hanging up Roxanne's and Scarlett's coats on the pegs in the hall. His younger daughter was pale, worry written all over her heart-shaped face, which, in turn, made Matt worry even more.

'Oh, Beatrix.' Roxanne pulled her niece into a hug, which made Trixie stiffen and Matt scowl. Trixie wasn't comfortable with physical contact, never had been. Roxanne knew that.

As usual, the dog failed to read the room and jumped up at Scarlett, wagging his tail and trying to lick her face. He then licked Roxanne's hand, to her obvious disgust. She had several cats, including one of those furless monstrosities, but she was not a dog person. Or a people person, for that matter. Matt pulled the dog away by the collar and Roxanne wiped her hand on her jeans.

'Mum will come home, won't she, Dad?' Scarlett asked, her eyes glistening with tears.

'Of course she will,' Roxanne answered for him.

He glared at his sister-in-law, but if she noticed, she pretended not to. Roxanne couldn't know for certain Leona would come home. She was giving Scarlett false hope.

'Did someone find Sydney?' Scarlett asked him, stroking the dog's ears.

'What do you mean?'

'You said Mum didn't come home after her run,' Scarlett said, 'but the dog's here. Did she go jogging without him or did someone bring him home?'

'Sydney came home by himself.'

He ushered Roxanne, Scarlett and Trixie into the living room. He was shaking, his whole body burning and shivering at the same time, as if he had the flu.

'Why aren't the police here yet? How long ago did you ring them? Did you give them directions? This place isn't easy to find, you know. Did you tell them Leona has been struggling with …?'

This was so typical of Roxanne, launching questions, one after the other, without taking a breath. Classic Roxanne, too, not to finish her sentences. But he knew what she was referring to. Leona's recent – and very public – fall from grace.

'They'll be here soon. I expect they recognised her name when I told them on the phone.' His voice sounded calmer than he felt, but he was sure everyone could hear the tremor in it even so. He needed to get a grip. He couldn't lose it, not in front of his daughters.

Roxanne plopped down on one of the sofas and gestured for the girls to sit on either side of her. He perched on the other sofa, ready to jump up again when the police arrived. The whole room was doused in an awkward silence, which, for once, his sister-in-law made no attempt to break. He was fiddling with his wedding band. He clasped his hands in his lap to stop himself.

He scanned the room. It was brimming with Leona's touch, her presence everywhere even in her absence. Her choice of décor – oak flooring; a wooden coffee table with two soft grey sofas facing each other across it, and matching armchairs at either end of it. The sofas and chairs were cluttered with cushions of various sizes and colours and a hodgepodge of prints adorned the walls – 'a pop of colour to zhuzh up the living room', as Leona had phrased it. At the far end of the room was an open hearth – he'd lit the fire. A low bookcase, stocked with magazines and books, spread the length of the wall nearest the seating area and above that was an obscenely large flat-screen smart TV. The overall vibe was homely.

Leona grinned at him from a framed, blown-up photo resting on top of the bookcase. The picture had been there for months – he still hadn't got round to hanging it on the wall. He'd taken the photo the summer before last, on holiday in Madeira. Leona was wearing a sarong over her bikini, standing on the beach, in sharp focus, while the ocean provided a blurred, turquoise background. Although her hair was scraped back into a ponytail, copper corkscrews leaked from under her straw sunhat. Even from where he was sitting, five or six feet away, he could make out the constellation of freckles along her nose and cheeks and – the part he liked best – Scarlett, Trixie and himself reflected in her sunglasses.

The faint crunch of tyres on the gravel in the driveway beckoned him back to the present. Tearing his eyes away from the picture, he glanced at Roxanne. She was deep in conversation with Scarlett and didn't seem to have heard the car approaching. The doorbell went, making him jump, even though he was expecting it.

'Maybe it's Mum,' Scarlett said. An invisible, icy finger jabbed his heart at the hopefulness in her voice.

'She wouldn't ring the doorbell,' Trixie pointed out. Her voice was barely audible and she was trembling. The situation was likely to get a lot more stressful. How would she bear up?

Moments later, he was sitting on the end of his sofa again. The two uniformed officers, who had introduced themselves as Sergeant Lucy Harris and Constable Owen Wright, sat in the armchairs. Harris looked to be in her early thirties, although her confident demeanour made her seem older. Wright was a fair bit younger – and rounder – than his superior. Either he hadn't showered that morning or else he was a sweaty individual – Matt had caught a whiff of body odour as Wright walked past him in the hallway.

Matt asked the girls to go upstairs to avoid upsetting them more and Constable Wright dispatched Roxanne to the kitchen to 'rustle up', as he put it, cups of tea for everyone.

Wright wiped his beefy hands on his trousers – a sweaty individual, then – and produced a notebook and pen from a pocket in his jacket. Harris cleared her throat and brushed her crooked fringe out of her eyes with her forefinger.

'Mr Walsh, I'd like to start by checking a few details you gave over the phone. You rang this morning to report your wife missing?' Harris said. He nodded. 'Full name: Leona Walsh, aged thirty-four? You haven't seen her since yesterday evening?' He nodded again. 'What time was it when you last saw her?'

'About five o'clock. She went out for a run.'

'Can you describe exactly what she was wearing?'

'Black leggings, a long-sleeved T-shirt, blue, I think. Pink-and-black running shoes. Nikes. She took a rucksack with her – she runs with it on her back – a small one, red.'

'What was in the rucksack?'

'Dog poo bags; the dog's toy: a plastic ball on a string; her mobile phone; keys: a door key and an intelligent car key and a few other keys on a Union Jack keyring. Um, that sort of thing.' He wasn't sure why he'd added so much detail. The police certainly didn't need him to describe Sydney's toy and Leona's keyring, but he wanted to be precise.

'Is it normal for her to go jogging in the dark?' Constable Wright asked, looking up from his pad.

'Yes. She runs almost every day. Usually in the evenings. She wears a headlamp.'

'Always the same route?'

'More or less. She tends to run at Wistlandpound Reservoir as we live so close – in the woods or around the reservoir. Sometimes she starts out from here, runs to the reservoir, around it and then back; sometimes she parks her car there, goes for a run, then drives home. Yesterday she took the car. She took the dog, too – she always does – but he came back alone about two hours later.' He was aware he was gushing. He wanted to get all the important information out. 'I don't know if she dropped him off and went somewhere else or if the dog came home by himself. Actually, I don't even know if she went to Wistlandpound. I just assumed that was where she went. It's where she always goes.'

'What makes you think she might have dropped off the dog and gone somewhere else afterwards? Has she done that before?' Sergeant Harris had taken over again and Constable Wright went back to feverishly scribbling notes.

'No. It's totally out of character for her not to come home like this. But …' He took a deep breath. He had to confess something, but he wouldn't come out of it looking good. 'We had a row last night,' he said sheepishly. 'My wife and I. She was about to go for a run and we had this huge argument. She stormed out and we haven't heard from her since. I thought maybe she'd decided to go somewhere to calm down. A friend's house, her sister's, maybe. But I've called everyone I can think of and no one knows where she is.' Hearing the panic rising in his voice, he forced it down a notch. 'I rang her, too – several times – but it went straight to voicemail each time. She must have turned off her phone. I thought she didn't want to speak to me.'

'And you haven't checked the car park at Wistlandpound Reservoir for her car?' Sergeant Harris asked. There was no note of disapproval in her voice, and yet he felt wrong-footed, as if he was under the microscope and every error he made would be magnified.

'No. I wanted to, but I couldn't leave Trixie – that's my younger daughter. She's seven. And I didn't want to take her with me. She was here when my wife and I had our fight and she's still shaken up.'

'OK. We'll have someone check that out immediately,' Harris said.

'Fight?' Wright questioned. 'Did you …' He must have caught the look his superior threw him because his voice trailed off.

Matt looked the constable in the eye. The officer hadn't made a good first impression on him. Not only did he smell ripe, but he was rather insensitive. 'It was a row. I didn't strike my wife, if that's what you want to know.' Matt's hand automatically went to his cheek. The red imprint of Leona's hand had branded his face last night, but this morning the mark had all but disappeared.

'So, you didn't go to the reservoir to look for your wife, even though that's where she usually goes,' Constable Wright said. He seemed to think he needed to play bad cop to Harris's good cop and it was grating on Matt's nerves. In other circumstances, Wright might have given Matt inspiration for one of his characters.

'No, I didn't,' Matt said through gritted teeth.

Harris asked him for the make and model of the car. He gave her the details as Roxanne came into the living room carrying a tray.

'And you think your wife had her phone on her? In her rucksack?' the sergeant asked as Roxanne set the tray on the coffee table. Matt wasn't sure if this was a question or an assertion – Harris's intonation rose at the end of nearly all her sentences.

'She often runs to music – she makes playlists and streams them from her phone, but even when she doesn't, she always has her phone on her, in case, you know, she injures herself running or something like that.'

'When was the last time you tried to get hold of her?'

'I rang her this morning again, just before I called the police. About eleven.'

'Right. We'll check the phone data. We'll need her mobile number.'

'Of course.' He looked it up in his own phone and read it out to Constable Wright.

Roxanne asked the officers how they took their tea and handed out the mugs, giving Matt a moment's breathing space. Wright was scrutinising him and Matt wondered what was going through the constable's head. Did Wright think he was acting suspiciously? Was he? He was anxious not to appear guilty. Of what, he didn't know. Did everyone feel this way when questioned by the police, even when they had nothing to hide?

Wright took a slurp of his tea, then set his mug down on the table. 'Do you think your wife's disappearance could have anything to do with the recent events she's mixed up in?' he asked.

He'd known this would come up, but the officer's brusqueness threw him. Did the man have no filter? He hesitated before answering, shoving his anger aside and fumbling for the right words.

Leona had been a local councillor for a number of years and she was also the election agent for the candidate standing as MP for North Devon in the upcoming general election – less than two weeks away. She'd wanted to stand for MP herself one day. But her future as a politician was looking bleak with allegations of fraudulent expense claims. The story and her photo had been splashed all over the local news on TV and online. Leona had been interviewed by the police, charged and then released pending further investigation, and no doubt pending trial. She'd had to resign from her post the previous week.

'Leona was—'

'My sister has struggled with mental health issues all her life. She suffers from depression and anxiety.' Roxanne certainly hadn't overthought how she was going to phrase what she wanted to say. 'This fake news obviously affected her frame of mind. She was devastated.'

Roxanne was probably wrong about the news being fake – Leona had admitted to him that there was some truth in the allegations against her – but the rest of what his sister-in-law said was spot on.

Harris and Wright exchanged a glance. Matt knew what they were thinking. He knew how this worked. Leona would be graded as high risk given her fragile mental health, and they would have to brace themselves for the inevitable media interest in this case. Leona hadn't quite slipped off the local news pages and now she was about to hit national headlines.

'I'll call this in and get the ball rolling,' Sergeant Harris said, jumping to her feet. 'There aren't many hours of daylight left and it's freezing out there.' Matt must have looked alarmed because she added, 'I know it's easier said than done, Mr Walsh, but try not to worry. Thousands of people go missing in the UK every year and nearly all of them are located within a couple of days.'

He was familiar with the National Crime Agency statistics, having looked them up for research purposes for one of his books. About one hundred thousand adults were reported missing in the United Kingdom annually – seventy-five per cent of them were found within a day; eighty-five per cent within two days. About ninety-nine per cent of them came home – or were found dead – within a year.

Which left one per cent. Matt had the unsettling presentiment that Leona would be one of the few to remain unaccounted for after one year. She wasn't coming home. She wasn't going to be found. Maybe not ever.

Chapter 2

Sunday, 1st December 2019: Day One

Sergeant Harris left the room to make the phone call. When she returned, she and her sidekick resumed their questions, firing them at him in rapid succession. Had his wife gone missing before? Could she have left of her own accord? Could she have gone abroad? Perhaps to get away from the media interest in the allegations made against her? Was she on medication? Would he check her bank statements to see if there was any unusual activity? Could he think of anything else that might be important?

These were easy questions. Matt was able to give answers without reflecting too deeply and without obsessing about whether he came over as suspicious. No, Leona had never gone missing before. This wasn't like her. He found her passport, putting paid to the idea she might have left the country. Leona wouldn't have tried to flee anyway. She was the sort of person who faced her problems head on. Yes, she was on medication – an antidepressant and a mood-stabiliser – but, as far as he could tell, she hadn't taken any medicine with her.

Leona kept note of her passwords on a sheet of A4 paper in a folder in her study. She'd made no secret of this, so, although he wouldn't normally spy on his wife or go through her things, he looked up the codes and checked through her bank statements online. Leona was a big spender – a squanderer – and there were several transactions he couldn't explain in the days and weeks before her disappearance, but nothing that struck him as abnormal for her. If he went further back, he'd no doubt come across a large sum of money or a dubious transfer connected to the embezzlement charges. The fraud investigators had everything they needed, according to Leona, and he couldn't deal with that right now.

When he came back into the living room, Sergeant Harris was on her phone. She ended the call and brought him and Roxanne up to speed. The police had found Leona's car – an ink blue Qashqai – in the car park at Wistlandpound Reservoir. There were no other vehicles. There was no sign of Leona.

'Leona has been graded as a high-risk missing person due to her vulnerabilities,' Sergeant Harris said. 'This means all the required and available resources will be deployed to find her as quickly as possible,' she explained.

Just as Matt had thought. But he knew what it really meant. He didn't need Harris to spell it out for him. The police considered there was a high probability of Leona coming to serious harm.

'I've spoken to the duty officer at the station and he has contacted the on-call superintendent,' Sergeant Harris continued. 'They're organising the first, immediate steps to be taken in order to locate Leona. They'll get the dogs out there immediately and they'll launch a more extensive search first thing tomorrow morning – if your wife's still missing. If that does turn out to be the case, CID will take over the investigation. But we're optimistic it won't come to that. We hope to find her alive and well before then.'

Officers were preparing to carry out a door-to-door, Harris told them, in the hope that one of their neighbours had noticed something useful yesterday evening. More officers had been tasked with a preliminary inspection of the paths and woodland around the reservoir before tomorrow's search got underway.

Matt should have found all this reassuring, but his heart was trouncing against his ribcage. The police were taking this seriously. But that hit home how serious it was.

'I need you to email me a recent photo of your wife, Mr Walsh,' Sergeant Harris said. 'It needs to be good quality and a good likeness. And in colour, obviously. We'll put up posters around the reservoir and surrounding area with your wife's picture on them, appealing for anyone with information or dashcam footage to come forward.'

He chose one he'd taken with his phone in the autumn, before the scandal. A close-up of Leona with a wide, white smile; curly auburn hair tumbling over her shoulders; and large green eyes looking straight into the camera. In it, Leona looked happy; she looked beautiful. The last time he'd seen her, she hadn't looked anything like that. A different picture was imprinted in his mind. Leona's face, contorted in rage, as they argued.

Snow had been falling – heavy and fast – for a couple of hours by this time and already about two inches of snow carpeted the driveway, hills and roads. From the sitting-room window, he took in this monochrome winter tableau that was dimming as daylight faded. Blizzards were forecast for the next day. No one would be out in these conditions; no one would see the posters. No one would come forward with information. His stomach clenched in fear, but he kept his thoughts to himself.

'What happens now?' he asked.

'Mr Walsh, would you mind if we had a quick word with your daughters?' Sergeant Harris said.

He hesitated. He felt an aversion to Constable Wright and didn't want him going near either of his girls. And he didn't want anyone to talk to Trixie.

'I don't know if that's a good idea. They're having a hard time processing this. Scarlett has only just found out her mum hasn't come home and—'

'It will just be a quick chat.' Harris's businesslike tone made it clear she wouldn't take no for an answer. 'You can come with me.'

Roxanne got to her feet, but sat back down when Harris said, 'Perhaps just Mr Walsh and myself? We don't want to overwhelm them.'

At least Wright wasn't going to accompany them upstairs. But Matt's relief was short-lived.

'Mr Walsh, do you mind if I take a look round?' the constable asked.

Matt's eyes darted from Wright to Harris and back to Wright. He wasn't sure if the constable was being nosy and wanted to explore the house – Matt choked back his retort that Roxanne could give him a guided tour – or if he was hoping to find some sort of evidence. Either way, he did mind.

Harris seemed to sense his reluctance. 'We might spot something that could lead us to Leona, give us a clue as to her whereabouts,' she said.

'I'll go with you,' Roxanne said to Wright.

Matt felt a rush of gratitude towards his sister-in-law as she accompanied Constable Wright through the kitchen towards the utility room and garage. Matt headed for the staircase, Sergeant Harris close behind him. Leona would have had a fit if she'd seen the two officers traipsing through her home in their clumpy boots.

Scarlett's bedroom door was ajar and Matt poked his head around it. Scarlett was lying on her bed, which looked like it hadn't been made since she'd last slept in it two nights ago. Her party clothes – a sparkly top, shorts and tights – were strewn on the floor. She was talking to someone on her phone.

'I've got to go,' she said and ended the call.

Spotting the police officer behind him, Scarlett sat up straight. She'd persuaded Leona to let her wear make-up on special occasions, and her face was streaked with the remnants of the mascara she'd applied yesterday evening. She still looked lovely. Her mother's green eyes, but Matt's dark hair.

God, he loved his daughters. He'd have done anything to spare them both from what they were going through, from what he feared lay ahead for them.

'Sergeant Harris would like to talk to you for a few minutes. Is that OK?'

Scarlett shrugged. 'Yeah, OK.'

'Hi, my name is Lucy.'

Scarlett hugged her knees to her chest. 'I'm Scarlett.'

'I saw you on your phone just now. Do you call your mum sometimes, Scarlett? Or text her?'

'Text, mainly.'

'When was the last time she sent you a message?'

'Yesterday. I've written since, but she hasn't texted back. I can show you, if you like?'

'That would be very helpful, if you don't mind.'

Scarlett shrugged again, tapped a couple of times on the screen of her mobile, then handed it to Sergeant Harris.

'May I?' Harris pointed at Scarlett's office chair. Scarlett nodded. Harris sat on the chair and wheeled it a few inches closer to Scarlett. 'Delivered, but not read,' she said aloud.

Matt took a step closer and tried to peer discreetly over Harris's shoulder, but he couldn't make out the messages. Harris scrolled through the most recent texts, then held the mobile out to Scarlett.

'If it's not too nosy of me, what were you doing on your phone just now?' Harris asked.

'I was on Snapchat.'

'That's the one where you post pictures that disappear?'

'Yeah. The minimum age is thirteen, so I'm allowed on it. I'm fourteen.' Scarlett sounded a little defensive.

If Matt had his way, she wouldn't have a mobile at all.

'I'm not very good at social media, but I'm addicted to word games. Words With Friends and Wordscapes,' the sergeant said.

'Yeah, so's my dad. That's how he starts his day. A mug of tea and word games.'

That wasn't how he'd started his day today.

'In that case, your dad and I have more in common than I thought,' Harris said.

Matt caught Harris's wink and the tight smile it elicited from Scarlett.

'He spends hours on social media, too,' Scarlett added.

'It's for work,' he said, half-jokingly, but both Scarlett and Sergeant Harris ignored him.

'Just be careful not to get addicted,' Harris said, standing up.

'Yeah, like that's going to happen.' Scarlett pulled a face. 'My dad limits my screen time. Parental control and protection on everything – phones, TV, tablets.' She rolled her eyes.

'That's not such a bad idea.' Harris handed Scarlett a card. 'Scarlett, if your mum contacts you, would you please let me know? My mobile number is on here. You can call or text. Or send a voice message. Whatever.'

'OK.' Scarlett took the card and set it on her bedside table without glancing at it. 'Do you think you can find her?'

'I hope so, Scarlett. We'll do our very best.'

Matt was grateful to the sergeant for not making promises she might not be able to keep. As he led the way along the landing to Trixie's bedroom, his mouth felt dry and his throat itchy. 'Is it really necessary to bother Trixie? She's—'

'Mr Walsh, I won't "bother" her for long. But if you want to find your wife – and I assume you do – I need to have a chat with everyone who lives with her.'

'Of course ... I ... Of course.'

He knocked on Trixie's door. Trixie's room was very different to her older sister's. Scarlett's was, quite frankly, a hovel, whereas everything in Trixie's room was neat and tidy. Too neat and tidy. Her teddy bears were assembled on top of the bookcase by size; her books were organised on the shelves by colour and then alphabetically. Her bed was made; her clothes, he knew, were hanging or folded neatly in her wardrobe. Posters of marine mammals were perfectly aligned on one wall; Trixie's artwork was displayed on the opposite wall. Pencil sketches, watercolours, charcoal drawings of all sorts of subjects – people, animals, flowers, landscapes, still lifes. The only thing her pictures had in common was the meticulous detail Trixie had injected into each of them.

Harris squinted at Trixie's initials in the corner of one of the paintings. 'Did you do these?' She sounded stunned.

Trixie put down the book she was reading, but didn't look up. She didn't speak, either.

'She's a budding artist,' he answered for her. 'She's very talented for a seven-year-old. She's been drawing since she could hold a crayon.'

'This would show incredible talent for an *adult*,' Harris said. She turned to Trixie. 'This is amazing, Trixie. I'm so impressed.'

'Thanks,' Trixie muttered.

'And I see you're interested in marine life.'

'My latest obsession.'

'Pardon?'

'That's what my mum calls it.'

'Trixie tends to focus on one hobby at a time. Not long ago, she was into origami. Now it's marine mammals,' he explained. 'Trixie, Sergeant Harris would like to talk to you for a minute. OK?'

'OK.'

'I know you must be very worried about your mum,' Harris began. 'Can you tell me when you last saw her?'

'Yesterday.'

'And what was she doing?'

'She was arguing with Daddy in the kitchen.' Trixie glanced at him, perhaps unsure if she was betraying him with her answer. He gave her a nod to show it was fine.

'Did you see her leave the house to go for a run after that,

Trixie?'

'No. Daddy said it would be better if I stayed in my room for a while, so I came upstairs.' Trixie still hadn't made eye contact with the sergeant. 'But she was wearing her running kit,' she added.

'Thank you, Trixie. That's very useful. I can see from your drawings that you have an eye for detail. Can you think of anything else that might be important?'

'Sergeant Harris, is this really …?' Matt stopped mid-sentence when Harris held up a hand.

Trixie thought for a moment. 'The dog was wet,' she said, knitting her eyebrows.

Matt's head spun from Harris to Trixie. He was surprised that his daughter had recalled that when, in his panic last night, he hadn't thought anything of it. She was right.

'The dog was wet?' Harris echoed. 'You mean it came home wet?'

'Yes. Sydney's fur was wet.'

'Thank you, Trixie. I'll bear that in mind. It may well be important,' the sergeant said, throwing a puzzled look at Matt. 'Trixie, Scarlett has a mobile phone. Do you have one, too?'

Trixie shook her head. She'd asked for a mobile for her last birthday, but he and Leona had agreed she was way too young. Trixie hadn't insisted.

'Your sister and your dad both have my phone number. If you think of anything, anything at all, you can ask them to get hold of me. OK?'

'OK.' Finally, Trixie looked up, but Harris had already turned and walked away.

Matt wanted to hug her, squeeze her tight, but he knew she wouldn't want him to. 'You did well, sweetie,' he said. Trixie picked up her book without responding. Matt followed the sergeant out of the room.

'It wasn't raining yesterday, was it?' she said as Matt caught her up on the landing. She turned to look at him, her hand resting

19

on the newel post.

'No.'

'But Trixie said—'

'Yes, Trixie's right. I'd forgotten that. It's strange, though, because the dog wouldn't swim when it's so cold. And we don't ever let him swim at the reservoir – it's forbidden.'

'And you didn't think to mention this until now?' Her tone was inquisitive rather than reproachful.

'No. I ... I'm sorry. I wasn't thinking straight.' Sergeant Harris nodded as if this answer, at least, satisfied her. 'Oh, God, if the dog went into the water ...' He didn't finish his sentence. It didn't bear thinking about.

'We should get going,' Harris said as they made their way down the stairs. 'There's not much more we can do today and it's getting dark.'

The snow was piling up outside at a terrifying rate. He didn't say what he was thinking, that if they dawdled much longer, they might have to stay over. He was sure they didn't want that any more than he did. Roxanne would spend the night. He'd insist on it. She didn't live far away, but she was a timid driver at the best of times. And she didn't have snow tyres.

Constable Wright was waiting with Roxanne at the bottom of the stairs. Matt wondered how much of his conversation with Sergeant Harris they'd overheard. Most of it, probably. Anyway, Harris would no doubt bring Wright up to speed, just as he would repeat everything to Roxanne. His sister-in-law shook her head gently, a sign Matt took to mean the constable hadn't found anything of note while he was snooping around the house. But he was holding something in each hand.

'Is this the dog's lead?' Wright held up the offending item.

It was obvious what it was and Matt was about to come out with a sarcastic comment, but he thought better of it. He got what Wright was driving at. 'Yes.'

'And harness?' Wright lifted up the harness in his other hand.

'They were hanging up on the pegs in the hallway, underneath the coats.'

Constable Wright *had* had a good poke around. He'd been thorough. 'Leona might have taken the lead and harness if she'd set off from here,' Matt said, 'but she doesn't need to when she drives as far as the reservoir. The dog stays beside her when she runs. He's very obedient.'

'Don't you have to keep dogs on the lead around the reservoir?'

Two paths wound their way around the perimeter of the lake. Theoretically, you had to keep your dog on a lead around the inner path, presumably so it wouldn't be tempted to go into the water. But Matt didn't dignify Wright with an answer. He took the lead and harness from the constable's hands, hung them back on the peg under the coats, then opened the front door for the officers. An unsubtle hint that it was time they got going.

Harris stepped outside, paused, then whirled round to face him. 'Oh, Mr Walsh?'

Judging from her tone, something important had just crossed her mind. In his novels, he often had a police officer ask the main suspect a particularly tricky question at the end of a chapter. He called it a 'Columbo moment'. He sensed this was what was about to happen and braced himself.

'What was the argument about?' she asked.

'Sorry?' He knew full well what she was referring to.

'With your wife? What were you arguing about?'

He needed to give an airbrushed version of this. 'I don't remember the details. We argue, quite often, Leona and I.' One of Harris's eyebrows leapt into her wonky fringe. 'Well, probably no more than most couples,' he added hastily. He should never have mentioned the damn argument.

'So you don't recall what it was about?'

'No, not really. Something to do with the kids, probably. We don't always see eye to eye on how to bring them up. Or money, maybe.'

According to Leona, he couldn't keep a poker face when he lied. She said he had a tell – but she wouldn't tell him what it was. Was he giving himself away?

Harris narrowed her eyes at him. She clearly didn't believe a word he'd just said. He stared her down. He couldn't possibly tell her the truth. If he admitted to Sergeant Harris what the row was about, it would give him a motive. The truth would convince the police he'd killed his wife.

Missing, Presumed Murdered
A True Crime Podcast Hosted by Gabriela Conti
Audio File 1
Interview with Roxanne Barrett, Leona's sister.
2024

This is the story of Leona Walsh, whose disappearance in December 2019 has remained a mystery for nearly five years. Join me as I explore the truths and lies in this case. I am Gabriela Conti and you're listening to **Missing, Presumed Murdered**, *a true crime podcast.*

Gabriela Conti: Roxanne, thank you for talking to me today. You must miss your sister very much and I appreciate this is painful for you.
Roxanne Barrett: Yes, it is.
GC: I can only imagine how hard this has been for you and your family. Has it made you closer?
RB: I've grown closer to my nieces, definitely. But my brother-in-law, well, that's a different story. The police suspected Matthew, you know. I mean, they had nothing on him. But they seemed to think he'd had a hand in this right from the start.
GC: How do you know they suspected him?
RB: Just the way they treated him, the way they questioned him, the way they looked at him. They searched the house, you know.
GC: I think that's normal procedure in a missing per—
RB: It's always the husband anyway, isn't that what everyone says? I mean, he had to be the obvious suspect.
GC: And what about you? Did you blame your brother-in-law for your sister's disappearance?
RB: Well, yes! If they hadn't had that argument, she wouldn't have gone missing, would she? She'd probably still be here today.
GC: Did you think Matthew Walsh was capable of foul play, though?

RB: Well, at the time, I wondered, but I couldn't be sure. I didn't like my brother-in-law, never have. Oh, he loved Leona, no doubt about that. But he said and did a few things that struck me as odd when she went missing.

GC: What sort of things?

RB: Well, for example, the dog came back without Leona, and he was wet, which made us think she might have gone into the reservoir for some reason and the dog went in after her. But the thing is, Matt didn't go to look for her. He said it was because he didn't want to upset Trixie any more than she already was – Trixie had witnessed their row, you see – but that just didn't hold water for me. Oops. No pun intended. He didn't go to look for her car, either. The police found it, parked at the reservoir. But you'd have thought Matt would have driven there to take a look, wouldn't you? It's only down the road. But, no, he didn't want to take Trixie with him and he couldn't leave her behind on her own. Then, of course, there was the fire.

GC: The fire?

RB: Yes. He lit a fire in the living room – an open log fire – while he was waiting for the police to arrive. I mean, who does that?

GC: It was a cold winter's day. Maybe that explains it? Or maybe he just didn't know what to do with himself while he was waiting.

RB: Maybe.

GC: So, you thought there was a possibility he—

RB: And finally, there was the way he was acting. It was really bizarre. At first, I thought he was being pessimistic. I was trying to reassure the girls, telling them everything would be all right, and he told me not to get their hopes up. He seemed to know what was coming next – the search, the investigation, the speculation, the media frenzy.

GC: I suppose with his experience in the police and the genre he writes in—

RB: No, it was more than that. Everyone else thought the row had been the last straw for Leona. She'd been under a lot of pressure.

We all assumed she needed some time out and she was on her own, cooling off somewhere. We expected her to walk through the door and die of embarrassment – sorry, bad choice of words – we knew she'd be mortified as soon as she realised how much fuss she'd caused by vanishing off the face of the earth. But Matt, well, he never considered the possibility she might show up at any minute. It was like he knew, right from the start, that she wouldn't be coming back.

Chapter 3

April 2024

'A Roman coin?' Gabi repeats in disbelief. 'Wow! That's exciting!' It comes out sounding ironic, which isn't her intention. She's genuinely interested in history and in the area.

Mick, the news editor, clicks his pen on and off. And then on again. As far as Gabi can see, he hasn't written anything – the only paper on his desk is today's edition of the *North Devon Echo* – but he has several chronic tics and irritating habits. 'Good. Glad to see you so enthusiastic for once.' His tone is equally ironic, but deliberately so.

He has a point. She used to be ambitious. She was driven. She had a rep for being tenacious, and she was proud of that. She'd envisaged herself one day working as a news correspondent for the BBC. Or ITV, she wasn't fussy. On TV. Or working for a major national newspaper based in London. She hadn't planned to spend her whole life working as a hack for the local rag. But that was before the pandemic. And before *him*. Or before he did what he did, anyway. Over four years later, and she still can't say his name. Even the sound of it in her head makes her feel sick. Darren Hughes.

'Oh, and Gabriela?' Mick leans back in his ergonomic swivel chair and rakes his free hand through his buzzcut. 'Take Joe with you. His spelling and grammar leave a lot to be desired, but he takes far better photos than you.'

Gabi groans inwardly. She'd rather go alone. No, that's not quite true. She'd rather go without Joe. But before she can protest, Mick shoos her out of the office.

She groans again – out loud this time – when Joe insists on driving. She's amazed he still has a valid licence. She's never known him to keep to the speed limit and she remembers him crossing the solid white lines to overtake along the link road on more than one occasion. She gets into his bright orange Vauxhall Corsa – God, it's like sitting inside a giant satsuma – fastens her seatbelt and checks it's done up. When Joe starts the engine, music blares out – some sort of angry hip-hop or rap. She reaches out and turns it down a notch.

'You can switch it off, if you like,' Joe says. She does. He turns to look at her through his clear blue eyes. She wishes he'd keep them on the road. 'Not a fan of grime, then?' he asks.

'What?'

'Dizzee Rascal? Not your bag?'

'Oh. No.' Definitely not her bag.

'What do you listen to in the car?'

'Babbel podcasts,' she admits, steeling herself for a scornful remark. But it doesn't come. Instead, an uncomfortable silence invades the car. She almost wishes she hadn't turned off Joe's dreadful music.

Joe has been at the *Echo* for at least seven years now. They hit it off immediately and she found the days raced by when they worked together. But their banter, which flowed so freely before, has dried up. Their jokes fall flat and they no longer poke fun at each other. They've winnowed down their conversation to safe subjects and small talk. It was easier when their flirting couldn't be taken seriously, when Joe was still blissfully unaware his girlfriend was cheating on him and Gabi was still under the delusion she was engaged.

'I'm learning Italian,' she adds eventually to break the silence.

'Right. Thought you *were* Italian.'

She scoffs. 'My grandparents were. They came to England in the 1950s, settled in Reading. My grandmother worked as a cleaner and my grandfather as a gardener. They'd be ashamed of me. I can't even cook dried pasta "*al dente*".'

He clearly doesn't know how to respond to that. He taps the fingers of his left hand on the gear stick. She gazes out of the window. Joe is careening round the bends on a narrow country lane that has lush green grass growing in the middle of it. Hedges and woodland flash by at an alarming speed. She closes her eyes, but as a wave of nausea breaks over her, she snaps them open again. They've reached the brow of a hill. A patchwork blanket of green and yellow fields is laid out in the valley below them. Beyond that, the thick blue stripe of the Bristol Channel underlines the cerulean sky. The car hurtles down the hill and she feels as if she's on a rollercoaster, her right foot pumping an imaginary brake in the passenger's footwell. She resists the urge to order Joe to hold the steering wheel with both hands. Preferably at ten to two.

They pass a sign pointing right for Wistlandpound Reservoir, three and a half miles away. Gabi glances down that road and her mind wanders along it – a brief detour down memory lane. The last time she was in this neck of the woods was nearly five years ago, when she investigated the disappearance of Leona Walsh. Gabi had been at school with Leona, although they hadn't been close friends – they hadn't been friends at all, in fact – and they'd long since lost touch, but the connection gained her access to the family that she would not have otherwise had. It was supposed to be the story that launched Gabi's career. But it hadn't panned out. She sighs. She holds Darren responsible for shattering her dreams – all of them – but deep down she knows she only has herself to blame.

'Didn't that family live out here somewhere?' It comes as no surprise that Joe has been reminded of the case, too. It was a major news story, both locally and nationally, for weeks on end. 'The missing woman? The Walshes, was it?'

'Yep. Blackmoor Manor.'

'Right. Blackmoor Manor.' Joe whistles through his teeth. 'Sounds posh.'

'It is. Massive house. Isolated. The husband and kids still live there, as far as I know.'

'I remember you were like a dog with a bone, determined to solve the mystery. I read all your pieces. I was a bit jealous not to be working on it myself, but someone had to cover the village fêtes and agricultural shows. They never found her, did they? The Walsh woman?'

'No.' She wants to tell him she knew Leona personally. She's tempted to tell him the whole story; she even feels like admitting why she dropped it. But if she spirals down that particular rabbit hole, she won't be able to climb back out.

'Must be really hard for the kids. Not knowing what happened to their mother, being brought up by their father. They must wonder if they're living with their mother's killer. Everyone else does.'

Gabi turns sharply to look at Joe. Sometimes it's as if he can read her mind. Those are the questions that writhe around inside her head, too. Did Trixie and Scarlett's father kill their mother? What's it like growing up with that doubt?

'What do you think happened to her?' Joe asks. 'Do you think he bumped her off?'

'Hmm.' She got to know Matt back then and she doesn't think he's a killer. But you never really know someone, as Gabi has learnt to her cost. 'You've missed the turning!'

'Bollocks!' Joe slams on the brakes, putting an end to their first actual conversation in months, reverses at high speed and turns onto the right road. The car is now bouncing over potholes that Joe could avoid if he would just slow down.

'This place,' Joe complains. 'Terrible roads, far too many sheep, too much traffic in the summer, crap weather all year round. I bloody hate it here.'

Gabi knows where Joe's dislike of the area really stems from. Joe relocated to North Devon from Bath because his girlfriend got a job working for a local pharmaceutical manufacturing business, if she remembers correctly. A couple of years ago, his girlfriend started having an affair with the CEO of the company. Joe found out and broke up with her. Gabi wonders if he'll move back to Bath one day. She hopes not, but she doesn't dare to ask him.

Joe pulls up in front of a cottage situated on a corner of the country road meandering through the small village of Benton. They've arrived – safely – at their destination. Gabi breathes a sigh of relief.

'This is it,' Joe says, grabbing his camera from the back seat. He gets out of the car and stands at the wooden gate at the bottom of the driveway.

Gabi joins him. The sign on the gate identifies the house as Rose Cottage. This is definitely the right place, although there's not a rose in sight. Apart from the chimney, poking up to the left of the thatched roof, the white cottage is perfectly symmetrical – two windows upstairs and two downstairs with the front door in the middle under a thatched porch.

'Quaint,' Joe comments, leaning his elbow on the gate and shooting a few photos.

The lawn is neatly mown either side of the narrow gravel driveway and there are flower beds with daffodils and tulips. But no sign of overturned earth. 'They must have been putting in the extension round the back,' she says.

They follow the high hazel hedge as it rounds the corner. Joe is tall and peers over it easily. She can just about glimpse the back garden if she stands on tiptoe. A square excavation site has been gridded and the area is surrounded by an orange net fence. Other than that, the garden is empty.

'It doesn't look like any work is being carried out here today,' she says.

'Rose Cottage. If there were ever rose bushes here, I'm guessing they've been dug up,' Joe comments.

Gabi thinks she must have spoken her earlier thoughts aloud.

They walk back to the front of the house and up the driveway to the front door. Gabi doubts anyone will be home in the middle of the day, but she knocks anyway. After a few seconds, the door opens and she finds herself face to face with a short, pretty woman about the same age as her. The woman is pregnant and Gabi's gaze is drawn to the large bump. She feels a pang of jealousy.

'Hello. Mrs Martin, is it? I'm Gabriela Conti and this is Joe Knight. We're journalists from the *North Devon Echo*.'

'Hello,' she says. 'Is this about the Roman coin?'

Her tone is friendly and Joe raises his eyebrows at Gabi. Gabi knows that having worked in a city, he's used to doorstepping and begging in order to get a decent photo. She's not above that sort of behaviour herself – in fact, she's been known to stoop to all kinds of devious tactics to get a good story – but people around here don't usually mind talking to journos. Most locals enjoy seeing their names in print. Plus, weeks can go by without a decent splash. Many of the articles they publish in the *Echo* are barely newsworthy, so it's not as if there's a pack of reporters hounding people at all hours of the day and night. Major news stories like the disappearance of Leona Walsh seldom happen in North Devon.

'Yes, we're writing an article about your discovery, Mrs Martin,' Gabi says, 'and we were wondering if we could ask you a few questions about it?'

'Of course. Do come in.' She leads the way through the house and into the living room. 'And it's Alicia,' she adds over her shoulder. 'I've been married for over a year, but I can't get used to being called "Mrs Martin".'

The living room is cramped, but bright. Joe and Gabi take

the armchairs.

'Would you like something to drink?' Alicia offers.

'Oh, no, that's fine, thank you,' Joe replies for both of them.

Gabi glares at him. She's dying for a coffee. Alicia sits on the sofa.

'Do you mind if I record our conversation?' Gabi asks, fishing in her handbag for her phone. She often just takes notes – it can be less intimidating – but Alicia seems at ease with their presence.

'No problem,' Alicia says.

Gabi places the mobile on the coffee table and taps the red record button. 'So, perhaps we could start at the beginning. When did you find this coin? And how?'

'Well, my husband and I decided to put in an extension, to make the kitchen bigger, you know? We love the cottage, but it's rather small. And the builders had just started work when they found this coin. It turned out to be a twenty-four-carat gold coin with the face of the Roman emperor Allectus on it. I'd never heard of him, to tell you the truth. Apparently, he died in about three hundred AD, or CE, as I believe we're supposed to say now.'

'That's unbelievable! We're talking – what? – over seventeen hundred years ago.'

'That's right.'

'Excuse me for asking this,' Joe cuts in, 'but do you have any idea how much the coin is worth?'

Joe is supposed to leave the questions to Gabi, but she tries not to mind. Besides, she's curious about that, too.

'A rough idea. A similar coin was found near a Roman road in Kent a few years ago and it fetched five hundred and fifty thousand pounds at auction,' Alicia says.

'Crikey! And is it finders keepers? I mean, do you get the money?'

If Alicia is thrown by Joe's intrusiveness, she certainly doesn't show it. 'So I've been told,' she says. 'The coin has been taken away to be cleaned up and examined and so on, but eventually we can sell it at auction or to a museum. I've got some photos of the coin. Would you like to see?'

Without waiting for an answer, she brings up the pictures on her phone. Gabi and Joe lean in to see.

'Ooh, these are great,' Gabi says. 'Would you mind emailing some of them to me?'

'Not at all.'

Gabi selects three of them, gives Alicia a business card and points at the email address at the bottom of her contact details.

'I'll do it straightaway before I forget,' Alicia says.

Gabi and Joe wait patiently while she sends off the photos. Gabi wonders why on earth Joe had to tag along. Alicia's photos will do the trick. Other than the square, shallow plot of earth in the back garden, what can Joe possibly take a picture of? She wouldn't put it past Mick to have insisted she take Joe with her as a matchmaking venture. He can be a little irritating, their boss, but he's a soppy romantic at heart. It's never going to happen, though. Once bitten and all that.

'What about your extension?' Gabi asks once Alicia's email shows in the inbox on her phone.

'Well, obviously we've had to delay the extension until the excavation is finished. There's a team of archaeologists working in the back garden.'

'Not today,' Joe comments wryly, perhaps thinking of a wasted photo opportunity.

'Do they think they might find something else?' Gabi says.

'They're checking in case.'

'Do you happen to have a contact number for the archaeologist leading the excavation?'

'No, I'm afraid not. But he's a professor at the University of Exeter. He should be easy enough to track down. Gareth Something.'

Gabi types a few words into her smartphone. 'Gareth Harvey. Professor of Archaeology,' she reads aloud, angling her phone towards Alicia so she can see the academic's profile pic.

'Yes, that's him.'

A phone number and an email address are displayed under Professor Harvey's photo. Gabi screen-grabs the page. 'That's great, thank you,' she says to Alicia, then to Joe, 'I'll get in touch with him and hopefully we'll get a good quote. Do you want to take some photos of the back garden before we leave?'

'You can go through the patio door in the kitchen,' Alicia says, pointing Joe in the right direction.

Gabi stops the recording and while Joe is gone, she makes small talk with Alicia, asking about her pregnancy and the baby.

'We'd hoped to have the kitchen in by the time he came along,' Alicia says, patting her bump. 'We'd have done it straightaway after moving in, but money was a bit tight back then.'

Gabi laughs. 'With a bit of luck, the coin will cover the price of the extension now.'

'Yes, actually, it will probably pay off our mortgage altogether.'

'That's brilliant!' Gabi says. 'When did you move in?'

'Nearly two years ago now. In the summer of 2022. The place was a bit run down. We're trying to give the cottage a bit of TLC. We've repainted it and I've been tending to the front garden.'

'It looks very nice. Hopefully you'll get your back garden and new kitchen sorted out soon,' Gabi says.

Joe comes back inside and closes the patio door. 'OK. We're good to go.'

Once they're outside, he turns to Gabi. 'I noticed on the way here that Rose Cottage is conveniently situated a stone's throw from the village pub,' he says. 'Fancy a swift pint?'

'No.' She watches his face fall. 'But I could murder a pie and chips.'

'My treat,' he says, brightening.

She wonders if a pub lunch will break the ice between them and get them back to where they were. She misses not feeling able to confide in him, gibe at him. But they barely say a word for the next half an hour. Sitting opposite each other at a wooden table by an unlit fire, they tuck into their pub lunches, studiously avoiding eye contact. Her steak and kidney pie is cold and her white wine is warm, but she eats up and drinks up in silence. Joe's paying, so it would be rude to complain.

Gabi ransacks her brain for something to say, but can't come up with anything. Absent-mindedly, she surveys the room. There aren't many people in the pub – an old man sitting on a high stool at the bar and a couple with a small dog at a table to their right. And a man sitting alone at the corner table.

With a jolt, she recognises him. She leans across the table towards Joe. 'Don't look now,' she whispers conspiratorially, 'but the guy behind you ... it's Matthew Walsh.'

Joe whirls round. Matthew Walsh's head is lowered. He's nursing an empty pint glass in his hands and staring into it. He doesn't look up. Joe turns back to Gabi, who rolls her eyes at him.

'I said, "Don't look now."'

'What's he doing here? We're way out in the sticks. Literally in the middle of nowhere.'

'I don't know. It's not exactly his local, but he doesn't live far away, as I said earlier. Like journos, some authors like to write in cafés. Perhaps he finds inspiration for his work in pubs. Or maybe he's waiting for someone.'

'Then they're very late. We've been here half an hour already. And he doesn't look particularly inspired. He certainly didn't come here for the food. It's disgusting.'

'It could just be a coincidence.'

'Hmm.' Joe's tone makes it clear he doesn't believe in coincidences. Neither does she, really, but she doubts there's any more to it than that. Joe glances over his shoulder, more discreetly this time. 'Is it my imagination, or does he look worried?'

Gabi scrutinises Matthew Walsh. His shoulders are hunched, his brow is furrowed and he's biting his lip. Joe's right. He looks very anxious indeed.

Chapter 4

Monday, 2nd December 2019: Day Two

Matt was having another restless night. He wasn't used to tossing and turning. He'd always slept well. On occasion, he would wake up with a brainwave for the book he was working on – a 'novel' idea, as he called it – which he would jot down on a piece of paper so he wouldn't forget his thoughts by the morning. But he invariably went straight back to sleep. Leona was the insomniac, always overthinking conversations and obsessing over tricky work situations. She would roam the house at night like a ghost, pacing up and down the living room, or sit for a while at the table in their farmhouse kitchen – her favourite room in the whole house – before coming back to bed.

He was shattered, physically and mentally, but sleep remained elusive. He glanced at the red digits of the bedside clock, glowing in the dark and taunting him. 2:03. Two in the morning. He heard Trixie creep into Scarlett's room. He made himself wait for twenty minutes, his eye on the time, then he got up and turned on the light in the upstairs hallway so he could check in on the two of them. They were both fast asleep in Scarlett's single bed. Scarlett's arm was hanging out of the bed, so he tiptoed into the room and gently placed it by her side, under the covers. He kissed each of the girls on the cheek, gently, so as not to wake them. Trixie's thumb was in her mouth.

Over a year ago, Leona had promised to redecorate Trixie's bedroom if she gave up sucking her thumb. As always, Leona had known which button to press. Trixie had been moaning for a while that her room was babyish. She stopped sucking her thumb on the spot and Leona gave the bedroom a complete make-over. She tore down the wallpaper frieze of princesses and fairies. Out went the pink Barbie curtains, replaced with plain lavender ones that matched the new bedsheets Trixie had chosen. Matt hung Trixie's pictures on the freshly painted cream walls. He bought her a desk. Trixie continued to do her homework downstairs, where he could help her, but she did her artwork upstairs from then on. She was thrilled with her new bedroom. But tonight, apparently, she didn't want to sleep in it. And she'd reverted to the infantile habit she'd given up. Poor thing. Who could blame her?

He went downstairs to make himself one of Leona's herbal teas. He flicked on the light and gave a shriek of alarm.

'Jesus, you startled me! What are you doing, sitting here in the dark?' Matt tried not to mind that Roxanne was sitting in Leona's place at the rustic, wooden table.

'Sorry.' His sister-in-law was obviously having trouble sleeping, too.

When he'd suggested she should stay over, she'd put up only a cursory protest. She would have been terrified driving home in such horrible conditions. He insisted she'd be better off here, where she'd get any news of Leona immediately.

He made some camomile tea for both of them and sat down opposite Roxanne. The dog hesitated at the doorway before coming into the kitchen and lying under the table at Matt's feet. Sydney was wary of Roxanne, for some reason. It was reciprocal. Some people just didn't like dogs, Matt understood that, but he tended to mistrust people his dog didn't like. Except for Roxanne. She was family.

For an hour or so, Roxanne reminisced about her and Leona as kids. Their parents had divorced when Roxanne was eight and Leona was six. After that, they saw their father less and less until they became estranged from him altogether. The way Roxanne told it, it was because of this that the two of them had been close since they were little.

But they'd also been very competitive growing up, as Matt knew. Leona had outshone her older sister – at sport, at school, at pretty much everything – and Matt got the impression Roxanne was still shouldering a cumbersome chip. She also seemed to believe that Leona had been their mum's favourite daughter. Matt couldn't confirm or contradict this. Their mum had died of pneumonia shortly before he met Leona.

Roxanne then went through all the scenarios she'd come up with to account for Leona's disappearance. Or nearly all of them – he got the feeling she wasn't sharing everything that was going through her mind. She slitted her eyes at him as she enumerated her theories, as if gauging his reaction. Did she think he had something to do with Leona's disappearance? Or was she as bewildered as he was? He couldn't tell – the two deep grooves that separated her eyebrows made her appear permanently suspicious. He tried to reassure her, but he wasn't very convincing. He was far too worried himself. He left Roxanne at the kitchen table, staring blankly at the clock above the door frame, and went back to bed, hoping Morpheus would finally come for him.

The hours until morning trundled by. Eventually he got some sleep before waking up from a nightmare. Leona, wearing a white see-through nightdress, was standing on the edge of a cliff, her back to him, as if she was about to jump to her death on the rocks below. Running towards her, he called out to her.

She turned to face him. 'You swine!' she shouted. 'You utter bastard!'

That part was real. As far as he knew, Leona didn't own a nightdress like that. But those were the last words she'd spoken to him. Or rather, screamed at him.

His sadness was tinged with anger, and he swiped at a rogue tear and resisted the urge to throw or break something. He got out of bed and pulled back the curtains, hoping the view over the moors would chase away the images and words that were lodged in his head. For as far as he could see – which was only about a hundred metres, the visibility was poor – everything was either white or grey. At least another eight centimetres of snow had fallen overnight. It had relented for now, but an army of dark clouds had assembled overhead, loaded with frozen ammunition and ready to attack. One thing was certain. The bad weather would accompany – and impede – the search.

As he stared out of the window, a Range Rover pulled up outside the front gate. They had a visitor. He pulled on yesterday's clothes, dashed downstairs and opened the front door. A tall, wiry man was standing on the doorstep, a gloved finger poised near the doorbell.

'I'm Detective Constable Andrew Chapman,' he said, removing his leather gloves to shake Matt's hand. 'I've been assigned as your family liaison officer.' The detective also took off his beanie, revealing a bald head and pointed ears. He made Matt think of Roxanne's Sphynx cat.

Matt didn't remember being asked if he wanted a FLO and he didn't relish the idea of having a complete stranger in his home, but if he objected at this point, he'd come over as inconsiderate or uncaring, or worse, guilty. 'Come in,' he said.

Roxanne and the girls joined them in the hallway. DC Chapman introduced himself again for their benefit. He was smartly dressed underneath a thick Puffa jacket, which Matt hung up on a hook in the hall.

'I'll be keeping you posted about any progress in the investigation, and I'll do my best to answer any questions you might have about what's going on,' DC Chapman said. He turned to Matt. 'I'm here to provide support and information to you and your family.'

This worked both ways, Matt knew. DC Chapman had omitted an important part of his job description: he was also tasked with gathering evidence and information about Matt and his family and passing it on to his colleagues.

'We were having breakfast,' Roxanne said. 'I'll make a pot of tea.'

They made their way to the kitchen and sat around the table. Roxanne coaxed Matt to eat something, but even the smell of toast made him retch.

He had no idea if he was expected to make small talk or if that would be deemed inappropriate. 'Terrible weather,' he said to Chapman. In this country no one could be criticised for complaining about the weather, not in any circumstances.

'It's not ideal,' Chapman said, which had to be the understatement of the year, 'but the search is underway. There are mounted police as well as police handlers with sniffer dogs scouring the area around the reservoir; we've got drones up and a police helicopter waiting to go up – as soon as the visibility improves – and I'm told the diving team are on their way.'

'To search in the reservoir itself,' Roxanne finished.

Scarlett looked horrified and Matt shot a reproving glance at his sister-in-law. He drank his tea in silence and left it up to Roxanne to exchange pleasantries with Chapman.

He'd planned to slip away for a while this morning, but now he had an unwanted guest, he felt as if he had to ask for permission. He was also reluctant to leave a police officer in the house while he was out. He popped upstairs for a shower and when he came back down, Chapman was in the living room, scanning the bookcase. Hearing Matt come in, he turned, a paperback – one of Matt's own novels – in his hands.

'So, where do you get your inspiration from?' Chapman asked, waving Matt's book at him.

'It depends. The news, sometimes. At other times, the setting inspires me—'

'Ah, yes. *Murder on the Moors,*' Chapman said, reading the title aloud. 'Not inspired by your time in the police force, then?' He sounded curious, but the question put Matt on his guard. How much did Chapman know?

'My career as a police officer was short-lived,' Matt said, although Chapman was no doubt aware of that.

'I haven't read any of your books. Yet,' he added as an afterthought.

'That's not the first one in the series.' Matt took the book from Chapman's hands and placed it back on the shelf.

'So, you're a multi-award-winning, number one *Sunday Times* bestselling author. Is that right?'

Clearly, he'd read Matt's bio on his website. It was a bit of an exaggeration. He had yet to hit a bestseller list. And although he'd been longlisted for a couple of awards, and felt he'd deserved to win both of them, he didn't actually make it onto either shortlist. Admittedly, Esther, his editor, wouldn't be too well pleased if she found out he'd inflated his success, but everyone embroidered their achievements on their CV, didn't they? This was no different.

There was no right answer to Chapman's question. If Matt confirmed it and Chapman did a little more research, he'd find out Matt hadn't been completely truthful. If Matt denied it and fessed up about embellishing his bio, it would also make him look dishonest. He couldn't win.

'Hmm,' he said noncommittally. 'Listen, I have to go out.'

Chapman's pointy ears visibly pricked up. His eyes flicked from Matt to the window, as if to say, *in this?*

'I have to look in on my mum,' Matt said, annoyed at feeling the need to justify himself.

His mother had been diagnosed with Parkinson's disease a few years previously. She was still fairly independent, but he had to take her some food and medication before she ran out of both or ventured out herself on foot in these treacherous conditions.

He also didn't want her to hear about Leona's disappearance on the news. He was glad of the excuse. The desire to get out of the house – to get away from it all, if only for an hour or two – was overwhelming.

Trixie came with him, but he left Scarlett with Roxanne. As the youngest and smallest Walsh, Trixie was usually relegated to the back seat, but as it was just the two of them, she climbed into the passenger's seat. He was about to ask her to get in the back – it would be safer given the slippery roads – but he let her stay put.

He drove out of the driveway cautiously, but with relief. There was no escaping the situation, though. It was just outside the nearest village – Blackmoor Gate – that he spotted her. Out of the corner of his eye, he saw Trixie point and gape.

'Daddy, it's ... Mummy,' she said.

He was already driving slowly, but he slowed even more as he approached and Leona beamed at them. The word 'MISSING' stretched across the top of the A4-sized poster in red capital letters with Leona's full name in slightly smaller, black capital letters underneath, then came the date she was last seen: 'SATURDAY 30th NOVEMBER', also in black caps; at the bottom was an appeal for people with information or dashcam footage to call 101. And right in the middle of the poster was what had grabbed their attention: the photo Matt had emailed Sergeant Harris yesterday at her request.

The posters were everywhere. In shop windows; along the roadside; on lampposts; on the bridge over the River Yeo; at the entrance to the supermarket and chemist they stopped at to get supplies for Matt's mum; above the pumps at the petrol station. He even saw a poster in the back window of a car. Everywhere he looked, his wife was smiling at him. Or perhaps she was baring her teeth.

Other than Leona, there wasn't a soul anywhere to be seen. No one was out and about on foot. Apart from the car with the poster in its rear window, he'd hardly seen another vehicle.

The locals were wise. They were staying safely indoors, working from home where possible, to avoid taking unnecessary risks. The schools were closed, so all the pupils were at home, too, no doubt delighted at having a few snow days. The thought he'd had yesterday corkscrewed its way back into his head: no one would see the posters; no one would even realise Leona was missing.

As if to contradict him, his phone started beeping with incoming texts, one after the other, which Siri proceeded to read out over CarPlay. Then his mobile rang. The caller ID came up on the dashboard screen – it was the mother who had dropped off Scarlett yesterday after the party. He reached out and tapped the red circle to decline the call, but it rang again. This time, it was their cleaner. He would call her back later. He switched his mobile to silent mode. When he got to his mum's, he looked at the screen of his phone. He had ten new voicemails. He tapped on the text icon. There were several unread messages from neighbours, friends, colleagues of Leona's, parents of Trixie's and Scarlett's classmates. He was wrong. Everyone knew about Leona's disappearance.

He made a mental note to post about Leona's disappearance on all his social media platforms as soon as he got a moment. He had a few thousand followers on Twitter, Facebook and Instagram. They would expect him to keep them in the loop. More importantly, he needed to keep them onside. People could be vile on social media.

His mum had found out seconds before they arrived that Leona was missing. 'I've just seen it on the telly,' she said as he and Trixie dumped the shopping bags in the hallway. 'The police have made an appeal. I was about to ring you, Matthew.' Her speech seemed more slurred than usual. He put it down to the shock rather than a worsening of the symptoms of her disease.

She wrapped her frail arms around Trixie. Trixie didn't hug back, but she didn't resist. The two of them had always had a special bond, but his mum's condition had strengthened that bond. Trixie often struggled to understand other people – their feelings and reactions. As a result, she could seem uncaring to those who didn't know her. But although his mother's difficulties were very different to his daughter's, Trixie was patient with her grandmother and empathetic towards her. Trixie seemed to 'get' her without having to make the effort she needed to make to understand everyone else.

They went into the kitchen, where his mum made a pot of tea. She poured a glass of orange juice for Trixie. Matt had a feeling he was going to be drinking a lot of tea over the next few days, a typically British response to everything, even a missing spouse, apparently. His mum's movements were slow and shaky, but he and Trixie both knew better than to offer to do it for her. She wanted to be as autonomous as she could, for as long as she could. Without saying a word, Trixie put some biscuits on a plate. He doubted Trixie had any more appetite than he did, but it would save his mum fumbling to open the packet.

She had lots of questions. Where did he think Leona was? What did he think had happened to her? What were the police doing to find her? How were the children coping? How could she help? He did his best to give her reassuring answers between sips of tea.

Matt felt as if he was suffocating. 'I'm going to pop outside, just for a minute,' he said. 'I need some fresh air.'

His mother looked at him, worry etched all over her face. He pulled on his coat and gloves and stepped outside. The cold air hit him like a punch in the face, which he felt he deserved. By the time he came back in, he was shivering and numb and feeling far worse than when he'd gone out. He checked his phone. The most recent call and text message were from DC Chapman, who had given Matt his mobile number earlier. It was a short text, asking Matt to ring him ASAP.

'Mum, Trixie and I should get going,' he said.

'Of course,' she said, getting to her feet with difficulty.

He called Chapman back as soon as they were in the car. 'It's

Matthew Walsh,' he said when the detective answered. 'I'm afraid my phone was in silent mode – it wouldn't stop ringing – and I missed your call.'

It was snowing again, the flakes coming at them so fast that even on high speed the windscreen wipers struggled to keep up. 'How soon can you get back here?' Chapman asked.

'Twenty minutes, maybe a bit more, given the roads and weather. I'm on my way now. Why? What's happened? Have you found something?'

But DC Chapman would say no more. 'My colleague will explain when you get here.'

Missing, Presumed Murdered
A True Crime Podcast Hosted by Gabriela Conti
Audio File 2
Interview with Detective Constable Andrew Chapman, recently retired police officer.
2024

This is the story of Leona Walsh, whose disappearance in December 2019 has remained a mystery for nearly five years. Join me as I explore the truths and lies in this case. I am Gabriela Conti and you're listening to **Missing, Presumed Murdered**, *a true crime podcast.*

Gabriela Conti: Detective Constable Chapman, I'd like to thank you for talking to me today. For our listeners, would you mind explaining how you came to be involved in this particular case?
DC Andrew Chapman: I was assigned to the Walshes as their FLO – family liaison officer – so I got to know Matthew Walsh reasonably well.
GC: And what did you make of him?
AC: I couldn't really suss him out.
GC: What do you mean by that?
AC: He could be charming one minute and quite arrogant the next. He had a bit of a temper.
GC: Oh?
AC: Yes, I saw him lose it on more than one occasion. And I didn't trust him.
GC: Why was that?
AC: So, he'd have these in-depth convos, and sometimes he'd tell me these wild anecdotes, but I could never figure out how much truth there was in them.
GC: An occupational hazard, maybe? He makes up stories for a living.

AC: Maybe. Have you read Murder on the Moors, *by the way?*

GC: That's the last one in the series, isn't it? The one that came out shortly before his wife disappeared?

AC: Yes, I didn't like it, personally, I found it hard to get into the story and the plot was really far-fetched. And even though Walsh used to be a copper, some of the police investigation bits were inaccurate. But that's not the point. The thing is, there are some disturbing events in the book, some elements that ... well, I won't give you any spoilers! But you should read it. You can make up your own mind.

GC: I did read it, actually.

AC: Then you know what I'm talking about.

GC: I'm not sure the novel proves anything. Do you really think he could have had anything to do with his wife's disappearance?

AC: Hard to say. But get this. On his website it says he's a multi-award-winning author whose books have all been number one Sunday Times *bestsellers*. Well, I checked him out. Both of those claims are false, you know. Ironically, his book crept onto the Sunday Times *bestseller* list – it spent one week in the number ten spot – thanks to all the exposure in the media when his wife disappeared. He's never won an award, though.

GC: I suppose it's a bit like adding qualifications you don't actually have to your CV, isn't it? Like pretending you passed GCSE French or Italian, when you can't string together more than three words in a foreign language.

AC: I suppose so, although this is more like saying you got a first in your degree when you flunked your A levels and didn't even make it into uni.

GC: It doesn't make him a killer, though, does it, bragging on his website, even if it's wishful thinking on his part rather than the truth?

AC: No, but it made me wonder. If he lied about that, what else was he lying about?

Chapter 5

Monday, 2nd December 2019: Day Two

Usually on a weekday at this time, mid-afternoon, he'd be in his study, beavering away at his computer, with Sydney sprawled at his feet and some film music – Hans Zimmer, John Williams or Ludovico Einaudi – streaming through the Bluetooth speaker. He was used to having the house to himself until the girls got in from school. But when he and Trixie got back, two more cars were parked in the driveway.

Roxanne's husband, Adam, was in the living room with Roxanne and Scarlett. The television was on. A 'BREAKING NEWS' banner was rolling across the bottom of a split screen, one side showing Leona's photo – the one Matt had provided for the posters – and the other showing the local newscaster.

Adam got up from the sofa and patted him on the back. 'How are you holding up, mate?' Adam didn't wait for an answer. 'The police made an appeal earlier. They've asked for anyone with information to come forward. Leona's now the main story on ITV News West Country.'

Matt's eyes were glued to the television. Leona's face had

disappeared, the image replaced by an establishing shot of Wistlandpound Reservoir. A chill washed over him, as if he was in the water, slipping under, and although he shut out Adam's voice and focused on the news item, he only caught snippets as he floundered to keep afloat: *Leona Walsh, local politician ... wife of renowned crime writer ... last seen on Sunday ... police ... concerned for her safety ... extensive search ... described as ... call ...*

'Do you want to sit down, mate?'

His head stopped spinning and he could breathe again. 'No, I'm fine.'

'There's someone to see you,' Roxanne said without taking her eyes off the TV screen. 'Another police officer. She's in the kitchen with DC Chapman.'

'Trixie, stay here with your aunt and uncle for a bit,' Matt said. 'Scarlett, take care of your sister for me, please.' He kissed her on the forehead. 'Are you OK, sweetie?' Scarlett threw him one of those looks teenagers do so well. 'No, of course you're not,' he said, squeezing her shoulder. 'Stupid question. Sorry.'

DC Chapman was sitting at the kitchen table opposite a woman Matt didn't recognise, presumably another plain-clothes CID officer. They were so deep in discussion that neither of them noticed him standing in the doorway. He didn't think much of the detectives' observational skills.

He cleared his throat noisily. The two officers got to their feet. The female officer was tall – almost as tall as Matt – despite her flat court shoes. Her chestnut hair was scraped back into a bun; she had a square chin and brown eyes. He'd have put her in her mid-forties, around the same age as him. But if he was right, she was ageing better than he was. He had less hair and more wrinkles than his author pic – taken and photoshopped several years ago – would have his readers believe, and he was developing a middle-aged paunch.

'This is Detective Sergeant Sophie Holland,' Chapman said. To Holland he said, 'I'll be in the living room.'

Holland turned to Matt. 'Take a seat, Mr Walsh.' Her voice was kind; her eyes sympathetic.

He did as he was told and that's when he saw what they'd found. Lying on the kitchen table, inside a large, transparent evidence bag, was a red rucksack. Either side of it were smaller evidence bags. In one of them was a mobile phone; in the other, keys. He gasped, his hands flying to his mouth. 'Those are my wife's,' he confirmed, before DS Holland could even ask. 'Where did you find them?'

'A police diver found the rucksack in the reservoir, in the shallows. The keys and the phone were inside the rucksack, just as you thought, Mr Walsh.'

'Oh, God. Oh, God.'

She leant towards him, resting her elbows on the table and her chin on her hands. 'Are you absolutely sure these items belong to your wife?'

He lifted the bag containing the phone and turned it over. He examined its contents again, just to make sure. It was the right make, it looked like the right model, but the real giveaway was the purple glittery protection case. Scarlett and Trixie had given Leona a brighter, cleaner version as a birthday present a few months ago. Then he peered at the bag with the keys inside. A door key and an intelligent car key on the same Union Jack keyring. Leona's. No doubt about it. 'One hundred per cent certain,' he said. 'The rucksack, the phone, the keys – they're all Leona's.'

The police had probably already got hold of the call data for Leona's phone, or at least applied for it. Finding the actual phone was unlikely to throw up any more clues.

'OK. Mr Walsh, here's what we know so far. You saw your wife at about five p.m., just before she went out for her evening jog. Two witnesses – an elderly couple, locals – saw the posters we put up around the village of Blackmoor Gate and came forward this morning. They sighted Leona, jogging around the higher path at the reservoir with your dog at around five-twenty. They were walking their dog, a Yorkshire terrier.'

'Is there any dashcam footage?' he asked.

'I was coming to that. A driver also came forward earlier this afternoon with dashcam footage that clearly shows your wife at the wheel of her Qashqai, shortly after five p.m., heading in the direction of Wistlandpound Reservoir.'

This was good. The witness accounts all corroborated his version of events. 'What about CCTV?'

If DS Holland was annoyed at him for asking the questions, she didn't show it. 'There's one home security camera between Blackmoor Manor and Wistlandpound Reservoir, but it wasn't working. There's no CCTV coverage at the car park or along the paths. Not all the possible exits on foot are covered.'

Matt understood what this meant. Leona could have left the reserve – voluntarily or forcibly – without being seen.

'There are cameras that monitor the wildlife around the lake,' DS Holland continued, 'but they're not helpful to us.'

'I see.'

'Taking into consideration your account, Mr Walsh, as well as the witness accounts of the couple, the dashcam footage and the fact we found Leona's rucksack in the water, our working hypothesis at the moment is that your wife, for whatever reason, went into the reservoir.'

She paused, perhaps to let him digest this.

'There were also some plastic dog poop bags inside the front pocket of the rucksack.' DS Holland apparently didn't consider it necessary to ask him to identify those. 'But you mentioned a dog's toy – a ball on a string?' Matt nodded. 'There was no toy or ball in the rucksack. How sure are you that it was in there when your wife set out for her run?'

Matt didn't answer straightaway. His breaths were shallow and fast, and he pulled at the clothing around his neck. 'As sure as I can be,' he managed after a few seconds. 'She never took the toy out of the rucksack, except to use it.'

The scenarios that Holland must have already considered went through his head. Leona had waded into the water after the dog's toy. She'd had some sort of problem – most likely, cold water shock. Or she'd very deliberately gone into the cold water with the intention of taking her own life. Either way, she hadn't come back out of the reservoir. She'd drowned. The elderly couple had spotted Leona running along the higher of the two circular footpaths, the one that led through the woods, further away from the water, but there were a few trails that connected the inner and outer paths, so the witness accounts didn't necessarily refute the police's main theory.

'The dog would probably have gone into the water with Leona,' Matt said. 'That would explain why he came home with wet fur.'

DS Holland nodded. Her face was impassive. He couldn't tell if she'd already thought of that. He had no idea if she found this theory convincing.

'At this stage, we don't suspect any third-party involvement in your wife's disappearance. But I'm keeping an open mind and we'll continue to search the woodland, too. Obviously, that task will be easier once the snow melts.'

Matt had checked the forecast. They could expect a further drop in temperature and yet more snow – it wasn't going to thaw any time soon.

A mobile phone buzzed to life. He stared at Leona's phone, but of course, it wasn't hers. DS Holland produced a phone from her pocket, looked at the caller ID and swiped the screen.

'DS Holland. ... How many? ... There's barely an hour or so of daylight left today ... I see ... OK. Thanks for letting me know.'

He tried to decrypt the conversation from Holland's side of it, but didn't get far.

Once she'd ended the call, she filled him in. 'Around one hundred people – members of the public, locals, mainly – have turned up at the reservoir to help with the search.'

One hundred people? In this weather? 'I'd like to go, too.' He nodded at the door to the living room. 'I think my family will want to come with me – my children, my sister-in-law and her husband.'

'I don't see any problem with you going, but I'm not sure if it's a good idea to take your daughters. It's below freezing and it could be traumatic for them.'

'You're probably right.'

'There's one more thing I need to talk to you about, Mr Walsh.'

'Oh?'

'A reward has been offered for any information that leads to finding Leona.'

'How much?' He clocked the expression on her face. That wasn't what he should have asked. 'Who put up the reward?'

'We don't know.'

'I don't understand.'

'It's an anonymous donor. They've offered thirty thousand pounds. It will be on the news, so I wanted to let you know. Can you think of anyone close to you or Leona who might offer that sort of money for information?'

'No.' He racked his brains. 'One of my fans, perhaps?' DS Holland gave him another disapproving look. Did she find him arrogant? 'Other than that, I have no idea who it could be.'

'It may be someone who has no connection whatsoever with you or your wife, Mr Walsh,' DS Holland said, 'someone who is simply moved by the news of Leona's disappearance. But we'll look into it.'

DS Holland rose, his cue to get ready to join the search. He led the way into the living room, where he explained to Roxanne, Adam, Scarlett and Trixie what was going on. He didn't tell them the police had fished Leona's rucksack out of the water. He'd tell Roxanne and Adam when they got back, but he wanted to protect the girls a little longer.

'I'll stay here,' Roxanne said.

'Are you sure?' Matt asked. Roxanne hadn't stepped outside since she'd arrived yesterday morning.

'Someone has to hold the fort, in case … you know.'

Adam took her hand and said to Matt, 'We'll both wait here

until you come back. Roxanne's right. Someone needs to be here. I'll get the fire going again.'

Matt hadn't realised the fire had gone out until Adam mentioned it, but now he could feel how chilly it was in the room.

'Can we come?' Scarlett asked, already on her feet.

'I think it might be better for you two to stay with Auntie Roxanne and Uncle Adam.'

Grudgingly and with a pout, Scarlett sat back down.

'Take Sydney, Daddy,' Trixie suggested. 'He might smell something.'

DS Chapman had told Matt that trained police sniffer dogs had been brought in, but to appease Trixie, he said it was a good idea.

'Do you think they'll find anything, Dad?' Scarlett asked.

He took a second to formulate his reply. 'I doubt it, sweetie, with so much snow, but there will be a lot of people searching.'

'What are they searching for?' Trixie asked.

'I don't know, my darling,' he said. 'I really don't know.'

A minute or so later, they were in the car, heading towards the reservoir. DC Chapman was sitting in the passenger's seat of Matt's car, his beanie back on his head. The dog was in the boot. DS Holland had left Blackmoor Manor in her own car to return to the police station in Exeter.

Matt drove down the lane leading to the reservoir. At the bottom, near the water's edge, a huge, rectangular police vehicle was parked. The police dive team van, no doubt. He was surprised they'd managed to manoeuvre it along the narrow, twisty access road. They'd recovered Leona's rucksack. That was quick work. And rather a shock.

Chapman was silent as Matt parked the car, lost, perhaps, like him, in his thoughts. Matt was mentally scrolling through a list of people's names – all the contacts he could conjure up – trying to work out who the anonymous donor was. He was convinced their identity would turn out to be important. But for the life of him, he couldn't imagine who it might be.

Chapter 6

Tuesday, 3rd December 2019: Day Three

Everything moved quickly after that evening at the reservoir, but Matt felt as if he was watching from a distance as events unfolded in slow motion. The house was often crammed with people, but it seemed empty without Leona. Those who did come to the house were mainly family members or police officers, but their friends stayed away, conspicuous by their absence, even though his phone pinged constantly with messages asking if he'd had any news.

He hadn't. He'd had no news of Leona whatsoever, but, by the third day, she was practically the only news. On television and on the radio; nationally as well as locally. Her disappearance was the main story, told on a sickening loop. The photo he'd provided for the poster cropped up on every channel and in every newspaper.

Leona was trending on social media, too: Facebook, Twitter, Instagram and YouTube. Everyone had a theory. Leona had waded into the reservoir with the intention of taking her own life; she'd rescued the dog in the water, but she herself had drowned; she'd been kidnapped; she'd deliberately gone AWOL to avoid facing the fraud accusations; she'd faked her suicide and left home of her own accord; she'd been murdered … by her husband, predictably. One YouTuber even suggested she'd been abducted by aliens.

To his relief, most of the comments were sympathetic; most of the unsympathetic remarks were relatively tame. The internet trolls weren't wielding their torches and brandishing their pitchforks en masse on any of the social media platforms. Not yet anyway. Compassionate messages had been flooding into his inbox via the contact form on his website.

He was also touched by how supportive the people in his community had been. Around a hundred locals had turned out the previous evening to help with the search until it was stood down because it was too dark. He recognised many of them the following morning – they'd come to resume the search, no doubt taking the day off work.

Schools had reopened, but there was no question of Scarlett and Trixie going back yet. He would have preferred them to stay at home, with Roxanne, by the fire. But the girls had insisted on coming this time and against his better judgement, Matt had given in. He'd told them to put on snow boots or walking shoes, and wear scarves and woolly hats as well as pull up their hoods. That way, not only would they be wrapped up warm, but also, if they were photographed, their faces would be less visible.

That morning, there were even more people – at a guess, as many as one hundred and fifty. And they weren't all locals. He arrived with the girls, Adam and the dog at first light, and yet the two car parks at the reservoir were already full. He counted three mini buses among the cars. One couple rushed up to them, presumably recognising him despite his obsolete author pic, to inform him they'd driven here all the way from Manchester to participate in the search. He thanked them and acted as if he found that completely normal until the woman asked if she could take a selfie with him.

'Maybe later,' he said over his shoulder as he walked away. 'Rubberneckers,' he muttered to Adam. 'Don't these people have jobs?'

'Don't these people have lives?' Adam chimed in.

It had stopped snowing. Finally. The temperature had crept up to a few degrees above zero, although the northerly wind meant it felt colder. The snow was several centimetres deep and would continue to hamper the search. Just as last night, police officers divided the volunteers into groups of about ten, each of them led by an officer wearing a high-vis jacket over their uniform.

Their group was ready to set off. They were to cover the higher of the two circular paths, through the woods, the path along which the dogwalkers had spotted Leona running. They were better equipped this time. Following the example of some of the previous evening's volunteers, he'd dug out some ski poles from the attic to use as probes and he noticed other people with sticks.

'What are we looking for, Dad?' Scarlett asked, an echo of Trixie's question the day before.

Drones with thermal cameras had searched the area throughout the night, according to DC Chapman, so it was safe to conclude they wouldn't find Leona herself under all that snow, even with so many people scouring the undergrowth with probes.

'Clues, sweetie,' he said. He threw a furtive glance at Trixie, who, despite her warm clothes, was shivering, her face flushed with the cold. He was worried about her. Then he turned back to Scarlett, lowering his voice so Trixie wouldn't hear, and added, 'Anything that might help us find Mum.'

Gabi was in the group behind Matthew Walsh's, tasked with checking the area to the right of the outer path around the lake, no easy job given the dense undergrowth. It took her group longer to advance and it soon became clear she had no hope of catching him up. She swore to herself and left her group, ignoring the group leader who called after her. She felt a small pang of guilt as she attempted to run towards Matthew and his kids, lifting up her knees, holding her stick aloft and sinking into the snow with every step. Everyone else had come here to help search for Leona, or for clues that might lead to locating her. Gabi, on the other hand, had come today with the aim of exploiting the tenuous link she had with the Walsh family – the fact she'd attended the same school as Leona – in order to get an exclusive. But seriously, what chance did they have of finding anything in these conditions?

She joined Matthew Walsh's group, inserting herself between him and the girl next to him, presumably his daughter, Scarlett. With the wind pinching their faces, they trudged side by side through the thick snow, in silence to begin with. She stole glances at him as they walked, sizing him up. He looked tired. Not just his face, with the dark rings under his eyes, but his posture. When they made eye contact, she gave him what she hoped would pass for a sympathetic smile, but he didn't return it. 'There's a good turnout today,' she began, wincing at her opening gambit.

He grunted in reply, his eyes back on the path in front of him. She launched into a monologue, hoping she was making all the right noises – so sorry you're going through this, keeping everything crossed they'll find your wife alive and well, et cetera. More grunts in response.

'Matthew, I went to school with your wife,' she said.

That got his attention. 'Oh?'

'We were in the same year, in the same house, in many of the same sets.'

'Were you two close friends?' he asked.

'Not particularly.' She laughed, but it sounded hollow. 'I wasn't very cool at school. I was rather – what did they call it then? – "square".'

'Oh?' he repeated.

So far, he'd spoken to her merely in grunts and monosyllables. Was he always like this or was it due to the stress of his wife's disappearance? Perhaps he was wishing she'd shut up. She could understand if he wanted to be left alone.

'Your wife was very popular at school.'

'But?'

Had she implied a 'but'? It wasn't intentional. Leona had been popular at school, but at the expense of some of her classmates. She'd been competitive and bitchy about girls she perceived as rivals. A bully, really, as Gabi knew to her cost.

'I was bad at sports, always picked last for the netball team, that sort of thing,' she said. 'Plus, I was a swot, which didn't help. So, no, we weren't close. But we knew each other quite well.'

He nodded knowingly, as if he understood what she hadn't said.

'I was wondering if you'd like to talk to me,' she said.

She pulled off one of her blue woollen gloves with her teeth, and delved into her jacket pocket for a business card. She introduced herself properly, but her words came out sounding incoherent, even to her, with her mouth full of wool. Matthew took the card and she took the glove out of her mouth.

He read her name aloud from the card at the same time as she repeated it. 'Gabriela Conti.'

'Gabi. I'm a journalist with the *North Devon Echo*. I thought you might like to get your side of the story across in an interview.'

His face clouded and he hesitated before taking the card. She'd obviously hit a false note.

His side of the story? That got his hackles up. Was she implying there was another side to this story? That he wasn't telling the truth? He stopped walking and stared at her in disbelief. She turned to face him and took a couple of steps towards him to stroke the dog. She was pretty, he'd give her that. She had long, sleek, dark brown hair, a shade darker than her eye colour, and flawless olive skin. She was wearing a blue woollen hat that matched her gloves, and make-up.

He was about to remind her they were supposed to be at arm's length from the next person in the group and stay alert, but he felt himself softening towards her and closed his mouth. This woman had been at school with Leona and although they hadn't been friends, she was trying to use that to get an interview. It was brash, but she seemed genuinely nice, and he told himself she was just doing her job. He pasted a tight smile on his face and pocketed the card. He'd throw it in the bin later.

Gabriela Conti remained glued to his side after that, like a piece of chewing gum on a shoe, separating him from Scarlett and Adam. She was way too talkative, but she had a mellifluous voice that he found calming, and she assured him they were 'off the record'. Even so, he weighed his words before saying anything to her and tried to say as little as possible.

From time to time, he nodded or mumbled to show he was listening. He was probably coming over as very cold, and he didn't want to appear rude, but he couldn't bring himself to chat to a complete stranger and he was worried that anything he did say might end up distorted and in print.

'And you must be Scarlett,' Gabi said, turning towards his daughter. 'I'm sure it's very hard not knowing where your mummy is. It's brave of you to take the day off school to help look for her.'

Scarlett either didn't hear or pretended not to. She'd had a meltdown that morning and she was understandably distressed by the whole situation.

It was Trixie who answered. 'We're not looking for my mummy.'

Gabi shot Matt a puzzled look. He explained about the thermal drones. 'I think the police are hoping to rule out the woods and trails around the reservoir.'

He didn't add what DS Holland had told him, that the police's working hypothesis was that Leona had gone into the reservoir, but Gabi's eyes flicked towards the lake. Evidently, she'd grasped the subtext. He, too, peered through the trees and thought he glimpsed a diver in the water. But it could have been a shadow or a trick of the light, or even a bird. The reservoir was massive – he'd read once that it covered an area of sixteen hectares and contained over one thousand five hundred megalitres. How long would it take the police divers to search it? The surface of the water was calm, but did that mean it was an easy job?

'Did Leona—?'

'How long have you been a reporter?' He wasn't asking out of curiosity, but in an effort to shift the focus away from his family and himself on to Gabi.

But before she could answer, a shout echoed through the woodland. He stopped in his tracks. Trixie took his hand. Even as a toddler, she'd been reluctant to hold an adult's hand – including his or Leona's – and as she gripped his hand, she squeezed his heart.

He found it impossible to work out where the shout had come from, but Adam pointed in front and to the right of them and said, 'It must be the group on the lower path.'

By unspoken agreement and despite the feeble protests of the officer in charge of their group, all ten of them picked up the pace. They stayed on course, but they no longer probed with their sticks or looked all around them as they went along, as they'd been instructed. Several metres further along, they spotted the other group near the wooden lakeside lookout.

'Stop here! Stay there!' The officer in charge of their search group instructed.

This time, everyone obeyed. Everyone except Matt and Adam.

Matt pulled his daughters to him and crouched down to them. 'Girls, I want you to stay here. With Gabi.' He looked up at her, a question on his face. She nodded. 'I'm just going to take a quick look with Uncle Adam. OK?'

The two of them crunched their way down the slope that connected the two paths. One of the volunteers was holding up his stick and something was dangling from the end of it. As they approached, Matt made out the object. It was a ladies' pink-and-black running shoe.

The officer leading the group was holding open a plastic bag. Matt and Adam stopped and watched as the volunteer lowered the trainer into it.

'Is that ... is that Leona's?' Adam breathed.

Matt checked Gabriela Conti was still with Scarlett and Trixie, well out of earshot. 'Yes,' he said. 'It certainly looks like it.'

'But they found her rucksack in the water.' Matt knew this, obviously. Adam was thinking out loud. 'How did it get here? Where's the other shoe? What does this mean?'

What did it mean? Matt was asking himself the same question, his mind whirring through the possibilities. Would this change the police's working hypothesis? Did it indicate foul play? 'I don't know, Adam,' he said.

They stared at each other. Neither of them knew what this meant, but they both feared the worst.

Missing, Presumed Murdered
A True Crime Podcast Hosted by Gabriela Conti
Audio File 3
Interview with Sergeant Craig Nash – Devon, Cornwall and Dorset Police Underwater Search Unit supervisor.
2024

This is the story of Leona Walsh, whose disappearance in December 2019 has remained a mystery for nearly five years. Join me as I explore the truths and lies in this case. I am Gabriela Conti and you're listening to **Missing, Presumed Murdered,** *a true crime podcast.*

Gabriela Conti: Sergeant Nash, thank you so much for talking to me today. I'd like to start by asking you to tell me a little about yourself and the diving team that was called out to search for Leona Walsh at Wistlandpound Reservoir.

Sgt Craig Nash: I'm fifty years old and I have sixteen years' experience as a police diver. We're a team of nine. Obviously, we weren't looking to rescue her – the water was very cold and she'd been gone far too long for that, she would only have survived a couple of hours in the water, at most. No, we were tasked with searching for a body. We started the dive on the first day with limited specific intelligence.

GC: You mean you didn't know where to concentrate your search?

CN: That's right. The reservoir covers forty acres, holds three hundred and forty million gallons of water and it's over twenty metres deep in places.

GC: And she could have been anywhere in the lake?

CN: Well, the working hypothesis at that time was that Mrs Walsh had waded into the water, for whatever reason, and that she'd drowned. If that was the case, we could assume her body wouldn't be too far from the edge. So, we started looking in the shallows around the perimeter.

GC: I imagine in a reservoir, currents aren't an issue, like they would be in a river?

CN: Well, yes and no. In the vicinity of the reservoir tower, the pipes, pumping and water release mechanisms can create dangerous currents underwater that are impossible to discern from the surface. But, yes, away from the tower and dams, reservoirs are generally free from the hazards you'd associate with rivers as there is no flow.

GC: And you didn't find a body. But you did find something belonging to the missing woman?

CN: Yes. We found a small rucksack, which turned out to be hers. It was a bit of a fluke we found it, really, but it was in the shallows right at the entrance to the reservoir, which was the very first place we looked.

GN: I suppose you don't normally find things as small as that?

GC: Unfortunately, most of our call-outs are to recover dead bodies. We're also called out frequently to hook up cars that have sunk so they can be winched out of the water. But we are sometimes tasked with finding small objects underwater. For example, we once had to locate a pocketknife. We believed it to be the weapon used in a murder. The suspect had lobbed it into the River Taw. We managed to find it and charge him. We've also recovered mobile phones on several occasions. But, like I said, we were looking for Leona Walsh's body. We didn't expect to stumble across her rucksack.

GC: Does that mean the visibility in the water at Wistlandpound Reservoir was good? Because it's drinking water, perhaps?

CN: No, not at all. We have projectors when we dive, but even if the water looks calm and clear on the surface, you can't see much underneath. At Wistlandpound, the visibility was one to two metres, at best. And, to be honest, the projectors don't always help. It's like driving with your headlights on full beam in the fog. No, you have to feel your way.

GC: *So, would it be impossible to search the whole reservoir?*

CN: *Well, after we found the rucksack and received confirmation that it belonged to Mrs Walsh, we initially concentrated our search in that area. But the shoe was found the next day a long way from where we'd found the bag, so it was hard to know where to look, really. We had sonar equipment, so we were able to conduct a systematic and exhaustive search.*

GC: *How long did the search go on for?*

CN: *Three weeks. It's a long time. We would have expected to stand down our underwater search after ten days or so, even if we hadn't found the body, partly because there's next to no chance of finding anything after all that time, but mainly because it's an extremely expensive operation. But the missing woman's disappearance was such a big deal, we had to make sure we couldn't possibly be criticised for our handling of it.*

GC: *So, after all that time and such a thorough search, how sure could you be that Leona Walsh's body wasn't in the water?*

CN: *We were pretty certain she wasn't in the water. You see, when a corpse decomposes, it produces gases and inflates like a balloon, so within a few days, the dead body floats to the surface. Admittedly, cold water slows down the decay, but unless the water is deeper than thirty metres or the body is caught under branches or rocks or something, which can happen in a river, but not so much in a reservoir, then it always surfaces eventually. No, the only way Leona Walsh's body could still have been in the water after we'd ended our search, was if it had been weighted and dumped overboard in the deepest part of the reservoir.*

Chapter 7

May 2024

At the *Echo* they're usually all overstretched and multitasking, but news is slow this week for some reason. Gabi doubts the copies she has filed so far today could actually be called 'news'. She has written a piece on a recent clog dancing event in Ilfracombe and another on the Great Torrington Mayfair. She has been stuck in the office all morning, and as it's open-plan it gets noisy, but right now it's fairly calm. She scans the room. Everyone else looks as bored as she feels.

She picks up her mobile to check the time. On the wall opposite her desk hangs a huge clock, but it stopped at some point during lockdown and no one has bothered to replace the battery. It ticked too loudly anyway.

'Time stands still in this place,' Mick now likes to joke, which always makes Mick himself laugh, if no one else.

Gabi briefly thinks about texting a couple of friends to see if anyone's free this evening. But there's no point. It's a weekday, for starters. Plus, most of her mates are married or living with their boyfriends and many of them have kids. They hardly go out anymore. Gabi's the only singleton. She needs to get a social life. Not tonight, though. Tonight, she'll get an Indian takeaway and eat it alone in front of Netflix.

She has a missed call from a number she doesn't recognise. The caller has left a voicemail, which she listens to. The quality of the recording is poor and the message cuts out several times so that she can't decipher what it's about. But she does catch the name of the caller. Alicia Martin. It's been a few weeks and it takes Gabi a second to place her. She listens again. This time, she makes out enough to get the gist.

She undocks her laptop and grabs her jacket from the back of her chair. On her way out of the office, she bumps into Mick. He's obviously just been out for a cigarette. He stinks.

'Where are you off to?' he asks, folding a stick of chewing gum into his mouth.

'Benton,' Gabi says. Mick furrows his brow. 'To the house where the Roman coin was discovered,' she clarifies.

'Ah, yes. Good idea. A human interest story, perhaps, as a follow-up? It's a bit like winning the lottery, isn't it, digging up that coin?'

'I … er … Actually, the owner of the cottage, Alicia Martin, left me a message to say there's been another find.'

'Oh.' Mick sounds disappointed. 'Is that worth reporting on, do you think?'

'Mick, this discovery … it's a big deal. It was previously believed that Roman influence stopped in Exeter.' She hopes Mick won't realise she's paraphrasing Professor Harvey, the archaeologist leading the excavation, whom she phoned and quoted in her piece last month. 'Plus, finding a Roman coin this far southwest, well, it challenges the boundaries historians had drawn up of the Roman Empire!'

'Yes, I read your article,' Mick says, vigorously chewing his gum, 'but I don't see what another coin brings to the table.'

'She didn't say they'd found another coin.'

'Well, what is it they've found?'

'I don't know.'

Gabi's heart sinks. Mick's bound to give her a different assignment and tell her to drop this one. And she's itching to get out of this place.

'Your idea of telling the story of the lucky couple, though, is a good one,' she says. 'Alicia said that one coin will probably pay off their whole mortgage. Perhaps I can kill two birds with one stone.' Mick looks puzzled again. 'What I mean is, I could look into this new discovery *and* do a feature on the lucky couple about how the coin will change their lives.'

'Great. Like it. Take Joe with you. Get some photos of the missus with her other half.'

'On it.' It's Joe's voice.

Gabi whirls round. How long has he been standing there? She's about to say she doesn't need a partner. Or a babysitter. But she closes her mouth. Secretly, she's quite glad she and Joe are teaming up on this, although she'd never admit that to Joe. Or Mick. She can barely admit it to herself.

'I'm driving,' she says to Joe once Mick is out of earshot.

'But your car is ... old and unreliable,' Joe argues.

Privately, she has to concede Joe is right. It has way too many miles on the clock and it has broken down four times so far this year.

'Also, mine's just out front,' he continues.

'Well, your car is ...' she trails off. The only adjective she can think of is 'orange', which isn't a great counter-argument. 'Anyway, we'll be far safer in my old car with me driving than in any vehicle with you at the wheel, believe me.' Someone in the office sniggers.

'Fair point,' Joe says. 'Are you insured for any car?' She nods. 'How about we take mine, but you drive?'

'Deal,' she says. Joe tosses her his keys and she just about manages to catch them.

There are several vehicles parked somewhat haphazardly in front of Rose Cottage, so Gabi pulls into the pub car park instead.

'There seems to be a lot more activity in the garden than the last time we were here,' Joe says, peeping over the hedge as they round the corner.

The hedge seems to have shot up a couple of centimetres since their last visit and Gabi is no longer tall enough to see over it, even on tiptoe.

Alicia opens the door when Gabi knocks. 'Ah, you got my message,' she says, giving them both a warm smile. 'Come in!'

Alicia leads the way to the living room and sighs as she sinks onto the sofa.

'Oh, I'm sorry. I'm forgetting my manners. Would you like something to drink? Tea? Coffee?' She starts to lever herself back to her feet.

'Not for me, thank you,' Joe says.

Alicia is visibly quite far along in her pregnancy now. Joe probably doesn't want her to go to any trouble. Gabi's parched, but she declines, too. Perhaps they can stop at the pub before going back to the office, like they did last time. The coffee there has to be better than the food.

'I should have rung ahead, Alicia, I'm sorry,' Gabi says. 'This is the second time we've just turned up.'

'No problem. I'm glad of the company, to be honest. They don't count.' She thumbs over her shoulder, in the direction of the kitchen door. Gabi assumes she's referring to the people Joe saw just now in the garden. 'I'm going mad waiting for this little monkey' – Alicia rubs her stomach – 'to come and meet us.'

Gabi resists the urge to dive straight in and ask what exactly is going on in Alicia's back garden, which is what she really wants to know. Instead, she asks politely, 'How long to go?'

'My due date was yesterday, officially. So, any day now.'

'I bet you can't wait.'

Gabi wonders wistfully if she'll ever have kids. At thirty-eight years of age, she feels her time is running out. Her mother has words of wisdom for her whenever Gabi pops in to see her: *Think about your biological clock, dear!* Or: *If you wait too long, you'll be too old to enjoy it when your kids are teenagers.* And her most recent gem: *Perhaps you should consider going it alone.*

Gabi steals a peek at Joe, expecting him to look uncomfortable at all this talk of babies.

'My sister had a baby last month,' Joe says. Gabi feels her mouth drop open, and closes it. 'The day after we came here, in fact.' He leans forwards in the armchair, extracts his mobile from the back pocket of his trousers and brings up some photos to show Alicia. 'This is my niece,' he continues. 'I'm meeting her for the first time this weekend.'

And Gabi thought she and Joe were getting better at talking to each other again.

She gives them a moment, then clears her throat. 'About your message, Alicia.'

'Ah, yes. You left your card last time you came, so I thought I'd give you a heads-up for your newspaper.'

Gabi's about to explain she couldn't make out the whole message, so she's not really up to speed, but Joe jumps in before she gets a chance.

'Who are all the people in your back garden?' he says.

'I'm not entirely sure,' Alicia says. 'Professor Harvey and some of his team, for a start. Come through and see for yourself.'

She rocks herself onto her feet and Gabi and Joe follow her into the kitchen, where the three of them stare out of the glass patio door.

'Two police officers, by the looks of it,' Joe comments. He turns to Gabi, bewildered.

She's no more enlightened than he is. There are people at work, wearing white suits, masks and gloves, most of them crouching or kneeling in the dirt, with brushes and other instruments. One is taking photographs and another appears to be sketching. Behind them lie several rectangles of green tarpaulin and beyond that some sort of marquee has been erected – a forensic tent, perhaps? The uniformed police officers are standing sentinel just outside the orange netting. There is now police tape around the square grid of the excavation site.

'What on earth have they found?'

'I told you in my message,' Alicia says. 'Bones.'

'Bones?' Gabi and Joe echo simultaneously.

'What sort of bones?' Gabi asks.

'Human bones.'

'Bloody hell!' Joe whistles through his teeth, turning his attention once again to the garden.

'What? They've found skeletal remains – actual real Roman bones – in your back garden?'

'Not Roman remains,' Alicia says. 'Professor Harvey says they're more recent than that. Much more recent.'

None of them speaks for a couple of minutes. Finally, Gabi says, 'Joe, you should take some photos. I'll see if one of the police officers will talk to me.'

But although both of the officers are happy to chat to Gabi, neither of them seems to know much more than what Alicia has just told her.

'The professor and his team were searching for Roman treasures when they stumbled on some human skeletal remains, so they called the police,' one of them informs Gabi. He has a walrus moustache she can't tear her eyes away from.

'They obtained a licence to unearth the body, which is what they're doing now,' the other officer tells her.

'What sort of licence?'

'From the coroner's office. By law – the Burial Act – you need a licence to exhume human bones.' His voice is patronising, as if everyone should be aware of this.

'Any idea if it's a male or female skeleton?' she asks.

To her surprise, the officers both laugh uproariously, but Gabi fails to get the joke she herself has apparently cracked.

'It hasn't been confirmed,' the walrus says.

'But we have a bet on it,' his condescending colleague adds.

'O-K,' Gabi says, drawing out the syllables. She doesn't bother to take down the officers' names. There's nothing remotely quotable in what they've just said. She makes an effort to catch the eye of one of the archaeologists, but although a couple of them look her way, they're obviously far too focused on their task to speak to her. She signals to Joe, then waits for him in the kitchen.

'They're making a hell of a mess of your rose garden,' Joe comments to Alicia when he comes back inside.

'Rose garden?'

'Yes. I figured you must have had rose bushes before all this happened.' He waves his hand in the direction of the excavation site that was once Alicia's back garden. 'You know, because of the name of your cottage.'

'Oh, I see. No. The cottage was named after the previous owner. She lived here pretty much all her life. I assumed you knew that.'

'How would we know that?'

'Everyone round here knows who this house belonged to.'

Gabi and Joe exchange a look.

'We don't,' Gabi says to Alicia. 'We're based near Barnstaple, so we don't know this neck of the woods that well.'

'Who was the previous owner?' Joe asks.

'Rose Walsh. She lived here until two years ago, when she went into a residential care home. She had Parkinson's disease, poor love. Anyway, that's when we bought the house. Her son, Matthew Walsh, sold it to us.' Alicia emphasises both his first name and surname.

Joe gasps, turning away from Alicia and staring at the garden. 'Matthew Walsh, the man whose wife went missing?'

Gabi follows his gaze. 'I think they might have just found her,' she says.

Chapter 8

Wednesday, 4th December 2019: Day Four

Once the search was underway, there was no getting away from the press. When Matt drove home that evening, the road leading up to the brow of the hill was clogged with television news vans, journalists and general busybodies. As he snaked past, a few of the reporters slapped the windows of the car. Trixie screamed, Adam shouted and Matt swore, which he wouldn't normally do in front of the girls.

The road was clear when Matt went to bed, but when he got up the next day, the vans were already back in position. From the bedroom window, he recognised the Sky News logo on the side of one of the vehicles. A press conference, in which he and Roxanne had insisted on making an appeal, was scheduled for later that day. Whether the televised appeal would help the police find Leona remained to be seen, but there was no doubt it would whip up even more media attention. Over the phone that morning, DS Sophie Holland had warned him what to expect.

'Generating public and media interest in a misper case can be a double-edged sword, unfortunately,' she said. 'On the one hand, increasing awareness about your wife's disappearance might result in a witness coming forward with a vital lead. On the other hand, we're inevitably going to be inundated with calls and false information, which can hinder us, as much as help us, in our investigation.'

He and Roxanne were driven to Middlemoor Police Headquarters, on the outskirts of Exeter, in an unmarked police car. Although she wouldn't be taking part in the press conference, DS Holland met them upon their arrival. She led them to a soulless, airless room with a nondescript carpet and a square table and four chairs. It was bigger than an interview room, but Matt half expected to see a one-way mirror on the walls and discover that the furniture was bolted to the floor.

They stood around nervously while the detective sergeant fetched them some coffee. She came back with two plastic cups and a stocky, stern-looking man who commanded the room from the moment he strode into it, swinging his arms and puffing out his chest, exuding confidence.

'Mr Walsh, Mrs Barrett, I'm Detective Chief Inspector Peter Carter. I'm the senior investigating officer in charge of this case.' He looked Matt in the eye as he shook his hand, squeezing a little too hard, then he turned his gaze to Roxanne as he shook her hand, too. His soft voice, three or four tones too high, belied his austere appearance. 'I'm so sorry not to have had the opportunity to meet you before now.' He gestured for them to take a seat at a table. 'I'm afraid press conferences can be unpleasant and gruelling, but they're an essential step in the investigation.'

DS Holland sat down next to DCI Carter, opposite Matt and Roxanne.

'The briefing will be led by Assistant Chief Constable Elizabeth Henry,' DCI Carter continued. 'She and I will outline the leads we're pursuing and the resources the police have deployed in the search and we'll also give the timeline for Leona's disappearance and other significant details. We'll keep this short and to the point.'

DS Holland took over. 'As you have both specifically asked to be involved, it will then be your turn to say a few words to appeal directly to the public for their help in finding Leona.'

Both officers had their eyes trained on Matt. For a moment, he felt like a naughty schoolboy, summoned to the headmaster's office to face both him and the teacher whose authority he had defied.

'Mr Walsh, both DCI Carter and myself agree that you should be the one to speak on behalf of your family,' DS Holland said.

'Of course.'

He sensed Roxanne seething beside him. She thrived on attention and would have loved to have the spotlight on her, even in a dire situation like this. Secretly, he was pleased he'd be the one doing the talking. He was keen to keep public opinion on his side and persuade any sceptics out there once and for all that he had nothing to do with his wife's disappearance. The last thing he wanted was the media maligning him and hounding his family. He'd prepared a draft of what he wanted to say, which DS Holland had abridged so that it was now only a couple of paragraphs in length.

'Don't I get my say?' Roxanne asked. She'd also penned a short speech, which she'd run by Matt earlier that day. 'Leona is my sister.'

'Mrs Barrett, we feel there's more impact when only one family member addresses the media,' DCI Carter said, 'but your brother-in-law will need your support, so your presence by his side, both figuratively and physically, is of the utmost importance.'

'It will be obvious what a close-knit family you are,' DS Holland added, 'and how desperate you are to find out what has happened to Leona.'

Roxanne turned to Matt. 'If you struggle to get out the words at any stage, I can take over,' she offered.

'Thank you.' He had a knot in his stomach, but he was confident it wouldn't come to that. He could hold it together.

'One more thing,' DCI Carter said. 'The conference will be

televised. It's also being livestreamed on both the Devon and Cornwall Police Facebook page and on our YouTube channel. Social media will be all over this, so our feeling is that it's better to incorporate this from the start. Some of the media outlets will no doubt also broadcast live feeds.'

DCI Carter stood up. It was time. They filed into the room at the end of the corridor and took their seats in the correct pecking order at a long table on a dais: Assistant Chief Constable Elizabeth Henry, Detective Chief Inspector Peter Carter, Matt, Roxanne. Behind them hung a long police banner. Next to that, the by now ubiquitous photo of Leona was being projected onto a giant white screen.

The room was jam-packed with journalists and their equipment, but it was a relatively small room and there were fewer reporters than Matt had anticipated. Hopefully, they'd been hand-picked and would give an objective account of the conference that was about to take place.

Identifiable by the name plaque in front of her, ACC Elizabeth Henry was in uniform: a dark blazer, a black-and-white chequered tie and her rank badge – crossed tipstaves surrounded by a wreath – on her epaulettes. She was clearly the visible face of the inquiry, albeit a rather wrinkled one that placed her firmly in her sixties.

'Thank you all for coming.' As soon as she spoke into a large orange microphone, everyone in the room hushed. She introduced herself, her colleague, Matt and Roxanne. 'Just to remind you, Leona Walsh went missing on the evening of Saturday, thirtieth November, four days ago. She was wearing ...'

The knot in Matt's stomach tightened. He hoped he wouldn't have to scurry from the room to the toilet. The rush of blood in his ears was deafening. He could hear ACC Henry's voice, but the words ran into each other and made no sense. He tried to focus, and after a minute or so, he was able to tune back in to what she was saying.

'Our search has been water-based with a police diving team,

who are working hard to explore every inch of the reservoir; air-based with drones and thermal cameras; and, of course, land-based with police, sniffer dogs and their handlers, mounted police and their horses as well as the numerous volunteers who have scoured the woodland thoroughly despite difficult conditions. All our efforts have been directed by police search advisors – PolSAs – and experts from the National Crime Agency.'

It sounded to Matt as if ACC Henry was being a little defensive, as if the police anticipated criticism of their handling of the case further down the line.

'I'll now hand you over to Detective Chief Inspector Carter,' ACC Henry concluded. 'Peter?'

'We've found two items belonging to Leona Walsh in the course of our search. Firstly, Leona's backpack, which was found in the water. It contained her house and car keys as well as her mobile phone. The second item is her shoe, a black-and-pink running shoe, of the make Nike.'

DCI Carter went into some detail about the evening when Leona had disappeared, but added nothing new or surprising to the mix. When Carter had finished, he and ACC Henry fielded questions from the journalists.

'Did Leona's mobile yield any clues?' one reporter asked.

DC Chapman, their family liaison officer, had already filled Matt in on this. On the day she disappeared, Leona had made plans for the near future. She'd created an event in the calendar of her mobile to have a working lunch the following week with some of her co-workers. She'd also sent text messages, arranging to meet up soon with a friend. The police seemed to assume that since Leona had made plans, she hadn't intended to commit suicide. But Matt had got the feeling there was something they hadn't told him.

'We are following up on data collected from Leona's mobile as we speak,' DCI Carter said.

The detective chief inspector was better at dodging questions than Matt himself. What was he withholding?

DCI Carter pointed at another journalist, as if he was anxious to get off Leona's phone, as it were, and on to something else.

'Has your working hypothesis changed now you've found a running shoe belonging to Leona in the woods?'

That was a good question, one Matt had been asking himself, too. According to the police's original working hypothesis, Leona, for one reason or another, had gone into the reservoir. Her trainer had been found near the lower circular route, but several metres from the lake. It didn't add up. Unless she'd taken off her shoes to go into the water. Although that wouldn't explain why they hadn't found the other one. Or why the one they did find wasn't discovered at the water's edge.

'We're keeping our minds open and constantly reviewing our hypotheses with each piece of evidence we collate,' DCI Carter said. 'We'll leave no stone unturned in our efforts to find Leona.'

'Do you suspect foul play?'

'Nothing so far suggests any criminal activity in relation to Leona's disappearance, but, as I said, we're keeping an open mind and exploring every possible avenue.'

'Leona's husband, Matthew, would now like to say a few words,' the assistant chief constable said. 'Leona's family won't be taking questions at this time.'

He was up. His heart stuttered, even though he was used to speaking in front of an audience at his book launches and events – far bigger audiences than this one, in fact. He'd done readings that were much longer than the short script he had to deliver today. But this was daunting – the intrusive clicking and flashing of the cameras and the inquisitive eyes of everyone in the room fixed on him.

He took a deep breath. He looked at his script, although he knew it by heart. 'I just want to say how worried we all are about Leona,' he began. 'It's totally out of character for her to be out of touch with us like this. We all want Leona back, safe and well, as soon as possible.' He paused to clear his throat. Roxanne placed her hand on his arm. 'Leona and I have two young daughters who are waiting for their mum to come home. My family and I would also like to say how much we appreciate everything that everyone is doing. We're grateful to the police and the local community, first and foremost, but also to those who have come from far and wide to offer their time and help.' He couldn't help thinking of the couple who had made the journey from Manchester and hoped he wasn't sneering. He lowered his head.

His mouth was dry. There was a glass of water on the table in front of him, but he couldn't possibly sip from it right now. It wouldn't be appropriate. For a second, he wondered if Roxanne might step in, but then he heard a loud sob to his left. He had to carry on.

He cradled his head in his hands. 'Our family is going through hell. We're going round and round in circles, asking ourselves what has happened to Leona. She can't just have vanished into thin air. We feel sure that someone somewhere knows something and we urge you to come forward if you have any information, however insignificant it might seem. Please help us to bring Leona home.'

And then it was over. Following ACC Henry's cue, he, DCI Carter and Roxanne stood to leave.

But a reporter at the back of the room also stood and without introducing himself or announcing what media outlet he worked for, he shouted, 'Would you agree, Mr Walsh, that there are certain uncanny similarities between the circumstances surrounding your wife's disappearance and the plot of one of your books, namely *Murder on the Moors*?'

Matt froze. Cameras were aimed at him like rifles and the reporters took their shots.

Assistant Chief Constable Henry leant towards her mic. 'We made it clear that Leona's family would not be answering any questions,' she snapped. 'Our press officer will help you with any further information.'

Matt was about to answer the journalist. He wanted to point out that contrary to the victim in his novel, there was no evidence to suggest his wife had been murdered by her husband. Or by anyone else, for that matter. Fortunately, DCI Carter propelled him towards the exit before he could make that mistake. But Matt caught Carter's grim expression before it was quickly replaced with a poker face and he knew the damage had already been done.

Chapter 9

Thursday, 5th December 2019: Day Five

Matt sat bolt upright in bed. What was that? Something had woken him. A noise. Had someone broken into the house? Then it came again. An ear-piercing scream. Trixie! He raced into her bedroom and smacked his hand against the light switch. Trixie was sitting up in bed, staring wide-eyed ahead of her. He followed her stare, but there was nothing there. He turned back to Trixie. Her pupils were dilated and she was gazing, unseeing, into space.

'Trixie, sweetie.' He sat on the bed and put his arm around her. 'You've had a nightmare.' She squirmed against him and kicked her legs under the bedclothes. She was scaring him, but he kept his voice calm. 'Trixie, wake up!'

She pushed him with both arms, a deep growl erupting from her throat. He withdrew his arm from around her shoulders and inched away from her, sitting on the edge of the bed now. Trixie's breaths were coming fast and she was thrashing her arms. He shook her gently, spoke more loudly, but that seemed to agitate her more. There was nothing he could do to rouse her.

After about ten minutes, although it felt much longer to Matt, she allowed him to hold her in his arms. She went limp. He peered down at her face. Her eyes were shut. Her breathing had become lighter and more regular. Gently, he lowered her upper body so she was lying down. He stroked her hair. Her face was flushed and damp with sweat. He fetched a cold flannel and held it to her forehead then her cheeks. When he was satisfied she was sleeping soundly, he tucked her in, turned on the bedside lamp, turned off the main light, checked in on Scarlett, who evidently hadn't heard a thing, and went back to bed.

He didn't sleep for the rest of the night and when he mentioned it at the kitchen table the next morning, Trixie remembered nothing of it, which was probably a good thing. When she asked what had happened, he played it down.

'You screamed a couple of times,' he said. 'You were asleep, but you had your eyes open. You must have been having a nightmare. I couldn't wake you up. You went back to sleep after a while.'

'It sounds more like a night terror than a nightmare to me,' DC Chapman said when Trixie had left the room. He was getting into the habit of arriving early in the morning while they were still at the breakfast table. He'd make a pot of tea, then pour a mug for himself before topping up Matt's. Once the girls had finished eating and gone upstairs, Chapman brought Matt up to speed with any developments in the inquiry. 'My son had night terrors for a while. He even walked in his sleep a couple of times.'

'Hmm. That's what I thought,' said Matt. He'd googled Trixie's symptoms during the night and had reached the same diagnosis. No doubt about it, Trixie's night terror was the result of the stressful situation they found themselves in.

Chapman was friendly enough. Occasionally, he eyed Matt suspiciously, but on the whole, he did his best to liaise, as per his job description, to fit in and around Matt and his family. Much as Matt resented his presence for several hours every day, Chapman was becoming part of the furniture. A fixture. They were even on first-name terms, at Chapman's suggestion.

Scarlett insisted on going back to school that day. She had a maths test and wanted to be around her friends. Matt wasn't keen, but he gave in on the condition she let him drive her to school instead of dropping her off at the bus stop. Trixie didn't want to go back to school yet, which was understandable. As far as Matt was concerned, she could take all the time she needed. DC Chapman – Andrew – offered to keep an eye on Trixie, which suited Trixie, so Matt left her at home.

When Matt got back, Chapman was in the living room, sitting on the sofa, one arm draped across the back of it, one foot resting on the other knee. He'd taken his shoes off, which Leona would have appreciated, and he was wearing socks with gingerbread men on them, which Matt might have found amusing in different circumstances. He clearly hadn't registered Matt come in and he made an ineffectual effort to hide the book he was reading. But Matt recognised the cover – *Murder on the Moors*. He glanced at the bookshelf, but his own copy was still on it. Did Chapman buy the book after the conference yesterday? Probably. Matt pretended he hadn't noticed what the officer had been reading.

'Andrew, I have some urgent work to do,' Matt said, heading for his study. How long was Chapman planning on sticking around today? 'Make yourself at home.'

His study was the room he liked best in Blackmoor Manor – the only room he'd had any say in decorating, although he'd consulted Leona on everything. Bespoke, solid oak, floor-to-ceiling bookshelves ran along one wall, complete with rolling library ladder. Trixie had organised the books by author – in alphabetical order – and then by date of publication. The view over Exmoor through the French windows was both inspiring and distracting. This was the one place he could shut himself off from the rest of the world. His sanctuary, his creative space. The only living soul welcome – or indeed *allowed* – in this room was Sydney, who kept him company while he wrote.

He closed the study door and booted up his laptop, which was hooked up to a large monitor. After yesterday's press conference, he was anxious to read the news. He often spent an hour or so during the day reading the news online, but today it would be all about him and his family. He hoped the press – and the public – would be on his side.

First, he brought up the latest articles about the case: the *Guardian*, the *Times*, to which he had a subscription, as well as some of the tabloids, and skimmed through them. The *Sun* had come up with a bad pun, embedded into its headline: MOBILE PHONE FOUND AFTER SYNCHING IN RESERVOIR. Not one of their best efforts, but it set the tone for the article. Matt's nostrils flared. How could they get away with such poor taste?

He also skimmed the most recent piece about the case in the *North Devon Echo*. A name jumped out at him. Roxanne Barrett. His sister-in-law. When did she talk to the press? She was quoted as saying, 'Something or someone is behind my sister's disappearance. Maybe even something close to home or someone she knew well.' Damn her! He scrolled back up to the top to find the byline. Heat flushed through him when he read the journalist's name. Gabriela Conti. He swore out loud, thumped his fist on the desk and jumped to his feet. Then he paced the room for a minute or two. He needed to get a grip. Roxanne had obviously been quoted out of context and she wasn't implying he'd had a hand in Leona's disappearance. He was overreacting.

Matt slowed down his breathing, sat back down on his swivel chair and googled 'Leona Walsh live press conference'. He wanted to check out the sort of comments that members of the public were posting while watching. More importantly, he needed to see how he himself had come over on screen.

A video of the conference was available on the Devon & Cornwall Police YouTube channel. He started watching, but it quickly became clear the comments had been disabled. Some of the media outlets present at the conference had also livestreamed the event and he clicked on the link to the Sky News Facebook page.

The first few comments were sympathetic:

Sending love to the family. I can't imagine what they're going through.

My heart goes out to the children.

What followed was a mixture. Armchair detectives felt compelled to make conjectures about what might have occurred or predictions about the outcome:

It's been more than 24 hrs. Ain't no way she's gonna be found alive.

Just because the dog was wet, it doesn't mean Leona went into the water.

There's no way she's in the river. They'll never find her, wherever she is.

She's defo been abducted.

She's done a runner to avoid paying back the money she stole.

Some viewers were critical of the police or made suggestions. Matt read them, cringing at the grammar mistakes and textspeak:

If the police had closed the nature reserve immediately, people wouldn't of trampled all over the crime scene.

Have U searched 4 a Fitbit / Apple watch?

Your investigation is full of holes.

One moron criticised Leona for running alone, at the same time and place every day, as if she'd knowingly put herself in danger by having a routine.

Once he and Roxanne appeared on the screen and he began to read out his appeal, one or two viewers continued to send hugs and love, or prayers, but most of them pointed the finger at him:

He looks as guilty as sin. He hasn't shed a tear. He can't even look at the camera.

Does the husband have an alibi?

His sister-in-law is crying and he's not comforting her. Where's his empathy?

Oh, the sick bastard. He's used inspiration from one of his books to bump his wife off.

And one witty dickhead had come up with a comment that had garnered over a hundred likes:

Has police officer turned crime writer turned to crime?

Matt swore under his breath.

People also had plenty to say on Reddit forums, which abounded with wild speculation and unfounded theories as well as personal experiences, some of which had happened years ago and none of which seemed remotely similar to what he and his family were going through. Matt swore, more loudly this time.

Finally, he went on Twitter to check the reactions to the press conference on there. One video in particular was trending. He clicked on the link. The video already had 253 retweets, 210 likes and 2.5K comments. Matt tapped the sound-on icon. A self-professed body language expert and behavioural specialist – the UK's No 1 in his field, according to his bio – was examining a screenshot of Matt from the news conference. Matt remembered the moment. His mouth had been dry, but he'd resisted the urge to drink from the glass of water in front of him. He had his arms wrapped around his stomach, fervently hoping he was going to make it through the short text of his appeal without having to run to the loo.

'When someone is hunched over like this, avoiding eye contact, with their arms folded across their chest, it indicates they have something to hide.' The guy didn't sound like the UK's leading body language expert – his accent had a strange Texan twang. 'They're not telling the truth, or at least, not the *full* truth,' the so-called expert was saying from inside a small square next to the still of Matt.

This was libellous! Haw dare he! Matt could sue him!

The main image switched to another screenshot of Matt, this time cradling his head in his hands. He remembered struggling not to break down at this point and wondering if Roxanne would intervene.

'Here, Mr Walsh is looking down, holding his head,' the

charlatan drawled. 'These are clear signs that he's lying.'

Matt snapped down the lid of his laptop and grabbed a glass paperweight that Leona had given him years ago. Jumping to his feet, he hurled it against the wall, where it smashed and fell to the floor, leaving a dent in the plasterboard. The dog leapt to his feet and cowered in the corner.

'Is everything OK?' Chapman's head appeared around the door. He hadn't knocked before opening the door to the study, which made Matt's temper rise higher.

'Fine,' Matt shouted, sounding anything but fine. He shooed Chapman out. Sydney sloped out, too, his head down and his tail between his legs.

Matt took a beat to calm down before going to say sorry to Chapman. In investigations like these, the husband was the obvious suspect, as everyone knew. Some people – members of the public as well as pseudo-experts like that idiot on Twitter – were bound to think he had something to do with his wife's disappearance. They would interpret his behaviour as confirmation of their suspicions, no matter what he said and did. But not everyone would share their tunnel vision.

When Matt stepped into the living room, DS Holland was there, so he had to apologise in front of her. He hadn't heard her arrive. Chapman had made tea, something he did several times a day. He knew Matt liked piping hot builder's tea with two sugars and he even used Matt's favourite mug every time – the one Trixie had given him for Father's Day with 'World's Best Dad' on it. Matt always washed this mug by hand instead of putting it in the dishwasher and Chapman followed his lead.

'Matt, DS Holland has an update for you,' Chapman said.

Wasn't it Chapman's job to give updates? DS Holland was the one who had asked them – him – questions ever since CID had taken over. This had to be serious. He looked questioningly at Chapman.

'It would be better if DS Holland told you herself what it's about,' he said, seeming to read Matt's mind.

They all sat down at the kitchen table, which had become the place where they discussed the case. The dog slipped underneath, licked Matt's hand and flopped down at his feet.

DS Holland took a sip of her tea. 'Does the name Toby Wigmore mean anything to you, Mr Walsh?'

'Should it?'

'I don't know. Does it?'

Toby Wigmore. Toby Wigmore. That would be a great name for one of his characters. Someone posh and pompous. 'No, I've never heard that name before and I don't know anyone called Toby Wigmore. I don't know any Tobies or any Wigmores. Who is he?' DS Holland arched an eyebrow. Damn! Toby was a gender-neutral name. 'Or she?' he added hurriedly.

'*He*'s the anonymous donor, the person who offered thirty thousand pounds for any information leading to finding Leona.'

'I see. No, I've never heard of him. You said it could be someone who had no connection with me or my family, though, didn't you? Someone who was sympathetic to what we were going through?'

'The thing is, Mr Walsh,' DS Holland began, 'we have reason to believe he did have a connection with a member of your family. It would seem that your wife knew him.'

'Was he a politician? One of her colleagues?' Matt asked. Infuriatingly, DS Holland took another sip of her tea. 'An employee, perhaps?'

'Not an employee. He's in politics, but not really a colleague of your wife's.' Holland leant forwards. Matt sensed she was about to drop a bombshell. 'Judging from the text messages we recovered from your wife's phone, Leona knew Toby Wigmore very well. They appear to have been in a relationship. Did you know your wife had a lover, Mr Walsh?'

'That's … that's impossible,' he said. His voice sounded completely foreign, even to himself. 'Leona would never be unfaithful.'

Neither Holland nor Chapman spoke. Questions raced through his mind, elbowing each other for attention. Did they know how long Leona had been cheating on him? What did this mean for the investigation? Would Leona's lover be a suspect in her disappearance?

And the most important question of all: would the police think his wife's infidelity gave Matt a motive to kill her?

Chapter 10

June 2024

Gabi is longing to know if the remains they've found at Rose Cottage are those of Matthew Walsh's wife, Leona. That might explain why Matt was in Benton the day she and Joe went to interview Alicia Martin, when they spotted him in the pub. Even if Matt doesn't know they've found human remains, everyone in the area knows about the Roman coin. He definitely knows they've been excavating the garden of the house his mother used to live in. If he did kill his wife and bury her there, he must be worried sick, more desperate than even Gabi herself to get an update. But would he have sold his mother's house if he'd buried his wife in a shallow grave in the back garden? He would have been taking one hell of a risk.

Gabi can't show up at the Martins' house unannounced again, especially as Alicia will be busy with her newborn baby by now. And Gabi has already rung Professor Gareth Harvey twice recently. He was evasive and curt both times, just as he had been the first time she spoke to him over the phone, when she rang him to get a quote for her article. She's worried he'll lodge a complaint with the editor if she pesters him again, not that Mick would take it seriously. He's also keen for Gabi to follow up on this story now he knows they've discovered bones and not another Roman artefact.

'Ideally, I want a double-page spread with all the juicy facts,' he'd told her in the editorial meeting that morning. 'Preferably with a decent photo this time so I can splash it on the front page.' He looked pointedly at Joe when he said that. 'The partially unearthed body or skeleton or whatever that they've dug up, for example.' The picture his description conjured up in Gabi's mind had made her shudder. Mick had to have been joking – there was no way they could run a photo like that – but he must have a very dark sense of humour.

Sitting at her desk now, Gabi decides to ring Alicia. But although Alicia answers, it's clear she's not up to having visitors.

'I'm exhausted,' she replies when Gabi asks her how she is. 'The baby never sleeps, I've got mastitis, so I'm struggling to feed him, and I'm an emotional yo-yo.' Alicia's voice cracks.

'I'm sorry to hear that, Alicia. I hope things get better and easier for you soon.'

'The main thing is the baby's OK,' Alicia says, obviously trying to put a brave face on it. 'My mum's coming to stay for a while, so that'll help.'

They talk about the baby – Louis – then Alicia says, 'Do you have any more information about the skeleton they found in the garden?'

'No,' Gabi says. 'I was about to ask you that, actually.'

'Oh. Well, I haven't heard anything for weeks. There were loads of people here for days on end – forensic scientists, crime scene investigators, Professor Harvey and his archaeology students, police ... They exhumed the body then excavated a larger area to check if there were any other bodies.'

Do the police suspect a serial killer? That would be a great story! But the police were probably just being thorough. 'And were there more bodies?'

'No. God. Can you imagine? If anyone comes back, I'll let you know, but I think it might only be to take down the forensic tent – it's still in the garden.'

Gabi thanks her, wishes her all the best and ends the call just as the office bursts into a discordant round of 'Happy Birthday'. It's Mick's sixtieth and someone – probably Cheryl, who works in the accounts department – has ordered a cake from a confectioner's in Boutport Street. Gabi would like to slink off home and take a cold shower – it's been a warm, muggy day and she smells a bit sweaty – but she's known Mick for a long time and he's good to her, so she ought to stick around for a bit.

Mick produces some prosecco and plastic goblets. Everyone cheers loudly and then ducks as he opens a bottle and the cork bounces off the ceiling.

Joe materialises at her side, a beautifully wrapped parcel with blue ribbon around it under one arm.

'Is this for Mick?' Gabi asks.

'No.' Joe hands her the gift.

'It's not for me, is it?' She realises too late that Joe only gave her the present to hold so he could juggle his cake and drink.

'Er … no. For Alicia. Well, her baby. I thought we could drop in and see her. It's a pair of pyjamas.'

'Oh.' Heat rises from her neck and her cheeks burn. She lowers her head. She doesn't look attractive when she blushes and she can't look at Joe. He must think she's foolish. 'I rang her just a few minutes ago. She's not feeling up to seeing us. She's completely in the dark about the dig anyway.'

'Dead end, then.' Gabi can't tell if Joe is joking or if it's a fortuitous choice of words. 'I'll take back the PJs and get a refund.'

Gabi looks at Joe, appalled.

'I'll send the present by post,' he amends, setting his plate on someone's desk and taking the parcel from Gabi. He puts that down, too, and steers Gabi by the elbow towards a corner of the room, where they don't have to shout to make themselves heard over the chatter and raucous laughter.

'That's a nice thing you did for Alicia,' Gabi says, 'buying her baby a present.'

'I didn't do it for her,' Joe says. 'I did it for you.'

'Oh.' Her face flames again. 'Why?'

'I know how obsessed you were with finding out what happened to Leona. I want to help you.'

'You're right. I was consumed by the whole story. Once upon a time. I thought I'd get the exclusive that would launch my career. I had my eyes set on better opportunities than the *North Devon Echo*.'

'I remember. So, what changed?'

She shrugs. 'Leona was never found. The country went into lockdown and the search for Leona more or less ground to a halt. Practically overnight, she became yesterday's news and tomorrow's fish and chip paper, so to speak.'

'Yes, but if this does turn out to be Leona Walsh's body, you could still get your story. We might finally find out what happened to her.'

Gabi sighs. This is what she has been telling herself, too. But she hasn't told Joe the full truth and she senses he knows there's more to this. How much can she tell him? How much does he know?

'Listen, Joe, I sort of decided to leave Leona's case and her family alone.'

'Does this decision have anything to do with your boyfriend's disappearance, by any chance?'

She's thrown by his candour. And his perceptiveness. He can read her like a book. She's feeling prickly now as well as sweaty. He's absolutely right, of course. Every time she probes into Leona's disappearance, she feels as if she's reopening a wound that's still festering under her skin. Darren's disappearance was nothing like Leona's, but the two missing people are somehow – *still* – intricately entangled in her head. Not that it's any of Joe's business.

'He was my *fiancé*. And yes, it's partly due to his disappearance,' she snaps. It has everything to do with Darren going AWOL, if she's honest with herself, but she's not going to admit that to Joe. 'I realised that people go missing for all sorts of reasons and—'

'I'm sorry. I didn't mean to offend you. Or to pry. I know your fiancé went missing, but that's all I know.'

Rumours tend to spread like wildfire around the offices of the *Echo*. Gabi assumed her colleagues must have known and gossiped about it, even if they weren't technically in the offices, as everyone was working from home when she found out what had become of Darren Hughes.

'You probably don't want to talk about it, so I'll—'

'No, that's OK,' she says. This isn't a story she enjoys telling, but she has missed feeling able to confide in Joe and lately they seem to be getting back on track. She takes a deep breath.

But just then Mick appears, armed with a bottle of cheap fizz to top up their plastic cups, followed by Cheryl, who arrives to ply them with more cake and usher them back into the fold, and the moment has passed. Gabi scans the room for Joe half an hour or so later, but he has already left.

Gabi tends to sleep badly after sparkling wine and although she only had one glass – or, more accurately, one plastic cup – of prosecco because she was driving, she tosses and turns all night. Her body cries out for sleep, but her mind goes into overdrive. She keeps replaying the aborted conversation with Joe. It has got her thinking about Leona and her career, which is a good thing, as she's been stuck in a rut for way too long. But also about Darren, whose memory is like an inoperable tumour in her brain. Thanks to an ongoing, combined treatment of self-pity, self-care, alcohol, chocolate and therapy, it has shrunk to a more manageable size, but she fears it won't ever go away completely.

For Gabi, when Darren vanished from the radar, the not knowing was far worse than the finding out. She'd come up with so many scenarios and it had been torture. Once she found out what had really transpired, it was shocking and heartbreaking and impossible to digest, but at least it was over. There was relief mixed in with all the other emotions. Gabi often thinks of those two girls, Scarlett and Trixie. Trixie was only little at the time; she must be almost in her teens now. And Scarlett was a teenager back then; she'd be an adult now. Would Scarlett and Trixie get some form of closure, even if the truth turned out to be the worst-case scenario? What would it do to them if they found out irrefutably that their mum was dead? And that their dad had killed their mum? It would be devastating for them. But wouldn't it be better to know?

Plus, it could be Gabi's big break. This would be a great hook. A killer angle. Literally.

She's still pondering her own unanswered questions when she shuffles into the railway station in Barnstaple, feeling far from refreshed after a virtually sleepless night, and buys a return ticket to Exeter.

On the train, she texts Mick to say she's got an appointment with Professor Gareth Harvey at the university. It's not entirely true. She's on her way to see Harvey, but he doesn't know she's coming. He may not even be there. It's June. Gabi's not even sure if there are still lectures and tutorials at this time of year. But if he's around, she has decided to butter him up, pretend she wants to write an article about him and his work, dressing it up so it sounds like a puff piece. Maybe that way she can glean some info on the ongoing investigation from him.

She intends to note down some questions on the train – she likes to be prepared – but she falls asleep. She wakes up with a jolt when the Tannoy sputters into life to announce, at an ear-piercing volume, the train's imminent arrival at Exeter Central. Sod it. She'll have to wing it. If he's there and accepts to talk to her.

Streatham Campus is about a mile from the railway station. Gabi decides to hoof it so she can gather her thoughts and come up with some pertinent questions for Professor Harvey.

The archaeology department is housed within the Laver Building – a rectangular block of reddish-brown bricks that resembles a large, unimaginative Lego construction. Inside the eyesore, the vibe is more modern, light and airy. A pretty girl in her late teens or early twenties with several tats and facial piercings points Gabi in the right direction.

'I'm one of his students,' the girl says. She's wearing cut-off denim shorts and black patent Dr. Martens. Gabi went to a different university – Brighton – around twenty years ago, but she herself wore a similar uniform. 'I've just come from his office. It's on the third floor.'

Gabi finds the office easily enough and knocks on the door.

'It's open,' comes the bark from inside.

Professor Harvey is sitting at his desk, a red pen poised in his hand.

'Hi, I'm Gabriela Conti – Gabi – from the *North Devon Echo*. We spoke on the phone?'

He looks far from pleased to see Gabi, but gestures for her to take a seat opposite him. He takes his time and makes her wait while he scribbles notes in the margin of the coursework he's grading.

She scans the room. A human skeleton model stands to the professor's right, practically looking over his shoulder, so close Gabi could reach out and shake its hand. It has a white lab coat draped across its shoulders. Towering stacks of lidded, transparent storage boxes line the wall behind the academic, each labelled with yellow stickers, and each containing bones. She squints, but can't make out the scrawled handwriting on the labels. A row of animal skulls – unlike the skeleton, they look real – sit on top of the storage boxes.

Harvey finishes one paper and starts marking another. Gabi takes out a notebook and pen – she doesn't dare ask if she can record their conversation – and clears her throat, but gets no reaction from Harvey. His frostiness is at odds with his looks. He has a gracious, rounded face, attractive stubble and striking blue-green eyes. She has to admit he's handsome, despite his overlong sideburns.

'Professor Harvey,' she begins when he finally looks up. 'I was hoping to write a piece about you and the great work you do here at the university, the archaeology department, that sort of—'

'Ms Conti,' he cuts her short, eyeing her reproachfully. 'Usually, I only receive people from outside the university by appointment. I don't have much time, so shall we cut to the chase? To what do I owe the pleasure of this unexpected visit?'

She won't allow Professor Harvey to intimidate her. 'I was wondering what more you can tell me about your dig in Benton.'

'Probably not a lot. What do you want to know?'

She sits up straight and maintains eye contact. 'How long had the skeleton been there?'

'I can't say.'

'You must have some idea.'

'It's recent. That's all I can tell you. It is definitely not Roman.'

She already knows that much. 'OK. Do you have any idea what the cause of death might have been?'

'No, I can't say,' he repeats.

'Can't say or won't say?' Her dislike of this man is growing. He's just as abrupt in person as on the phone.

'Look, Ms Conti—'

'Gabi.'

'—I'm an archaeologist, not an anthropologist. Or a forensic scientist, for that matter. It's up to them to determine time elapsed since death, cause of death, age of the skeleton, et cetera.'

'How do they do that? Carbon dating?'

'Carbon dating, Ms Conti, as everyone knows, is used only for ancient remains.' His voice drips with condescension. 'No, they will take into consideration soil composition and pH balance, insect activity, and so on and so forth.'

Gabi writes that down. 'I know you checked the surrounding area for other bodies and found none. Did you find anything else at all?'

'Yes, we used radar, but we found no other bodies. We did, however, find a watch – a Garmin – with a metal buckle and a plastic strap. Now, is there anything else? I have a ton of marking to get through.'

'Do you happen to have any photos of the dig you could email me?' Gabi asks. This might be pushing it, but she may as well give it a go.

'No. Now if that's all, Ms Conti, as I said, I have work to do.'

She doesn't know whether to burst into tears or thump the professor. She puts her pen and notepad back into her handbag and gets to her feet. 'Just one more question. Where is the skeleton now?'

'With the Home Office forensic pathologist,' he replies without looking up, already back to his marking.

He hasn't really answered her question. She could contact the local hospital and public mortuaries to ask if they've officially identified the body, but it would be a waste of time. They won't divulge any info over the phone to a journo.

'Thank you so much for your time, Professor.' She manages not to let too much sarcasm seep into her voice.

The student she spoke to earlier, the one in the Dr. Martens boots, is still in the entrance hall, chatting to some of her friends. She smiles as she sees Gabi. Gabi smiles back and heads for the main doors. Then she stops, turns around and walks towards the student.

'Hi again. Sorry to interrupt, but I was wondering if I could ask a question or two.' She hands the girl a business card. 'My name's Gabi. I'm a journalist.'

'I'll catch up with you later,' the student says to her friends, then to Gabi, 'I'm Freya. Is it about the archaeology course here?'

'No, it's about a recent dig Professor Harvey was in charge of in a village called Benton. Do you know—'

'Oh, yes. I was one of the diggers,' Freya squeals. 'So exciting!'

A surge of hope lifts Gabi. 'Do you happen to have any photos?'

The student pulls a mobile phone out of the back pocket of her shorts and stands shoulder to shoulder with Gabi as she swipes through the photos in the camera roll. Freya has several pictures of a partially unearthed skeleton, fitting Mick's specifications precisely. Alicia did say bones, but Gabi expected a dead body, something recognisable, even if it was badly decomposed. The remains in the photo look more like the skeleton model in Professor Harvey's office. They don't seem real. Gabi swipes through them, fascinated as much as she is repelled.

'This is all that's left after five years?' she says, more to herself than Freya.

'I don't think they know yet how long the skeleton had been there, but yeah, that's all that remains of it. And bits of clothing, a watch and what's left of a shoe, that sort of thing.'

Gabi selects some less gruesome, more publishable photos of Harvey's team hard at work and asks Freya to email them to her. She needs one that's not too graphic for her article. While she waits for the emails to arrive in her inbox, she says, 'I didn't get much out of Professor Harvey. He more or less threw me out of his office.'

Freya guffaws. She has a laugh like a leaf blower. 'He's a bit of a cold fish until you get to know him,' she says. 'He's a great teacher, actually. Experienced, interesting, good leadership skills, good communication.'

Gabi harrumphs. 'Are we talking about the same professor?'

Freya laughs again. 'I'll put in a good word for you.'

Gabi's about to tell her not to bother, but thinks better of it. 'Perhaps I came on a bad day. He was busy marking papers. Maybe *you* can tell me something about the skeleton?'

'Not much, I'm afraid. Our job was essentially to exhume the remains. The rest is up to the anthropologists.'

Gabi's heart sinks. That's what Professor Harvey said, albeit more brusquely.

'All I can say for sure is that the skeleton was relatively recent, but I have no idea how recent,' Freya continues, 'and that we're looking at female skeletal remains.'

Gabi thinks she has misheard. 'Female?'

'Yes. That will have to be confirmed, but you don't need a microscope to determine the sex. You can tell that from the eyes, jaw and pelvis.'

Gabi remembers the two police officers in Alicia's back garden who had bet on the sex of the skeleton. Now she gets the joke, although she still doesn't find it remotely funny.

As Gabi heads back to the station, she thinks about Leona Walsh, casting her mind back to when they were at school together. Leona was intelligent, athletic and popular, but she could be rather mean, a bully. Gabi, who was hopeless at team sports but who got higher marks than Leona in every subject except P.E., had been Leona's target more than once. Her nemesis. She remembers coming home once with chewing gum stuck in her hair; on another occasion with paint on her uniform; and on yet another occasion with bruised shins after Leona whacked her accidentally on purpose with her hockey stick during a match, even though they were on the same team.

Did Leona turn out to be a good person? A nicer person than she was at school? She was a local councillor, who allegedly submitted forged invoices – thousands of pounds worth – while in office. She had probably made some enemies over her lifetime.

But she also had two little girls who loved her. And as far as Gabi knows, Leona did nothing to deserve her fate, that is, *if* the remains found in the garden of Rose Cottage in Benton are those of Leona Walsh. It seems likely that they are, but Gabi's not quite convinced. Something doesn't add up. Gabi resolves to get to the bottom of the Leona Walsh case. This time, she won't stop until she finds out the truth.

Chapter 11

Friday, 6th December 2019: Day Six

When Matt went to wake Scarlett for school the next day, Trixie was sleeping next to her older sister, her thumb hanging out of her open mouth. She woke up, too.

'Hop back into your own bed now, sweetie,' he said to her.

To his dismay, Trixie burst into tears. Was something frightening her? Was it something in her bedroom that had triggered her night terror? Or was there something that reminded her of it?

'Hey, it's OK. Auntie Roxie's here. She'll look after you while I take Scarlett to school.'

Only Trixie called Roxanne by the diminutive of her name – to her face, that is. Roxanne hated it. She insisted on calling Trixie by her full name – Beatrix, which Trixie couldn't stand. It was a sort of longstanding joke between them. But knowing her aunt was here didn't soothe Trixie.

'Do you want to sleep in my bed for a while?' Matt asked.

Without taking out her thumb, Trixie nodded. He scooped her up and carried her into his bedroom. She curled up into a ball, looking tiny and lost in the double bed. He kissed her on the forehead and tucked her in.

Although Scarlett was dressed in her uniform when she came down for breakfast, she wasn't nearly as enthusiastic about going to school as she had been the previous day. She complained she was tired; Trixie had woken her up in the middle of the night when she'd come into her room and got into her bed. But Matt got the feeling there was more to it.

'You don't have to go if you don't want to. Perhaps it's too soon to go back every day,' he suggested.

'I can't stay cooped up here all day. I'll go mental. I need something to take my mind off everything, you know?' She sounded older than her fourteen years, but she didn't sound convinced.

'Did something happen at school yesterday? Did your test not go well?'

'It went fine.'

He waited. That was often the best way to get Scarlett to talk. If he quizzed her, she tended to clam up.

Sure enough, as they put on their coats and shoes in the hallway, Scarlett said, 'Keira Sutton hasn't invited me to her birthday party.'

He'd never heard her mention this classmate before, but that obviously wasn't the point. 'Well, sweetie, maybe she thought it wasn't a good time for you,' he said gently. Secretly, he was relieved she hadn't been invited. It wouldn't look good for his daughter to be celebrating anything when her mother hadn't even been missing for one week. He was increasingly worried about the media's growing fascination with him and his family.

'That's not why I didn't get an invite. It's because her parents want her to have nothing to do with us.' Scarlett glared at him as though this was entirely his fault.

He felt sad for Scarlett and mad at the Suttons, whoever they were. Only the day before, Harriet Clark, the head teacher of Trixie's school had rung to say they'd replaced him in the literacy project, which had been his idea. She'd made it sound as if this was temporary and for his benefit, but now, because of the Suttons, doubt skulked into his mind. Was this how it was going to be from now on? Would they be ostracised because some keyboard warriors were vilifying them? He didn't know what to say to Scarlett, and so, stupidly, said nothing.

'I'll wait in the car.' Scarlett stomped out of the front door, signalling that the conversation was over.

The number of media vans and cars crammed into the lane was outrageous. Roxanne had warned him, but this beggared belief. There were twice as many vehicles as last time he'd ventured out. His palm pumping the horn, he opened his window a fraction and hollered for the journalists to move their vehicles and let them through. It took several minutes. He eyeballed the reporters through the dirty window of his car. The cheeky bastards took photos and shouted questions and pressed their faces up against the windows of the car as Matt weaved his way past. His knuckles white from gripping the steering wheel, he resisted the urge to leap out and deck a few of them. He'd have a word with DC Chapman when he showed up and find out what could be done to keep these inconsiderate pillocks from blocking their road and invading their privacy.

Scarlett hardly uttered a word, and when he dropped her in front of school, late, she swung her bag over her shoulder and strolled away from him without saying goodbye. His heart heavy, he headed home. He dreaded facing the newshounds again.

Driving up the hill to the house was as much of an obstacle course as the descent had been. There was still no sign of Chapman when he got home. And Roxanne wasn't in the kitchen or the sitting room. He called her name a few times before she heard him and called back. She was in the utility room.

'What are you doing in here?' he asked. Roxanne had her back to him. She was bending over, putting on a load of laundry.

'Beatrix wet the bed,' she said without straightening up or turning round. 'I realised when I saw a pair of pyjamas discarded on her bedroom floor.' That explained what Trixie was doing in

Scarlett's bed. And why she didn't want to go back to her own room when she woke up. 'She's in the shower.' Roxanne pressed the start button, then whirled round to face him. 'You should take her to see a counsellor.' Her tone was accusatory, as if he could have prevented this. He couldn't seem to do or say anything right this morning.

He bristled at his sister-in-law's parenting advice. What made her such an expert? She didn't have any children. He almost came out with a remark along those lines, but he bit it back. Roxanne and Adam didn't have kids because they couldn't. Something to do with both Roxanne's dysfunctional ovaries and Adam's low sperm count. Roxanne loved Trixie and Scarlett, and doted on them, even though she must have been reminded every time she saw them of what she herself didn't have. And Roxanne had a point. Trixie was struggling to process everything that was going on. They all were.

'Trixie does get professional help, Roxanne,' he said, 'for her … difficulties. But I'll mention it to the therapist, OK? In the meantime, I think it's best not to make a big deal out of her wetting the bed in case that makes it worse.'

Roxanne nodded, seemingly pacified. He offered her a hot drink and a biscuit, but she shook her head. They went through to the living room and sat on the sofas.

'Did you know about this Toby Wigmore guy?' he asked. Leona confided quite a lot in Roxanne, but would she have told her sister she was cheating on him?

'What about him?' Apparently not. 'Who the hell's Toby Wigmore?'

Good question. He'd spent a couple of hours the previous night trawling the web trying to answer it. Wikipedia had been fairly forthcoming. Toby Wigmore was the Conservative MP for Beckenham, although that could change with the general election in a few days' time. His 'official portrait' showed a smug-looking man with greying hair, a dark monobrow and unnaturally big ears, wearing a dark jacket over a pink shirt and a pink-and-grey-striped tie. He was forty-eight years old, married – to a fellow Conservative councillor – with one grown-up son, and the University of Sheffield was listed as his alma mater. He was a former rugby player, which might have explained the ears. Leona certainly hadn't been attracted to him for his looks.

'The police didn't tell you? He's Leona's lover, so they say.'

Roxanne's jaw dropped open and she gaped at him, rendered speechless for once. He'd been too blunt, but there was no way of whitewashing it. For a split-second, he saw Leona in her sister's face. Like Leona, Roxanne had high cheekbones, a long, narrow nose and striking green eyes. But while these features made his wife breathtakingly beautiful, they somehow made his sister-in-law look a little scary. And Leona's eyes reminded him of emeralds, whereas he associated Roxanne's eyes, which were flashing wildly now, with the colour of envy.

When Roxanne finally found her tongue, she said, 'That's so typical of Leona! She only thinks about herself! Isn't one man enough for her?'

They were on the same wavelength, for once. He'd been asking himself the same thing, over and over.

As quickly as it had slipped, Roxanne's concerned-older-sister mask was back in place. 'Could this ... what's his name—'

'Toby Wigmore.' His hands balled into fists as he spat out the name.

'Whatever. Could he have something to do with her disappearance, do you think?'

'I don't know. He's the anonymous donor, the one who has offered thirty grand for info leading to Leona's whereabouts.'

'Really? Well, if he wants Leona's safe return and is prepared to pay that amount of money for her to be found, he's unlikely to have had a hand in her disappearance,' Roxanne reasoned.

'Unless he knew the police would find out he was sleeping with Leona at some point and the reward is a double bluff.'

Roxanne threw him a look of disdain. 'You've been reading – and writing – too many bad whodunnits.'

He didn't take the bait, mainly because Trixie came into the kitchen, effectively putting an end to that conversation. Roxanne buzzed around her niece, making her breakfast, producing a comb from somewhere and running it through Trixie's wet hair and talking non-stop. Trixie looked calmer than an hour or so ago, apart from the grimaces she made every time her aunt tugged at a knot.

The doorbell went. DC Chapman had arrived. Although they had no official routine, he apologised for being late. 'I had to take my daughter to hospital for an X-ray this morning after she fell and hurt her arm in the playground at school yesterday,' he explained, shrugging out of his coat and pulling off his beanie. 'Fortunately, there were no bones broken.'

Chapman was clearly hands-on when it came to raising his kids. They had that in common. Chapman had mentioned his wife once, but Matt had no idea what she did for a living.

'Sophie … DS Holland is on her way,' Chapman said.

Matt lit the fire in the living room. Roxanne and Trixie were sitting on the sofas. Trixie had a rug over her and was watching Netflix. He hoped it was age-appropriate. Being so much younger than Scarlett, Trixie got to watch series and films with sex, swear words and violence that Matt found unsuitable, not to mention disturbing. Just a few weeks ago, on Hallowe'en, he'd caught her watching a horror film with Scarlett that was, in Matt's opinion, beyond scary. Leona hadn't considered it a big deal. He glanced at the TV screen. Some American high school series. It looked tame enough. Roxanne would step in if necessary.

When DS Holland arrived, she, DC Chapman and Matt sat at the kitchen table. The kitchen, it seemed, was everyone's preferred place for important discussions.

'Just a quick visit, Mr Walsh,' Holland said, declining Matt's offer of tea. 'It's about your wife's running shoe.'

'The one that was found at the reservoir? Or the missing one?'

She ignored his question. 'It's squeaky clean.'

'I'm sorry?'

'I said, it's squeaky clean.' She was wearing her hair loose today – it suited her – and she tucked imaginary wayward strands behind her ears with both hands at the same time. 'You'd expect a running shoe to have bits of grit and gravel and dirt stuck in the tread pattern of the soles, but there's nothing.'

'I don't understand,' he said, although he was beginning to. 'Those trainers weren't new. Is that what you're implying?'

'Not exactly.'

He suspected her silences were deliberate, her superpower, to make him talk. DC Chapman didn't say a word. He looked uncomfortable, as if he really didn't want to be privy to the grilling Matt was getting.

Matt should have kept quiet, too, but he couldn't help himself. 'Leona cleaned her shoes after each run,' he said. It was true. Leona was a bit OCD about her running shoes. She would never put them in the washing machine, claiming that would damage them, so instead, she used warm water and detergent and scrubbed them with a brush after each run, then dried them in the airing cupboard. 'Could that explain it? Or perhaps there was no dirt because of the snow. That might be why her trainer was clean.'

'It wasn't snowing on the Saturday evening when, according to you, she went for a run at Wistlandpound Reservoir.'

He shrugged. There were also two witnesses who placed Leona at the reservoir last Saturday evening, but he didn't point that out. Instead, he decided to play DS Holland at her own game, saying nothing until she broke the silence.

It took a while. 'Shall I tell you what I think?' she asked eventually, staring him down with her dark brown eyes.

He could tell from her expression she no longer felt sorry for him, as she'd seemed to when DC Chapman first introduced her. She now doubted him, suspected him. 'Please do.'

'I think the shoe was planted there.' She paused, expecting him to ask why or by whom, perhaps. But he was way ahead of her and waited it out. 'Possibly by the person who took her,' she said as if she was continuing her sentence. 'To make us look in the wrong place.'

'Took her? Let me get this straight. You're now saying there was foul play?'

'We'll be pursuing this line of inquiry.'

'But I thought—'

'As I told you before, with each new piece of evidence, we revise our working hypothesis.' Then with a change of tone that almost implied her question didn't follow on from what she'd just said, she asked, 'Mr Walsh, would you have any objection to us having another look round your premises?'

What could he say? If he refused, they'd think he had something to hide. They'd only come back with a Section 8 PACE warrant. For all he knew, they already had a search warrant up their sleeves and would present it the instant he declined. 'Of course not,' he said, affecting an amiable tone. 'Anything to help find my wife.'

He showed DS Holland out. They exchanged a few words about the swarm of journos in front of the house.

'I'll see what I can do about that,' Chapman offered, grabbing his coat from the peg in the hallway. 'I doubt I can get rid of them, but I'll ask them to move back from the house, give your family some privacy, see if I can get them to move their vehicles out of the lane.'

'Thanks, Andrew,' Matt said. He didn't rate Chapman's chances.

Matt closed the door behind the police officers and sighed. He wanted to ask Chapman if there was any more on Wigmore, but decided to look into it himself. He went to Leona's study, dug out the folder with the passwords and within minutes, he'd booted up her laptop and was in.

He found what he was looking for almost immediately. Leona had clearly deleted all Wigmore's emails from her inbox, but there were a few recent messages still in her Sent folder. There were also a few messages – from nearly three years ago – in the Bin. Matt used the search bar to bring up their correspondence and started reading. Some of the emails were tender; some were sexually explicit; some contained selfies. He stumbled on a nude selfie Leona had evidently taken in front of the full-length mirror in their bedroom. Grabbing the waste basket at the foot of the desk, he retched, but managed – just – to keep his breakfast down.

He had no idea how long he sat on Leona's chair, scrolling through her emails, but after a while, he could take no more; he'd seen more than enough. He massaged his temples – he had a headache coming on – and his nausea had barely subsided. He wanted to delete every single message between Leona and Wigmore on the computer, as though that would erase Leona's affair and rewrite their marriage in its place, a palimpsest. But the illicit love story would remain documented somewhere in the ether, even if he obliterated all their correspondence from the cloud, too. And it would look suspicious to the police if he gave in to that urge.

He was surprised they hadn't already taken Leona's laptop – perhaps they would now they were going to conduct a more thorough search of the house. But he imagined they'd gleaned as much information from the mobile phone they'd fished out of the reservoir inside her rucksack as he had from Leona's laptop. That had to be how they'd found out about Toby Wigmore in the first place. He'd sensed they were keeping something from him, something to do with Leona's phone. He'd been right. How he wished he'd been wrong.

As far as Matt could tell, Leona and Wigmore's relationship had begun a few weeks after they met at a Tory party conference in London three years ago. They'd met up mainly in London hotels, but also at least once in Wigmore's secondary home in Southend-on-Sea. This property had incurred some structural damage due to dry rot. Reading between the lines and judging from the immense gratitude Wigmore expressed, along with a photo of his penis that Matt would never be able to unsee, Leona had paid for the dry rot treatment. How much had that set her back?

In the more recent emails he'd skimmed, Leona and Wigmore fantasised about living together in the house in Southend one day. It was more of a long-term plan – Leona had made it clear to Wigmore that the girls were too young for her to leave Matt; Wigmore was keen to avoid a scandal that could ruin his political career. But who knew what the two of them had said to each other, face to face or over the phone?

The police now believed there might have been third-party involvement in Leona's disappearance. But these emails proved Leona had intended to leave him for her lover. Could Leona have left home of her own accord? Surely the police were considering this possibility. Objectively, in either scenario, it seemed unlikely Leona would be found – alive or dead – in the area around the reservoir, or indeed anywhere in the area at all. And yet, faced with mounting public pressure, the police had promised to redouble their efforts and expand the zones they were searching.

Leona had been missing for six days and there was no concrete lead, no clue whatsoever, no trace of her. Matt got the feeling the police were looking for a needle in a haystack. In the wrong place.

Missing, Presumed Murdered
A True Crime Podcast Hosted by Gabriela Conti
Audio File 4
Interview with Harriet Clark, head teacher of Blackmoor Primary School.
2024

This is the story of Leona Walsh, whose disappearance in December 2019 has remained a mystery for nearly five years. Join me as I explore the truths and lies in this case. I am Gabriela Conti and you're listening to **Missing, Presumed Murdered***, a true crime podcast.*

Gabriela Conti: Mrs Clark, thank you for talking to me today. You're the head teacher at Blackmoor Primary School, where Trixie was a pupil. Is that correct?

Harriet Clark: Yes. The year Trixie's mother went missing, Trixie was seven years old, poor love, so she would have been in Year 3. Her sister had also been a pupil at Blackmoor Primary School, but that was before my time. Scarlett was a good pupil, though, by all accounts.

GC: And what about Trixie? Was she a good pupil, too?

HC: She excelled in some subjects, maths, for example. Her reading skills were also way higher than average. And she was an amazing artist. But she had certain difficulties. She was a visual learner and had a terrific memory, but she struggled to understand verbal instruction, for example. Her social skills were a little lacking so she didn't make friends easily with her classmates. We worked closely with a special educational needs coordinator. Trixie was very keen to improve in the areas where things didn't come so naturally to her, like communication. She was also working with a professional outside of school.

GC: Do you mean she was autistic?

HC: It's difficult to diagnose a child with autism. It's not like there's a blood test for that. And, to be fair, Trixie's symptoms, if that's the right word, were fairly mild. As far as I'm aware, the specialist Trixie was working with didn't diagnose her as autistic. Moreover, many parents don't like labels like 'autistic' or 'on the spectrum' or 'neurodiverse', and if that's the case, we follow their lead. We consider each pupil to be an individual with individual strengths and needs, and we do our best to take any difficulties our pupils may have into account.

GC: *Did you know Trixie's parents well?*

HC: *We knew Trixie's mother more by reputation, really. Oh, I wasn't referring to the money scandal. I just meant, well, Leona Walsh was a local councillor. She was well known in the community; she was invested in the area.*

GC: *What about Trixie's father? Did you know him well?*

HC: *Hmm. Well, I thought so at the time. Now, with hindsight, I think I probably didn't know him as well as I believed. Do you ever really know someone? Or what they're capable of? We saw a lot of him when Trixie was a pupil at Blackmoor Primary. It was Matthew who drove Trixie to school and picked her up. He often volunteered to help out and accompany us when we took our pupils on educational day trips and so on. I suppose because of his job as an author, he could be flexible about his working hours. And he set up the Literacy Project with the teachers of Years 4 and 5. The idea – it was his idea, initially – was to find fun ways to encourage pupils to read and write. Matthew came in once a week to run that. It was very successful. In fact, we still have the project today.*

GC: *Without Matthew now, obviously.*

HC: *Yes. We had to dispense with his services a long time ago, years before all these recent developments. I don't think he was even a suspect at the time, but we received phone calls and emails from worried parents just a few days after his wife went missing. They didn't want their children to participate in the project anymore if Matthew Walsh remained involved with it. So we had no choice. He had to go.*

Chapter 12

Saturday, 7th December 2019: Day Seven

They had to leave the house for a few hours while the police searched it. Roxanne took Scarlett and Trixie to her place, but Matt needed some time to himself, so he decided to take Sydney out for a long, overdue walk. He put on a pair of walking boots and a waterproof coat, then slipped out the back door to avoid the journalists, who hadn't moved an inch, despite Chapman's efforts. If anything, they'd multiplied.

He chose one of Leona's favourite routes – across the moors, and through Heddon's Mouth Wood. When the weather was good, they would walk as far as the clifftops and stare out across the Bristol Channel at the South Wales coastline before turning back and stopping at Hunter's Inn for a beer on the way home. He wouldn't get that far today, and certainly didn't intend to stop off anywhere for a beer, but it would do him – and the dog – good to get some fresh air. He imagined Leona by his side as Sydney bounded ahead.

Most of the snow had melted, although some large white patches clung stubbornly to the hilltops. The frost glistened in the sun's spotlight, and icicles, dangling from the branches of the trees, shimmered. The air was chilly despite the sun. Matt took in the perfect, panoramic view, like a wintry, glittery scene on a Christmas card. It had a calming effect on him. Until he remembered it was less than three weeks until Christmas Day itself. Leona had been missing for a whole week. That was a long time. Statistically, her chances of being found were diminishing by the day and the chances of her being found alive were virtually non-existent. How could they possibly get through Christmas this year without Leona, let alone celebrate it?

Closing his eyes, he offered his face to the sun. He wasn't at all religious – to anyone who asked, he described himself as agnostic, though, really, he was more of an atheist. But he said a silent prayer. Thrusting his hands into the pockets of his coat – he'd forgotten his gloves – he felt something inside one of the pockets: a piece of paper or cardboard. He was about to take it out and look at it, but he remembered what it was. Whistling for the dog, he turned and walked home.

Although the police had promised not to disturb their belongings more than necessary, nothing was in its place. Drawers upstairs and downstairs had been rifled, or more likely, the contents had been tipped out and then thrown back in. The books were in the wrong order on the shelves, both in Matt's study and in the living room. The messiness accentuated the emptiness. Leona kept the house spick and span, meticulously tidy. In the girls' rooms, it looked as if nothing had been touched, which was a relief, but he imagined the police had just been more careful about putting everything back the way it was. Trixie would have thrown a tantrum if her things had been in disarray. As he'd anticipated, their computers had been taken. Matt's car was also gone. DS Holland assured him everything would be returned very soon.

When everyone had gone, Matt rang Roxanne and asked if she could keep the girls with her for a bit longer, then he spent the next hour or so tidying, trying to shake the feeling that their home had been desecrated.

As Matt was finishing up, his mobile went. The caller ID showed it was DC Chapman. He was spending the weekend with his family, but he'd promised to check in. Matt sank into an armchair and took the call.

Once they'd got through the formalities, he told Chapman about the search. He also gave him a watered-down version of what he'd discovered on Leona's laptop. This was back to front. Here he was, updating Chapman, and yet Chapman was the one who was supposed to keep him up to speed about the investigation.

'What do *you* know about Wigmore?' Matt asked.

'So, as you know, Leona paid him thirty thousand pounds for structural repairs to his secondary home in Essex—'

'Thirty grand?' He'd had no idea it was that much. There must have been a hell of a lot of structural damage. That was one mystery solved, at least. This was undoubtedly what Leona had spent the embezzled money on.

'I know!' Chapman said. 'Oh, the irony.'

They obviously weren't on the same wavelength and it took Matt a few seconds to see why this was ironic. Of course. The same amount as the reward money Wigmore had put up.

'Deliberate or coincidental?' Matt asked.

'Who knows? Perhaps the guy has a sick sense of humour.' The comment made Matt feel as if Chapman was on his side, and he appreciated that. 'He claims he was going to pay her back and he'd saved the money to do just that.'

'He's trying to keep himself out of trouble,' Matt said.

'I'd say so. It's not going to work,' Chapman said. That made Matt smile to himself. 'Obviously, there's an ongoing inquiry into the fraud charges against your wife,' he continued, 'but for the moment, we've found nothing to suggest there's a connection between those allegations and her disappearance.' Maybe that was why DC Chapman hadn't gone into detail before about Wigmore.

That and the fact it was a tricky topic. 'It is, however, one of the avenues we're exploring.'

Once Matt had ended the call, a disquieting silence seemed to descend on the room. He was used to being by himself during the day, but there had been so many people here over the past week. Now he was alone again, he felt it keenly. Alone and lonely. He switched on the television, not only to provide some background noise, but also to catch up on the latest news about Leona. He feared the worst, but he still wasn't prepared for what he saw.

Sky News was broadcasting their own reconstruction of Leona's disappearance to 'raise awareness about Leona's last known movements'. A shaky camera held on the shoulder; dramatic voice-over narration; a female actress, who bore a passing resemblance to Leona, dressed in running clothes; and filmed in broad daylight with the sun bouncing off the water, snow loitering on the ground and obstinately hanging on to the trees – nothing like the conditions on the day Leona went missing. The report was amateurish and sensationalist, and presented nothing new.

But the BBC lunchtime news told a different story. An irate, elderly local man was bemoaning the damage to his garage, which had been broken into during the night.

'It's uncalled for. And unfair,' he shouted into the journalist's microphone. 'It's also very frightening. Even though I can't afford it, I'm considering hiring a private security firm so I can feel safe in my own home.'

The next image was of the on-location reporter, standing next to the elderly man, in front of his garage.

'In total, six homeowners, living within a four-mile radius of Wistlandpound Reservoir, have reported forced entry to their garden sheds, garages or barns,' she said in a suitably grave tone.

The scene cut to a shot of the same reporter in front of another home, her mic held to the face of a woman, presumably another victim. 'I'm very sorry someone has gone missing,' the woman said, looking directly into the camera and sounding anything but sorry, 'but her disappearance has nothing to do with me. It's not *my* home that needs to be searched.'

'The community here is a tight-knit one,' the reporter concluded, 'but, as you can tell, the locals are struggling not to feel resentful of the unwanted attention this high-profile case has attracted.'

The next image showed a face Matt recognised. The officer's name appeared on the screen before Matt could pluck it from his memory. Constable Owen Wright.

'We've been called out on numerous occasions within the past three or four days to disperse groups causing a nuisance,' he said. 'Instagrammers and YouTubers have been playing private detectives, peering through people's windows, trying the door handles of local residents' homes, and, in some instances, actually breaking into people's private property.'

Matt scowled at Wright and switched channels, catching the end of the live ITV lunchtime news. It more or less picked up from where he'd left off on the BBC news.

'This recent spate of breaking and entering is not the only example of amateur sleuths carrying out their own vigilante investigations into the disappearance of Leona Walsh,' the news anchor was saying. 'Armchair detectives have posted online all sorts of conspiracy theories about Leona's disappearance; members of the public have come to Wistlandpound Reservoir to make reels or take selfies for social media; "psychics" have also travelled to the place where Leona Walsh was last seen alive to use their "gifts" to uncover the truth. Detective Chief Inspector Peter Carter, the senior investigating officer in charge of the investigation, had this to say …'

DCI Carter filled the screen. He was wearing a suit and standing in front of a building Matt couldn't identify.

'We would strongly urge people from outside the area to stay away,' he said in his slightly high-pitched voice. 'Social media sleuths, both online and on site, are obstructing our inquiry into Leona's disappearance and wasting valuable police time and resources. The behaviour of these individuals is not only disrespectful to Leona Walsh's family, but in some cases also unlawful. Any criminal acts will of course be investigated.'

Matt stayed tuned and watched ITV News West Country. Leona's disappearance was still the main story, but the angle was different. The images were of his home, during his absence, with the police stomping in and out of the house. Blue-and-white tape stretched across the entrance with the words 'POLICE LINE DO NOT CROSS' clearly visible. He assumed it was to keep the journalists out, but it made Blackmoor Manor look like a crime scene. Matt sat up ramrod straight and swore. He'd come in the back door when he'd returned from his walk. Was the tape still there?

The news bulletin was short and to the point. 'Police searched missing woman Leona Walsh's family home this morning. The thirty-four-year-old mother of two disappeared one week ago today.'

The footage showed uniformed police officers ducking under the blue-and-white tape to carry out boxes, presumably containing some of their belongings that he hadn't yet noticed were gone, as well as his and Leona's computers.

The report concluded, 'Police refused to comment when asked if Leona's husband, the renowned crime writer Matthew Walsh, was now a suspect.'

He stabbed the red button on the remote control and stormed out of the living room. He yanked open the front door. The tape had been cut or torn in the middle, but it was still there. He removed it and wound it up, looking daggers at the mob of journalists and busybodies who were snapping photos of him with their phones and cameras. He was overcome with loathing, disbelief and fury. There were rows and rows of people. At the front, some of them were leaning on the front gate or the wall. They weren't physically crossing the boundary into his property, but this was a clear invasion of his privacy, an intolerable intrusion. He wanted to shout at them all to fuck off. He managed

– just – to swallow down the invective, but he couldn't refrain from slamming the front door when he went back into the house.

He threw the bundle of tape on the floor and stamped on it, an animalistic growl erupting from his throat. Then he sank onto the stairs, where he sat for several minutes, trying to slow down his breathing and his heart rate. The tears hadn't come on the day of the televised appeal, but they came now. As his body became racked with sobs, a curse went round and round his head. It wasn't directed against the journalists. It was aimed at his wife. *Damn you, Leona! Damn you!*

Swiping at his cheeks with his sleeve, he got to his feet and walked over to the wooden pegs on which his coat was hanging. He reached into the pockets and pulled out the business card he'd felt earlier when he was out on his dog walk.

Standing in the hallway, for seconds, maybe minutes, he turned the card over and over in his hands. The vitriolic comments some viewers had posted during the press conference flashed before his eyes. The head teacher at Trixie's school no longer wanted him to run the Literacy Project, and the parents at Scarlett's school didn't want their kids to have anything to do with his daughter. He was the police's main suspect. Christ, even his sister-in-law didn't completely trust him. He'd been inundated with emails, most of which he'd deleted without opening, and no one he knew ever called his landline – he never gave out the number – but it hadn't stopped ringing and he'd had to unplug it. Similarly, the calls to his mobile never stopped – he left it in silent mode most of the time. But few of their friends had called or texted, especially over the past couple of days. None of them had actually dropped in to see how they were doing.

Just as he'd feared from the start, the tide was turning. It had only been a week, but already public opinion was shifting against him. He was becoming a pariah, a suspect, an enemy. He was well aware of how detrimental this could be to his career in the current age of cancel culture. But, far more importantly, he needed to clear his name so his girls wouldn't suffer.

He looked down at the card. *Gabriela Conti*, he read. *North Devon Echo*. Perhaps Roxanne had been right to talk to the press. She'd just said the wrong thing. He'd been avoiding them, but it was time to let the media in and get them onside. Who was it that said 'Whoever controls the media, controls the mind'? It was time for a bit of mind control. He needed help to set the tone for this story, before the plot developed any further. He fetched his mobile and punched in Gabriela Conti's number.

Chapter 13

Saturday, 7th December 2019: Day Seven

Gabi wasn't sure exactly what she'd expected, but it wasn't this. Standing at the gate, she stared at Blackmoor Manor. It was both showy and austere; inviting, and yet imposing. Isolated. It made her think of a building at a boarding school, like the one she'd attended as a day pupil on the edge of Exmoor. Or a haunted house. The wayward, bare branches of some climbing plant or creeper – Gabi couldn't identify it – blended in with the façade, the grey stone offset only by the yellow lights glowing from inside. It was five p.m., and it was dark outside, making it impossible to see inside, even into the rooms where the curtains weren't drawn. This house had a history. It had a story to tell. What secrets were contained within these walls? Were there clues hidden somewhere in the manor's rooms that could reveal what had happened to Leona Walsh? Would they ever discover any tangible trace, any concrete proof?

Matthew Walsh had warned her there was a pack of press hounds in front of the house, but by the time Gabi arrived, there was only a smattering of her fellow journos hanging around.

Most of them had probably called it a day and gone to the pub. She thought she recognised one or two of the loiterers, so she kept her head down as she unlatched the gate and strode up the drive, hoping they'd assume she was a family friend rather than one of them. She could barely contain her excitement. Matthew Walsh had called *her*, Gabriela Conti. He wanted her – in his own words – to 'shape the narrative'. He'd promised her an exclusive. She'd dropped everything and driven straight out here. If everything panned out, this could be the story that defined her career.

The door opened immediately when she rang the bell. Matthew Walsh ushered her inside before she could speak. He was wearing a navy-blue woollen jumper, his stubble was several days old and his hair was unkempt. He looked even more exhausted than he had on the two occasions she'd seen him before – at the reservoir and at the press conference. She'd been there, in the conference room at the police headquarters in Exeter. She'd watched him read out his appeal, cringed as he made a right balls-up of it. No wonder he needed her to talk up his character.

'I'm a little late. I'm so sorry. I got lost,' she gushed as Matthew Walsh took her coat.

'Most people get lost when they come here for the first time. Did the satnav try to direct you across a field?'

'Er, no. My car doesn't have a satnav – it's way too old for that – and I couldn't get an internet connection on my phone to use Google Maps.'

'Ah. Well, it's not any easier to find Blackmoor Manor with a satnav or an app, to be honest.'

He led her into the living room and gestured at the armchairs and sofa for her to take a seat. 'My daughters are staying at my sister-in-law's for a few days,' he said, 'so it's just you and me. Would you mind if I opened a bottle of wine?'

She shot him a sideways glance. It sounded a bit like a come-on, but surely that was the last thing on his mind.

It must have sounded bad to him, too, because he added, 'It's been a tough day. A tough time. A total bloody nightmare and that's putting it mildly. I need a drink.'

She sat on an armchair and set up her phone, ready to record. The fire was lit and she watched, mesmerised, as the flames licked the logs. Matthew came back with a bottle of Burgundy in one hand and two glasses in the other.

'Will you join me, Gabi?' he asked, already pouring some wine into the glass he'd placed nearest her on the coffee table.

She was about to decline. It was way too early to drink. Plus, she was driving. But Matthew looked lost and lonely as well as stressed. The least she could do was accept a drink to keep him company.

'Just a drop for me, Matthew, please.' She held out her hand to stop him pouring, waited while he poured wine into his own glass, filling it almost to the brim, then asked, 'Is it OK with you if I record this?'

He nodded. 'Of course. And call me Matt,' he said.

'OK.' She tapped the red button on her phone. 'Shall we start at the beginning?'

'As good a place as any, I suppose.'

'Can you walk me through the last time you saw Leona, just before she went missing?'

Gabi knew the facts, but Matthew – Matt – might add something she wasn't aware of. She listened attentively as he talked about the row that Trixie, his daughter, witnessed; about Leona setting off for her run in the car, with the dog, but not coming home; about him ringing round their friends before phoning the police the following morning. He went into a lot of unnecessary detail for some of it, but he seemed to soft-pedal other parts. There was something about his story that didn't sit right with her, something a bit off. She got the impression he was telling the truth, but not the whole truth. What was he leaving out?

Even though she was recording their conversation, she took notes while he spoke. She remembered everything better if she wrote it down. From time to time, she glanced up and appraised him. Matt's chin had an arrogant tilt to it, offset by quite a cute cleft. She was impervious to this man's charms – she only had eyes for her fiancé – but she could see how women would find him attractive. He gave you the impression he could take care of you and needed you to take care of him at the same time.

'When you rang me, Matt, you said the police suspected you of killing your wife. What makes you think that?'

He took a gulp of his wine. 'A few things. Firstly, the police always look at the spouse or partner. It's often the husband. It's a cliché, but it's true. Then, Leona and I had a row that evening, as I mentioned. I should never have told the police about that. Initially, they latched on to the idea that she'd deliberately upped and left after our disagreement.'

The same idea had entered Gabi's head. 'What was the argument about?'

'The police asked that, too. Honestly, I can't even remember. That's how trivial it was.'

There it was again, that evasiveness. If it had been Gabi – if her partner had gone missing – she would have played their last conversation on a loop in her head, trying to work out if there was a clue in there somewhere and regretting she hadn't had the chance to make amends.

'It was nothing that couldn't be sorted out or that would make Leona want to leave me on the spot, if that's what you're thinking,' Matt said. It was indeed what she'd been thinking. 'Leona can be … argumentative,' he continued. 'We bicker a lot, but always talk things through once we've both cooled down.'

'OK. Is that all they've got? The police, I mean.'

'No, there's more, unfortunately,' Matt said. 'The shoe they found—'

'Leona's trainer? At Wistlandpound?'

'Yes. It was clean. No grit stuck in the soles of the shoe. Leona scrubbed her shoes after each run, which might explain it, but the police think the shoe was planted.' He raked his hand through his hair, making it even more dishevelled. 'They seem to think *I* planted her shoe.'

'What for?'

He shrugged. 'Beats me.'

Matt paused, slugging more wine, so she prompted, 'And the book. *Murder on the Moors*. I was at the press conference when that came up. In what ways does your wife's disappearance resemble the plot of your novel?'

Matt looked pensive. She couldn't tell if it was an act. He had to have been struck by the similarities between his own novel and the drama playing out in his life right now. Or was he weighing his words before he answered?

'It's the last book in the series and it hasn't been out that long, but I finished writing it some time ago now. I've written a standalone since then. It's funny, you read your own book so many times, you practically know it by heart by the time you send off the final draft to your editor. But it's surprising how quickly you forget it once it's done and dusted. It's not released until a year or so later. Um … let's see.'

At this point, he actually stroked his chin thoughtfully with his free hand. A chortle rose up inside her, but she managed to bite it back.

'The book kicks off with a search for a missing woman, mother of two children,' Matt continued. 'She's the main character's wife. He's the main suspect. But, you know, there are autobiographical elements in every book. Generally, I mean, not just mine.'

'Any other similarities?'

Matt hesitated again. 'None that spring to mind, not off the top of my head.'

This time, it wasn't just an impression. She *knew* Matt was glossing over the facts. She'd done her homework. She'd waded through the bloody book. In it, Walsh used obscure words that she'd had to look up – he'd probably looked them up himself, she'd bet he wouldn't have a clue what they meant if she asked him now – and he wrote long, descriptive passages that, as far as she could see, served only to pad out his chapters. Some scenes were so graphically violent that many reviewers on Amazon had cried out for trigger warnings.

'The missing woman in your novel was killed, wasn't she?'

'Yes.' Matt looked sheepish. 'By her husband.'

If you asked Gabi, *Murder on the Moors* was a bit meh. The husband, a former police officer turned crime writer, shot his wife dead on the moors with a shotgun and left her body as food for scavengers. The 'twist' at the end was that the whole novel had purportedly been written by the crime writer's main character who had committed murder rather than the crime writer himself – a story within a story. She hadn't seen the twist coming, but she'd been underwhelmed even so.

'You know, I used to be a police officer and I've been writing thrillers for many years now,' Matt said. 'If I wanted to commit the perfect murder, I could. But I promise you, I did not murder my wife.'

She believed him. The part about being capable of committing the perfect murder anyway. She wasn't sure if she believed he didn't kill his wife, even though he was convincing in proclaiming his innocence. Then again, maybe the man doth protest too much.

Matt leant back into the sofa. 'There's more,' he said with a sigh. Before Gabriela Conti arrived, he'd debated whether to bring this up. It was hard to talk about it and he felt like a fool. But it was bound to get out at some point. And it might be important. It might also help to keep the public sweet.

'Go on.'

'Leona had a lover.'

He noticed Gabi sit up straighter, all ears. The readers of the *Echo* would love this. This was his life, but for everyone else it would be juicy gossip. And it would sell newspapers.

'Toby Wigmore,' he continued. 'A Tory MP with big ears and a small penis.'

Gabi's mouth twitched at the corners, as if she was trying to suppress a giggle. He chuckled, a little nervously, and she burst out laughing. He smiled. She had an infectious laugh.

'I won't ask you how you know that,' Gabi said.

He wouldn't have told her anyway, but God he wished he could get that dick pic out of his head. 'Can you forget I said that last bit?' he asked. 'It's the alcohol talking.' He felt his face redden, but he couldn't be sure if he was blushing or if it was the wine combined with the heat from the fire.

'Probably not,' Gabi said, 'but I can promise not to print that detail.'

'Thanks.'

He drained his glass and set it on the coffee table. Gabi had taken only a couple of sips of her wine and didn't need a top up. He badly wanted another glass, but he fought the urge to reach for the bottle. He'd wait until Gabi had left.

'The rest of it will leak to the media eventually, you know that, don't you?' Gabi said, her expression serious again. 'This will be impossible to keep under wraps.'

'Yes. That's why I'm telling you. I want you to break it. As gently as possible.'

'OK. Matt, were you aware your wife was cheating on you?'

'No,' he said. 'I feel stupid, because their affair had been going on for three years. But I genuinely had no idea, never even suspected it was going on.'

'But it gives you motive, doesn't it? If the police think you knew.'

'Exactly. But between you and me, if I'd known my wife was having an affair, I'd have killed *him*, not *her*.'

He shouldn't have said that. The wine was numbing his brain-to-mouth filter. Gabi didn't seem to know how to respond. She jotted down something in her notebook. He tried to read upside down, but her writing was too small. He scrabbled for something to say.

But Gabi got there first. 'On the other hand,' she said, 'this guy could be a suspect. Are the police looking into him? I mean, he might have abducted her.'

'Or she may have left me to be with him. Yes, I believe they're looking into him. Perhaps less in connection with her disappearance and more because they suspect Leona may have given him the money she misappropriated – allegedly.'

'I see.'

Seeing her take more notes, he added, 'I'm not sure how much of that I'm actually allowed to share with you.'

'What I can't confirm with other sources, I'll phrase carefully,' Gabi said. 'I'll do my best to check out Toby Wigmore, too.'

'He's a politician. There should be plenty of dirt on him,' Matt comments.

That wasn't what Gabi meant – she had no intention of digging up any dirt on Toby Wigmore; she just wanted to look into his relationship with Leona. But no matter how she spun it, this would be massive. She was about to break news, just a few days before the general election, about a Conservative Member of Parliament having an extra-marital affair with a mother of two who has disappeared. She was going to have to word her article carefully to minimise the injuries to Matt in the fallout. Did he realise how explosive this would be? She didn't share her thoughts with him. He clearly needed an ally and she got the impression she was gaining his trust.

She wasn't sure how much she trusted him, though. He seemed to oscillate between saying the first thing that came into his head and giving his replies careful consideration so that some of what he said came out sounding dodgy, but the rest of it seemed rehearsed. Plus, he was twiddling his wedding band round his finger, a nervous tic, perhaps. Or could it be a tell? Was he lying? Had he known about the affair all along? He'd seemed furious

– murderous, even – when he'd told her about Toby Wigmore, but his reaction was certainly natural, given the circumstances.

'What's Leona like?' she asked. 'I mean, I knew her at school, but that was years ago.'

Matt sighed. 'I love my wife,' he said. 'She's driven, smart, beautiful, funny. She's the love of my life, my anchor.'

Gabi sensed an implicit 'but'. 'It's OK,' she said. 'We can keep this off the record if you want.' She made a show of ending the recording on her phone.

'She has her flaws, like everyone else,' Matt said. 'She can be difficult; she can be unkind. Temperamental.'

That sounded more like the Leona that Gabi used to know.

'She has mood swings and bouts of depression,' Matt continued, 'but when she's on form, she lights up the room. And when she trains her spotlight on you, it makes you feel like you're the only person who matters to her. I'm lost without her, Gabi, to tell you the truth.' His face crumpled. 'Completely lost.'

She studied Matt. He certainly looked untethered. Actually, he looked as if he was about to cry. He pulled his jumper over his head. It was hot in here with the fire burning. As his T-shirt rode up, she averted her gaze. She turned back to catch him eyeing the bottle of wine longingly.

'Can you dig out some photos, Matt? Ideally, pictures of Leona with you and your daughters.' The photo of Leona that had been used in every news bulletin and on all the posters was printed in indelible ink on the insides of everyone's eyelids. It was getting old. Gabi needed to have something fresh, something exclusive. She needed photos that would tell a story and show who Leona was, focusing on her good side and her achievements, obviously. 'Oh, and maybe a school photo? I'm thinking of starting my article by saying I went to school with Leona.' Having a personal connection with the missing woman would imbue her article – or articles – with authority and authenticity.

'Anything to help,' Matt said, getting to his feet.

She wondered what he meant by that. Anything that would help her? That would help her to help him? That would help find Leona?

While Matt was hunting for photos, Gabi scrolled through the different scenarios in her head. Drowned. Murdered. Abducted. Absconded. That was it. There were no other possibilities. With every day that passed, it seemed less likely they would find Leona alive. Gabi was beginning to wonder if they would find her at all.

Chapter 14

Thursday, 12th December 2019: Day Twelve

Gabi's feature had come out earlier that week, three days after her interview with Matt. Illustrated with some of the photos Matt had selected, it painted a portrait of the Walshes as a loving family. So far, Gabi only had Matt's word to go on and she hoped it was an accurate representation.

With a bit of luck, this article would be the first of many. There seemed to be an unspoken pact between Matt and her, a transaction. She had to present him positively – or at least objectively – and he would give her exclusive interviews. She was ravenous for more. She wanted to reveal new facts about the case, but there was nothing ground-breaking in this piece. She couldn't include the fact Leona's trainers were suspiciously clean – not without a quote from the police, and she hadn't been able to get one.

She'd kept back the part about Leona's affair with a Conservative MP. Deliberately. At Mick's suggestion. That revelation was to be published in next week's edition of the *Echo*. That way, it wouldn't be eclipsed by Thursday's general election, which was all anyone could talk about.

'Hold the front page,' Mick had said in the editorial meeting, scratching the inside of his ear. One of his favourite expressions coupled with one of his annoying habits.

Gabi checked the time on her phone. She sighed. Darren had rung the night before last to say he'd had to postpone their weekend away. Work. Again. She knew that his job – he was a corporate executive in a multinational mining company – was varied and demanding, even if exactly what he did was beyond her. She knew he'd make it up to her, but she couldn't help feeling bitterly disappointed. She should have been at Bristol airport right now, on her way to a three-day break in Brussels, not on her way home from a day trip to Beckenham. She should be sitting on the plane, not on the train. Pleasure, not business.

Mick had persuaded her to go to Toby Wigmore's constituency today, on election day itself. It had turned out to be a total waste of time. She managed to take one half-decent photo of the MP that wasn't blurred, but she ended up using his Wikipedia photo, in which he was sporting a baby-pink shirt under a grey suit jacket. Matt was right about the man's ears. They were enormous. She'd also failed to get a usable quote from Wigmore about his relationship with Leona Walsh. She managed to get close enough at one point to ask him, but he refused to comment.

She saved the document to the desktop of her computer. She'd wait to find out if Wigmore held on to his seat in Beckenham before she filed copy. He was expected to be re-elected. Would he be forced to resign? Perhaps only days after the general election? Gabi felt guilty about the role she was about to play in messing up this guy's career. She didn't want to hurt him or his family. But the news would break sooner or later, one way or the other.

The train stopped at Taunton. Gabi looked out of the window at the deserted platform. Half an hour left to Exeter St David's, where she would change for Barnstaple. Her tummy rumbled. She could do with something to eat. And a beer. Was there a food trolley on this train? Or a restaurant carriage? She turned to ask her neighbour, but he was asleep. She would have to disturb him to get out of her seat, or clamber over him, so she stayed put.

She had one of Matthew Walsh's novels in her bag – he'd given her a signed copy of the first novel in the *Moors* series the other day. She'd started it on the train from Exeter to London this morning, but although she'd only read the prologue and the first chapter, she wasn't sure she could bear to read any more of it. Certainly not this evening.

Her mind returned to Toby Wigmore and the election results. And from there to Leona's role as a local councillor. What would Google throw up about Leona's career? Could there be a political motivation for Leona's abduction or – God forbid – assassination? As Gabi had already shut down her laptop, she took out her phone. She scrolled through everything she could find on Leona. As far as Gabi could see, there was nothing to suggest a link between Leona's disappearance and her profession. But she would have to look more thoroughly into the embezzlement allegations as well as into Leona's relationship with Toby Wigmore before she ruled out the possibility.

She put her phone back into her handbag, leant back and yawned. An image came to her as she closed her eyes for a few seconds. The same picture everyone saw, everywhere. The photo of Leona that had been used in all the television appeals and printed in every newspaper in the country for the past twelve days. Leona, with undulating coppery hair and piercing green eyes, lips stretched into a broad grin across perfectly aligned, pearly white teeth. Leona looked so happy, so carefree, as if she believed bad things could never happen to beautiful people. That image had marked the nation. No wonder this case was so high profile.

But the fact Leona was an attractive, middle-class, white woman wasn't the only reason her disappearance had attracted unprecedented media attention. Thousands of people went missing in the UK every year. Why was this case generating such a media circus? Gabi took her notebook out from her handbag and started to take notes. She would write a piece on this at some point. Ideas careened through her mind, answers to her own question.

The Christmas-card, sleepy village of Blackmoor Gate, where Leona and her family lived, provided the ideal backdrop. It was an incongruous setting for a crime to be committed and it lured busybodies from all over the country to the area. In addition, people were more obsessed than ever with true crime – a real-life conundrum to solve. The fact no one knew, in this instance, if a crime had actually been committed, simply added an extra layer to the mystery. And Matthew Walsh was a crime writer, which was a nice twist.

On top of all that, social media offered the perfect platforms for wannabe detectives and armchair sleuths to share outrageous and often injurious conspiracy theories, and air criticisms and accusations, fortified by the relative anonymity and invisibility of their online personas.

But perhaps one of the main reasons this case was so incendiary was that most missing persons turn up – alive or dead – within a few hours, a couple of days, tops, whereas Leona was still unaccounted for after almost two weeks.

And soon, there would be even more interest in the case. Gabi's scoop about Leona's affair would see to that.

Missing, Presumed Murdered
A True Crime Podcast Hosted by Gabriela Conti
Audio File 5
Interview with Toby Wigmore, former Conservative MP for Beckenham.
2024

This is the story of Leona Walsh, whose disappearance in December 2019 has remained a mystery for nearly five years. Join me as I explore the truths and lies in this case. I am Gabriela Conti and you're listening to **Missing, Presumed Murdered***, a true crime podcast.*

Gabriela Conti: Thank you for agreeing to talk to me, Mr Wigmore. I know you haven't given any interviews to the media since Leona Walsh went missing and I appreciate you taking time out of your busy schedule to talk to me.

Toby Wigmore: Hummph! It's hardly a busy schedule, Miss Conti. Not anymore. I lost my seat, as I'm sure you know. I was forced to resign because of this whole … beastly business.

GC: I'm sorry, Mr Wigmore. This must all have been very hard on you.

TW: It was, actually. Not only did I lose Leona, but the ensuing scandal also cost me my job and my wife in the space of about six months. And, of course, my London home, which was … er … in my wife's name.

GC: That's why you're living here, in Southend-on-Sea, I assume?

TW: Yes, that's right. Leona and I were very much in love. We planned to live here together one day. I'm … sorry.

GC: Would you like a tissue, Mr Wigmore?

TW: No, no. Just had a speck of dust in my eye.

GC: How did you meet?

TW: At a Conservative party conference in London. She was

absolutely beautiful and I was infatuated. Love at first sight. I could never understand what she saw in me, truth be told.

GC: *Hmmm. So you began an affair?*

TW: *Yes. I wasn't in the habit of cheating on my wife, I'd like to make that crystal clear, but Deidre and I had been married a long time; we'd got into a bit of a rut, probably even before our son flew the nest. Then Leona came along. And, well, that was that. Obviously, Leona and I were both doing our damnedest to make sure nobody got hurt – my wife or Leona's family, especially her daughters. They were still so young. So, the idea was to wait for the right time, no matter how long it took.*

GC: *I imagine if you had left your wife for Leona, that would have affected your political career, too?*

TW: *Undoubtedly, Miss Conti. As I said, we had no immediate plans to be together, but we hoped to have that chance one day.*

GC: *Did you and Leona ever discuss your … other halves?*

TW: *Leona and I didn't have any secrets from one other.*

GC: *What did she tell you about her husband, Matthew Walsh?*

TW: *The man sounded like a frightful bore. According to Leona, he was big-headed and far more interested in himself than in her.*

GC: *Did she talk about her children, too?*

TW: *Yes. She always said Matthew was a better father than she was a mother, but Leona could be rather self-deprecating. As far as I could tell, she did a lot with her daughters; she loved them dearly. She wouldn't have done anything to hurt them, so there was no question of us getting divorced from our respective spouses.*

GC: *Did Leona say anything that made you think Matthew might harm her?*

TW: *Well, she was terribly afraid of his reaction if he should find out about our relationship. But I don't think she thought for a moment he would kill her, if that's what you mean.*

GC: *So you think Matthew may have found out about your affair?*

TW: *I prefer to refer to it as a relationship. 'Affair' sounds so sordid. That's what the police believed, isn't it? That Matthew Walsh found out about Leona and me.*

GC: *Mr Wigmore, I'd like to ask about the anonymous reward you put up when Leona disappeared. Was it a coincidence that you offered thirty thousand pounds – the same amount of money Leona gave you to repair the dry rot in this very house, here in Southend?*

TW: *It was a loan. Leona didn't give me the money; she lent it to me. I had amassed that amount to pay her back, so it seemed right to offer it as a reward for information that would help with the search. So, no, to answer your question, it wasn't a coincidence.*

GC: *How would you respond to people who insinuated that you offered thirty thousand pounds because you were aware she'd embezzled thirty thousand pounds with false expense claims? The police – and the press – accused you of trying to keep your ears clean … I beg your pardon, I meant your nose.*

TW: *It's total bollocks, excuse my language. I should have sued the tabloids for slander.*

GC: *You mean libel.*

TW: *Whatever. I had no idea the money wasn't Leona's. I'll have you know, Miss Conti, in the end, I used the thirty thousand pounds to make full restitution for the money Leona allegedly embezzled.*

GC: *I didn't know that. One last thing, if I may. Did you ever see a darker side to Leona?*

TW: *I don't know what you mean.*

GC: *Well, was she ever … volatile? Temperamental? Did she have a violent temper, for example?*

TW: *Steady on! I don't know what you're implying, Miss Conti, but I never witnessed any erratic behaviour. Leona Walsh wasn't perfect. She could be a little irritable. But I wouldn't say she was volatile or temperamental. Nothing like that. Where did you get that notion from? If anything, he was the one with a violent temper, not her.*

Chapter 15

Wednesday, 18th December 2019: Missing for two weeks and four days

DC Chapman rocked up to the house even earlier than usual. When Matt opened the door, he burst inside and practically bounced from one foot to the other as he took off his beanie and gloves. Matt took his coat and clocked his demeanour. It was clear something had happened. But he couldn't tell if it was good or bad news.

Did it have anything to do with the embezzlement charges? It was odd – that had been such a hot potato in the local press – up until Leona had gone missing. The issue hadn't completely fizzled out, far from it, but the police and media didn't seem to consider it relevant to Leona's disappearance and it appeared to have been relegated to the background.

'I don't want to get your hopes up,' Chapman said, 'but we've received a promising lead.'

So it had nothing to do with the allegations against Leona. But Chapman wouldn't say anything else until they were sitting at the kitchen table. Matt had spent so much time in this room lately, he was beginning to hate it, even though it had been Leona's favourite room and had her stamp all over it. A country kitchen with its rustic, wooden table; the glossy, easy-to-clean tiles Leona had purposefully chosen for the kitchen floor; the large, round Roman numeral wall clock that ticked far too loudly; the Aga cooker Leona had insisted on buying, but never used – he did all the cooking.

'I'd like to show you some footage from the security camera at Withypool village shop,' Chapman said, extracting a tablet from his bag. It took him a moment to get set up.

Matt knew the shop, on the edge of Exmoor. They'd stopped to buy bread and cheese for a picnic once, before hiking up to Dunkery Beacon. It was a blustery day, but they'd had so much fun. It was a short walk, and Trixie, who must only have been four or five at the time, was so excited when she spotted the wild ponies. He smiled wistfully to himself at the memory.

'This was taken yesterday.' Chapman angled the tablet so Matt could see the screen. 'The shopkeepers – a husband and wife – came into the station this morning after watching this several times together and deliberating last night. They were afraid of wasting police time.'

'Is this ... What ...?' Matt couldn't get his words out.

'It's a possible sighting of Leona,' Chapman said. 'I need you to take a look.'

Matt watched it twice, his heart thrashing against his rib cage. The camera was behind and above the shopkeeper, so he could only really see the top of the customer's head. He didn't recognise her clothes. But it looked like Leona. Same length and style of hair, same gait when she walked up to the till.

Chapman was looking at him expectantly. 'She bought some fudge and a chocolate bar, apparently.'

'Leona has a sweet tooth,' Matt said. Leona wouldn't keep chocolate in the house to avoid temptation, but every now and then she'd crack and he'd have to drive eight miles to the nearest late-night garage to fetch her a family-sized packet of Maltesers or a bumper bar of Dairy Milk. 'Show me again.'

Chapman obliged.

'I can't be sure,' Matt said after analysing the grainy black-and-white images, without blinking, for the third time. 'It could be her. But it doesn't make any sense. Why would she be in a local village shop? Alone?'

It didn't fit any of the theories. If she'd left him willingly, she'd hardly be holed up somewhere just a few miles away, popping out because she needed a quick sugar fix.

'Do you want to ask your sister-in-law what she thinks?'

Roxanne seemed to have taken up residence at the manor, although she went home to Adam at night. Matt had no idea how she'd wangled the time off work. He didn't really like her being there all the time, but he didn't complain. She would make herself useful or make herself scarce, according to what was needed. She didn't get under his feet. He felt as if she was spying on him, but he put that down to paranoia on his part. He found her upstairs, cleaning the girls' bathroom.

'You don't need to do that,' he said.

'Someone needs to,' she retorted. He couldn't argue with that. 'Sorry. That was out of line. It makes me feel better, doing a mindless task.'

He knew what she meant. At the moment, he appreciated chores like ironing, not because he cared what he looked like – that ship had sailed – but because he could numb his brain and function on autopilot. He cooked every evening for the same reason, even though no one ate much. They'd all lost several stones in weight between them over the last fortnight.

He told Roxanne about the security camera footage and she followed him downstairs.

'If it's not Leona, it's an uncanny resemblance, don't you think?' she said after viewing the video.

It couldn't be Leona. This was just wishful thinking. He

shouldn't have let Roxanne get her hopes up. He should have kept her out of it. 'I don't want the girls to know about this,' he said to Chapman.

But, of course, the whole nation knew by early afternoon – it was on the lunchtime news. The girls were both at school, but someone would blab.

Matt was in the car, on his way to pick up Trixie, who had gone back to school that very day, when his editor, Esther, rang. She lived and worked in London, but even she had heard the news. She asked how he was and spouted all the right platitudes, then she got to the reason she'd called.

'*Murder on the Moors* is flying off the shelves, Matthew. It sold one thousand six hundred and sixty-three copies this week, according to Nielsen BookScan,' she announced. 'And it has stormed onto this week's *Sunday Times* fiction paperbacks bestseller list at number ten.'

He used to check his Amazon rankings religiously, at least twice a day, sometimes more. And he'd badger his agent to request regular sales updates from his publishers, even though it had been a long time since he'd written a book that had earned out his advance in royalties. It was an obsession. But he hadn't even wondered how well his books were doing since Leona disappeared.

'Matthew? Are you still there?'

'That's great,' he managed.

It didn't feel great. This was his dream come true, his main goal since he'd become a published author, but it meant nothing without Leona there. It was precisely because Leona wasn't there that he'd become a *Sunday Times* bestselling author. Her disappearance had given his books exposure. Until then, he'd really been only a mediocre mid-lister. That journalist's comment about Leona's disappearance mirroring the plot of the last book in the *Moors* series had hooked potential readers more than any eye-catching cover or London Underground billboard could. Wannabe detectives and general busybodies were no doubt scrutinising his every sentence, reading things into what he'd written that weren't there. No publicity was bad publicity, it would seem.

'I wanted to let you know, Matthew,' Esther said. 'I thought it might cheer you up a little in spite of everything you're going through right now. Let's hope there's more good news on the way. I'm keeping everything crossed they'll find your wife soon.'

Harriet Clark, the head teacher at Trixie's school, said something similar when he arrived to pick up Trixie. 'We're all hoping and praying that this sighting means Leona will be home very soon,' she said.

She hadn't looked him in the eye since she'd barred him from running the Literacy Project. She clearly thought the possible reappearance of Leona in a nearby village shop meant he'd had nothing to do with her disappearance after all.

He had hoped the news about his wife's affair would take the heat off him a bit and point the finger in Wigmore's general direction instead. But although Gabi's article yesterday had provoked some Tory-bashing with Wigmore as the main target, it had also sparked more speculation that Matt had killed his wife when he found out about her indiscretions.

Shortly after he arrived home with Trixie, Scarlett's friend's mother pulled into the driveway. Through the living-room window, he saw her get out of the car and walk towards the front door. She hadn't done that since the time she'd driven Scarlett home after the birthday party, when Leona had first gone missing. She continued to pick up Scarlett from the bus stop after school and drop her off at Blackmoor Manor on her way home, but she'd made no effort to speak to him. He'd texted his thanks a couple of times, and he could see from her read receipts that she'd received his messages, but she hadn't replied.

'Please let me know if there's anything I can do,' she said when he opened the door. The same offer she'd made before.

People had been avoiding him, telling their kids to stay away from his daughters, and now, all of a sudden, everyone believed he was innocent. He was above all suspicion.

It turned out to be only a temporary reprieve. DC Chapman's phone rang while Matt was prepping dinner. Chapman left the room to take the call and returned a minute later with a long face.

'The shopper in the video has come forward,' Chapman said. 'She recognised herself when she watched the news.'

Chapman went on to describe it – rather euphemistically – as 'a disappointing development'. A false lead that dashed everyone's false hopes.

Since the day of Leona's disappearance, Matt had been caught up in a plot worthy of one of his novels, life imitating art, rather than the other way round. But now he was finding it harder and harder to keep a grip on reality. And he had no control over how the scenario would play out. He wanted to imagine a different sequence of events, based on what might have happened if the shopper with the sugar craving had turned out to be Leona. Perhaps his story could have had a happy ending.

When Chapman and Roxanne had gone, Matt and the girls ate dinner in the living room in front of *Hotel Transylvania 3* – Trixie's choice. It had a PG rating, so Matt was watching it with them, but he couldn't concentrate on the animated film and found his mind wandering to Leona.

They'd celebrated their tenth wedding anniversary in August. They'd got a babysitter – or childminder, as Scarlett insisted they called her, and went to a restaurant. Leona looked beautiful. Radiant. They laughed, reminisced, planned their next summer holiday, and all the while, Matt couldn't wait to get home, get rid of the childminder and take off Leona's clothes. The memory of that night was tarnished now. Leona was probably thinking of her lover while she made love to him.

Scarlett was nearly five when he and Leona got married; she'd been a flower girl at their wedding. Scarlett hadn't been planned. Leona, over ten years his junior, was only twenty when she realised she was pregnant – so young. He was absolutely delighted, but it took her a little longer to accept she was going to become a mum.

Leona suffered from severe postnatal depression after Scarlett was born and it took six years before she felt ready to try for another baby. She'd spent her entire pregnancy with Trixie dreading what would happen afterwards, but the second time around, there wasn't so much as a hint of the baby blues. Leona's moods had never been so stable. She'd never been so happy.

Scarlett and Trixie had finished eating and snuggled into him. He put an arm around each of them and kissed them one after the other on the top of their heads. Scarlett wrapped her arm around his waist and Trixie didn't push him away. His whole world was right here, his babies on either side of him, everything that was important to him was contained within these four walls. Everything except Leona. He was petrified of what his life without her would be like. He couldn't picture it. He was staring down the barrel of emptiness.

It was late by the time he got Scarlett and Trixie to bed. He tucked in Trixie first. She rolled into a foetal position and put her thumb in her mouth. Lately, she'd been sleeping with her night light on – the one she'd had as a toddler, a cat curled up and sleeping soundly. She was still wetting the bed, almost every night. He'd bought a protective sheet for the mattress and he left the landing light on so Trixie could come and get him.

'Sweet dreams,' he whispered.

He went to say goodnight to Scarlett.

'Do you think they'll find Mummy?' she asked.

He pondered what to say for a few seconds, something along the lines of: *hopefully we'll at least find out what has happened to her*, but before he could say anything, Scarlett amended her question and this one stumped him. Floored him.

'Do you think Mummy is still alive?'

Scarlett had stopped calling Leona 'Mummy' ages ago. She found it too babyish. But like Trixie, who had taken up sucking her thumb again, Scarlett seemed to be reverting to childish ways. The girls needed their mummy. And she wasn't there. He was doing his best and Roxanne was pitching in. But they were poor substitutes for the real deal.

For the longest time, he didn't answer. He didn't want to lie to Scarlett. Of course, he was capable of being dishonest. He could lie convincingly. The trick was to stick as close to the facts as possible, blend morsels of the truth in with the falsehood. But he'd always prided himself on being candid with his daughters. Perhaps the situation called for a white lie, but he didn't know if he could bring himself to tell one.

He liked to think his wife had left him and was alive and well somewhere – even if it was with that Tory knob, Toby Wigmore. He preferred that version to the alternative. God knows, Leona had been tempted to walk out on him in the past, on several occasions. But she would never have left the girls. And the truth was, he knew she was dead. Statistically, she had to be dead by now. She'd been gone too long. He already thought of her in the past tense and was worried he would slip up when he was talking to DC Chapman or DS Holland. Or to Roxanne.

There was no sugar-coating this. 'No, I don't think so, sweetie,' he said eventually. 'Mummy would never have left you and Trixie like this with no news for over two weeks. She loved you both so much.'

He didn't add what he was thinking – the answer to Scarlett's first question – that if they did find Leona now, it would be her body.

Chapter 16

June 2024

Gabi wakes up with one hell of a hangover. She opens her eyes, but instantly snaps them shut again. Apparently, she has forgotten to draw the curtains and the sun is streaming in through the windows. It hurts. Bloody hell, her head hurts. How much did she have to drink last night? Not that much. Not enough to deserve this headache, that's for sure. She really is a lightweight. This is not a great start to the weekend.

A realisation pierces through her grogginess and she sits bolt upright, groaning loudly as pain slices through her head. There's a body next to her. A man's body. In her bed. Squinting at him, she sees he's breathing. That's good. She doesn't know why she wondered, even fleetingly, if it might be a dead body. She was dreaming about Leona Walsh's remains, so that may be why. Or perhaps it's because she feels half-dead herself.

She has no recollection of taking anyone to bed last night; no recollection of even getting into bed. The quilt covers him from the waist down, but on the top half, he's not wearing any clothes. Is he naked? His face is turned away from her, but she recognises him a split second before he speaks, without moving, without even turning towards her. Joe. That makes sense. It was the office summer party yesterday evening. A few of them – Joe, Mick, Cheryl and Gabi – went on to a club. Gabi was probably the youngest in the group, but she's still far too old for that sort of thing. She should have known better.

'Good morning,' he says. There's no hint of embarrassment in his voice. In fact, he sounds cheerful.

She grunts in reply. An image comes back to her. She kissed him. They were outside, hopefully alone. She won't be able to face her co-workers if it's common knowledge at the *Echo*. 'Did we …?' It was a good kiss. 'Did we …?' A long kiss that made her knees turn to jelly. Although, that could have been partly due to the alcohol.

He props himself up on his elbows and looks at her. She can see he's amused. 'Did we have sex?' he supplies.

She nods, then winces.

'No, we didn't.'

'Oh, thank God,' she says. Is it her imagination or does he look a little miffed? 'Why not?'

'Well, I'm not in the habit of having sex with women who have passed out. And I like to think if you and I had sex, you might remember the experience. All right if I take a shower?'

He rolls out of bed. He's wearing boxers, she notes with relief. And he's got a really fit body. Toned muscles. She tries not to stare.

When he has finished in the bathroom, she goes in. She rummages in a cupboard and finds a packet of painkillers. She downs two tablets, drinking water straight from the tap. Realising she's thirsty, she gulps down more water. Next, she peels off her pyjamas, hoping she put them on herself last night, and steps into the shower.

She expects Joe to be gone by the time she comes out, but when she emerges, in her dressing gown, a towel wrapped around her head, looking totally bedraggled, he is barefoot, making himself at home in her open kitchen, wearing the same T-shirt and jeans as last night, cooking breakfast. On Sundays, she usually has a lie-in and makes herself brunch, so her fridge was stocked with bacon, eggs, mushrooms and tomatoes, ready for tomorrow morning. The smell of bacon makes her feel nauseous and ravenous at the same time. Joe points at the bar stools. She unravels the towel and throws it on the sofa, then obediently takes a seat at the breakfast bar.

Moments later, they're sitting side by side, sipping coffee and eating a full English breakfast. She eats hers slowly, worried she might not keep it down. Neither of them says anything, but it's a companionable silence rather than an awkward one. For her, at least. Is Joe feeling uncomfortable? She hopes not. Once she's finished eating, she feels a lot better.

'I need to change into some clean clothes,' Joe says. 'I could pop home and come back, if you'd like to spend the day together? We could go for a walk on the beach, or from Valley of the Rocks to Lynton?'

'I can't,' she says. She sees Joe's face fall. 'Not today. I do like the idea of a walk on the beach, though. With you. Are you free tomorrow?'

He brightens. 'Yes. That works for me. I should probably get go—'

'Another coffee first?'

He makes it while she pulls on some clothes. This time they sit next to each other on the sofa, his leg just touching hers.

It's now or never, she thinks and takes a deep breath. 'His name was Darren,' she begins. 'My so-called fiancé's name was Darren Hughes.' She spits it out, hating the sound of it. She hasn't said it aloud for … it must be about four years. 'We lived together, although he was often away on business.'

'Why do you call him your "so-called" fiancé?' Joe asked.

'He asked me to marry him, he'd bought a ring, I said yes.' They'd also talked about starting a family, but she doesn't tell Joe that bit. 'We even fixed a date for the wedding.'

She pauses, but Joe seems to sense she doesn't want him to prompt her. She hasn't answered his question, but he says nothing. He just sets his coffee cup on the table and turns towards her.

'He disappeared as we went into lockdown. Poof!' She makes a gesture with her hands, like a magician. 'Vanished into thin air. No phone calls, no texts, nothing. It's almost impossible in this day and age to keep such a low digital footprint, but I couldn't find any trace of him online. Hughes is a common name, which made it harder. I reported him missing to the police, but locating a middle-aged man wasn't a priority for them at the time. They were busy making sure everyone was staying at home, avoiding non-essential contact and travel.'

She takes a sip of her coffee. Her hand is shaking.

'But you found out what happened to him?' Joe asks.

She nods. 'When it became clear lockdown and Covid restrictions were going to continue for the foreseeable, he got in touch with me – wrote me an email. He'd been missing for almost a month by then, but he was alive and well and had been ghosting me all that time. He was in Somerset, he told me, at home … at his *other* home, with his wife. She'd just given birth to their first baby.'

That was the hardest part to digest. Not the fact he had a wife, but that he'd had a baby. Gabi was thirty-five when her relationship with Darren came to its dramatic end. She's now pushing forty. She always thought she'd have kids by now.

'Bloody hell!' Joe whistles through his teeth.

Gabi has noticed this habit before. It doesn't bother her, not like most of Mick's habits, which she finds intensely annoying. On the contrary, she finds it endearing. And she appreciates Joe's solidarity.

'He'd been leading a double life,' she continues. 'I was an unwitting mistress. We'd been together for nearly two years. I thought we were engaged. He knew my friends. Christ, he even met my mum.'

Joe must think she's stupid. She expects him to ask her if she saw any red flags because of course she did. Darren didn't like having his photo taken; his parents were supposedly dead and his brother lived abroad; she'd met only one of his friends, who clearly didn't approve of her, although she couldn't understand why at the time; no matter how often she tried to glean information about his job, he was guarded about it, as if he was some sort of undercover agent rather than a company executive; he was also secretive about his mobile and laptop; he shunned social media; his phone seemed to play up an awful lot when he was away; and his accounts of where he'd been and what he'd done didn't always add up. This was all strange and it had niggled her constantly, but he'd given her plausible explanations and it only made sense to her in hindsight. She really had been incredibly naïve. She'd been in love.

But Joe doesn't ask how she missed the signs. Instead, he says, 'I'm really sorry, Gabi. I had no idea. What an absolute shit!' He sounds angry on her behalf. 'He makes my ex-girlfriend look like a saint.'

She leans into him and he puts his arm around her shoulder. 'I don't know how you would even begin to get over something like that,' he says.

'Mainlining Ben & Jerry's Chunky Monkey helps a lot,' she says into his armpit, surprising herself by being flippant despite the lump in her throat.

'Don't let him prevent you from pursuing your goals,' he says. 'Don't let anyone stop you.'

She tilts her head and kisses him on the cheek. 'I won't. What you said – just now and the other day – you got me thinking.'

'Uh-oh. I didn't mean to make you think,' Joe says jokingly.

She hits him playfully on the arm. 'I'm not going to let my so-called *ex*-fiancé continue to trample on my dreams. I've decided to make a podcast.'

'A podcast? About the Leona Walsh disappearance?'

'Exactly.'

'That's a great idea!'

'That's what I thought! I've invested in some equipment – mics, headphones, that sort of thing.' She has spent about three hundred pounds of her own savings and Mick has promised to inject some more money into her project. He's also checking out the legal side of things. She has spent hours skimming online articles and watching YouTube tutorials on how to make good quality podcasts. 'I already have loads of material from before that I need to edit. Ideally, I'd like to get the pilot episode out there fairly soon. My podcast will have much more impact if listeners can follow what's going on in real time.'

'This is brilliant, Gabi! I can help, if you like. I know a bit about editing and recording – I play the guitar in a band and we've recorded some songs.'

Gabi knew this and was hoping he'd offer to help. 'I was thinking perhaps you could compose some creepy music for the intro,' she says, waving her arms around in her excitement.

'Definitely! It would be my pleasure.'

'I'm going to see Matt – Matthew Walsh – today,' she continues, her words coming out in a rush. 'He must know they'll identify the remains from the garden any day now. He might talk to me.'

Joe's smile inverts to a frown. 'Is that wise?'

'Yes! By the time we get confirmation the remains are those of Leona Walsh, everyone will be all over it. If I want a story, I'll have to wheedle it out of Matt before we reach that point.'

'I'll come with you. You might be in danger.'

'No,' she says. 'I'll be fine on my own. I'll see you tomorrow.'

'Gabi, there's a strong probability the man is a murderer. Please tell me you don't still think he's innocent. I'll stay in the car if you like.'

Until they found the body in Benton, she did believe Matt was innocent. She was never one hundred per cent sure – how could she be? Matt prevaricated about lots of things in their interviews as well as telling a few outright lies. But she has always given him the benefit of the doubt.

But if the body does turn out to be Leona's, which looks highly likely, then who else could have killed her and buried her at Rose Cottage? Gabi has already mulled this over. Again and again. She's well aware Matt is probably guilty after all. She has arranged to meet up with him today because she's hoping he'll admit it to her.

'He trusts me; I trust him,' she says. 'He won't talk to me if you come with me.'

Joe argues some more, but she's not having it. She doesn't need a bodyguard.

Gabi left her car in town last night so she could have a few drinks. She regrets that now – the drinks, that is, not leaving the car. Joe, who – sensibly – didn't drink and whose car is now parked in front of her maisonette, offers her a lift. She packs some equipment into a rucksack and they head outside.

'Your carriage awaits, madam,' he says, opening the passenger door of his tangerine Vauxhall Corsa for her.

She takes a disdainful look at the car. 'I think my carriage has turned into a pumpkin,' she mutters.

It's a short drive from Sticklepath, where Gabi lives, to Barnstaple town centre. When Joe drops her off, she gives him another kiss on the cheek. He drives away, tooting his horn.

She keeps a portable alcohol tester in the glove box. She's pretty sure she's under the limit, but she'd better check. She turns the device on, breathes into it until it beeps, then waits until the LCD screen shows the result. It's negative. She's good to go.

But her car doesn't start on the first go. Or on the second attempt. She's not superstitious, but she wonders if it's an omen. It may not be safe for her to go to Blackmoor Manor alone. She might be walking into the lion's den. She hears Joe's voice in her head. *You might be in danger.* She should have taken him up on his offer to come with her.

She turns the key a third time and the car splutters into life.

She laughs at herself for getting spooked. Her car not starting means only one thing: she needs a new one. She sends Matt a text message to let him know she's on her way and then sets off for Blackmoor Manor.

Chapter 17

June 2024

As Gabi drives past the Old Station Inn car park, half a mile from Matt's house, she spots Joe's car. She could hardly miss it. Her phone pings with an incoming text seconds later. She thinks it might be from Joe, but, although she's itching to check, she doesn't glance at her phone. She doesn't drive when she's over the limit, nor does she use her mobile while she's at the wheel. She doubts her old banger would hold up well in an accident. It would probably fold like an omelette. Plus, she has reported on more road traffic accidents than she can count. She waits until she has pulled up in front of Blackmoor Manor to read the text message.

Waiting down the road.
Let me know when you've finished / if you need me.
Jxx

Smiling to herself, she sends a thumbs-up emoji and gets out of the car.

She stands at the front gate, trying to peer through the ground-floor windows, but she can't make out any movement from inside the house. There are lights on upstairs and downstairs, though. The first time she came here, it was dark and cold, the taste of winter in the crisp air. Today the sky is a cobalt blue with barely a cloud to be seen; it's going to be a scorching summer day. And yet, the house seems more forbidding than welcoming.

She surveys the front garden, which was once well-tended and is now overgrown. Riotous rhododendrons jostle with snarled weeds and the lawn clearly hasn't been mown for some time.

Matt opens the front door. He has let himself go, too. The last time she saw him was at Benton that day. In the pub. It has now been four and a half years since Leona went missing. Matt looks like he has aged a decade in that time. His hair is in desperate need of a cut; his eyes are bloodshot; deep furrows crisscross his face like scars; it's not yet midday, but already he has a five o'clock shadow; and he's stooping, as if the weight on his shoulders is too much to bear.

Matt eyes Gabi warily. When Leona first went missing, Gabi rang from time to time or texted. He imagined she was angling for some inside info rather than checking to see how he was doing, but he appreciated her calls and messages. Apart from family – Roxanne and Adam and his mother – Gabi was pretty much the only person who kept in touch. But he hasn't seen or heard from her for ages. The past few years have taken their toll. He's well aware he cuts a pitiful, diminished figure, and he can see this reflected in her eyes.

'Long time no see,' he says, gesturing for her to go into the living room. It comes out sounding reproachful, which is not how he means it. The coronavirus imposed a hiatus on a lot of things, including the police inquiry into Leona's disappearance. And no doubt Gabi's investigation into it, too. She was bound to put two and two together and turn up on his doorstep eventually.

She's dogged in her pursuit of a story; thirsty for her big break. Or she used to be.

'I'm sorry about that,' she says.

'Oh, no, don't be.'

He sinks onto the sofa and Gabi perches on the armchair. She's clearly ill at ease. Is she scared of him?

'Did you come alone?' He regrets the question as soon as he has asked it. It sounds predatory. What must she be thinking?

'Yes. Well, sort of.' Gabi's neck goes red, as if she has a rash, and it spreads upwards to her cheeks. He has embarrassed her. 'Joe – that's my colleague – is waiting for me at Blackmoor Gate.'

'He thinks I'm dangerous.'

It's a statement, not a question, but Gabi answers. 'He's concerned for my safety, yes.'

'Are you concerned for your safety?'

'No, Matt. Of course not.'

He can't tell if she's being honest. 'I take it this isn't a social visit.'

'No, Matt,' she repeats. 'Are you OK with me recording our conversation?'

'Yes,' he says, remembering Gabi recording them on her phone in the past. As well as taking notes. Perhaps she has a bad memory. Perhaps it's just the way she has been trained for her job.

'I wonder if I could trouble you for a glass of water.'

'Yes, I'm sorry.' He leaps to his feet. 'I'm forgetting my manners.'

When he returns, a glass of water in each hand, Gabi has set up a laptop and two large mics on stands. He sets the glasses on the coffee table and sits down, staring at the mic pointing towards him.

'What's all this?' he asks, waving his hand at the equipment Gabi is setting up.

'Matt, my aim has always been to report the events surrounding your wife's disappearance objectively. I think it's fair to say that I've never painted you in a bad light,' Gabi begins.

It's true. She hasn't.

'I was interested in your story,' she continues. 'I still am. Podcasts have become incredibly popular since lockdown and I'd like to make one about Leona's disappearance. With your permission, I'd like to use the recordings I've already made of my conversations with you and add to them. The mics will give a far better sound quality.'

He's used to speaking into microphones – he's done it at crime writing festivals and also for local radio stations – but today, for some reason, he finds the raised mic pointing at his face daunting. He's being silly. It wasn't intimidating when she used her phone to record their previous conversations. This is no different.

'Ideally, I'd like more interviews with you, but also with other people – potential witnesses, family members – your sister-in-law and your daughter, for example.'

'I want you to leave Trixie out of this. She's only twelve. She's struggling.' Looking around to check Trixie hasn't crept downstairs to eavesdrop, he lowers his voice. 'Her mother's disappearance has messed her up. Understandably.'

'I meant Scarlett, actually.'

'Obviously, I would prefer for you not to approach Scarlett, either, but she's an adult, so you must ask her. She doesn't live here anymore, though. She moved out when they found the … She moved out a couple of weeks ago. She's at her aunt's.'

'So, are you happy for me to use our interviews to make a podcast?'

'Happy might be stretching it.' Things are going to get worse. A lot worse. Regardless of whether he gives Gabi permission to make her podcast, he's going to be headline news. Any day now. The sword of Damocles has been hanging over his head for a while, but it's about to fall. It would be good to have someone fighting his corner. 'But I have no objection.'

He hears the ding as she taps a key on her laptop to start recording. She also extracts a notebook and pen from her handbag and sets them on the arm of her chair.

'OK, then. Can we start with Rose Cottage?' she asks gently. 'What can you tell me about that?'

He sighs. 'It was my childhood home. I didn't want to sell it. I was brought up there, mainly by my mum – my father died when I was eight. Pancreatic cancer.'

'I'm sorry.'

'My mum lived in Rose Cottage, as you probably know, until two years ago. She had Parkinson's disease. I helped her out as best I could, but her condition deteriorated rapidly during the lockdowns and, well, it got to the point where she could no longer live alone. I would have liked her to come here, to Blackmoor Manor, but she couldn't have managed the stairs to the bedroom. There are workarounds, I know, stairlifts and so on, but, well, she needed full-time care, so I found a residential home for her.'

'I'm so sorry,' Gabi repeats.

She leans forwards, reaches out and pats his arm. Her gesture surprises him and moves him, too. Trixie isn't one for cuddles and Scarlett has moved in with Roxanne and Adam, and he can't remember the last time he had any physical contact with another human being.

'Thank you. She's doing OK,' he says. She's not, but he doesn't know what to do with Gabi's sympathy. His mum did her best to adapt to her new environment and now she's fighting against her disease with every ounce of energy she has. But the only way is downhill. 'She's in good hands.' This part, at least, is true. The care home is full of empathetic, hard-working members of staff. Well, not *full* – they're short-staffed – but the carers do a fantastic job.

'So, you sold Rose Cottage,' Gabi prompts.

'As I said, I didn't intend to sell it. Ever. I was planning to do it up a bit and rent it out as a holiday home. But although Leona's disappearance caused a sudden surge in book sales, it was temporary and I haven't written a word since she's been missing.'

'Writer's block?'

'Yeah. I lost my mojo along with my muse,' he says wryly.

'Without Leona's salary, too … financially, my only option was to sell Rose Cottage. If only I'd known …' He forces a chuckle. 'The answer to my problems was in the grounds of the house all along.'

Gabi looks at him blankly for a moment, then she says, 'Ah, you mean the Roman coin.'

He knows Gabi's next question will be about the bones and he braces himself for it, but Gabi leans forwards and taps a key on her laptop, presumably to pause the recording, then smiles at something over his shoulder. He turns around to follow her gaze. Trixie is standing in the doorway. With her strawberry blond hair, green eyes and freckles, she's a younger version of his wife. Leona used to call Trixie her 'mini me'. Trixie even has some of Leona's mannerisms – her slow smile and the way she bites her lower lip when she's concentrating, for example. Whenever he sees Leona in Trixie, his heart breaks a little bit more. He's sure Gabi must see the likeness.

'Hello, Trixie,' Gabi says warmly. 'Do you remember me? I'm Gabi.'

'Hi. Yes,' Trixie says shyly. 'I remember you. You're a reporter.'

'That's right.'

'Everything OK, sweetie?' he asks.

'I've finished my homework. I wanted to know if I could go out for a while with Nola.'

'Yes, of course. Come back before dinner?'

'I'll be back way before then.'

When Trixie has left, Gabi starts up the recording again. She also picks up her pen, although Matt's pretty sure she hasn't written anything in her notebook so far.

'She's grown up a lot,' Gabi comments.

'Yeah. And she has a friend – Nola. A girl who lives just down the road and whose parents don't mind her hanging out with Trixie.' Seeing Gabi knit her brows in confusion, he adds, 'I'm sorry. That's me being resentful. Trixie didn't really have any close friends before Leona went missing – she had difficulty socialising – but Scarlett did. Scarlett's friends weren't allowed to see her. Their parents warned them to stay well away from her. Scarlett became an outcast. It was devastating.'

'I can imagine. That's terrible. Has the situation improved?'

'Well, Trixie has a best friend and Scarlett says she doesn't have any close friends, but she has mates.'

'So, you're on speaking terms with Scarlett? Even though she has moved out?'

'I call her every day and occasionally she picks up, but she's not very talkative when she does.'

He has told Gabi nothing but sob stories, one after the other, since the moment she arrived. He doesn't want her to think he's wallowing in self-pity. And he doesn't want her to pity him – that would be even worse.

He shrugs. 'Understandable, I suppose. Roxanne blamed me for Leona's disappearance and, after a while, it rubbed off on Scarlett.'

'So you feel like your sister-in-law has poisoned your daughter against you.'

Not his exact words, but these are no doubt the words that will worm their way into Gabi's next article. That's what it amounts to, so there's no point in him splitting hairs over semantics. 'You could say that.'

He could also say that Roxanne is slowly succeeding in setting Trixie against him, too – she seems more and more wary of him these days – but he keeps this to himself.

They talk about Scarlett and Trixie for a while. Gabi must be desperate to know what he has to say about the second discovery in the grounds of Rose Cottage – but she seems genuinely interested in his daughters and they're his favourite topic of conversation. He's quite happy to distract her, keep her from discussing the elephant in the room.

If he was writing this scene for one of his novels, this is the bit where the police would arrive to arrest him before Gabi could ask him to explain the bones in his mother's back garden. Saved by the doorbell. Reviewers and bloggers have often criticised his books for being chock-full of clichés. He almost wishes the police would come and get him. He's sick of this feeling of impending doom. He might actually feel better once it's done and dusted.

Gabi feels sorry for him. He's had a hard time and that's putting it mildly. She didn't know his father had died when he was little. She knows what that's like – hers died when she was young, too, drank himself into an early grave. And since Matt's wife has gone missing – which she can also relate to – he's been having financial difficulties on top of having to deal with his mother's bad health and his elder daughter leaving home.

She wonders how to broach the subject of the human remains in the garden. She thinks Matt's evading the issue, deliberately skirting around it, but he must know that's why she's here. She scribbles circles and wiggly lines on her pad, trying to think of a way to get their conversation back on track.

In the end, Matt's the one who gives her the cue. 'Gabi, I have nothing to do with Leona's disappearance,' he says.

'Are you saying they found someone else's bones in the garden of Rose Cottage? That they aren't Leona's remains?'

'No. No, that's not what I'm saying. They're Leona's ... bones. Obviously.'

'How do you know that if you didn't kill her?'

'It's just ... they're bound to be ... It's her, it has to be Leona. What I'm saying is I didn't kill my wife. Please, Gabi ...'

He trails off. She gets the impression he's not pleading with her to help him or to depict him from a flattering angle when she writes up her piece; he's begging her to believe him.

She leans forwards. 'If you didn't kill her, then who did?' It comes out as a whisper.

Matt looks down at his hands and fiddles with his wedding ring. Gabi is surprised and touched that he still wears it, but why wouldn't he? To all intents and purposes, he's still married. Until he's officially widowed. She looks down at her own hands, remembering the engagement ring that she'd once worn on her finger.

'I don't know. It's a set-up, Gabi,' he says. 'Someone is trying to frame me.'

Chapter 18

June 2024

Matt keeps glancing out of the living room window, expecting several police cars and vans to roll up, blues and twos and the whole caboodle. Will they knock at the door politely or knock it down with a battering ram?

He'd been interviewed a few weeks after Leona went missing. The police hadn't arrested him – they'd asked him, tritely, to assist them with their inquiries – but it had been crystal clear they suspected him. He hadn't even contacted a lawyer, anxious not to do or say anything that would make him look guilty – or guiltier – in anyone's eyes. He stuck it out, answered their questions, repeated over and over that he had nothing to do with his wife's disappearance. They couldn't arrest him. They had nothing on him. Any evidence against him would have been circumstantial at best. They couldn't even prove Leona was dead. Not without a body.

All that was about to change. He would be arrested any day now. Maybe even any second or minute.

'Who would frame you, Matt?' Gabi's question breaks into his thoughts. 'Do you have any enemies?'

Gabi is the first person to call in and see him in months and she's here professionally. He has no friends at all anymore. Members of his own family – and Leona's – have turned against him. Roxanne's husband, Adam, checks up on him from time to time. And his mum's on his side, but that's about it. Even Trixie is on her guard around him now. But he can't say any of this to Gabi. She'll think he's pathetic.

He scoffs. 'These days I have more enemies than friends,' he says.

'But what about back then? When Leona went missing, everyone who knew you spoke very highly of you. You were popular in the community.'

'It didn't take long for the tide to turn, though, did it?' he says. 'Before long, everyone thought I was behind Leona's disappearance, including the police. *Especially* the police.'

'Yes, I always found that strange. You used to be a police officer. Didn't you have any allies in the force?'

She's looking at something in the corner of the room, over his right shoulder. He knows without turning around what it is. The enlarged photo of Leona that used to sit on the top of the bookcase, leaning against the wall. The one he took the year they went on holiday to Madeira. He has finally got round to hanging it on the wall.

'Do you know why I left the police force?' he says.

'No. Tell me.'

'I was on the beat one evening when Sandra, who was also a PC, and I were called out to this house on the Forches estate in Barnstaple. A man was threatening his wife. She was the one who had called 999. He'd had far too much to drink – we could smell the alcohol on his breath and seeping out of his pores. He had a knife. There was other stuff going down that night and it took a long time for back-up to arrive. We had to restrain this guy – Gary Pearson, he was called – while we waited. We were terrified one of us or Mrs Pearson could get seriously injured.'

'Go on,' Gabi prods when he pauses.

'Well, that's precisely what happened. He wrestled himself free and stabbed Sandra in the abdomen. She died in the ambulance on the way to hospital.'

'That's awful. I'm so sorry,' she says. 'What happened to Gary Pearson?'

'He took off, but he was apprehended a few days later. He went to prison. He's probably out by now. Unless he's back inside for something else.' He can hear the venom in his tone. God, how he loathes that guy. Prison is too good for scum like him. He should be hanged, drawn and quartered.

'So this incident, losing your colleague, that's why you left the police force?' she asks.

'I didn't resign immediately. But after the incident, I wasn't the same. I struggled with anxiety and PTSD. I had to give up frontline duties and work in the North Devon Constabulary control room headquarters. Eventually, I was medically discharged. I started writing. Diaries to begin with. But I soon turned to thrillers. It was therapeutic, cathartic, whatever. Some sort of escapism or exposure therapy. I write about crime, but I feel removed from it. It's paradoxical, but writing about danger makes me feel safe.'

Her eyebrows knit into a stitch. She must think he's going off on a massive tangent.

'But, yes, that's why I left the police force and became a crime writer.' He looks over the mic into her eyes. 'I always wondered, don't ask me why, if the two incidents – the knife attack and Leona's disappearance – might be connected in some way.'

'How?'

'I don't know. It's silly. Maybe the connection is only in my head. The two worst experiences of my life. Losing my colleague, then losing my wife.'

'Did you discuss this with the police?'

'No. No point. As far as the police were concerned back then, I may as well have plunged the knife into Sandra's stomach myself. They blamed me. I blamed myself as it was, so that was ... well, it was one of the things I had to deal with.' He tries to keep the bitterness out of his voice. 'I bet if they could get me for murdering Leona, they would see it as poetic justice for Sandra.'

Gabi frowns at him. 'I get that you think some of the officers investigating Leona's disappearance might have had it in for you because your colleague died on your watch, Matt,' she says. 'But surely you don't think the police are setting you up?'

'No. No, of course not.' Matt doesn't sound convincing or convinced, not even to himself. 'But I don't think they considered the possibility that someone else might have harmed Leona. As far as I know, they never had another suspect. Only me. I don't know who might want to frame me. All I know is someone is stitching me up.'

He's desperate for Gabi to believe him – he needs an ally – but he's not thinking straight and he's talking bollocks. He knew Gabi was coming today. He should have worked out what to say beforehand.

'What is it that makes you think you're being framed?' Gabi asks.

'When Leona went missing, the police searched the house,' he says. 'Twice. The first time it wasn't really official. One of the first responders – a constable – had a look around, ostensibly to see if anything in the house might provide a clue to Leona's whereabouts.' He takes a sip of his water. He's not thirsty, but he needs a few seconds to gather his thoughts. 'When the house was searched for the second time – by CID officers – they searched more thoroughly. They also seized Leona's computer and mine.'

'Go on,' Gabi says when he takes another mouthful of water.

'The police asked me about my internet search history.'

'Oh?'

'Apparently, a day or so after Leona disappeared, I'd looked up the rate of body decomposition in soil. I visited several different websites, according to the police.'

Gabi looks at him intently, her tweezed eyebrows now arched into circumflexes. He can't tell if her expression is one of surprise or disbelief.

'And you didn't?' she says.

'No. Definitely not. Seriously, Gabi. If I'd buried my wife after researching …' He breaks off. 'God, it's just … I can't even think about it. I would … I wouldn't …'

'You'd have deleted your browsing history.'

'Well, obviously. I'm not stupid.'

'So you think this "evidence" was planted.'

'I can't think of any other explanation. Can you?'

Gabi doesn't answer his question. Instead, she asks one of her own. 'Who had access to your computer before the police took it?'

'Theoretically, no one,' he says. 'Apart from me, only the dog comes into my study. I don't even allow the cleaner inside that room. I tidy and clean it myself.'

'Is the computer password-protected?'

'Yes, but my password is written on a Post-it, stuck next to the trackpad on the computer itself.' He can imagine what she's thinking. What kind of idiot does that? And he's just told her he's not stupid.

'So, basically, anyone who came into the house could have used your computer,' Gabi concludes.

Gabi loads her rucksack into the boot, gets behind the wheel and plugs in her phone to charge it up. She's stunned when her car roars into life and a man and woman start arguing in Italian through the speakers. She pauses the Babbel app on her phone, sends a quick text to Joe and sets off to join him. On the way, she replays in her head snippets of what Matt has told her. Something doesn't sit right with her. Once or twice, he changed the subject to dodge her questions. She had zero control over the interview, despite having planned everything out in advance. Nothing new there, though. Every time she interviews him, Matt is the one pulling the strings. What is it that's niggling her? She tries to put her finger on it, but draws a blank.

Her mobile rings just as she parks alongside Joe's car. She turns off the ignition and signals to Joe that she'll just be a minute. Then she looks at the caller ID.

'Today is just full of surprises,' she says aloud to herself, swiping to take the call. To Gareth Harvey, she says, 'Good morning, Professor. To what do I owe the pleasure of this unexpected phone call?' She gets a kick out of paraphrasing his own line back at him.

'Good morning, Ms Conti.' He sounds friendly, for once. Perhaps his student – Freya – did put in a good word for Gabi, as she promised. 'I've just had confirmation ... I thought you'd like to know ...' Gabi waits, amused. He isn't usually this inarticulate, either. 'Gabriela, I've just had a phone call from a contact of mine at the Home Office ...' Gabi waits with bated breath. 'You can't quote me on this,' he warns, 'but the remains we excavated at Rose Cottage in Benton have been confirmed as those of Leona Walsh.'

It shouldn't come as a shock, but Gabi's heart skips several beats, then starts up again, too fast. She has another scoop! This will be a major news story and she's going to be the one to break it. 'Thank you, Professor Harvey. This is ... It's ...' Now she's the one who's tongue-tied. She takes a deep breath. 'It's very kind of you to let me know. You have my word. I won't reveal you as my source. Thank you, again.'

Professor Harvey doesn't reply and she realises he has already ended the call.

The evidence is stacking up against Matthew Walsh. Five years ago, the police had only circumstantial evidence, if that. There was no way of making anything stick, no way of building a concrete case against him. Now they have a body. His wife's body. Buried in the grounds of his mother's house, no less. After he'd supposedly searched for information about body decomposition in soil. This all points to Matt. This all points to murder. And yet, Gabi still wants to believe him. But how can he possibly be innocent?

Joe taps on her window. She winds it open a few inches, then the lever sticks. Joe says something, but his words are drowned out by the howl of sirens. Seconds later, three police vehicles streak by, one of them an unmarked car with a blue rotating light on the roof, all heading in the direction from which Gabi has just come, towards Blackmoor Manor.

Missing, Presumed Murdered
A True Crime Podcast Hosted by Gabriela Conti
Audio File 6
Interview with Scarlett Walsh, Leona's daughter.
2024

This is the story of Leona Walsh, whose disappearance in December 2019 has remained a mystery for nearly five years. Join me as I explore the truths and lies in this case. I am Gabriela Conti and you're listening to **Missing, Presumed Murdered**, *a true crime podcast.*

Gabriela Conti: Thank you for agreeing to talk to me, Scarlett. I realise that this is very hard for you.

Scarlett Walsh: I want to know what really happened to my mother. That's why I'm doing this. I need to know if my father is responsible.

GC: I understand. It's torture, not knowing for sure, isn't it?

SW: Yeah, totally. Like you're stuck in limbo.

GC: What was it like, growing up with that doubt? How do you cope with that?

SW: You don't. I didn't. Cope, I mean. It just never went away. Everyone assumed my dad was guilty of something. No one came to the house anymore. He became an outcast, but so did I. So did Trixie, but she's introverted and it didn't bother her as much. People looked at us differently, like we were all deformed or contagious or something. My friends weren't allowed to see me anymore. Their parents seemed to think if my dad was evil, then maybe I was, too. The apple doesn't fall far from the tree. That's actually how I learnt that expression. Keira Sutton's mother said it to me.

GC: I'm so sorry, Scar—

SW: And school was just awful.

GC: *In what way? Were you bullied?*

SW: *The other kids called me names, pulled my hair, kicked my chair, that sort of thing. A lot of the teachers made jokes about me, in front of me, to make the pupils laugh. I was, like, left out. A lot. Ignored. Like I was invisible. I preferred that to the name-calling and stuff.*

GC: *What do you mean, 'left out'?*

SW: *Never picked for the netball team, that sort of thing.*

GC: *Ah, I know what that's like. I was bullied a bit at school, too. And I was always picked last. I was rubbish at netball.*

SW: *I wasn't. I was really good. And in class, no one would sit next to me. The maths teacher fetched a table and a chair one time from the classroom next to ours rather than ask a pupil to sit in the empty chair next to me. My marks dropped at school. I flunked my A levels last year. When I was little, I wanted to be a lawyer. That has been my dream ever since I was about nine years old. I'm working as a dog walker right now, earning peanuts, until I can get my act together.*

GC: *I'm so sorry, Scarlett. People can be very cruel.*

SW: *Can I ask you a question?*

GC: *Of course.*

SW: *Do you think he did it? Do you think my dad killed my mum?*

GC: *Honestly? If I had to say, one way or the other, I'd be inclined to give him the benefit of the doubt.*

SW: *Why?*

GC: *I don't know, really. Admittedly, he's adept at stretching the truth, but—*

SW: *Lying, you mean.*

GC: *Lying, yes. I think that goes with the job, making up stories. But I got the impression when he said he didn't kill your mum, that he was telling the truth. What do you think, Scarlett?*

SW: *I think he's probably guilty. Like, ninety-five per cent chance. I know it's supposed to be innocent until proven guilty, but he lies about everything, all the time. Plus, he used to boast he could commit the perfect murder, and I just think, well, everything points at him, you know? But I guess that even now he's been arrested, I'm still hoping it wasn't him. I've lost my mum. I feel like I've lost my dad, too, but if he didn't do it ... I wouldn't have to lose him.*

GC: *Your dad seems to think you might have been swayed by what your aunt says. Do you think she might have influenced you? Could that be the reason why you don't believe in your dad anymore?*

SW: *Aunt Roxanne thinks Dad's as guilty as sin. For her, there's not even, like, a shadow of a doubt. But I'm capable of making up my own mind. I sat on the fence for a while, I suppose, but, well, he's the obvious suspect, you know? I can't see who else could have done it. Like I said, I hope I'm wrong. But even if I am, I just want to know the truth.*

Chapter 19

June 2024

Thanks to Gabi's quick thinking and Joe's breakneck driving, they manage to snag a video and some photos of Matt's arrest at Blackmoor Manor. Matt offers no resistance as he's led down the driveway, cuffed and flanked by two police officers, and followed by three more.

Passing Gabi, Matt looks directly at her – or into the camera of her phone, she's not sure which – and says, 'I didn't kill my wife. You have to believe me.'

As Joe drives back to the restaurant car park, more slowly now, Gabi makes a phone call. She wants to let Roxanne know what's going on before she and the girls learn about it online or in the news. Roxanne has nothing to say, for a change. She merely thanks Gabi for letting her know, then ends the call. Then Gabi uploads the video to the rag's X and Instagram pages. She wonders what this development means – for them, for Matt, for his daughters.

The bones in Benton have been identified as Leona Walsh's remains and Matthew Walsh has been arrested on suspicion of murder. And she and Joe are the only ones on this story for the moment. She's buzzing with excitement, but at the same time, she can't help feeling heartbroken. Poor Matt. His words echo in her mind. *I didn't kill my wife. You have to believe me.* This looks for all the world like an open-and-shut case; everything is pointing at Matt's culpability. And yet Gabi clings to the slither of hope he's innocent. Is there any chance he really was set up? And, if so, by whom?

'Looks like he's guilty,' Joe says, as if reading her thoughts. 'Hardly any doubt about it now.'

Gabi says nothing.

'Surely you don't still believe him, Gabi?'

'I want to believe him,' she says. 'Don't you think there's even a small chance …?'

Joe turns to look at her. She wishes he'd keep his eyes on the road. 'Nah. I have a pretty good built-in bullshit detector and it's gone way off the scale.'

Gabi sighs. She has always been bad at reading people, a poor judge of character. Just look at how she was taken in by Darren.

At the wheel of her own car, she sifts through what she knows, trying to find something that might indicate Matt is innocent. No stone unturned. That's what the police promised in their efforts to find Leona four and a half years ago. But did they really explore every avenue? Or was their investigation contaminated by tunnel vision, their focus exclusively on Matt? How closely did they look into Leona's lover, Toby Wigmore? How seriously did they look for any other possible suspects?

Gabi herself investigated a possible political incentive for Leona's disappearance, but got nowhere. Locally, Leona had a visible profile – she was a local councillor and she was working as the election agent for the North Devon candidate when the scandal broke. She must have put a few people's backs up, assuming the fraud accusations were founded. But despite the shame Leona's alleged embezzlement brought on the local government, no one Gabi spoke to had bad-mouthed her. Leona seemed to have been genuinely popular with her co-workers and friends. She didn't appear to have any enemies. And misappropriating thirty grand would hardly be an offence worth killing someone over. Gabi looked into the fraud allegations, too. Although the claims appeared to be founded, Gabi couldn't find a link, not even a tenuous one, with Leona's disappearance. Another blind alley.

But what about the knife attack Matt told her about? When he was a police officer, Matt lost his partner before his very eyes. He thinks the assault and Leona's disappearance might somehow be connected, although he can't be sure if the association was just in his head. Could the knife assault be a lead? It's definitely worth checking out.

The traffic is slow going as Gabi approaches Barnstaple. She drums her fingers on the steering wheel, mentally composing the article she'll write. Joe is waiting for her when she gets home. She parks and gets out of the car. He follows her inside. As soon as she has kicked off her shoes, she boots up her laptop and starts to type, her fingers flying over the keyboard. Joe stands behind her and reads over her shoulder, but she shoos him away. So, instead, he plies her with coffee and waits patiently for her to finish. When she's satisfied with what she has written, she shows it to him.

'It's good, Gabi,' he says when he has read it. 'Really, really good. Wow! This is going to make waves!'

Joe makes a few suggestions and Gabi tweaks her copy. Then he takes his mobile out of the back pocket of his jeans and emails her the photos he took of Matt's arrest. She selects one of the photos and adds it to the article. She also adds Joe's byline to hers. Then she uploads the piece to their online paper and sends the link to Mick.

They have lunch together – cheese toasties, Gabi's fridge and food cupboards are almost bare. Then Joe, in need of a change of clothes, and probably something more substantial to eat, goes home after arranging to pick her up tomorrow to go for a walk at Saunton Sands.

Once he has left, Gabi listens to her interview with Matt in which he told her about losing his colleague. She flicks through her notepad until she finds the page on which she jotted down the names and details – Matt's partner, Sandra; Gary Pearson and his wife, the Forches Estate, Barnstaple. If Matt testified against Pearson, would Pearson still hold a grudge by the time he got out of jail? Could Leona's death have been some sort of revenge killing? Gabi swipes away the thought as soon as it enters her head. It's too far-fetched.

She has no idea when the incident took place and berates herself for not thinking to ask Matt at the time. She does a couple of sums on the calculator app on her mobile – she has never been good at mental arithmetic. The average prison sentence for murder in the UK, Gabi knows, is between fifteen and twenty years, so the assault must have happened before 2004 for Pearson to have been released and to have had a hand in Leona's disappearance in 2019. But according to his author bio, Matt joined the police force when he was eighteen. He's now fifty.

If the assault took place near the beginning of Matt's career in the Devon Constabulary, she may not find any trace of it online. The *Echo* didn't exist at all until fifteen years ago and the *North Devon Journal*, the main paper in the region, and their main rival, only went online a year or two before the new millennium.

She types 'Gary Pearson', 'stabbing' and 'Barnstaple' into the search bar and clicks on the first result that shows up. It's an article on the *Echo Live* website, dated 27 December 2018. It's not exactly what she was looking for, definitely not what she expected – she can tell that from the headline: 'POLICE KILLER GARY PEARSON DIES IN PRISON ON BOXING DAY'. As she skims it, words and phrases grab her attention, as if highlighted: *HMP Guys Marsh … 25-year sentence … convicted of murder … Exeter Crown Court … April 2002.*

She scrolls back to the top to reread the article, more carefully this time, in case she has missed something.

The Ministry of Justice has confirmed that Gary Pearson, 35, died on Boxing Day at HMP Guys Marsh in Dorset, where he was serving a 25-year sentence for the murder of police officer Sandra Greene. As with all deaths in custody, there will be an independent investigation by the Prisons and Probation Ombudsman.

The cause of his death isn't clear, but how he died is of no interest to Gabi. What matters is that there's no way he could have had a hand in Leona's disappearance. At least, not directly. He died a year before she went missing. There's nothing to connect Sandra's death to Leona's disappearance, as far as Gabi can see. Unless Matt has associated them because both incidents were absolutely horrific for him. Or because they both took place at Christmas time. This is pointless.

She's about to snap down the lid of her laptop when she spots the discrepancy. How did this not leap out at her the first time? She reads it aloud this time.

Pearson was convicted of murder at Exeter Crown Court in April 2002. PC Sandra Greene, 26, and her colleague PC Matthew Walsh, 28, were called out to the Forches Estate in Barnstaple for an incident of domestic abuse. As the two officers attempted to restrain Pearson, who was armed with a kitchen knife, PC Greene received a fatal stab wound to the neck.

Is there a mistake in the article? She doesn't recall the incident – she was still at school in April 2002 and there's nothing extraordinary about the news item itself. It's the sort of everyday filler used as padding in news pages, online as well as in print. Gabi looks at the byline. Cath Ward. She knows Cath. She used to work for the *Echo*, but she now works in London – for the *Times*. She left shortly before Leona's disappearance. She'll email Cath to ask what she remembers. But Cath's a good journo. Gabi has never known her to make mistakes.

Is Gabi the one making a mistake? Has she misremembered what Matt said? She closes the page and clicks on the audio file again. It takes her a moment to find the right section. *As far as the police were concerned back then, I may as well have plunged the knife into Sandra's stomach myself.* And a few seconds later, he says it again. *He wrestled himself free and stabbed Sandra in the abdomen.* He said it twice! The stomach. The abdomen. Not the neck.

Gabi grapples for an explanation. Maybe Sandra was stabbed in the stomach and then the neck. That makes sense, although it's odd Matt didn't mention that. He'd remember the details, surely, if he witnessed his colleague being brutally stabbed. Or perhaps Matt was traumatised and blanked out the event completely. He did say he suffered from PTSD after the incident. Or could he have confused reality with an incident in one of his books?

All these theories seem plausible, but something about this doesn't add up. Gabi can't shake that now familiar feeling that Matt is hiding something, skipping part of the story. But what reason would he have to lie?

Chapter 20

June 2024

Gabi doesn't expect Cath Ward to get back to her immediately. It's Sunday, after all. She's probably spending quality time with her family. And yet, Gabi can't help feeling disappointed when, by mid-morning, there's still no reply to the email she sent last night.

She has been trying to unplug and unwind more at weekends, but even as she enjoys her stroll along the beach, hand in hand with Joe, her fingers are itching to take out her phone and check her emails again.

One of the problems with being a journalist in the digital age is that it's hard to disconnect. Your work doesn't stop when you leave the office. Technology has irrevocably transformed the way news is distributed and consumed. Journalists have to provide real-time reporting as events unfold. In the evenings, Gabi updates articles online and follows up stories on their social media platforms. She tries to give in-depth analysis. Anyone with a smartphone and a social media account can post newsworthy content nowadays, so speed is vital. Gabi feels like she's a permanent competitor in a race without a finish line.

When she needs quotes and interviews, people tend to be freer at weekends and in the evenings, which makes it even harder to switch off and have some downtime. As if to prove her own point, she has arranged to see Scarlett again later today.

Joe buys Gabi a latte in the Beach Shop and they sit at a window table and look out at the sea. It's a sunny day and the beach is packed. The waves are good, too, and there are lots of surfers in the water.

She waits until Joe pops to the loo before giving in to temptation and taking out her phone. Cath Ward evidently works at weekends, too – her reply is sitting in Gabi's inbox. It's short and to the point. Cath does remember the knife attack. She covered Gary Pearson's trial at Exeter Crown Court. She's adamant that the victim, Sandra Greene, died of a single stab wound – to the neck. So Matt's account of events is inaccurate. But Gabi still can't work out why.

Combe Cottage is situated down a muddy track near Mullacott Cross, on the outskirts of Ilfracombe. Gabi came here recently to interview Scarlett and Roxanne for the podcast. Even so, she almost misses the turning. The cottage is a stone building, a converted barn, no doubt. From the outside, it looks pretty, but small – a lot smaller than Blackmoor Manor.

Roxanne opens the door with a scowl on her face and her hair all over the place. She leads Gabi into the sitting room. It's even messier than Gabi remembers. Ornaments clutter every available space; washing hangs on a clothes horse next to the radiator. Photos dangle lopsidedly on one of the walls and a large mirror above the electric fire reflects a rather dusty image of the room. In spite of the disorder, or perhaps because of it, the room is cosy and welcoming.

'Scarlett's popped out to fetch some groceries,' Roxanne says. 'She should be back any minute. Have a seat. I'll make us a cuppa. Remind me how you take it?'

Gabi would prefer a coffee, but she doesn't dare ask. She finds Roxanne intimidating. 'Milk, no sugar, please,' she says, perching on the edge of the sofa.

There's cat hair everywhere, even though the only cat Gabi can see, curled up on the armchair, is bald. She nearly ran over a black-and-white cat outside last time she came. Perhaps that cat belongs to Roxanne, too. She hears the roar of the kettle in the adjoining kitchen as she sets up her recording equipment.

Trixie materialises in the doorway. Gabi stares. Gosh, she really does look like her mother. Gabi remembers being struck by the likeness last time she saw Trixie. Trixie must be around the same age now as Leona was when Gabi first met her. It's like looking at a ghost.

'Hi, Trixie. How are you?' she says.

Trixie doesn't answer. Gabi can hardly blame her. What an idiotic question. The poor girl's world has been turned upside down. Again.

Trixie sidles closer to Gabi. 'Can I ask you a favour?' she says, looking down at her hands, clasped in front of her.

'Of course. Anything.'

'Could you look after Sydney for me?'

Sydney? Gabi throws Trixie a puzzled look, but Trixie doesn't seem to catch it.

Roxanne comes back into the room. She sets a mug on the coffee table in front of Gabi, slopping some tea over the rim, dangerously close to Gabi's laptop. Roxanne either doesn't notice or doesn't care. The table is decorated with several stains and marks. She pushes the cat off the armchair and sits in its place. 'Beatrix, you can't ask Gabriela to look after the dog,' she says.

The hopeful expression wilts on Trixie's face.

'Ah! The dog. I didn't know what … who you were talking about.' Gabi likes dogs well enough – she grew up with a golden retriever – but her house is small and Australian shepherds need a lot of exercise.

'I've had to move in here, you see, because my dad has been arrested,' Trixie explains. 'Auntie Roxie has five cats, so Sydney couldn't come with me.' Tears well up in her eyes and threaten to spill down her face. She sounds and looks so much younger than her twelve years.

'Where's Sydney now?' Gabi asks.

'He's at the animal shelter in Ilfracombe. Please?'

'Trixie!' There's a gentle warning in Roxanne's voice.

Gabi's house might be small, but it's definitely a lot bigger than a kennel or a cage at the dog shelter. And she has just promised to do anything for Trixie. 'It's Sunday. It's probably closed, but I'll get the address from your aunt and go and pick him up as soon as it's open.'

'It's open today until four. It's two o'clock now.'

'In that case, I'll go and get him when I've spoken to Scarlett. OK?'

This seems to satisfy Trixie, who smiles her thanks, reels off the address in Ilfracombe, including the postcode, by heart, then turns and leaves the room.

'How's she doing?' Gabi asks Roxanne.

'She's adapting. Slowly. Beatrix was feeling increasingly uncomfortable living under the same roof as her father – she was conflicted and confused – but she finds herself out of her comfort zone as soon as her routine is disturbed, so having to move to a new home isn't ideal.'

'It must be terrible for her.'

'It's terrible for all of us,' Roxanne says.

'The girls are lucky to have you.'

'That's nice of you to say, but I'm the one who feels lucky.' Roxanne leans towards Gabi and adds in a conspiratorial tone, 'I always wanted kids. Leona had two beautiful daughters – she always got everything she set out to get.' She gives a dry laugh. 'And I couldn't … conceive. And now they're living with me.'

Gabi doesn't know what to make of that. She remembers

thinking last time she saw Roxanne that she seemed jealous of Leona. What was it she said? Something about Leona rolling in it and having more money than sense, and yet squandering so much that she needed to pilfer more money. There's no love lost between Roxanne and her brother-in-law – that much is obvious. But did Roxanne resent her sister, too?

Roxanne is looking at her, clearly waiting for her to speak. Thankfully, Scarlett arrives at that moment and saves Gabi from having to think of something to say. She dumps a cotton Bag for Life on the floor – presumably containing the groceries.

'I'll leave you both to it,' Roxanne says, and, picking up her mug of tea in one hand and the shopping bag in the other, she heads back into the kitchen and closes the door behind her.

Gabi doesn't ask how Scarlett is. She can see from the girl's gaunt, pale face that she's not doing well. 'Thank you for talking to me again today. I'd like to pick up from where we left off last time, if that's OK with you,' she says. Scarlett nods and Gabi hits a key to record their conversation. 'Last time we talked, you said you believed your dad probably killed your mum. What do you think his motive was?'

Scarlett shrugs. 'Because he found out about her lover, I guess,' she says.

'Did your dad ever say to you, before your mum went missing, that he knew she had a boyfriend? Or anything that made you realise in hindsight that he knew about Toby Wigmore?'

'No. Nothing. But I was young at the time. He'd hardly have confided in me.'

'No, but you might have overheard your parents arguing about it or something.'

'I mean, I sometimes overheard them arguing, but I don't remember an argument specifically about that.'

The bald cat jumps up onto Scarlett's lap. It really is very ugly. Gabi can hear it purring from where she's sitting. She hopes the mic won't pick it up.

'What sort of things did your mum and dad argue about, Scarlett?'

'Oh, you know, they would argue about what Trixie and me were allowed to do, or not, what punishments to give us when we did something wrong – Mum was stricter than Dad; about Mum's job because she said Dad didn't take it seriously, even though she earned more than him; about money – Dad said Mum spent money like water. Mum said Dad needed to get a real job and earn a decent salary. That sort of thing.'

'And did they argue a lot?'

'Not a lot, no. Sometimes. Quite often, I suppose. But ...'

'But?'

'But every once in a while, they had, like, these massive fights.'

'Fights?'

'Yeah.' Scarlett pauses. Gabi wants to prompt her again, but waits it out. She remembers Matt telling her ages ago that was often the best way with Scarlett. Pushing her made her clam up. Scarlett looks at the mic, as if seeing it for the first time. Gabi's about to offer to stop the recording, to go off the record, when Scarlett continues, 'Dad lost his temper easily. And Mum ... well, she'd get ... hysterical and throw a hissy fit. But the rest of the time, they got on well, you know? They used to, like, kiss and hold hands, even in front of us, in front of the TV and stuff. Trixie and me, we found it a bit gross.'

'Scarlett, I have to ask ... did your dad ever hit your mum?'

'Oh, no. His bark's worse than his bite.'

'So you wouldn't describe him as violent, even though he had a quick temper?'

'No. He was never violent.'

'And yet you think he probably killed your mum?'

'Yeah. I think everyone has the potential to murder someone if they're pushed too far. If he found out Mum was cheating on him, I think that might have made him snap. But I never actually, you know, witnessed Dad being violent towards Mum.'

Scarlett pauses again. Gabi needs to change tack. She flicks through her notebook, looking for the ideas she jotted down before coming today.

But before she can find the right page, Scarlett adds, 'If anything, it was the other way round.'

Gabi looks up sharply. Did she hear that correctly? 'What did you say?' she asks.

At first, Scarlett doesn't answer, perhaps thinking she has already said too much. Then she says, 'Can we stop now? I mean, I'm not comfortable with where this is going. I don't want to, like, speak ill of the dead, you know?'

'Sure,' Gabi says reluctantly and stops the recording. She wants to press Scarlett for more detail. But she can't risk losing her trust or upsetting her. She shuts down her laptop and packs up the equipment, stealing glances at Scarlett, who is biting her nails.

If anything, it was the other way round. What did Scarlett mean by that? There's only one person Gabi can ask. But she has no idea when she'll get to talk to him again.

Chapter 21

June 2024

Matt is taken to the new custody centre at Middlemoor in Exeter. Four and a half years ago, when the press conference was held next door at the police headquarters, it was under construction. Now it's completed and fully functioning, a sustainable, state-of-the-art building, lots of glass on the façade and a spacious, airy vibe inside.

He knows how this works. He has been arrested, so the clock is ticking. Theoretically, the police will have to charge him or release him within twenty-four hours. In practice, this is likely to be much longer once extra time is granted, first by the superintendent and then by the magistrates' court. He could be here all week.

He also knows he'll face several rounds of interviews. At first, the officers will behave professionally and be friendly. They'll ask easy questions. Deceptively easy. Matt needs to be on his guard. The officers will aim to lure him into a false sense of security, then set traps for him to fall into. And by the time the interrogations start to resemble the Spanish Inquisition, they'll be trying to catch him out, catch him in a lie.

The custody sergeant takes Matt's fingerprints and a DNA sample. She also takes his possessions – his phone, the watch that Leona gave him for his fortieth, his wallet and his belt. She tells him he's entitled to free legal advice from the station's duty solicitor.

'No,' Matt says. 'No need. I know a defence solicitor. Could you call … damn, I can't remember his name. It's either Peter Oliver or Oliver Peters, something like that.'

The custody sergeant throws him a look that says, *Know him well, do you?*

'It's Patrick Oliver,' Matt says as the guy's name comes to him.

Adam used to play squash with Oliver and put Matt in touch with him ages ago. The solicitor has helped Matt out on several occasions, patiently and promptly responding to emails every time Matt needed information to write the court scenes in his books with some degree of authenticity. Matt has listed him in the acknowledgements of at least three novels in his *Moors* series and was contemplating dedicating his last book to him, but in the end, at Trixie's suggestion, he dedicated it to Sydney.

So, to answer the custody sergeant's unspoken question, no, Matt doesn't know the defence solicitor well. He has never met the man. He doesn't know how he's going to pay him, either. Of course, Patrick Oliver may refuse to represent Matt, in which case Matt will ask for the duty solicitor.

The custody sergeant escorts Matt down a white corridor with two bright orange stripes running parallel along the length of it. The wall at the far end is a matching orange. His cell door is a blue that pops, between duck egg and turquoise on the colour chart. Leona would have known the name of that particular shade. Matt gets the feeling he's in a nursery.

The cell is less vibrant. Tiled walls; a low toilet; a handwashing station built into the wall; a long bench. All white. Leona once told him that white walls and furniture make a room look big. It's not working here. He sits on the bench, wrinkling his nose as the smell of bleach assails his nostrils.

Matt half expects Patrick Oliver to send a paralegal in his place, so he's a little surprised when the man himself shows up, an hour or so later. The custody sergeant fetches Matt from his cell and takes him to a private room the size of a walk-in wardrobe, where the defence solicitor is waiting for him.

'Matthew,' the man says, 'I wish we could have met in different circumstances.' He gestures for Matt to sit.

'Patrick ...' Matt wants to blurt out that he had nothing to do with his wife's disappearance or death, but there's no point. The solicitor doesn't need to be convinced of Matt's innocence; he'll act in Matt's best interests whether he believes Matt's guilty or innocent. 'Thank you so much for coming,' Matt says instead.

'Now, I've obtained disclosure from the police, Matthew,' the solicitor says, clearly keen to get down to business, 'and they seem to think the evidence against you is fairly strong. I get the impression they haven't told me everything. They're keeping a trick or two up their sleeves.' Matt nods. This works both ways. He has no intention of telling the police everything, either. 'Why don't you walk me through it all, starting from the very beginning?'

Matt has had time to think about what to say. A lot of time. Nearly five years, in fact. He has run through the whole sequence of events in his head countless times, starting from the night of Leona's disappearance and ending with her body being unearthed in his mother's garden.

He has also had lots of time to decide how to play this, to consider his options and work out his next steps. He could confess and get this all over and done with, enter a guilty plea at the first opportunity and avoid a trial, go straight to jail without passing go. Whether he pleads guilty or not guilty, he's under no illusion: he's going down. He's looking at a life sentence either way. But if Matt pleads guilty and shows remorse, perhaps the judge will be more lenient, and set a lower minimum sentence.

He has no idea how long their consultation lasts. It seems like a long time, but it's probably less than an hour. Patrick Oliver takes notes while Matt talks, asking questions for clarification from time to time.

Finally, Oliver says, 'I would suggest our best plan of action is for you to answer – as succinctly as possible – the questions that you were asked in voluntary interviews when your wife first disappeared.' Matt nods again. 'That way, you'll be seen to be cooperating,' Oliver continues. 'Any questions they ask this time that they haven't asked on record previously, however, I would advise you to answer "no comment". You have the right to remain silent, remember, and you mustn't risk saying something that might be contradictory, or worse, incriminatory. Don't forget that anything you say can be used against you in court.'

Matt is allowed a short break, which he spends in his cell. He anticipates the questions the police will ask. Many of them, they'll already have put to him in the past. And he must give the same answers. The problem is, Matt's truth has become peppered with little fibs over the years and his story differs slightly, depending on who he's telling it to. He has scaled down what he has revealed to his daughters; depicted himself in the best possible light when talking to Gabi and Adam; omitted certain details when talking to the police; reimagined parts of it in his own head. He's struggling to keep track of all the versions. He feels as if he's creating a choose-your-own-adventure book that contains numerous plot holes, but only one outcome.

Despite all the glass outside, there's no window in the interview room. Rows of fluorescent ceiling lighting strive to make up for the lack of natural light.

Two officers, both wearing smart casual clothes and police lanyards, follow Matt and his solicitor into the room, and Matt's heart trips over a beat or two as he recognises one of the officers: DS Sophie Holland.

'Mr Walsh, Patrick,' she says, gesturing for the two of them to take their seats next to each other on one side of the table.

DS Holland's use of the solicitor's first name throws Matt, but he quickly recovers. Oliver is here to represent him. He and the DS are bound to know each other; they've certainly worked on the same cases, from different sides, in the past.

Matt sits down next to his solicitor on chairs that look quite attractive – polished wooden seats and backs – but that are really uncomfortable. The two officers take their seats opposite them. Matt stretches out his legs and accidentally kicks DS Holland under the table. He tries to inch his chair back a bit, but it won't move. It must be fastened to the floor. Is this room designed to be daunting? If so, it's working. Matt is suitably intimidated. Or is it supposed to be welcoming, coax the prisoner into confessing? If that's the case, the effort is lost on Matt. The last thing he feels like doing is talking.

'This interview will be recorded on video,' DS Holland begins.

Matt looks around for the camera and spots it on the wall, angled down at him. DS Holland identifies herself. Her colleague, a male detective constable, says his name, clearly, for the recording. Matt is on high alert, attentive to every detail, and yet the detective constable's name seeps in through one ear and flies out of the other. Stress, no doubt. He squints to read the DC's name on his lanyard, but it's too small to make out, even from just across the table.

'Would you please state your full name and date of birth?' DS Holland says to Matt.

As he predicted, the interview kicks off with simple questions and the atmosphere is almost informal. He can feel the beads of sweat forming on his forehead and hear his heartbeat in his ears, but everyone else seems relaxed. DS Holland leads the interview while her colleague – Matt couldn't remember his name if his life depended on it – studiously takes notes and periodically grunts his encouragement. Holland manages to strike the right balance between professional and familiar. Clearly, this is not her first gymkhana. Matt takes his time before answering each question, careful not to offer any more information than the police already have.

Then there are questions about Leona. They're not trick questions; Holland says she wants to establish some background. She's probably asking about Leona to put him at ease, maybe even to get him to lower his guard. But these questions are hard. He has talked as little as possible about Leona for months, maybe even years, as if not verbalising his thoughts will help ease the pain. She's on his mind All. The. Time. And now he's mentioning her name, bringing her back to life by talking about her out loud and reliving memories of their life together, his grief threatens to overwhelm him.

After a while, Patrick Oliver requests a break. They agree to call it a day. Matt is to spend the night in his cell. Eight long hours. He estimates that he sleeps for about eight minutes before he wakes with a jolt in the early hours of the morning. In his dream, he was digging in the garden at Rose Cottage. At first, he assumed he was digging a grave for Leona, but it turned out he was digging a hole for himself. A metaphor, then. Or a warning.

He can't get back to sleep and spends the rest of the night agonising over what will happen to him. He doesn't want to go to prison. He wants to go home. What scares him the most, is what will become of Scarlett and Trixie. He feels like he's already lost Scarlett, and he has been losing Trixie for some time, too. The thought of not being part of his daughters' lives anymore torments him. He vomits in the toilet. He can't stop heaving, long after there's nothing left to throw up.

Chapter 22

June 2024

The interviews resume in the morning. Is it Matt's imagination or does DS Holland eyeball him as he sits down on the hard wooden chair? Her round brown eyes seem to bore into him as she reels off the names of the people present and the time for the recording. It's disconcerting, and again, Matt misses the DC's name. It shouldn't bother him, but it does. He doesn't like the feeling he's in the room with people who know – or, at least think they know – all his dirty secrets while he knows nothing about them, not even, in the case of the detective constable, his name.

'Mr Walsh,' she begins, 'I'd like to clarify a few points.'

Matt nods. Best to show willing.

DS Holland's voice hardens. He's not imagining it. She has dropped the nice act. 'There seem to be certain … inconsistencies in your account,' she says.

It's stuffy in this tiny room. Matt pulls at the clothing around his neck, gasping for air. It's as if he can feel the noose tightening.

'Firstly …' She opens a folder, licks a finger and flicks through some pages. Matt's sure she knows exactly where she's going and this is just for show. 'Firstly, your internet search history. You visited' – she consults her file again – 'four different websites altogether to look into the rate of body decomposition in soil.'

'Yes. You see, I'm a plotter, not a pantser.' Seeing DS Holland's eyes narrow at him, he clarifies, 'I need to plan out my novels in detail and do extensive research before I start writing. I can't just wing it as I go along.' Matt's aware he's offering up information that the DS hasn't actually asked him for. It's nerves. He needs to give concise answers. Otherwise, he'll tie himself in knots.

'I see,' DS Holland says, although her tone suggests she doesn't. 'So, you're saying you looked up body decomposition in soil as research for one of your books?'

'It was a long time ago, but that's the most likely explanation I can come up with,' says Matt. That was better. A wishy-washy, sit-on-the-fence answer.

'OK. But here's our problem.' She glances towards the DC, who nods. 'The "research" was done the day *after* you reported your wife missing.'

'As though you had a body on your hands and needed to get rid of it,' the DC adds.

Matt shrugs. He remembers giving a different account to Gabi, telling her someone was stitching him up. He's getting confused. 'In that case, I don't know. Writing was the last thing on my mind when Leona went missing. I've barely written a word since she disappeared. I didn't do any work at all in the weeks – maybe even in the months – following Leona's disappearance. Someone else must have looked it up on the internet from my computer.'

'But you told us no one else goes into your office.'

'No one else is supposed to go in there, that's true. But I don't keep my study door locked. And, rather stupidly, I keep my password on a piece of paper Sellotaped next to the trackpad of my computer, so anyone could have used it. And it's a laptop. It may not have been in my study when it was used. It might have been somewhere else in the house.'

He has dug himself out of that little hole nicely – he winces at the choice of words in his head – but he mustn't get complacent. He can tell from DS Holland's expression she doesn't believe a word of what he has just said.

'While we're on the subject of soil, Mr Walsh,' the DC puts in, 'how do you explain that the soil on your Wellington boots in the garage of your house was a match for the soil in the garden of Rose Cottage, the house where your mother lived at the time of your wife's disappearance?'

Matt shrugs. 'I did the gardening there sometimes,' he lies.

DS Holland turns to another page in her file. She takes her time, a tactic, no doubt, meant to destabilise him. Matt tries not to let it get to him, but he's consumed with nerves.

'The next point is about the dog's lead and harness,' DS Holland says at length.

Matt knows what's coming. He can justify this, too.

'Your wife often ran with the lead around her waist attached to the dog's harness. Is that correct?'

'Yes, although as I've said before, if she took the car to Wistlandpound Reservoir, she didn't necessarily need the lead and the harness. Sydney's a very obedient dog. He stays by her side when she jogs.'

'Right. Now, you said the dog came home by itself. Was it wearing the harness and lead when it showed up at Blackmoor Manor?'

'No. Leona took the car that evening. She didn't take the harness and lead.'

'Which would explain how they were found by Constable Owen Wright in your house, hanging on the coat pegs.'

It's not a question, so Matt stays mute.

'But here's the thing,' DS Holland pauses. For effect, probably. 'We have two witnesses – two dog walkers – whose statements contradict that version of events. They both clearly remember …'

Matt feels faint. For a few seconds, the noise of blood rushing through his ears drowns out DS Holland's voice. He reaches for his glass of water and takes a sip. Then he takes a deep breath. But the knot in his stomach tightens. Please, no. He can't throw up in here, in front of DS Holland, Patrick Oliver and DC Whatshisname. He needs to hold it together.

'So which is it, Mr Walsh?' DS Holland is saying. 'Did your wife take the harness and lead or did she leave them at home?'

'She left—'

'My client has already answered your question,' Patrick Oliver interjects.

'Can you see the discrepancy, Mr Walsh?' the DC says. 'How do you explain that?'

Matt shrugs again, a gesture that hopefully conveys that he doesn't think it's up to him to find an explanation. 'It was dark. The dog walkers were elderly. They must have been mistaken.'

'Uh-huh.' DS Holland clearly isn't buying that. 'Finally, there's the blood,' she continues. Matt stiffens. 'As you know, Mr Walsh, traces of your wife's blood were found in the kitchen, notably on the floor. You said …' She flicks through the pages in her folder. Matt recognises the prompt. She wants him to finish her sentence. He waits. 'You said your wife cut herself while cooking,' DS Holland says eventually.

'Yes, I remember her cutting her hand when she was chopping an onion, a few days before … some time before she disappeared.' They haven't told him how much blood. Would Leona cutting herself account for it?

'But your sister-in-law, Roxanne Barrett, told us Leona never cooked.'

'She also said Leona did all the gardening, including at your mother's house,' the DC adds.

'There were only *traces* of blood,' Patrick Oliver says, apparently thinking along the same lines as Matt. 'And accidents do happen in the kitchen.'

'Leona *rarely* cooked, that's true,' Matt says. 'I did most of the cooking. Perhaps that's why she cut herself – lack of practice. And I rarely do the gardening, but I have helped Leona out on occasion, both at Blackmoor Manor and at Rose Cottage.'

Matt's confident he has explained away the discrepancies, but he feels far from smug. Oliver is right. They do have some fairly compelling evidence against him. Some of it is flimsy, but the prosecution can spin a convincing story with it even so. And the fact Leona's body was buried in his mother's garden doesn't look good. It doesn't look good at all.

At his solicitor's request, they take another break. A guard brings Matt lunch in his cell. It's revolting, but he forces himself to eat it and then struggles to keep it down.

The interrogation resumes in the afternoon. This time Matt catches the name of Holland's subordinate. Detective Constable Hawkins. The police have found out the cause of death and DS Holland and her underling fire questions at him like bullets. He answers 'no comment' more and more. There's one question that DS Holland repeatedly bombards him with, albeit with slight variants on the same theme: *Did you kill your wife, Mr Walsh? Why did you kill your wife, Mr Walsh? Where did you kill your wife, Mr Walsh?* He stonewalls these questions each time with a categorical silence.

Matt feels exhausted and sick. He understands how suspects might crack. It's tempting to confess, even if you didn't do it, just so it will stop. He thinks about changing his story. He even contemplates telling the whole truth. But he has been over this in his mind. He has weighed up the pros and cons, again and again, and each time he resolves to stick to his guns. What happened is not all his fault and he's not about to confess to a crime he didn't commit. But he can't shut out a little voice in his head, that sounds uncannily like Leona's, telling him he should confess to the crime he did commit.

Matt gets regular breaks – Patrick Oliver sees to that – but each time he finds himself alone in his cell, he panics. Full-on panic attacks where he can't catch his breath and feels as if the floor is pitching and the walls are closing in around him.

They can't hold him here forever, but when he gets out of this cell, he'll be taken to another one – no doubt about that. No doubt in his mind, either, that once DS Holland and her crony have finished here, the CPS won't hesitate in their decision. The evidence against him is compelling. He will be charged with murder.

It takes DS Holland and DC Hawkins three and a half days to break him. Matt has nothing left in the tank and is on the point of breaking down and crying in front of the police officers and his solicitor. He hasn't slept. He has barely eaten. It feels like his head is clamped in a vice, its jaws tightening. He can't take any more.

'Shall I tell you what I think?' DS Holland leans forwards and places her hands on the table, her fingers interlaced.

She must like that phrase. She used it on him before, a long time ago, when she more or less accused him of planting the shoe. He can remember that conversation almost word for word.

'I think you had a row with your wife—'

'We have a statement from your younger daughter to that effect,' DC Hawkins chips in.

'Leave Trixie out of this,' Matt growls.

'The row got out of hand,' DS Holland continues. 'In a fit of rage, you grabbed the knife and stabbed her. Then, instead of phoning for an ambulance, you watched her bleed to death.'

'That's not what happened,' Matt says. 'That's not how it happened.' His voice is almost inaudible; he barely hears it himself. For several seconds, no one says anything. Did he speak or was he only thinking?

'Mr Walsh, are you ready to tell us the truth now?' DS Holland's voice is soft, cajoling, her eyes sympathetic once more.

Before Matt can answer, Patrick Oliver jumps in. 'I'd like a moment with my client,' he says, placing a restraining hand on Matt's arm, a warning not to say any more.

'Of course.' DS Holland smiles sweetly, first at Oliver, then at Matt. 'Interview suspended at …'

Oliver gets to his feet and Matt follows his lead. He's desperate for this to be over, but he knows this is only the beginning. And it won't end well.

Missing, Presumed Murdered
A True Crime Podcast Hosted by Gabriela Conti
Audio File 7
Interview with Mr Edward Draper and Mrs Margaret Draper, retired, dog owners.
2024

This is the story of Leona Walsh, whose disappearance in December 2019 has remained a mystery for nearly five years. Join me as I explore the truths and lies in this case. I am Gabriela Conti and you're listening to **Missing, Presumed Murdered**, *a true crime podcast.*

Mrs Margaret Draper: Don't mind Bentley. His bark is worse than his bite.

Gabriela Conti: Oh, that's fine, Mrs Draper. I'm not scared of dogs. I expect … Bentley, is it? I expect he can smell the dog I'm looking after on me.

Mr Edward Draper: Shall I shut him in the kitchen? He's going to be barking on your recording, isn't he?

GC: You're right, Mr Draper. Would you mind?

ED: Not at all.

GC: OK. Let's start, shall we? Here we go. Thank you both for giving this interview. You were both out, walking Bentley on the evening of Saturday, 30th November 2019. Is that right?

ED: Yes, that's right. We've been over this with the police. Several times.

GC: I know you have, Mr Draper, and I'm sorry to ask you again, but this time it's for the readers of the North Devon Echo.

MD: We read the Echo, *don't we, Edward?*

ED: Of course, of course. Yes, we do.

GC: I wonder if you would mind telling me why you were at the reservoir at that time of day? I mean, I know you live nearby, but it was cold and dark. Do you usually walk Bentley in those conditions? He's a Yorkshire terrier, isn't he? They don't need a lot of exercise, do they?

ED: *Yes, he's a yorkie. They don't need as much exercise as big dogs. We used to have German shepherd dogs when we were younger, didn't we, Margaret?*

MD: *Yes, we did. Now they do require a lot of exercise.*

ED: *We're amateur astronomers.*

GC: *Sorry?*

ED: *You asked why we were out at that time of evening. We like stargazing. The sky was very clear that night.*

MD: *Oh, yes, it was. For days after that, you couldn't see a star in the sky because it was so overcast – but that night it was really clear. We saw the twins.*

GC: *The twins?*

ED: *Castor and Pollux. The constellation of Gemini.*

MD: *And Jupiter was very visible. And Aries, Perseus—*

GC: *I see. Did you drive to the reservoir or did you walk there?*

ED: *We walked.*

MD: *We live literally just around the corner.*

GC: *And at what time did you see Leona Walsh?*

ED: *It must have been at sixish. A quarter past, maybe? No later than that. She was running along the outer trail. She was just starting her run and we were on our way back home. She was with her dog, an Australian shepherd.*

GC: *Was the dog loose or was he on a lead?*

ED: *It was on a lead. Mrs Walsh had the lead around her midriff and it was clipped on to the dog's harness.*

MD: *We saw Mrs Walsh quite often during the winter, nearly every time we went out to look at the stars. Didn't we, Edward?*

GC: *And can you be absolutely sure you're not confusing that particular night with a different one? Could the dog have been loose that night, but on the lead a different night?*

ED: *No. We're getting on, Miss Conti, but we're not senile.*

GC: *I beg your pardon, Mr Draper. I didn't mean to imply—*
MD: *There's something strange, but we only realised afterwards. Edward didn't think it was important because we couldn't be sure, but … I don't know.*
GC: *What is it, Mrs Draper?*
ED: *It's not important, Margaret.*
MD: *The thing is, we walked past the two car parks on our way home and we didn't see any cars. Afterwards, we saw on the news about her car – I can't remember the make, but it was blue, apparently. They said it had been found parked at the reservoir.*
GC: *You're right. That is strange.*
ED: *As my wife said, we can't be sure. Mrs Walsh may have parked her car at the far end of one of the car parks. We might not have seen it in the dark.*
GC: *It's unlikely, though, isn't it? You'd think she'd park at the end nearest the trails. Were there any other vehicles in the car park?*
MD: *No. Not that we saw. I remember saying to Edward, as we walked past the car parks, that apart from Mrs Walsh, there was no one at the reservoir. Not a soul. Hardly surprising, really. It was cold and dark and late. Edward, perhaps we should tell the police.*
ED: *Margaret, we've been through this. It's not important.*

Chapter 23

July 2024

Gabi is desperate to find a way of going to see Matt. He has been put on remand and is being held in HMP Exeter, where he's awaiting trial. Exeter is only an hour and a quarter's drive from Barnstaple. But Gabi knows from experience that applying to visit a prisoner as a journalist is a tricky and lengthy process. Plus, visits by the media are only allowed in exceptional circumstances, such as when the prisoner claims there has been a miscarriage of justice.

The only way she can see him is if he adds her to his visitor list and she visits him as a friend, socially rather than professionally. This process, too, is likely to take a while. A few weeks at the very least. She doesn't know if she'd be using up visiting time he could spend with his family. Do Scarlett and Trixie visit him in prison? She hopes so. But if they do, maybe Matt won't want to see her.

She signs up to Email a Prisoner and types an email to Matt on her computer. It costs forty-two pence. She keeps her message short and sweet. She asks how he's holding up and if there's anything she can do. She asks if he has any spare visiting hours for her to come and see him. She tells him she's looking after the dog. She refrains from asking what she really wants to know: what was Scarlett implying? She'll wait until she can do that in person. Prison staff probably check all incoming and outgoing emails and she wants hers to be printed out and handed to Matt, not deleted.

Over the next few days, she checks her emails regularly. Matt hasn't replied. Then one day, she thinks to check her spam. She has received an email from Matt and another one from the prison itself. She opens them one after the other, reads them and smiles. Matt has made a request for a secure video call. It's scheduled for the day after tomorrow. She rereads the information in the second email more thoroughly. The app works on a tablet or smartphone, it says; not on a computer. She grabs her mobile, creates an account and downloads the app. It can take up to twenty-four hours for her account to be verified, but hopefully, she'll be up and running in time. She still hopes to be able to visit him at some point, to talk to him face to face, but this is the next best thing.

Gabi has opened the app and is ready at least a quarter of an hour before the video call is due to start. She's no technophobe – in her line of work, you have to get your head round technology, but she's nervous the internet signal won't be strong enough or the app will turn out to be incompatible with her phone. But right on time, she hears the audio notification that signals the call is connecting, then Matt's pixelated face appears and slowly comes into focus.

Stubble encroaches on his cheeks and chin; his eyes are red and sunken, the rings underneath so dark, it looks as if he has cried after applying a heavy coat of black mascara and eyeliner.

Gabi keeps the niceties to a minimum. They only have half an hour. As soon as she feels it's polite to do so, she asks what has been on her mind for the past few weeks.

'Matt, I went to see Scarlett not long ago,' she begins.

'How is she?'

Gabi already knows from Matt's email the other day that the girls haven't been to the prison for a visit. Not yet anyway. How can she answer Matt's question? Scarlett is scarred by her mother's disappearance, defined by it. She has been bullied and ostracised because of it. Her career goals have been demolished by it. She's trapped in a nightmare that's still ongoing; her ordeal isn't even close to an end. She needs to know the truth.

'She's a remarkably resilient young lady,' Gabi says, because she can't say any of the thoughts that have just streaked through her mind. 'She's er … um … doing as well as can be expected.' *Which is not well.* Matt nods. He has grasped the subtext. 'Listen, Matt, Scarlett said something I'd like to ask you about.'

'OK. Go ahead.'

'I asked her if you were ever violent towards Leona. I'm sorry, it just sort of cropped up in our conversation. Scarlett said you had a quick temper, but you were never violent. Then she said, and I quote' – Gabi picks up her notebook and consults it, but it's really just a habit. She knows Scarlett's words by heart; she has replayed them over and over in her head – 'she said, "If anything, it was the other way round."' Gabi looks up, back into the screen of her phone, to gauge Matt's reaction, but his expression is impassive. 'She wouldn't elaborate,' Gabi continues. 'And I didn't want to press her. I thought maybe you could tell me what she meant by that?'

Matt doesn't answer. One side of his mouth twitches and he lowers his eyes. He looks hurt. Has she overstepped the mark? She's being super nosy, prying into a personal matter that probably has nothing to do with what happened to Leona. It has nothing do with Gabi; it's really none of her business. She expects him to end the video call. She's about to apologise before he goes, ask if it's OK if she continues to write to him. But then he focuses his gaze on her again and she hears him take a deep breath. She's aware she's holding hers.

'The first time it happened, it was during the night,' Matt begins. 'I was fast asleep. I assumed Leona was, too, and put it down to an involuntary movement during a bad dream. I thought maybe she was being attacked in her nightmare and she was defending herself, you know? I joked about it the next day. Leona had given me a black eye. She seemed mortified and made me put ice on the bruise.

'Then one day, I was helping her with the gardening. I'm not at all green-fingered. The garden was very much her domain, like the kitchen was mine. Anyway, I deadheaded a rose that looked past it to me but Leona said it was in perfect bloom. And she slapped me. She was really apologetic afterwards and swore it wouldn't happen again. But a few weeks after that, we had a row about money – she said I wasn't earning my keep; I said she was spending way too much. Always a bone of contention between us. So, she picked up a cookery book and walloped me over the back of the head with it as I was sitting at the kitchen table. It was only then I wondered if that nocturnal incident might have been deliberate.'

Gabi stares at Matt. Is he telling the truth? After his initial hesitation, it has all tumbled out fluidly, as if he has recited lines learnt by heart. He has recounted his story in a detached way, as if it happened to someone else. But he hasn't broken eye contact. And she can't see why he would lie about something like this. Plus, the Leona she once knew had a mean streak. Her bullying verged on violence at times, like the time she bashed Gabi in the legs with the hockey stick. Matt's account is certainly plausible.

'I've never told *anyone* that before,' Matt says. 'It's my shameful secret.'

Gabi gets it. Years ago, one of her co-workers wrote a feature on two men, both victims of domestic abuse. They'd insisted on anonymity. They'd talked about shame, too, as well as social stigma, stereotypes, low self-esteem. Gabi needs to tread carefully. This must be traumatic and painful for Matt, especially if he's never opened up about it before.

'But there is support available for male victims, Matt. You could have got help.'

Matt did consider getting help, a long time ago, but ruled it out. He shakes his head. 'It's not easy, when you're a woman, to admit you're the victim of domestic abuse,' he says. 'Imagine what it's like when you're a man. Men are supposed to be able to stand up for themselves. It's even more complicated once there are kids involved. No, Gabi, my only option was to keep quiet. My main fear wasn't for myself in any case.'

He hears her intake of breath. 'You mean Scarlett and Trixie? Did she—'

'No! She never laid a finger on the kids. That's not what I meant. I was worried that one day – with my short fuse – I might … hit Leona back.'

There's more to this, but Matt can't tell Gabi anything else. He has already said way too much. He studies Gabi, through the screen, but he can't read her. She must have expected this when she asked him what Scarlett meant and she doesn't look shocked. Her expression isn't one of disbelief, either. Does she believe him? He hopes so. She's pretty much his only friend now, apart from Adam, whose friendship with Matt is curtailed by his marriage to Roxanne.

Perhaps Gabi is right. Maybe he should have sought help and spoken out. He's not convinced it would have helped him then, but it might have helped him now. If he'd told someone this story – his GP, for example – or taken a photograph of his body with bruising, his lawyer could have built a case around self-defence. Or manslaughter.

'Is that what happened, Matt? Is that what happened that night?' He can hear Gabi's voice, but the words don't make sense and fail to infiltrate his thoughts.

Could he say he was defending himself? Would it work? Is it

too late to go down that road? He bats away the idea. If his lawyer argued self-defence, Matt would have to admit to concealing the body. He would still be looking at a prison sentence for preventing a lawful and decent burial. Besides, everyone would want to know why he didn't bring up any of this before. A sentence from the police caution plays in his mind: *It may harm your defence if you do not mention when questioned something you later rely on in court.*

No, his mind has run amok. He couldn't possibly say his wife used to abuse him and one day he retaliated and killed her – accidentally – and he buried her in a place she loved. Scarlett is struggling to keep afloat. This would push her under. And he would lose Trixie for good. Besides, Matt's a firm believer that it pays to be economical with the truth, but, as everyone knows, the most convincing lies are those that stick the closest to the truth, and there are two or three lies in there somewhere – maybe more – that stray too far.

Gabi looks at him pointedly. Either Matt hasn't taken in what she has just said or he's chosen to ignore her question. 'Is that what happened, Matt?' she repeats. 'You had an argument just before Leona went missing. Did—'

'The argument we had that night had nothing to do with Leona's disappearance,' he says. He must hear the vehemence in his own voice because he dials it down a notch and adds, 'Or her death.'

'OK.' She's pushing this too hard, just like she did with Scarlett. How can she calm him down, regain his trust?

'And the same goes for everything I said just now about Leona … sometimes … hitting me. It has nothing to do with what happened to her. What I told you, I told you in confidence. I don't want you to write anything about it in one of your articles.'

'You have my word. This stays between you and me.'

That seems to mollify him. A bit. Gabi has one more question on the tip of her tongue. She wants to ask Matt what really happened to Leona. Will he change his story now the remains have been identified? She examines Matt. He looks exhausted. Crushed. Frightened. Maybe now isn't the time. She already feels she has gone too far. As if to reinforce that impression, a notification pops up on the screen to indicate they only have two minutes left. She'll have to wait until next time to ask that one.

She tries to lighten the tone. She promises to email him and send letters, and says she hopes to visit him in person soon.

'Gabi, I wonder if I could ask you a huge favour,' Matt says.

'Yes. I'm happy to help if there's anything I can do.'

'Would you mind popping in to see my mum? She must be lonely. I'm worried about her.'

Gabi has already tried to get into the home to see Matt's mum – she wanted to interview her for the podcast – but she was refused access. She can't tell Matt this, though. 'I don't know if they'll let me in,' she says. 'It's not like I'm family, and your mum doesn't even know me.'

'No, but you're a friend of mine. I've already emailed the care home to let them know you're coming. I hope you don't mind.'

'Not at all. If they have no objection to me visiting, I'll go. Perhaps I can take the girls with me.'

Gabi watches as relief washes over Matt's haggard face. She hoists Sydney onto her lap and waves at Matt with a paw. She feels silly, but it elicits a smile from Matt. Then their time is up.

The screen of her phone goes blank for a second or two, then her mobile rings. The caller ID shows it's Professor Harvey. Surprised, Gabi swipes to take the call.

'Hello, Professor Harvey,' she says. 'I can't thank you enough for your tip-off—'

'I've been following your articles, Ms Conti,' he cuts in. 'Great work.'

Bloody hell. Was that a compliment? 'Thank you.'

'I have another one for you,' he says.

'Sorry, another what?'

'Another "tip-off". If you're interested.'

A heady mixture of anticipation and curiosity hits her like an occasional drag on a cigarette. 'Of course.'

'But you didn't hear it from me.'

'Of course not.' Gabi squeezes her phone between her ear and her shoulder and grabs her pen and notebook.

'I've spoken to my contact again.' He pauses.

Gabi gets the impression he's deliberately stringing this out, enjoying the suspense he's creating. She wants to snap at him, tell him to spit it out, but she bites her tongue. She needs to keep him sweet. 'Yes? Go on,' she says. 'Please.'

'The post-mortem examination is complete and I thought you might like to know that the cause of death has been established.'

Gabi drops her pen, but doesn't pick it up. She presses the phone hard against her ear, hanging on to his every word. And as he tells her how Leona died, a piece of the puzzle slots into place.

Chapter 24

July 2024

Professor Harvey ends the phone call, without so much as a goodbye, like last time he rang. Gabi stares at her mobile, gobsmacked. Not at the professor's rudeness, but at what he has just revealed. She should have recorded the call with Harvey on a voice memo. Then again, he wouldn't have agreed to it. He made it clear she didn't hear this from him. And she would never have recorded the conversation without his knowledge, not even for her own use. No matter. Some of the medical terms might escape her and possibly some of the measurements, too, but she recalls most of what the academic said verbatim. She bends down to pick up her pen from the floor and scribbles everything she can remember in her notebook. Then she rings Joe. She has to tell someone about this. It's huge.

'Hi, gorgeous,' he whispers. 'I can't really talk right now. Can I call you back?'

'Where are you?' she asks. 'Can you come round?' She paces up and down the living area. The dog follows her and almost trips her up.

'I wish! You might be working from home today, but I'm at a primary school near Okehampton that offers free music tuition to its pupils. It's going to be quite a story.' He mimics Mick as he adds, 'Hold the front page!'

It's a great impersonation – Joe sounds just like Mick, but Gabi's sense of humour has gone AWOL and she doesn't laugh. She stops pacing and plops onto the sofa. Sydney puts his head on her knees and stares up at her through doleful eyes – one blue and one brown.

'What's up?' Joe asks. 'How did your video call with Matthew Walsh go?'

'Fine. It's the phone call I got from Professor Harvey afterwards that's troubling me.'

'Ah. I can come round later, after work, if you like? Shall I bring pizza?'

Gabi has not done the shopping. She'd intended to make something healthy, but now cooking is the last thing on her mind. 'I'd prefer curry,' she says.

'Indian takeaway it is. See you later.'

Sydney puts his two front paws on Gabi's lap and licks her face. She pushes him down and he whines. Trixie has sent Gabi several emails, detailing Sydney's routine: what he eats, what he needs and lots of other info. With each message, Gabi has bought more canine supplies – dog food and treats from the pet shop; a lead, dog poo bags and chew toys from Tesco's; she has even bought Sydney a rather expensive dog bed from Amazon, although that turned out to be a complete waste of money. Sydney sleeps on the sofa. Gabi has tried to forbid it and make him sleep on the floor and she's sure the dog has understood, but he's not having it. Even though she has bought him chew toys, Sydney has ripped open two of her cushions. Apparently, Sydney requires intellectual stimulation – otherwise he gets bored and naughty – but Gabi's not sure how to go about catering to that particular need. She'll have to ask Trixie for suggestions.

Sydney jumps onto the sofa now and pushes his head under Gabi's arm. He is to have one long walk or two shorter walks every day, whatever the weather.

'You want to go for walkies, don't you?' Gabi says. Apart from taking out Sydney early this morning for a 'potty walk', as Trixie calls it, she hasn't walked the dog yet today. A walk will do them both good.

Sydney wags his bobtail. Trixie has explained the dog's short tail is genetic. She didn't want Gabi to think it had been docked. Gabi puts on some trainers and a denim jacket, and stuffs some dog poo bags into the pocket of her jeans as Sydney bounds around her. Then she fetches the lead and fixes it to Sydney's collar.

They walk towards the River Taw, then along the riverbank, crossing at Long Bridge and on to Rock Park, where Gabi lets Sydney off the lead. Sydney finds a stick and drops it at Gabi's feet. She throws it for him. The sun comes out and she takes off her jacket and ties it around her waist.

Gabi takes some photos of Sydney, who is surprisingly photogenic, and emails them to Trixie. She hopes the twelve-year-old won't find them upsetting – she must miss her dog. Gabi just wants to reassure her that Sydney is being well looked after.

After they've played fetch for a while, Gabi clips the lead back onto the dog's collar and they head back. She feels as if she has wasted her time. Sydney seems to have far too much energy left and the fresh air hasn't cleared Gabi's head, either. She can't stop thinking about her short phone conversation with Professor Harvey. Is she jumping to conclusions? She's starting to doubt herself and can't wait to see if Joe comes up with the same explanation as she has.

When she gets home, she wipes the dog's paws, makes herself a coffee and sits at the little table in the corner of the living area that serves as her desk. She boots up her laptop and types a short article. She mentions the cause of death, careful to use phrases such as 'is thought to' and the adverb 'reportedly'. It feels like poor journalism, but she can neither name her source nor risk publishing defamatory information. Mick would not be pleased. She sticks to the facts as Professor Harvey presented them, although she doesn't go into as much detail. Above all, she refrains from any analysis. She can share her thoughts with Joe, but she can't print them. She adds her byline and emails the copy to Mick.

The doorbell goes just as she's sending the email. The noise makes the dog bark, which in turn makes Gabi jump. There's a tantalising smell emanating from the bags Joe carries into the tiny hallway of her house. Gabi realises she hasn't eaten much since breakfast. She's starving.

While Joe loads two plates with Indian food in the kitchen, Gabi opens the fridge and takes out a bottle of white wine. She rummages through the drawers, hunting for the corkscrew. Her tummy rumbles and her mouth waters at the smell of aloo gobi and pilau rice. She serves them a large glass of Chardonnay each to wash it all down and sits on the bar stool.

'Out with it,' Joe says, setting down the meals and cutlery and taking his seat next to her. 'What did Professor Harvey say?'

'He rang with the cause of death,' Gabi says, her mouth full.

'For Leona Walsh?' Joe turns and stares at her, his fork pausing mid-air.

'Yes. She died of a single stab wound to the abdomen.' Gabi lets that sink in.

'The same way Matthew Walsh's colleague – what was her name? Sandra? – died? His wife died the same way as his partner?' Joe sounds incredulous.

'No! That's just it. Matt *said* Sandra Greene had died of a single stab wound to the stomach. She was actually stabbed – once – in the neck.'

Gabi observes Joe. He looks pensive. He shovels a forkful of food into his mouth and seems to mull over what she has just told him while he chews.

'That's weird,' he remarks at length.

Gabi tries not to feel frustrated. She has been ruminating on this all afternoon and Joe is a bit slow to put two and two together.

'So, according to Gareth Harvey, Leona was stabbed with a sharp, single-bladed knife, most likely a kitchen knife,' Gabi continues. 'She would have bled out. He said the rate of exsanguination – his words – from sharp force trauma depends on the injury. If the knife penetrates an organ, this can accelerate death.'

'And did it penetrate an organ?'

'Hang on.' Gabi slides off the stool and fetches her notebook from the coffee table. She flicks through to the last page, on which she made notes after Professor Harvey's phone call. 'The wound was approximately ten centimetres deep. The knife penetrated the fifth intercostal space – I'm pretty sure that's what he said – and, in all likelihood, the left diaphragm and liver.' Gabi looks up. Joe has put down his fork and is focusing all his attention on what she's saying.

'How on earth can they determine that nearly five years after her death?' he says, shaking his head in wonder. 'It's incredible.'

'Probable extrusion of the intestines,' Gabi continues, wrinkling her nose. Maybe Joe has stopped eating, not because he's listening to her, but because he has lost his appetite. She should have waited until after dinner to tell him this. 'The professor said, judging from the depth and angle of the wound, the knife didn't puncture the aorta, which would have resulted in almost immediate death, a few minutes at most. But he was unable to say how long it would have taken her to die from the wounds she did sustain. Several minutes, maybe up to an hour, was his best guesstimate. He felt sure that she would have had a chance of survival if she'd been given urgent medical assistance.'

'Walsh didn't call for an ambulance.'

Gabi sighs. Joe's still missing the point.

'He watched her bleed out and die.'

'Professor Harvey said it was a very bizarre way to kill someone,'

Gabi says. 'A single stab wound to the abdomen that she could have survived.'

'Probably not premeditated, then?'

'That's what I thought,' Gabi says. She's convinced something about this doesn't add up, but she doesn't have the expertise to work out what. Maybe Matt and Leona did have an argument that got out of hand after all.

'OK, so let's get this straight,' Joe says, evidently thinking out loud. 'Matthew Walsh claimed his partner – Sandra Greene – died of a single stab wound to the abdomen. In fact, this is how his *wife* died, not his partner.'

'That's right,' Gabi says. Now he's getting there. 'Matt told me he got the feeling the two incidents were connected – his colleague's assault and Leona's disappearance, but he thought the connection might just be in his head, possibly because they were the two most traumatic events he'd ever experienced.'

'So, what are you thinking?' Joe asks. 'That it was a slip of the tongue? Did he confuse the two incidents? He said Sandra was stabbed in the stomach even though he knew it was in the neck because he was thinking of his wife? He knew full well that his wife was stabbed in the abdomen because he's the one who killed her. Is that it?'

'That's exactly what I'm thinking,' Gabi says, relieved Joe is thinking along the same lines as she is. It's as if it confirms her suspicions about Matt, validates her conclusions. 'The reason Matt associated Leona's disappearance with the knife attack on his colleague is that both women died in a similar way – from a single stab wound. Matt probably watched them both bleed to death.'

'Christ! No wonder the two incidents are linked in his mind.'

For a moment, neither of them speaks. Then Joe gets up and reheats the food in the microwave, first Gabi's plate, then his own. He also tops up their glasses. Gabi's no longer hungry, but she polishes off her meal even so. Then she takes several gulps of Chardonnay.

All this time, Gabi has been clinging to the belief that Matt was telling the truth – mostly. She wanted him to be innocent. She gave him the benefit of the doubt. She befriended him to get the story, but now she feels angry, as if he has betrayed her trust. He has been lying to her all along, manipulating her into bigging him up in the media in an attempt to keep public opinion on his side.

But Matthew Walsh is clearly getting tangled up in his own web of lies. He has slipped up; he has given himself away.

Chapter 25

July 2024

Gabi imagined a foreboding place with black wrought-iron gates designed more to prevent its elderly occupants from wandering out than to keep potential intruders from breaking in. The care home, near Swimbridge, is nothing like that. From the outside, it looks like a large private residence with clean cream walls on the first storey façade and stone cladding on the ground floor. Gabi follows Trixie up the ramp and through the automatic doors.

A fair-haired receptionist in her forties is sitting at a high desk in the entrance hall. When she smiles, Gabi notices lipstick on her teeth. 'Good morning,' Gabi says and introduces herself.

The woman clearly recognises Trixie, greeting her by name as she jiggles the mouse to bring the computer to life. She scrolls through something on the monitor.

'Here you are,' the receptionist says triumphantly, angling the screen so Gabi can see it, too, and then tapping a long, manicured fingernail on Gabi's name. She fills in the date and time in a ledger then turns it the other way up and pushes it towards them. 'Can you both sign in here?' She points at the column where their signatures are required. Gabi can't help feeling ashamed of her own ragged nails as she takes the pen. To Gabi, the woman adds, 'And can I see some ID, please?'

Gabi hands over her driving licence. The receptionist glances at it and nods.

'Rose is in her bedroom,' she informs them.

They pass a spacious lounge with laminate flooring, red armchairs and several windows offering views over rolling green hills. The doors are open and Gabi peers inside at a group of residents sitting around a television that is turned up loud. It's at least two degrees too warm in here and there's a strange smell of overcooked vegetables mixed with polish, but other than that, the whole place gives off a comfy, welcoming vibe.

Gabi's phone sounds with a text notification just as they arrive at Rose's bedroom door. She rummages in her handbag for her mobile and gestures for Trixie to go on in. The text is from Roxanne to ask if Gabi can drop Trixie home after the visit. A spark of irritation rises in Gabi. Roxanne was supposed to pick up Trixie from the care home. Mullacott Cross isn't exactly on Gabi's way home – it's a massive detour – and, more importantly, she hadn't planned to go home after visiting Rose Walsh. Today is Matt's plea and trial preparation hearing at the Crown Court in Exeter. Gabi was going to race there, with Joe, and hopefully make it in time.

She hammers out a reply, but then deletes it instead of sending it. Taking Trixie back to Combe Cottage isn't asking a lot. It's the least Gabi can do. Those poor girls are about to go through hell. Again.

There's no need for Gabi to go to Exeter. It's not like she can take photos of a dishevelled, badly shaven Matt appearing – briefly – in court. He's obviously going to plead not guilty, but he's been proclaiming his innocence from the very start, so that will hardly be a scoop. She's covered enough murder trials to know there will be no bail application today – the judge won't decide on that for a day or two. Plus, she's absolutely livid with Matt for manipulating her and lying to her, and she wouldn't want him to think she's in court because she's being supportive.

She calls Joe and explains the situation.

'I'll go by myself,' he says.

'Are you sure? I mean, it would be different if this was the actual trial, but it won't matter if no one from the *Echo* is there for the plea and trial preparation hearing, surely?'

'No, I'll go. I'll call you as soon as it's over.'

'I'll make you dinner, if you like?'

'Perfect.' Gabi can hear the smile in Joe's voice, even in that single word, and she smiles, too. 'See you later.'

She fires off a quick text with a thumbs-up emoji to Roxanne, activates the silent mode on her phone and knocks on Rose's bedroom door.

The bedroom is small, but bright and nicely decorated. There's a single bed; a television on the wall; a table with a kettle, mugs and a vase of flowers on it; a little fridge in the corner of the room; a large window with a wide sill on which photos of Matt, Scarlett and Trixie are displayed; a door that is ajar through which Gabi glimpses an en-suite bathroom. Rose is sitting, slumped on an armchair next to the table.

'Hello, Mrs Walsh, I'm Gabi.'

'Hello, dear. It's … lovely to … meet you.' Her speech is slow and slurred, her voice frail. 'Matt has … told me … about you. Thank you … for com … ing to see me and for bring … ing my grand … daughter with you.' It takes several seconds for her to get out those few sentences.

'You're very welcome, Mrs Walsh,' Gabi says.

'Please, Gab … riel … ela, call me … Rose.'

'Nice to meet you, too, Rose. Call me Gabi.'

She sits down on the only chair at the table, setting her handbag on the floor beside her. The kettle roars and then clicks off. Trixie pours milk into two mugs. Gabi hopes one of them is for her.

She's parched. It's hot in this place. It's making her throat dry.

Trixie asks Gabi how she takes her tea and hands her a mug. She pushes the other one across the table, close to Rose. Gabi can see from here that Rose's tea is very milky and the mug is only half full. Trixie sits on the edge of the bed so that her knees are touching Rose's and she holds her hands over Rose's trembling hands to steady them as the elderly woman drinks. Then Trixie takes the mug and sets it back on the table. Trixie's relaxed around her grandmother.

Nearly five years ago, when they first met, Matt told Gabi about Trixie's difficulties. Gabi has always been careful not to touch Trixie, even though the girl sometimes looks as if she could do with a hug or a pat on the arm. But Trixie doesn't pull away when Rose strokes her hair or holds her hand. The two of them are clearly very close.

'I r-read all your art ... articles in the *North Devon Echo*, dear,' Rose says to Gabi, nodding towards the newspaper on the table.

Gabi follows Rose's nod. The newspaper is open at the page on which Gabi's latest article is published – about men as the overlooked victims of domestic abuse. The video call with Matt prompted Gabi to look into the issue and raise awareness. She wanted to show that men, as well as women, can find themselves on the receiving end of physical, emotional, verbal and even sexual abuse. She spoke to a volunteer at a hotline – a man who was once himself a victim and who now gives advice on how to get out of an abusive relationship. She also interviewed a woman who runs a shelter near Tiverton that accepts male survivors of domestic violence. Her piece has generated a lot of interest, judging from the numerous comments posted to their online edition, the *Echo Live*.

'This is a v-very int ... eresting article,' Rose says, tapping the page.

Gabi studies her. But if Rose knows that Matt was the victim of physical abuse at the hands of Leona, there's nothing in her face to show it. Matt did say that Gabi was the first person he'd ever told.

Trixie, who has barely said a word on the way here and who seems completely uninterested in Gabi's article, changes the subject. She tells her grandmother all about school, Sydney and living at Roxanne's. Gabi listens.

According to Matt, Rose's mind is still sharp, but from time to time she turns to Gabi and asks the same question: 'When is Matthew coming home?'

Gabi isn't sure how to answer that. Matt is Rose's only son, her only child. She's obviously very worried about him, but Gabi doesn't want to tell Rose a lie, not even a white lie. Matt could be home as early as the day after tomorrow if the Crown Court judge grants him bail. But equally, he could be remanded in custody until his trial and end up spending the rest of his life, or most of it – at the very least, the rest of Rose's life – behind bars.

The first two times Rose asks the question, Gabi replies honestly. She doesn't know when Matt will come home. But the third time, she's not sure if Rose has forgotten she has already asked the question or if the answer she was given wasn't good enough.

'That depends on whether he is granted bail,' Gabi says.

'Is that possible?' Trixie asks. 'Do you think they'll let Dad come home until his trial begins?'

Perhaps Trixie has overheard Roxanne and Adam discussing this. Or perhaps they explained the next steps to her. For several seconds, Gabi says nothing. She's acutely aware of two pairs of eyes boring into her and the hum of the fridge, which seems to crescendo. She wants to give an honest answer and she wants to avoid getting Trixie's and Rose's hopes up. How likely is it that Matt will get bail? Gabi has already considered this question.

A few months ago, there was a riot at HMP Wakefield, a category A prison in Yorkshire, notorious for housing the most dangerous and violent criminals in the country. The riot resulted in the deaths of two inmates and one prison guard, with another prison guard seriously injured. It also reopened the debate about prison overcrowding in the UK. At the moment, it seems to Gabi, defendants are released on bail where possible, even when they've been charged with murder, as long as they've had no previous conviction and as long as they're unlikely to commit another crime while on bail or abscond. This could work in Matt's favour.

But Gabi recently covered a story about a man from Bideford who killed his mother-in-law – and then himself – while on bail, awaiting trial for allegedly murdering his wife. The man was to be tried at Exeter Crown Court. The story hit the headlines locally and the incident was also reported in some national newspapers. This could work against Matt. There's no way of predicting his fate as far as bail is concerned. The judge could decide either way.

'I don't know, Trixie,' Gabi says.

'He didn't … do it, you … know,' Rose says sluggishly. Gabi has to lean towards her to make out her words. 'He didn't k-kill Le … ona.' Rose sounds so adamant, even with her hesitant speech.

'I know.' Gabi winces because now, with those two words, she has told a lie, and not just a white lie. She knows nothing of the sort. She no longer believes there's the slightest chance Matt's innocent.

She has thought long and hard about what Matt said, about his mistake. But what can she do about it? She can't print it. And she can't tell the police. His slip of the tongue doesn't prove anything. Except to Gabi. To her, it proves that he's guilty and that he's been lying to her all along.

Gabi's keen to talk to Rose. She's convinced Matt's mother knows more than she's letting on. She must do. Leona's body was buried in her garden. How can she not know something? Ideally, she'd like to interview Rose for the podcast, despite her hesitant, garbled speech. But Gabi will have to come back alone. There's no way she can probe into what Rose knows in front of Trixie. Gabi is on Rose's visitor list now. She'll arrange to pop in and see Rose again soon.

As she and Trixie exit the care home, Gabi suggests they stop off at her place to take Sydney for a walk together. Trixie jumps at the chance. It strikes Gabi as a little ironic that Scarlett is working today, walking other people's dogs. Trixie's not as chatty as she was with her grandmother, but she makes a huge fuss of the dog, and even smiles a little, and Gabi gets the impression the walk does her good.

She's sorely tempted to ask Trixie what she remembers about the night Leona was last seen, about the row she witnessed. Does she know something important? She was only seven at the time, but surely she remembers the last time she saw her mother. Maybe Trixie knows something that she hasn't revealed because it didn't seem relevant to her at the time. But Gabi doesn't want to spook Trixie.

Once they've turned round and are heading back to Gabi's house, however, curiosity gets the upper hand. Trixie's no longer a little girl. And Gabi can sound her out gently. 'Trixie, can I ask you something?' she says.

Trixie shrugs. 'Yeah.'

'I was wondering about the last time you saw your mum, when she and your dad were arguing.' They're walking side by side and Gabi sneaks looks at Trixie to judge her reaction. Trixie doesn't seem disturbed by the subject Gabi is tentatively bringing up. 'Do you remember anything about that evening? Do you remember what your parents were arguing about?'

'No. I remember them shouting at each other, but not what they were shouting about. I don't think I even knew at the time what the row was about. They were making a racket. I can't stand a lot of noise. When people shout, I tend to cover my ears. And Dad sent me upstairs, out of the way.'

'And is there anything about that evening that you didn't mention to the police, but that might be important?'

'I told the police everything,' Trixie says. 'I don't like to think about that night.'

'No, no. I can only imagine how hard it must be for you,' Gabi says. 'And you told the police the truth, did you?'

'Yes,' Trixie says. She doesn't sound defensive, which surprises Gabi. 'I'm not good at lying, so I pretty much always tell the truth,' Trixie continues. 'No one tells me secrets; I can't keep them. Everyone can see if I try to lie or hide something.'

Gabi doesn't know how to respond to that. Eventually, she hazards a question. 'And do you think your dad is telling the truth, Trixie?'

'People say my dad stretches the truth,' Trixie says, 'but I can never tell when he does that. I can't tell when people lie to me. Dad tries to be honest with Scarlett and me, that I do know.'

Gabi's aware she may be going too far, but this might be her only chance. 'And what did your dad tell you and Scarlett about that night?'

'He said he didn't kill my mum.'

Gabi turns to study her. Trixie isn't lying – Gabi's certain of that – but she doesn't sound convinced.

Gabi is driving Trixie home when her phone goes. She lets it ring out. She's looking for a new car, but still hasn't found one, and she has no hands-free system in this heap of junk. It's bound to be Joe. Gabi is itching to pull over and take the call, but she can't possibly discuss Matt with Trixie in the car.

She stops in a layby and calls Joe back once she has dropped Trixie at Combe Cottage.

'Gabi, you won't believe what just happened!' It sounds as if Joe can hardly contain his excitement.

Damn it! Has she missed out on something? 'Try me.'

'Matthew Walsh pleaded not guilty to murder and not guilty to wounding his wife, but he—'

'Well, there's no surprise there. That's what we—' Gabi talks over Joe. She stops as what he says registers. She must have misheard. 'What? Can you say that again?'

'He pleaded guilty to preventing the lawful and decent burial of Leona's body,' Joe repeats.

No, she heard correctly the first time, but it doesn't make any more sense the second time. 'Hang on … So, he's claiming he didn't hurt her and he didn't kill her, but he did get rid of her body. Is that it?'

'Yep. That about sums it up.'

'But … but …' Gabi can't get her head round it. 'Does that mean he's going for self-defence?'

'I assume so. That's what I figured when he entered his plea. Self-defence or manslaughter, maybe.'

Gabi can't think what to say. She doesn't know what to think. Thoughts are hurtling incoherently through her mind, colliding with each other. Something about this is way off kilter. Why didn't Matt say it was self-defence before? Unless she's the one who gave him that idea when he admitted Leona used to hit him. Or was that a lie, too? What the hell is Matt playing at?

Missing, Presumed Murdered
A True Crime Podcast Hosted by Gabriela Conti
Audio File 8
Interview with Rose Walsh, Matthew Walsh's mother.
2024

This is the story of Leona Walsh, whose disappearance in December 2019 has remained a mystery for nearly five years. Join me as I explore the truths and lies in this case. I am Gabriela Conti and you're listening to **Missing, Presumed Murdered**, *a true crime podcast.*

Gabriela Conti: Hello, Rose. Thank you for talking to me today. I was hoping we could start by talking about your daughter-in-law, Leona.

Rose Walsh: L-Leo ... na? Matthew loved her ... very much, but she c-could be ... difficult.

GC: In what way?

RW: Moody. Merc ... urial. She would f-fly into a rage with no ... warning.

GC: And did Matt – Matthew – argue a lot with her?

RW: They didn't ... argue much in f-front of me, although she sometimes ... shouted at him. I don't ... know what went on behind closed doors.

GC: And what about you? Did you get on well with Leona?

RW: Oh, yes, dear. She was like a ... d-daughter to me. Her own ... mum d-died shortly before she met Matthew. Between you and ... me, I don't think she had an easy time of it ... growing up.

GC: No, Matthew told me her parents divorced when she was little and she didn't see much of her father after that.

RW: No. He sent money for the s-school fees for Leona and her s-sister, but the girls d-didn't see him often. Leona d-didn't ... have the best ch-childhood. And I think she was a d-difficult ...

child, too. Demanding.

GC: *What was Matthew like as a child?*

RW: *Ah, he had a ... vivid im-imagination. He was my only ... child. My beloved husband, Henry, p-passed away when Matthew was ... young.*

GC: *Yes, he told me his father died of pancreatic cancer when he was eight. That must have been very difficult for you both.*

RW: *It was. Matthew often p-played alone. He was never inter ... ested in boys' toys like Lego or model planes. My f-fault, I expect. I had no inter ... est in that sort of thing myself. Matthew l-liked to help me c-cook and he liked b-board games ... Cluedo and Scrabble. He was g-good at jigsaw ... puzzles. He lived in a ... fantasy w-world a lot of the time and he wrote stories and po ... poems from a young age. He s-started to write shortly after his father died.*

GC: *It sounds like he was destined to become an author.*

RW: *Yes, I sup ... pose he was. An author or a p-policeman. I am a f-fan of Agatha Christie, and Matthew read all her n-novels, too. Did you know, dear, that ... Matthew was in the p-police for a f-few years before he became a writer?*

GC: *I did know that, Rose, yes. Matthew told me he left the police force because his partner, Sandra, was stabbed.*

RW: *Yes, nasty b-business. He's h-had a rough time of it al-altogether.*

GC: *You must be terribly worried about your son, Rose. Oh, I'm so sorry. I didn't mean to upset you. Would you like to stop? We could continue another time, if you like.*

RW: *I'm fine.*

GC: *Are you sure?*

RW: *Yes. I am very ... worried about Matthew. I'm worried about my g-grand ... daughters, too, partic ... ularly Trixie. She's still so young. They n-need their father.*

GC: *Yes, they do, Rose. Matthew's a very good father. You're very close to Trixie, aren't you?*

RW: *Yes. I like to think I'm c-close to both Trixie and Scarlett, but Trixie and I have always been as … thick as thieves. And Matthew l-lives for his ch-children. He would do any … thing for them.*

GC: *Are you sure you're all right, Rose? Would you like some water? Here, let me help you.*

…

RW: *Thank you.*

GC: *Rose, Matthew has been charged with some very serious crimes.*

RW: *He didn't … do it. He didn't … kill Leona.*

GC: *If he didn't kill her, Rose, who did?*

RW: *I don't know. But he said he d-didn't kill her and I b-believe him. If he says he d-didn't do it, then he didn't d-do it.*

GC: *Rose, Leona's body was buried in the garden of the house you used to live in and Matthew grew up in. If your son didn't kill Leona, how did her body end up in the grounds of Rose Cottage?*

RW: *He b-buried her there.*

GC: *Sorry? Who did? Who buried her there?*

RW: *Matthew.*

GC: *Are you saying Matthew buried Leona's body in your garden?*

RW: *Yes.*

GC: *Are you sure? How do you know that?*

RW: *Matthew has m-many … talents, but g-gardening is not … one of them. He was doing the … g-garden … ing, at n-night, in the w-winter.*

GC: *But you said Matthew didn't kill Leona.*

RW: *I said he didn't … kill her. I d-didn't say that he didn't … bury her. I-I'd like to stop now, dear. I'm tired.*

Chapter 26

Saturday, 30th November 2019

Matt wanted to bury her on the moors. Leona loved the moors. It was the main reason they'd bought the house. The remote location didn't scare her. On the contrary, she relished the peace and quiet. And she adored the view. Nearly every morning, she would pull back the curtains in their bedroom and stand for a minute or two drinking in the wild landscape while he propped his head on his elbow and appraised her from the bed, his sleepy eyes adjusting to the light. They would stroll together across the moors at the weekends, usually with one or both of the kids, but, lately, now that Scarlett was old enough to keep an eye on Trixie for an hour or two, or when Roxanne came round, they'd found themselves alone on a few occasions, just the two of them and the dog. Sometimes they would talk non-stop; at other times they'd walk in silence – that comfortable silence that comes from years of marriage. Sydney would bound in front of them, ecstatic about all the smells and eager to go out whatever the weather.

The weather was one of the reasons he couldn't bury her on the moors. They were having a very cold spell and the ground was frozen. It would be like trying to dig up concrete, at least until he got through the surface. And Matt's shovel wasn't up to the job. Neither were his muscles or his back. The weather wasn't going to improve any time soon – the forecast was for heavy snow.

In the last book in his series, the main character had simply and callously left his wife's body on the moors for scavengers. Exmoor offered an abundance of places where a body could be dumped and probably never found, but there was no way Matt could do that. Leona loved the ocean, too, but Matt didn't have a boat. Nor did he have sea legs. So, that wasn't an option. Leona deserved a proper burial – or as near to proper as possible – and he wanted to keep her close to him, to her family.

So, he had to come up with another plan. He knelt on the kitchen floor, at Leona's side, gazing at her lifeless form. Tears rolled down his cheeks and dropped onto her face as she stared, unseeing, back at him. He closed her eyelids, one after the other.

'I'm sorry,' he whispered out loud. 'I'm so sorry, Leona.'

There would be a time for mourning, but now was not it. He was struggling to think straight, but he had to make an effort. He couldn't afford to slip up. Before long, the police were going to be watching his every move. He was bound to be their main suspect. Husbands always were.

He thought about storing Leona's body somewhere, then burying her in the garden. Ideally, in a spot he could see from their bedroom window. That way, she'd be in a place she loved – the grounds of Blackmoor Manor – near the people she loved. He couldn't bear to think of her all alone.

But that would be far too risky. He decided to bury her in the garden of Rose Cottage. Leona hadn't thought much of the house – she'd said it was poky and the lighting was bad – but she'd loved his mum. And she'd tended to the garden there, just as she'd done the gardening at Blackmoor Manor. Two summers ago, he'd bought a storage shed, some tools and a lawnmower from B&Q for Rose Cottage so Leona wouldn't have to keep carting everything from one house to the other. He would leave Leona's body in the shed and bide his time, just for a little while – until the heat died down and the weather warmed up. Then he would have to act fast. He didn't need to be a crime writer to know he couldn't leave a body in the shed for long once the temperature rose above zero.

He got to his feet and washed the blood off the knife at the sink. Then he put the knife in the dishwasher and put on the quick wash cycle. He stood for a minute or two, gripping the worktop to keep himself upright.

Blinded by tears, he stumbled upstairs. Leona's maternal grandmother had crocheted stacks of shawls and blankets during her lifetime and they still had about a dozen of them in the airing cupboard that they never used but didn't have the heart to throw out. They wouldn't be missed.

Leona's trainers were also in the airing cupboard. She'd put them in there to dry after scrubbing them. The sight of the shoes, as he opened the cupboard door, made Matt double over, in physical pain, as if he'd been punched in the stomach. He stayed bent in two, until he could catch his breath. Then he straightened up, grabbed three blankets under one arm and the trainers in his other hand. From the wardrobe in their bedroom he unzipped some of those plastic clothes bags in which Leona hung up her dresses and coats. He took everything back down to the kitchen.

He checked Leona's pockets, but other than a used tissue, there was nothing in them. Then his heart clenched. She was wearing her sports watch. She always tracked her runs with the GPS function. Would it give him away? He tried to think rationally. What had Leona done when she got home – before they started arguing? She'd washed the dog outside – it had rolled in fox poo, apparently – then she'd washed her trainers in the utility room. It was OK. If the watch was still on her wrist, she hadn't uploaded the data to her running app. It took him a moment to work out how to turn off the damn thing. He left it on her wrist.

He wrapped her up in the woollen blankets, as if to keep her warm. She always felt the cold. With the help of some duct tape, he enveloped her in the clothes bags – a makeshift body bag.

It wasn't until he'd finished that he noticed he'd forgotten to put her shoes on her feet. They were lying behind him, on the floor. Too late now. Perhaps, though, it was a blessing in disguise. The police would expect him, as a crime writer and former police officer, to channel his expertise and set up the perfect crime scene. But if he included some inconsistencies – a couple of clues that didn't quite add up – then he'd be less likely to fall under suspicion.

By the time he hoisted Leona's body into the boot of his car, he was physically and emotionally drained, and he had a splitting headache. But he had to keep going. He put his wellies into the boot, then closed it, gently, as if he didn't want to disturb Leona.

He needed to concentrate. What was he forgetting? Her mobile! It wasn't on her – he'd gone through her pockets before he wrapped her up.

Then he remembered her mobile had run out of juice – Leona had sworn, in front of Trixie, which Matt hadn't been happy about. He'd held his tongue, anxious to avoid an argument – Christ, the irony. He'd been concerned about Leona going for a run without her phone. She could pull a muscle or twist her ankle or something. There wouldn't be many other people out in the dark and cold. She might need him to come and get her. He'd offered her his mobile, but she'd refused, insisting she wouldn't need to be rescued.

Where was her mobile? She kept her charger in the drawer of her bedside table. He took the stairs two at a time and stopped at the top, gasping for breath, as if he'd just run several kilometres. Sure enough, Leona's phone was charging by her side of the bed. It was switched off. Even with his head pounding and his mind in turmoil, he realised this was a stroke of luck. The police would attempt to track Leona's last movements by triangulating her mobile phone. He rang Leona's phone from his own mobile and left a message, saying he was sorry and asking her to call him. His voice wobbled all over the place, but that didn't matter. He would tell the police he'd had an argument with Leona – at least he'd be telling one truth. That would explain why he sounded distraught. It would also act as a good bluff. The police would hardly think he'd murdered his wife if he admitted to having a row with her. Then he pocketed Leona's mobile, leaving it switched off, and left his own – switched on – in its place.

While he was upstairs, he checked in on Trixie. He'd given her some of the cough medicine he'd been prescribed last winter when he'd had bronchitis. He'd spent three nights coughing non-stop and sleeping very little, which had prevented Leona from sleeping, too. She'd sent him to the doctor and banished him to the guest room. The cough mixture knocked him out that night and he and Leona both slept well. Trixie was out for the count now, too. He wasn't proud of drugging his daughter, but needs must. He wouldn't be gone long, but he couldn't risk her waking up during his absence.

He picked up one of Leona's trainers, making a mental note to get rid of the other one. If he burnt it in the fire, it would probably smell or leave some residue in the embers. He would put it in the shed at Rose Cottage and bury it with Leona. He grabbed the little rucksack, containing some dog poo bags and the dog's toy, that she always took with her when she went jogging. He put the phone in the main compartment.

As he was leaving the house, he thought to take a torch with him. Something was niggling him – he was sure he'd forgotten something, but he couldn't think what.

For a split second, he panicked, thinking Leona must have the key to her Nissan on her. But he reminded himself again that he'd checked her pockets. And she hadn't driven to Wistlandpound. She'd set off from home. He went out to the hall and sure enough, her keys were sitting in the dish on the console table, where she kept them. Both sets. He put one set – the one with her house keys on the same fob – in the front pocket of her rucksack and left the spare in the dish.

He wore leather gloves while driving her Qashqai to the reservoir so as not to leave fingerprints. He didn't like driving with gloves on, even in the winter, but if he wiped the steering wheel of Leona's car, it would efface her fingerprints as well as his, which would look suspicious. He was fairly sure there was no CCTV on the way to Wistlandpound. There was an activity centre near the lake, where there might be security cameras. But they would probably be focused on the entrance to the centre rather than on the road itself. He should be all right.

He parked the Qashqai in the car park and took the torch with him, even though it was such a starry night he didn't really need it. He walked to the water's edge. He was about to throw Leona's rucksack into the reservoir, but he hesitated. Would the dog's toy make it float? He took the toy out and shoved it into his coat pocket. Then he lobbed the rucksack as far as he could into the water. He heard a discreet splash. He watched for a while as the rucksack floated away from him, carried by the wind. His heart skipped a beat. Did it matter if it stayed floating? The bag would be found anyway, whether it drifted or sank – sooner rather than later, that was all. But just as he reassured himself with this thought, the rucksack disappeared under the surface.

He walked half a mile or so around the lake and left Leona's trainer near the birdwatching lookout. He knew the shoe would be found – although if it snowed like it was forecast, it might take a while – but he wasn't sure what the police would infer from the clue he'd planted. The rucksack would make it look like Leona had gone into the water. If he left both of her shoes by the water's edge, that would suggest the same thing. But one shoe, a little further back from the reservoir, might provide a red herring. Hopefully, it would send the police off in the wrong direction for a while, searching for other clues around the lake. It would buy him some time.

He walked home – briskly, as he was anxious about Trixie, although he didn't think she'd wake up. He also had some cleaning to do. And he needed to cover his tracks.

On his way, he stopped in front of a house, as isolated as his own. The bin had been put out for the following morning. He opened the lid and unknotted the bin bag. He put the dog's toy inside, wrinkling his nose as he pushed it down under the rubbish. Then he knotted the bag again and silently closed the lid.

As soon as he got home, he rang Leona again. This time he didn't leave a message. He would send a text message in a few minutes, then ring once more in the morning before ringing round their friends. And Roxanne.

In the meantime, he got to work in the kitchen. Thank goodness Leona had insisted on those shiny tiles. They were lethal – he'd almost slipped over a few times, but at least they were easy to clean. He'd need more than warm, soapy water, though. He knew from his research for his books as well as from experience what he needed. Hydrogen peroxide. Ages ago, Scarlett had had a nose bleed and he'd tried to get the bloodstains out of the rug in the living room. The hydrogen peroxide had done the trick, but not only had it removed the stains, it had also discoloured that part of the rug beyond repair. They'd thrown out the rug. But he still had some hydrogen peroxide in the cupboard under the sink. He'd tell the cleaner next time she came that the tiles were looking grubby in here so that she'd scrub them with bleach, too. Hopefully, between the two of them, they'd remove every last drop of blood.

He'd have to clean the car thoroughly, too, maybe even take it somewhere for a full valet service, as soon as he got the chance, once he'd taken out … afterwards.

Matt had shut the dog in the living room – even though he was still a bit wet from being washed – so he wouldn't get blood on his paws. He could hear him whining from the other side of the door. It was way past Sydney's dinnertime and he'd been for a run with Leona earlier. He must be hungry. The dog food and bowls were in the kitchen with Matt. He fed Sydney in the living room, then finished up in the kitchen.

It was only as he was emptying the last bucket of water down the sink that he noticed the sports bottle upside down on the draining board. Leona always took a drink when she went running and wore the bottle around her waist in a belt. He paused, the bucket still in his hands. Then he put down the bucket, opened one of the cupboards, spotted the belt and tidied the water bottle away with it. It wasn't important. If the police thought to ask, he'd say Leona took water with her in the summer, but not necessarily for a short run in the winter.

He'd been planning to take Leona's body to Rose Cottage that evening and leave her in the shed, but he hadn't thought this through. It was three o'clock in the morning now. Leona's car wouldn't have been spotted by anyone on the way to Wistlandpound Reservoir at night and it was unlikely to show up on any CCTV, but the same couldn't be said for his own car if he drove to his mother's place in Benton and back.

He'd have to wait until tomorrow, possibly even the day after that, after he'd called the police rather than before. That way, he wouldn't wave any red flags. He had to take some shopping to his mum soon anyway. He'd just have to put the shopping bags in the back seat instead of in the boot. He shuddered as he visualised Leona, wrapped in plastic clothes bags and blankets. It wasn't how he wanted to remember her, but it was a picture he knew he wouldn't ever get out of his head.

He spent the rest of the night bawling his eyes out like a baby, sitting on his bed, hugging his knees and rocking back and forth. Sydney wasn't allowed on the bed, but he'd jumped up when he heard Matt crying. Matt didn't have the energy to push the mutt onto the floor. He tried not to make too much noise so as not to wake up Trixie, and now and then, when he was overcome with sorrow, he sobbed into the pillow – Leona's pillow, which smelled of her face cream and citrusy shampoo.

'I'm sorry, Leona,' he said aloud, over and over again. 'I didn't mean it. I didn't mean to … I'm so sorry, Leona.'

But at times he felt sparks of anger catch inside him and flare up like matches. He was shocked and scared and unspeakably sad. But he was also furious. This wasn't all on him. Leona had brought this upon herself.

Chapter 27

November 2024

Gabi finds the time until the trial long, but imagines Matt finds it even longer. She keeps in touch with him by email, but can't bring herself to talk to him face to face, either via video call or by visiting him in person. He has used her and she feels stupid and angry. She has so many questions she wants to ask him, but she wouldn't believe him, no matter what he answered. She'd be surprised if he was allowed to discuss his case with her anyway. He seems to have steered clear of that topic in his emails – they must be checked before they're sent out.

The four months between the plea and trial preparation hearing and the beginning of the trial have given Gabi ample time to interview people for her podcast – witnesses, members of Matt's family as well as experts such as DC Chapman, the family liaison officer assigned to the Walshes, and Sergeant Craig Nash, the Underwater Search Unit supervisor. She and Joe have spent hours editing. The pilot episode aired some time ago and the rest of the episodes are almost ready to go. Gabi has decided to wait until the trial is over before airing the next one, though.

During that time, she has also done her homework, examining similar cases and the sentences the defendants were given. Matt has been charged with murder and with preventing the lawful and decent burial of a dead body. He has pleaded guilty to the second of these charges, which means that he'll be sentenced for it after the verdict is returned in his murder trial.

She can hazard a good guess at the story Matt intends to use for his defence. Right from the start, he admitted he and Leona had had a row. Knowing Matt, he'll say it got out of hand, that his wife attacked him – she was frequently violent towards him – and he defended himself, grabbing a knife to threaten her, but not in the aim of killing her. He may get lucky. The jury might return a verdict of not guilty for murder. If the jurors believe Matt acted in self-defence, he'll be acquitted. Of murder, at least.

Matt can't avoid a custodial sentence altogether and, theoretically, he could be looking at a life sentence for preventing a lawful and decent burial. In practice, as far as Gabi can see from her research, it's rare to be sentenced for this crime alone. It's usually an added count, going together with homicide. She has found a couple of cases online where the defendants were found not guilty of murder but guilty of preventing the lawful and decent burial of the victim. In both instances, they were sentenced to three years' imprisonment.

Gabi can't see the jury buying the self-defence story. But will they convict him of murder? In a few days' time, it will all be over and they'll know. Matt's fate will be determined.

The trial is being held in the Exeter Law Courts, in Southernhay Gardens. It's a recent, modern building – with gleaming white walls and lots of glass, both inside and out – comprising both a County Court and a Crown Court venue. Until about ten years ago, criminal court cases were heard at the old law courts at Exeter Castle. The courtrooms in the new building are larger and airier, but somehow some of the solemnity has been lost. Or perhaps Gabi has just become used to covering murder trials over the years – she's attended a fair few during the course of her career – and the atmosphere no longer rubs off on her in the same way. She's got a feeling, though, the atmosphere at Matt's trial will be electric.

On the day the trial is to begin, Gabi is up early, hours before she needs to be. She tiptoes around the house barefoot so as not to disturb Joe, who is still sound asleep in her bed. He has mooted the idea of them moving in together. It has only been a few months, but she's madly in love, both with Joe and with the idea of living with him. He has met her mother on a few occasions now. He has had no trouble winning her over, no mean feat given that Gabi's mother hates men. Not that Gabi would listen if her mother had reservations about Joe, but still. Her mum didn't think much of Darren – she made no secret about that – and she turned out to have a point. So Gabi's relieved that Joe has met with her mother's approval.

How she and Joe both managed to wangle permission from Mick to attend the trial, Gabi doesn't know. They plan to get there in good time, at least an hour before the start of the court's sitting hours, in case there's a long queue to get through security. There might well be; Matt's case has become a high-profile one. Gabi herself has had a hand in that. There will be other reporters and perhaps some of Matt's family as well as some curious members of the general public. Plus, there will be other trials in progress in other courtrooms.

Gabi makes herself a coffee and sits on one of the bar stools. She turns on her phone. Three missed calls. All from her mother. That's strange. Her mum doesn't often call her. She seems to think it's up to Gabi to ring. Gabi calls her back, but there's no answer. She leaves a message, reminding her mum the trial starts today and promising to try and get hold of her again this evening.

Gabi and Joe are eating breakfast when her mobile goes. The caller ID shows it's from her mum's number, but when Gabi answers, it's not her mum. As Gabi listens, she feels the blood drain from her face.

'The North Devon District Hospital?' she says. She catches the worried look Joe throws her and gives him a tight smile. 'Please tell her I'm on my way,' Gabi says to the caller, hanging up. 'My mum,' she explains to Joe. 'She's had a heart attack.'

A lump forms in Gabi's throat and she blinks back tears. They've never been as close as Gabi would have liked, but her mum's pretty much the only family Gabi has got. A sixty-five-year-old non-smoker, who goes for daily walks along the South West Coast Path and does a weekly yoga class, her mother is not really a prime candidate for heart trouble. Gabi's shocked. And worried.

But it's more than that. She's disappointed, too. This is really bad timing. She shouldn't have that thought at a time like this, but she can't help it. She has been working on this story since Leona disappeared five years ago. She could see the finish line, but now she sees her dreams fading. Again.

Joe puts his strong arms around her and strokes her hair. 'Do you want me to come to the hospital with you?' he asks.

'No,' Gabi says, although she'd very much like him to accompany her really. 'Someone needs to be there. In court, I mean.'

'OK, if you're sure,' he says. She nods against his chest. 'I'll keep you up to speed. Let me know how your mum is, OK?'

Gabi eases herself reluctantly from Joe's embrace and less than a minute later, she's on her way. The traffic is hell. Total gridlock going through Barnstaple towards Raleigh Park, in the direction of the hospital. Has there been an accident? Or is it always like this on Monday mornings? The offices of the *Echo* are in the town centre and Gabi never comes this way. At one point, the line of cars is stationary for several minutes. She breaks her own vow never to touch her mobile while she's at the wheel and texts her mum to say she'll be there as soon as she can.

Gabi finally reaches the hospital and pays for the car park. She walks briskly to the entrance, only to be informed by the receptionist that visiting hours begin at ten o'clock. Gabi has an hour to wait.

'A nurse called me this morning on behalf of my mum,' she says. She can hear the frustration and anxiety in her voice. 'She had a heart attack last night.'

The receptionist relents, asks for Gabi's mum's name and directs her to the Victoria Ward on level four.

The nurse Gabi spoke to on the phone is very sympathetic and allows Gabi to sit at her mum's bedside. Her mum is asleep. While she waits for her to wake up, Gabi tries to read her book – she always carries a paperback in her handbag – but she can't concentrate. Her thoughts pitch between the courtroom and the hospital. She drags her chair round to the other side of the bed so she can hold her mother's hand – the one that doesn't have the cannula in it.

From time to time, Gabi checks her phone, but there's no news from Joe. In the public galleries, where the press benches are, you're allowed to take in your mobile as long as you don't use it to take photos or record the proceedings.

Her mum wakes up – briefly – around lunchtime. She smiles at Gabi and squeezes her hand, then promptly goes back to sleep. Gabi leaves her to get lunch in the cafeteria downstairs on level two. The food looks and smells good, and Gabi realises to her surprise that she's hungry. She guzzles down a jacket potato with coleslaw, Cheddar and baked beans. She's already feeling wired and has drunk far too much caffeine today, but she has another coffee. She takes the stairs rather than the lift back to her mum's ward.

Her phone rings as she reaches her mother's bedside and her mother's eyes snap open. Gabi takes the phone out of her handbag and sends the call to voicemail, registering as she does that it's Joe who is calling. Damn.

'You gave me a scare, Mum,' Gabi says.

'I had a bit of a fright myself,' her mum says. 'It was lucky Joan had popped round.'

'Joan?'

'My neighbour. You know Joan. She called the ambulance. I'm feeling as right as rain now.'

Gabi's mum's Devon accent is quite pronounced, much stronger than Gabi's, perhaps because Gabi went to a private school. Her mother could never have afforded it, but Gabi got a scholarship in the eleven plus exams. Gabi's mum has lived in North Devon her whole life and gave birth to Gabi in this very hospital.

Her mum is quite chirpy, which is a huge relief. There's no TV on the ward itself and she jokes that she wants to be home in time for *Tipping Point*, *The Chase* and Richard Osman's *House of Games*.

'I think you can knock that idea on the head for today, Mum,' Gabi says, just as her phone beeps with a text message. She resists the urge to read it.

Later that afternoon, the doctor comes by. He has sparse white hair and his face is crisscrossed with lines. He doesn't appear to be wearing well.

'We've had the results of your blood tests, Mrs Conti,' he says to Gabi's mum. 'Your cholesterol is sky high. We'll get you started on statins and that should prevent any further heart attacks.' He goes on to assure her there's probably nothing seriously wrong, although they'll run more tests before she's discharged.

Gabi's mum barely waits until the doctor is out of earshot before commenting, 'He's got one foot in the grave himself, that one.'

Gabi smiles. It hasn't taken her mum long to get back to her old self. 'I need to ring Joe, Mum,' she says. 'Are you all right if I pop out for a sec?'

'Of course! Go ahead.'

'What did I miss?' Gabi asks as soon as Joe picks up.

'Not much,' he says. 'The jurors were sworn in – six women and six men. The judge – The Honourable Mrs Justice Alexandra Roberts – gave them preliminary instructions, you know, told them only to discuss the case among themselves and warned them to stay off the internet and that sort of thing. I've updated all our social media platforms.'

'So they didn't get as far as the prosecution's opening speech?' she asks Joe.

'No. I imagine they'll kick off with that tomorrow. Honestly, if you've got FOMO, there's no need. You haven't missed anything.'

'Any idea how long the trial is likely to last?'

'Two weeks, according to the judge. Now, how's your mum?'

'She's fine,' Gabi says. 'In good spirits. Doesn't appear to be in any pain.'

'That's good. I'm on my way back from Exeter. Shall I meet you at yours?'

'Yes, please! See you in a bit.'

Gabi's mum is sitting up eating dinner when Gabi goes back into the ward. She puts down her fork as soon as she spots Gabi.

'I'm going home now, Mum, but I'll be back again tomorrow at ten, when visiting hours begin.'

But her mum's not having it. She shakes her head. 'I completely forgot what day it was. Matthew Walsh's trial began today, didn't it? I'm so sorry.'

'That's OK, Mum. Joe went. Nothing much happened.'

'You've been following Leona Walsh's disappearance for years,' she says. 'You have to attend this trial.'

'No, Mum. It's not important. I'll—'

'I'm in good hands. I feel fine. There's no point in both of us hanging around here twiddling our thumbs while we wait for them to give me the all-clear. Don't you dare come back here tomorrow! You can give me a ring in the evening—'

'But—'

'—and let me know what happens in court. It's a crying shame we no longer have the death penalty in this country. That murdering bastard should be hanged for what he did. Or strung up by the balls. Let's hope he at least spends the rest of his life languishing in a prison cell.'

Gabi doesn't know what to say to that. Or what to think about it. Matt way well spend the rest of his life languishing in a prison cell. Gabi hopes he will if that's what he deserves. Let the punishment fit the crime. Or crimes.

Chapter 28

November 2024

Matt's day starts off in exactly the same way as yesterday, giving him the unsettling impression he's trapped in Groundhog Day. He is driven from His Majesty's Prison Exeter to the Law Courts in Southernhay Gardens. The windows in the van are too small and too high. He can see only overcast sky and bare treetops and the occasional flash of the upper floors of tall buildings. The van stops and starts as it moves through rush-hour traffic. It's a short journey, which Matt reckons should normally take about ten minutes, but which must take them at least half an hour. Or perhaps it's just time going by slowly. Eventually, he feels the van go down a ramp, a signal he recognises from the previous day – they've reached their destination.

He's held in a tiny, unventilated cell in the bowels of the building. The floor and walls are painted – green and yellow, respectively, presumably in a futile effort to brighten up the windowless room and make it less claustrophobic.

He knows the drill now. A short wait before he is led to a consultation room, barely larger and no less depressing than his holding cell, for a brief chat with his barrister, Simran Takhar KC. She tells him what to expect in court that day and gives him general advice on how to look and where to look, especially when he himself takes the witness box in a few days' time. Then he is taken back to his cell until the court session begins.

Matt doesn't really know what to make of Simran Takhar KC. He has met with her three times now, including their talks in the consultation room, and each time she has come over as calm, soft-spoken and unassuming. Matt hopes this shows confidence rather than timidity. She's petite and slim, which does nothing to make her seem more assertive. He'd be hard pushed to guess her age. She looks as if she's barely old enough to have qualified as a barrister, let alone taken silk. Her wig looks spanking new, too, in better condition than Matt thinks it should for an experienced lawyer. But Patrick Oliver assured him that she's one of the best defence barristers around.

A female judge and a female defence barrister. Matt has no idea if this will work in his favour, or against him. It should make no difference whatsoever, but he's afraid they'll both sympathise with his late wife. He's fairly sure Simran Takhar doesn't believe a word of his story. Her dark brown, almost black eyes seem to look at him – look *through* him – as if she knows not to take him at face value.

Today the wait in his cell is long. Is there a problem? Or does it just seem as if time has stopped? Matt wipes his clammy palms on the trousers of his suit and then swats at the beads of sweat on his forehead. He would pace up and down if there was any room. Instead, he sits on the hard bench and ruminates. He feels lonely, but strangely, not alone. Leona might be dead, but she hasn't disappeared. At times, she hovers over him, like a spectre; at others, she glows before him, like a guiding light. He can feel her presence now, her ghost sitting beside him. But he can't tell if she's mad at him or on his side. Is anyone on his side?

At last, he hears the door to his cell being unlocked. The same two men have come for him as yesterday, wearing the same uniform of crisp white shirts and dark trousers. He is led up the steps, bracketed by the guards, his legs threatening to give way as he nears the top.

Court Number Four is a brightly lit room and as he enters it, he's dazzled for a few seconds after the dim gloom of his holding cell. He knows what to do. He pulls down the seat of the plastic folding chair and sits between the officers in the dock. He's surrounded by shatterproof glass and feels like a goldfish in a bowl. Except he's not swimming round and round; he's drowning.

His barrister and her junior are already there, huddled together, discussing something that Matt has no hope of making out from here. Are they talking about him? Or something else entirely? They both look up and nod at him, then turn back to their discussion. The Crown Prosecution Service lawyers are also present, as well as the clerk, who is sitting in the row in front of the seat the judge will occupy.

The usher asks them all to rise and the judge enters, wearing her red robes. The Honourable Mrs Justice Alexandra Roberts. Even from the other end of the room and from his position on a raised platform, Matt can tell she's tall. Taller still, in her high heels. Matt would find her intimidating if it wasn't for her red robes, but he can't help thinking she's just a fake beard short of a Father Christmas costume. She takes her seat, at the front of the court, underneath the Royal Coat of Arms, behind her on the wall. She asks for the jury to be brought in.

Out of the corner of his eye, Matt watches the jurors file in. Six men and six women. He has memorised which of them took a religious oath when they were sworn in yesterday – three of them swore by Almighty God and two of them by Allah – and which of them chose to affirm instead. Not that he knows what to infer, if anything, from this. Even without looking at them directly, he can feel their doubting eyes on him, sizing him up. These twelve people will determine his fate.

As the barrister for the prosecution begins his opening speech, Matt fixes on the back of his head – the little plaits in his wig. A realisation hits Matt like a blow to the stomach and for a few seconds, he is winded. This is it. His trial has begun.

There's a sudden sneeze from above him. He's supposed to look straight-ahead – that's what his counsel has told him to do – but his eyes flit up to the public gallery, where the spectators and journalists are shuffling in. Yesterday it was packed. But to Matt's disappointment, it appeared to be full of reporters, busybodies and true crime addicts. He didn't recognise a single person, not one friendly, familiar face in a sea of inimical ones.

Then he sees her. Gabi. She's with her colleague, the one who snapped photos of him when he was arrested at Blackmoor Manor. Her presence is a comfort to him, even if she's there in a professional capacity. And then his heart floods with love as he spots Adam and Scarlett. He's relieved Trixie's too young to be admitted in the public gallery. This would be way too upsetting for her. If he'd had his say, Trixie wouldn't set foot in the court building at all, but his legal team have made it clear that's not an option. Thankfully, because of her age, special measures will be put in place and she'll give evidence via video link from a separate room. Roxanne also has to give evidence. She's not allowed to attend Matt's trial as a spectator until after her stint as a witness for the prosecution. And even then, she may not want to. But Scarlett and Adam are here. That's more than enough to buoy Matt up, keep him afloat.

Gabi takes her seat in the public gallery and scans the courtroom. Matt is looking up at her from the dock. She gives him a tight smile. Last time she saw him, he looked haggard, his face encrusted with greying stubble and his eyes red from lack of sleep. Today he's clean-shaven, but he looks no less gaunt or grey; his face is wan and the jacket of his suit hangs off him as though it's several sizes too big.

The prosecution barrister – Donald Dewberry KC – is on his feet, making his opening speech. He cuts a grandiose figure in his horsehair wig and wizard-like robe. The barristers' wigs and gowns, Gabi knows, date back to the Restoration period. In modern law courts such as this one, they seem incongruous to her, contrasting with the innovative design of the place. She has to admit, though, that the fact the British judicial system is so firmly rooted in tradition also inspires confidence. You get the feeling justice will be served. She certainly hopes it will be in this trial.

Donald Dewberry doesn't appear at all self-conscious in his vaguely ridiculous outfit. He's a natural orator, clearly comfortable in his surroundings and with an audience. Gabi notes with amusement that he emphasises all the adjectives and adverbs in his speech.

'Leona Walsh was a *good* mother and a *loving* wife,' he's saying. It doesn't sound like they've missed much. 'She was a *respected* politician and an *upstanding* figure in her community.'

Upstanding might be stretching it, given the embezzlement allegations. The same thing is going through Joe's mind, Gabi would bet on it. Not that the charges were ever proven. No date was ever set for Leona's trial – due to Leona's disappearance or lockdown, Gabi doesn't know which. Now her body has been found and the money restituted by Wigmore, that's no doubt the end of the fraud charges.

'Ladies and gentlemen,' Donald Dewberry continues, 'you will hear the defendant claim that he acted in self-defence, that he should not be found guilty of this *atrocious* act.'

So she was right. Matt's barrister intends to argue self-defence.

'The prosecution case is that on Saturday, the thirtieth of November 2019, the defendant had a *heated* argument with his wife and *deliberately* stabbed her in the stomach, *fatally* wounding her. He did not call for an ambulance, but instead left her lying on the kitchen floor and watched for some time as she suffered *excruciating* pain and *eventually* bled to death.'

Gabi looks from the prosecution counsel to the jurors. They all have their eyes riveted on him, hanging on his every word. Do they believe his story? Will Matt's lawyer manage to convince them he acted in self-defence and used reasonable force?

Donald Dewberry KC calls his first witness, Dr Sebastian Cavendish, the Home Office pathologist. He's around the same age as Professor Harvey, which makes Gabi wonder if they were at school or university together. Is that how they know each other? Dr Cavendish reads the oath and remains standing.

The prosecutor refers the jurors to the bundle in front of each of them. Gabi wishes she could see what the file contains. There are photographs of the alleged crime scene, that much is clear, maybe also photos from the post-mortem. The jurors' heads are down so she can't even assess from their faces how revealing or grisly the photos are.

With the help of his expert witness, Donald Dewberry paints a vivid – and rather gruesome – picture of the badly decayed, largely skeletonised remains of the victim. Dewberry then has Cavendish establish the cause of death.

'Sharp force trauma,' the pathologist says, then adds, 'Leona Walsh received a single, fatal wound to her stomach from a sharp instrument.'

There's a collective gasp of shock from the jury when Dr Cavendish says it might have taken Leona up to an hour to die. Gabi listens attentively, but for most of his testimony, there's nothing new. Professor Harvey has already given her the bullet points. Gabi takes notes anyway, scribbling so fast that her handwriting is barely legible, even to herself. Recording equipment inside the courtroom is forbidden, so there's no chance of her using anything from Matt's trial for her podcast. She notices that the judge also takes notes – constantly – either typing on her laptop or jotting on a pad.

The prosecution barrister steers Dr Cavendish on to the murder weapon. 'Five years is a considerable amount of time,

Dr Cavendish, but you have explained how you, as a forensic pathologist, are able to ascertain important, irrefutable information about the cause of death, even after such a long period. Were you also able to determine from the post-mortem you carried out what sort of weapon was used to kill the victim?'

'Yes, indeed. Leona Walsh was stabbed with a single-bladed knife,' Dr Cavendish says.

'What sort of knife?' Dewberry asks.

'A kitchen knife, in all probability. A sharp knife, one that is used to cut vegetables or meat.'

'Dr Cavendish,' the Crown barrister continues, 'I'm now going to ask you some questions about exhibit SH slash one, which will be the court's exhibit one, a kitchen knife that was recovered from the defendant's home.' Donald Dewberry holds up a protective sleeve, a transparent one, through which a knife is clearly visible. He asks the usher to hand the exhibit to the witness.

Gabi steals a furtive look at Joe, who turns towards her briefly, his eyes wide, then turns his attention back to Donald Dewberry. Gabi's mind is whirring. She edges forwards on her seat. A knife?

'Dr Cavendish,' Donald Dewberry continues, 'in your professional opinion, could this knife be the one that was thrust into Mrs Walsh's body?' He stresses the word 'thrust'.

Gabi shudders.

Dr Cavendish turns the knife over in his hands, examining it. But it's just for show. It must be. 'The stab wound, as far as we can make out from damage to the bone and so on, certainly appears consistent with the shape and dimensions of this knife,' Dr Cavendish asserts.

The prosecutor then asks the usher to pass the exhibit to the jury, followed by the judge and the defence counsel. It makes Gabi think of a game of pass the parcel or hot potato. Except that this is no game. This is no parcel or hot potato. It's the probable murder weapon.

Until Leona's body was discovered a few months ago, no one

knew how she'd died. In fact, until then, no one knew for sure she was dead. Everyone had been looking for Leona; no one was looking for a murder weapon. So the knife can only have been found recently. Matt can't have disposed of it very well if it was found in his own home. Why didn't he get rid of it?

'No further questions, My Lady,' Donald Dewberry says, butting in on Gabi's thoughts.

Matt's representative stands to cross-examine the prosecution's expert witness. Simran Takhar KC is a pretty woman, whose poise belies her small stature. She speaks slowly and clearly.

'Dr Cavendish, you say the wound appears to have been almost ten centimetres deep. Is that correct?'

'Yes.'

'And in your expert opinion, how much force would have been needed to cause an injury of around ten centimetres with a knife such as exhibit one?'

'That depends,' Dr Cavendish says. 'The sharper the knife, the less force is needed. This particular knife is very sharp. A knife this sharp would have slid into the body with relative ease.'

Gabi thinks she can see what Matt's barrister is driving at. Self-defence is about reasonable force and if the knife wasn't 'thrust' into Leona's body, but rather 'slid' into it, the act of stabbing looks less violent, perhaps even unintentional.

And, indeed, Simran Takhar proceeds to put the case to Dr Cavendish that the defendant was acting in self-defence and that no evidence indicates the knife was 'thrust' into the victim's stomach.

The pathologist doesn't help out Matt's barrister a lot. After nearly five years have elapsed, it seems that it's possible to determine a surprising amount of information about how the victim died and the instrument used to kill her, but not so much about how the knife itself ended up inside her. He's also unable to say for sure how sharp or blunt the knife was. But the lawyer has made her point.

'No further questions, My Lady,' Simran Takhar eventually says.

She has no doubt toned down in the jurors' minds the violent image painted by the prosecution barrister's wording. That was probably the best she could hope to achieve. For now. A little damage limitation. The prosecution is telling a compelling story and Gabi can tell from the jurors' faces that they're lapping it up. Even Gabi herself is convinced they're finally nearing the truth – the real version of what happened to Leona Walsh.

Chapter 29

November 2024

By the next day, Gabi's mum is out of hospital. She has insisted on looking after the dog, although Gabi thinks it may be the other way round. She didn't like to think of Sydney cooped up on his own all day in her maisonette. She also hated to think of her mother alone. Her mum won't be up to walking the dog, but at least they'll provide company for each other. Her mum's neighbour, Joan, has promised to call in, too.

Sitting in court today, Gabi is more focused, less agitated. Yesterday, she felt as if her body was in one place while her mind was in another. Joe's the one who has been updating their socials and who has written the latest article about the trial for the *Echo Live*.

To kick off the proceedings this morning, the prosecution calls one of the investigating police officers, Detective Sergeant Sophie Holland. Gabi consults her notepad, where she has jotted down the reference number for exhibit one. SH/1. Sophie Holland's initials. So, the knife was found by the detective sergeant. Gabi is on full alert.

Donald Dewberry KC takes DS Holland through the searches that were carried out at Blackmoor Manor, the details of which were officially recorded each time. He refers her to various reports. There isn't a sound from the public gallery as the spectators are kept on tenterhooks. Surely everyone wants to know what Gabi herself is desperate to find out: where exactly was the knife found? Dewberry directs the police officer towards that very question.

DS Holland's answer comes as a bit of a shock. 'I took it from a wooden knife block in the defendant's own kitchen,' she tells the barrister, who pauses before pursuing with his questions, perhaps to allow the jurors to mull that over.

Gabi is reeling. Did Matt stab Leona with a knife from his own kitchen and then keep that knife in his house, in plain sight, all this time? She wouldn't put it past him. A wave of nausea surges inside her with her next thought. Has he been using this very knife to chop carrots or slice tomatoes?

Of course, there's no evidence to confirm this is the knife that killed Leona, as DS Holland admits under cross-examination. It just happens to be about the right length. But despite Simran Takhar's best efforts, Gabi's sure the jurors are convinced exhibit one is indeed the murder weapon.

After lunch, it's Trixie's turn to give evidence. The Honourable Mrs Justice Alexandra Roberts stands up and shrugs off her gown, then, sitting back down, she takes off her wig and runs her fingers through her short, dark hair. She asks the barristers to remove their gowns and wigs, too.

Because she's a child, Trixie gives her evidence via video link. There are several television screens angled towards the jury, the judge and the barristers. From her position in the public gallery, Gabi can make out Trixie's face on one of the monitors.

To begin with, a statement, made by Trixie at the time of her mother's disappearance, is read out to the court. Then a slightly dishevelled Donald Dewberry gently asks Trixie if she remembers anything now that she didn't say then.

Trixie is fidgeting and looks terrified. She glances to her left, off-screen, before replying. There must be someone there with her, to support her.

'No,' she says.

Dewberry then asks her a few questions, to verify everything she said in her statement. Gabi doesn't get why he does this. Is he trying to get the poor kid to contradict herself? If so, it doesn't work. But maybe he's just trying to put Trixie at ease. Or lull her into a false sense of security.

'In your statement, Trixie, you said that your mum was about to go out for a run,' Dewberry says, clearly aiming for a soft voice, but overshooting. 'What made you think that?'

'She was wearing her running clothes.'

Dewberry asks her to describe the running clothes. He enters another exhibit – the trainer found at Wistlandpound Reservoir, and asks Trixie if she recognises the sports shoe.

'It could be my mum's. I'm not sure,' she says. 'It was a long time ago.' She looks as if she's about to burst into tears and Gabi's heart goes out to her.

'Now, you said that your mum was about to go out for a jog, Trixie. But could it be that your mum had just come home from her run?'

Trixie appears to ponder this question. 'It's possible, yes.' Then she adds, 'I was only little. I don't remember.'

Dewberry carefully probes a little further, but Trixie doesn't remember what her parents were arguing about and knows nothing that can shed more light on what happened at Blackmoor Manor that evening. The jurors are left to fill in the blanks.

Even though Gabi listens to every word uttered in that courtroom, she finds much of the rest of the trial uneventful. Court sitting hours are from ten a.m. to four p.m., but by the time a morning break, a lunch break and at least one afternoon break are deducted from that, the days seem rather short.

Over the next few days, the prosecution calls more forensic experts as well as some sort of voice analysis expert, who also takes the witness box to deconstruct the 999 call Matt made to report his wife missing. The expert points out red flags and interprets hesitancies and voice modulations as signs of faked concern. But on the recording, Matt sounds genuinely distraught, and the jurors look as nonplussed as Gabi feels by the jargon the expert uses.

The testimony of the bloodstain pattern analyst is just as unconvincing. Traces of blood – Leona's blood – were found on the kitchen floor, but 'traces' turns out to be the operative word. When cross-examined, the prosecution's witness admits he would have expected more blood, much more blood, if a fatal stabbing had taken place there.

One afternoon is almost completely taken up with legal arguments over whether certain evidence, arguably bordering on hearsay, is admissible or not. The jury isn't present for this part and Gabi contemplates taking a break herself. It's not exactly riveting stuff and she doesn't think the evidence in question proves much one way or the other.

In fact, Gabi gets the feeling that the prosecution case is crumbling, despite a good start. Donald Dewberry KC has clearly already played his trump cards – the testimony of Dr Sebastian Cavendish, the Home Office pathologist, and exhibit one – the knife recovered from the wooden block in Matt's own kitchen. It's all been going downhill since then.

Joe voices Gabi's own thoughts during their lunch break that day, while they sit in a nearby café, drinking their coffees. 'I thought the prosecution would have stronger arguments,' he says. 'I figured this would be a clear-cut case. Seriously, what have they got on him? A few drops of Leona's blood on the kitchen floor and a knife that may not even have been the actual murder weapon? That and the fact that Matt has a tendency to tell the odd porky pie? A liar does not a murderer make.'

'I know. I've been wondering about that,' Gabi says. 'Uggh. This coffee is revolting. I think most of the evidence they had against him proved he buried his wife. The fact she was buried in his mother's garden spoke volumes; he looked up body decomposition in soil on the internet only hours after she went missing. Christ, there was even a soil match on his Wellington boots. But now he's actually admitted he buried her, the case against him seems to have come apart at the seams. The only thing in dispute is whether Matt stabbed Leona intentionally. The prosecution has to prove he deliberately thrust the knife into her.'

'*Slid* the knife into her,' Joe reminds her, 'with relative ease.'

'Hmm. It sounds almost as if it was an accident.'

'I think that's what Matt's barrister wants us to imagine.' Joe takes a sip of his coffee and screws up his face. 'You're right. This is vile.'

'The prosecution has got nothing that shows premeditation,' Gabi continues. 'Matt has no motive – there's nothing that proves he knew about Leona's affair. Because he's changed his story and has pleaded guilty to preventing a lawful and decent burial, there's no more evidence now than right back at the start, when Matt was the prime suspect but the police didn't have a body.'

'Perhaps Roxanne will have something to say,' Joe suggests.

'Roxanne always has something to say,' Gabi mutters wryly.

Matt spends lunchtime in his cell. The food they bring him – on a plastic tray with blunt plastic cutlery – is cold. It's some sort of meat with pasta in tomato sauce. It doesn't taste too bad, but it seems to clot into stodgy lumps in his mouth, making him gag. Matt's hand shakes as he lifts the fork to his mouth. It feels like swallowing ping pong balls, but he forces himself to eat. He needs to build up strength and he can't afford to lose any more weight. Long gone is the middle-aged paunch Matt used to have. His stomach is concave. He can't remember the last time he really enjoyed a meal. He hasn't finished eating this meal when the two guards come to escort him back up the steps to the dock.

Matt has never been so terrified in his life. His stomach is in knots. With every stage of this trial, it feels as if he's one step closer to losing everything – his freedom, his life, his children – for good. Right now, the odds are stacked against him. He hopes this might change once the prosecution case has closed and it's Simran Takhar's turn to present the defence case and tell Matt's side of the story.

He's fairly sure Roxanne is the final witness to be called up for the prosecution – his barrister has run him through the batting order. Last Matt knew, Roxanne was an atheist, unless she's recently found God. But she raises her right hand and swears a religious oath.

At first, his sister-in-law is convincing, but she has little of any importance to say. Donald Dewberry's questions focus on Matt's strange behaviour on the morning he reported his wife missing as well as on his character. Roxanne describes him as dishonest, saying he has a tendency to exaggerate and even tell unmitigated lies. She makes Matt look really bad, but he can't fault her portrayal of him.

However, Roxanne doesn't do so well during cross-examination.

'Would you describe your sister's relationship with the defendant as a close one?' Simran Takhar asks.

'Yes, they seemed close. My brother-in-law clearly loved my sister, but they had fierce rows.'

'And did you yourself witness any of these rows?'

'Er … no, not often. They didn't tend to row in front of me. Leona would sometimes confide in me about their arguments afterwards.'

'What sort of thing did they argue about?'

'Things that most couples argue about, I suppose. Money, the kids, chores.'

'It's true to say that you never saw the defendant behaving violently towards his wife, isn't it?'

Roxanne pauses, as if pondering the question, but Matt knows she won't lie, especially not under oath. 'No, I didn't. But he had a violent temper.'

'Violent, Mrs Barrett? What do you mean by a "violent" temper? You've just told the court that you have never known your brother-in-law to be violent towards your sister.'

'I mean he has a tendency to fly off the handle.'

'I see. And would you agree that Leona also had a temper, a tendency to fly off the handle?'

'Yes. She could be argumentative and aggressive. She was also depressive.'

Matt tries to keep his eyes front, as his barrister advised, but he can't resist a sideways glance at Roxanne, sitting in the witness box. He's not sure why the prosecution called her as a witness. She has managed to paint him in a negative light, but she's now tarring her sister with the same brush. By describing Leona as argumentative, aggressive and depressive, Roxanne doesn't seem to realise she's paving the way for Matt's defence.

After Roxanne's evidence, that's it for the prosecution's case. And that's it for the day. Gabi and Joe head downstairs to the ground floor with Adam and Scarlett. Joe has told Gabi that Adam and Scarlett didn't come on the first day, the day Gabi spent by her mum's side at the hospital, but they've been here every day apart from that, like Gabi herself. Gabi studies Scarlett. How is she holding up? Does she want her father to be convicted or acquitted? But Scarlett's expression gives nothing away, and Gabi doesn't dare ask, especially not in front of Adam.

'Gabi, I'm looking for a place of my own to live,' Scarlett says as they reach the foyer. 'I can look after Sydney once I've found somewhere.'

'Oh.' Gabi is surprised at how disappointed she feels. She should be pleased for Scarlett. She's getting on with her life, making plans. 'That's great, Scarlett,' she manages. 'For you and Sydney.'

'In the meantime, he's being well looked after,' Joe says.

'See you tomorrow,' Adam says as they exit the court buildings.

Tomorrow the defence case will begin. It's Matt's turn to give evidence. So far, even though Gabi finds some of the evidence a bit thin, it's not looking good for Matt. But Matt's a good liar, as Gabi now knows. Can he convince the jurors he's innocent? Is there still a chance he'll get away with murder?

Chapter 30

November 2024

Patrick Oliver, his solicitor, and Simran Takhar, his barrister, both felt the defence case would be too weak if Matt didn't give evidence. He had to take the witness box, no question about it. But they were dubious about how convincing he would be. Takhar said – although not in so many words – that Matt would screw up; Oliver was afraid Matt would come over as arrogant. Matt was keen to give evidence, to tell his version of events. He was confident he could pull it off.

Now he's up, he's less sure of himself. He thought his lawyers would coach him so he could more or less recite by heart the answers he was supposed to give on the big day. But that's not how it played out and nothing has prepared him for this.

He senses the jurors' accusing eyes glued to him as he affirms, hoping the believers among them won't hold his lack of religious convictions against him. He's aware, too, that Scarlett is present again today, sitting next to Roxanne, who has joined Scarlett and Adam in the public gallery now that she has been heard. Of all the people in the courtroom, it's his daughter's judgement he fears the most.

He remembers to look directly at his barrister and at the jury as he answers his barrister's questions. He tries to speak up and enunciate, reminding himself she's not out to trap him, but he can hear the quaver in his own voice.

'How long were you married to Leona, Mr Walsh?' Takhar asks.

'We got married in 2010, but we'd been together much longer than that. Our elder daughter, Scarlett, was almost five when we tied the knot. She was a flower girl at our wedding.'

Christ, if there are any serious Bible bashers in the jury, he won't get their votes. A child born out of wedlock.

'And how would you describe your marriage?'

'It was a loving one. I was very much in love with my wife.' Matt leaves it there. Everyone knows Leona was cheating on him when she died. He can hardly say she was in love with him, too. 'I thought of us as a team. Team Walsh. Leona, myself, the girls.'

'Did you and your wife argue a lot, Mr Walsh?'

'Yes, we did. I don't think we argued more than many couples, and we always made up before we went to bed – that was a rule between us. But, yes, we did have some pretty fiery rows.'

'Did you ever strike your wife during one of these "fiery rows", Mr Walsh?'

'No. Never.'

He's glad Takhar won't turn that question inside out. It never occurred to anyone, except Gabi, that *Leona* used to strike *him*. It might have strengthened his case if he'd used the domestic violence angle as part of his defence. If people had believed him. But he doesn't want this to come out. He has his reasons.

'Can you walk me through what happened on the evening of the thirtieth of November 2019? Did you and your wife quarrel that evening?'

'Yes, we did. I can't remember what it was about – something completely trivial, I'm sure of it. Leona had just come back from her run. We had this huge row, so I sent Trixie, who was there, in the kitchen with us, upstairs to her room. Then the argument got out of hand. Leona had been under a lot of stress. She'd been accused of … misappropriating funds at work and thought her political career was over. That night, she just … she just lost it.'

Matt hears his voice crack and swallows down the lump in his throat. He can't go to pieces, not in the witness box.

'What do you mean by "she just lost it"?'

'She lost her temper, lost control, lost her mind. She threatened to kill me. She wasn't talking sense. She even threatened to kill herself.'

'She threatened to kill herself? Had she made threats like that before?'

'No. I don't think she meant it. But she wasn't in a good place. She was on antidepressants and she wasn't herself.'

'What happened next?'

'She grabbed a knife from the wooden block on the worktop. She was brandishing it at me. I tried to wrench it off her and somehow it ended up inside … in her … stomach.'

'Mr Walsh, can you be more specific? How did the knife end up in your wife's stomach?'

'My hands were on the knife when I … realised … when it hit me. I must have stabbed her. I stabbed her. But I don't know how … we reached that point. I didn't mean to. I was trying to twist the knife out of her hands. I was trying to protect myself.'

Matt is in danger of losing it himself. He takes several deep breaths.

'Can you describe what happened after you realised your wife was wounded?' Takhar asks him when he has pulled himself together.

'The next thing I knew, Leona … my wife was … she was dead,' Matt says. 'I immediately thought of my children. Their mother was dead and I would be the obvious suspect. My fingerprints were on the knife. If I was arrested … if I was convicted, then my daughters wouldn't have a mother or a father.'

'So what did you do?'

'I made a terrible decision. I was panicking. I thought if I could cover it up, if I could make it look like my wife had gone missing, then maybe I wouldn't go to prison for something I didn't intend to do,' Matt says. 'And my daughters would still have one parent.' He hopes that last bit doesn't sound too much like an afterthought.

It's only when Matt hears a loud, embarrassing snort that he realises he's crying. He's such a cry baby. Do all men blubber like this? He sits up straighter in his seat, swipes at his face angrily with the sleeve of his jacket and tells himself sternly to get a grip. He's grateful when the judge suggests a short recess, even though this will mean going back to his cell.

Gabi has to hand it to him. It's a performance worthy of an Emmy nomination. After the recess, when Matt's barrister has finished asking her questions and the prosecutor gets to his feet, Gabi studies each of the jurors in turn. Are they taken in by him? Does the matronly woman with the outlandish sense of dress feel sympathy for him? Is that a tear shining in the eye of the girl in her twenties with multiple face piercings? One of the men is barely looking at Matt, his head down and his pen flying across the paper in front of him as he feverishly takes notes. What's going through his mind?

Gabi imagines Matt is about to get a grilling from Donald Dewberry KC. But Matt seems to have regained his composure. He has a determined, suitably meek look on his face and is no longer sniffing and weeping.

'Mr Walsh, your wife – the victim – was *seriously* wounded. Why didn't you call for an ambulance?'

'Leona asked me not to,' Matt says.

'Your wife was seriously wounded, but she asked you not to call for an ambulance?' Dewberry's voice is infused with a mixture of incredulity and scorn.

'She gripped my arm as I knelt beside her on the kitchen floor. She said, "Stay with me." She seemed to want to make up before … before she died. I told her I had to call for an ambulance, but she said no.'

Gabi glances at Scarlett. She's terribly pale. Roxanne puts her arm around her and pulls her in tight, practically smothering her, as if that will shield her from what's coming next.

'So, how long did it take your wife to die?' the prosecution barrister continues.

'Not long. A minute or two, maybe. Five, tops. I made the mistake of … pulling out the knife. She … the blood … it poured out after that. Profusely.'

Matt confirms exhibit one is the knife that ended up in his wife's stomach, but although Dewberry attempts to get a clearer picture of how exactly it happened, that chapter of Matt's story remains a little blurred. Gabi wonders if it's deliberate on Matt's part.

Dewberry asks Matt about the argument and puts it to him that they were rowing because Matt had found out about his wife's lover.

Matt denies it. 'I didn't find out that my wife had a lover until after she died.'

The questions keep coming at him. But he has an answer – a good one – for everything. Dewberry has Matt go over every step he took in disposing of his wife's body and covering up the incident. He asks Matt how he made the body bag; what clues he planted to mislead the police; how he cleaned up both the kitchen and his car; when and where he buried his wife. Matt goes into detail, looking candidly at the jurors, seemingly horrified at his own actions.

At first, Gabi can't see where the barrister is going with this. Matt has pleaded guilty to preventing the lawful and decent burial of his wife, so surely none of this evidence is in dispute?

But then Dewberry gets to the point. 'Even though you were in shock, you went to great lengths to cover up the fact that the victim – your wife – died at your hands. And yet, you *scrupulously* set up a scene to tell a completely different story, one with an open ending. Is it not the case that this murder was *premeditated* and that you thought everything through beforehand, down to the smallest detail?'

Gabi remembers Matt telling her something in one of their interviews. *If I wanted to commit the perfect murder, I could.* She shivers, suddenly cold, as if the temperature in the room has plummeted. Is that what he did? Does that explain how he acted with such meticulousness? Had he planned to kill Leona all along?

Matt doesn't falter. 'I used to be a police officer,' he replies, 'and I've read – and written – so many crime novels, it was almost second nature to me, covering up my wife's demise. I was in shock, yes, terrible shock. I was devastated, crying my eyes out, a complete mess. It was late at night and I couldn't think straight. But I was acting on autopilot. I kept going; I kept telling myself I was acting in the interests of my daughters. That thought spurred me on.'

The first expert witness to be called up for the defence is Dr Maureen O'Reilly. She's a pretty, slim redhead, in her early to mid-fifties. She has been present in court through some of the trial. Gabi's surprised. She thought witnesses weren't allowed in court before giving evidence, but that obviously doesn't apply to expert witnesses for the defence.

Dr O'Reilly remains standing in the witness box, just as the expert witnesses for the prosecution did. Her credentials are quickly established. Like Dr Cavendish, she's a forensic pathologist. She has twenty-five years' worth of experience. To begin with, Simran Takhar's questions and Dr O'Reilly's evidence merely confirm the findings of the Home Office pathologist.

'Now, Dr O'Reilly,' Matt's counsel says after a while. 'You didn't conduct the post-mortem on Leona Walsh's body, but have you ever conducted similar post-mortems?'

'Yes. I have established the cause of death as sharp force

trauma on six occasions,' Dr O'Reilly says, her Irish lilt somehow making a gruesome subject more palatable. Some of the jurors lean forwards, eager to hear more of what she has to say. Gabi follows suit.

'Would you mind explaining that in layman's terms?' Matt's barrister asks.

'I have examined the bodies of six victims who were stabbed to death.'

'And were all of these deliberate deaths?'

'Yes. In fact, three of the victims were deliberately stabbed to death by their spouses.'

'And of those three victims, were there any similarities with the results of the post-mortem carried out by your colleague, Dr Cavendish, on the body of Leona Walsh?'

'Well, actually, there was one notable difference. The three victims I examined who were murdered by their spouses had been stabbed multiple times.'

'Multiple times. Is this surprising?'

'No, not at all. In a *crime passionnel* – a crime of passion – that is to say, a violent crime such as when the husband stabs the wife or vice versa, there is a lot of anger and jealousy, so the perpetrator commits their crime in a frenzy, in the heat of passion. It's not a premeditated crime; rather it is provoked, for example, when one spouse discovers their partner in bed with someone else.'

'I see. And one last question. Have you ever examined the body of a victim who was killed by his or her spouse with a single, deliberate stab wound?'

'No, never. It would be a highly unusual method for a murder. I would expect there to be several stab wounds, not just one.'

'No further questions, My Lady,' Simran Takhar says.

Donald Dewberry stands to cross-examine the witness. 'Dr O'Reilly,' he says, 'you say you have been working in this field for twenty-five years, and yet during the course of your career, you've never encountered a dead body where the cause of death was determined as a *single, deliberate* stab wound. Do—'

'No, that's not quite what I said,' Dr O'Reilly interrupts. 'I said a single, deliberate stab wound administered by the victim's spouse. There was one occasion when I performed an autopsy on a dead body and established the cause of death as sharp object trauma with only one stab wound – to the stomach, coincidentally. That single stab wound proved to have been fatal.'

'I'm sorry. I misunderstood,' Dewberry scratches his wig, evidently still perplexed. 'Err, ... but this was a *murder* case ... was it not?'

'No. In that particular instance, the deceased was found alone, with a knife in her own hand. It looked as if she'd committed suicide. My conclusions were consistent with that hypothesis. Her fatal wound was indeed self-inflicted.'

Dewberry is obviously thrown. Gabi watches as he opens and shuts his mouth.

Dr O'Reilly spells it out for the barrister and the jurors. 'The woman had killed herself, by pushing a knife into her own stomach.'

Gabi gapes at Joe, whose eyes look like they're about to pop out on stalks. Matt's words just a few hours ago echo in Gabi's head. *She even threatened to kill herself.* Was this orchestrated? Is this how Matt and his barrister had planned it? Gabi can't see Simran Takhar's face, but judging from Matt's expression, he can't believe his good luck. It really does seem as if that just slipped out by chance during cross-examination.

Donald Dewberry does his best to regain control of the situation, to show that the case Dr O'Reilly has just described has absolutely nothing in common with Leona Walsh's case. He manages to lessen the blow by getting Dr O'Reilly to point out that there were tentative marks on the body in the case she mentioned, as one might expect in a suicide by stabbing whereas there were no hesitation marks on Leona Walsh's body. Dewberry also gets Dr O'Reilly to confirm that stabbing oneself is a relatively rare method of suicide.

But the damage is done. Gabi can tell from the jurors' astonished expressions. And from the slightly smug expression on Matt's face. The pathologist has sown a seed of doubt; she has planted an alternative image in the minds of the jurors.

And perhaps that will be enough.

Chapter 31

November – December 2024

It's almost over. The final day of his trial opens with the prosecution's closing speech. Donald Dewberry KC oozes confidence as he recaps the evidence against Matt. Matt no longer makes the effort to look straight-ahead of him, but assesses each of the jurors in turn, trying to gauge their reactions. Do they think he's guilty? All he needs is a reasonable doubt. Just one detail that doesn't quite add up in the minds of the jurors – or some of them – and he could be acquitted of the murder charge. As Matt once wrote in one of his novels, the British judicial system is less about truth and more about proof. Or words to that effect. In this case, Matt knows, there are big, gaping holes in both the truth and the evidence.

His own barrister is just as persuasive as her learned friend. Matt has to admit that his first impression of her – as a mousy, timorous woman – was wrong. His solicitor, Patrick Oliver, was right. If anyone can get him off, she can.

Of course, Matt won't be striding out of the main door when the verdict comes in. No matter which way it goes, he'll be going to prison for covering up his wife's death. He's resigned to that fact. Best-case scenario, according to Patrick Oliver and Simran Takhar: he'll be found not guilty of murder and sentenced to three to four years for preventing the lawful and decent burial of a dead body. He could be out in eighteen months to two years. Worst-case scenario: he'll be found guilty of murder and spend the rest of his days in prison and never see his mother again and only ever see his daughters if they accept to visit him.

Matt fidgets during the judge's summing up. The Honourable Mrs Justice Alexandra Roberts has said very little during the trial itself, but this is clearly her moment. She obviously loves the sound of her own voice and waffles on and on, reminding the jurors of pretty much everything they've heard, as if they're incapable of remembering the details for themselves. It's an insult to their intelligence, if you ask Matt.

It's about three-thirty in the afternoon by the time the judge has finally finished summing up and so there will be no verdict before Monday. Matt will have to fret in his cell in HMP Exeter over the weekend.

Patrick Oliver comes to see him on the Saturday. Ostensibly, his solicitor has come in a professional capacity. But Matt senses he's here as a friend and appreciates Oliver taking time out of his weekend to offer his support.

'How long do you think it will take for the jury to return a verdict?' Matt asks him.

'It could be as soon as Monday morning or it may take days,' Patrick Oliver says.

'Is it true that if the jurors come back quickly, it's more likely to be a not guilty verdict?' Matt asks.

'That's what they say.'

The solicitor hasn't really answered the question, but Matt drops it. No one can predict how long the jury will be out. And no one can predict whether Matt will be found guilty or not guilty. All anyone can do now is wait and see. But, for him, the wait is interminable.

Gabi and Joe arrive at the Exeter Law Courts shortly before ten on Monday morning. It's the 2nd of December, almost exactly five years since the day Leona Walsh was reported missing. Gabi's mum is looking after Sydney for the day again. She has even insisted on cooking dinner for Gabi and Joe. Her mum's not known for her culinary skills, despite the numerous cookery books in her kitchen, but Gabi's grateful for the offer and relieved that her mum is feeling better.

They wait in the café, although Gabi will be glad to see the back of it. The cups are dirty, the benches uncomfortable and the waitress is unpleasant. It's their last day. If the verdict isn't returned today, she and Joe won't come back tomorrow. Mick keeps complaining about the amount of time this court case has engaged two of his best journos. Gabi has made an arrangement with the security guard, Dan. It's been the same guy nearly every day and they're now on first-name terms. He will text them as soon as the verdict is in. Spectators have come and gone during this trial – presumably due to work commitments for most people – but Dan has been careful to let in the family first, followed by the journalists and the regulars. Gabi's keeping her fingers crossed the jury will reach a decision today, but if not, thanks to Dan, she'll be one of the first people to find out the verdict anyway.

It's shortly after two p.m. and Gabi's on her fifth or sixth cup of insipid tea – the coffee is just too disgusting in this place – when her phone beeps with a text. She glances down at the screen, then up at Joe. 'Here we go,' she says.

Roxanne, Adam and Scarlett haven't come today. Trixie had been going to her friend Nola's house after school while Roxanne was in court, but Roxanne wanted to be with her younger niece when the verdict was returned. And perhaps it was all getting too much for Scarlett. She looked broken on Friday as they left the

Law Courts. Gabi has promised to call Roxanne as soon as this is over and let her know the verdict – and the sentence, if the judge passes sentence today. She can't even imagine what Matt's family are going through, especially Scarlett and Trixie.

There's not a sound in Court Four, not even a cough or a sneeze. You could cut the tension with a knife. A suitable idiom, given the circumstances.

Everyone rises as the judge enters. She sits down, which is everyone else's cue to sit down, too. She asks the clerk to bring in the jury. Once the jurors have taken their seats, the clerk gets to his feet and asks the foreperson to stand.

The foreperson is a short man with round, tortoiseshell glasses. He has a loud, baritone voice, which strikes Gabi as at odds with his slight build.

'Have you reached a verdict on which you're all agreed?' the court clerk asks him.

Gabi holds her breath as the court clerk goes through each individual count and asks, 'Do you find the defendant guilty or not guilty?'

Gabi's eyes are glued to Matt. He doesn't flinch, not even when the final verdict has been delivered.

Matt is found not guilty of murder, but guilty of manslaughter. And, of course, he has already pleaded guilty to preventing the lawful and decent burial of a body.

Again, the judge has plenty to say, but eventually gets to the point. Matt is sentenced to a total of eight years for manslaughter and two years, to run concurrently, for preventing a lawful and decent burial. Gabi's no expert, but he'll probably serve only half of that. Which means he'll be out in four years.

For once, Roxanne is speechless when Gabi relays the news. Gabi doesn't add what she's thinking. Roxanne is probably thinking more or less the same thing. Leona was thirty-four when she died, almost exactly five years ago. It seems like yesterday. Eight years – or, more realistically, four years – doesn't seem like much for taking a life, no matter how that life was taken. After several seconds of silence, Roxanne thanks Gabi and ends the call.

'I guess no one will ever know what really happened,' Joe says on the drive back to Barnstaple.

Matt has given Gabi elements of the truth, like pieces of a jigsaw puzzle. She should be able to fit them together and see the completed picture, but she can't shake the feeling there's still a key piece missing. Now it's all over and once all the podcast episodes have aired, Matt might be willing to tell her everything. The whole truth. He has nothing else to lose. But she can't forgive him for using her, for lying to her. She doubts she'll keep in touch. She doesn't want to see him again.

'I expect you're right,' she says. 'We'll probably never know exactly what really happened to Leona.'

Chapter 32

March 2025

Joe has more or less moved into Gabi's house in Sticklepath, but they need a bigger place, with a garden, for the babies. That's what they've taken to calling the dogs from the rescue centre in Ilfracombe they chose to rehome. Gabi was heartbroken when Scarlett reclaimed Sydney, so she decided to adopt a dog. Her heart broke a little bit more at the centre, so she and Joe ended up bringing home not one, but two pooches, both of indeterminate heritage and in urgent need of obedience training.

Gabi's podcast has been a huge hit and she's hopeful it will be shortlisted for a British Podcast Award. The last episode aired just a few weeks ago. She has never been so close to achieving her goal of moving to London and working for the BBC or ITV or even a major national paper. But now she's in a position to take the shot, she finds the goalposts have moved. She's happy, here, with Joe. She's also getting on much better with her mother, whose 'brush with death', as her mum describes her heart attack, seems to have made her more mellow. Gabi doesn't want to move away. Who in their right mind would want to leave North Devon? She hasn't travelled much, but this has to be one of the most beautiful places in the world.

Joe had tried to insist. 'You have to follow your dreams,' he'd said. 'You can't give up now. Not when you're so close. Listen, I'll come to London with you, if you want.'

He must really love her to even contemplate following her to the other side of the country considering what happened last time he relocated because of his girlfriend's job.

'I'm already living my dream,' she'd said. 'I can make podcasts anywhere. I can freelance, work from home a bit more and look after the babies. I can still aim to be a BBC or ITV correspondent – for the South West. Anyway, I couldn't leave my mum.' She chuckles. 'Or Mick, for that matter.'

So it was decided. They'd buy a house together, here, in North Devon.

'Blackmoor Manor is up for sale,' Joe comments now. They're both sitting on the sofa with their laptops on their knees, trawling through the websites of local estate agents. He whistles through his teeth. 'Wow! It's way over our budget.'

'Really?' Gabi leans towards him and peers at his screen. 'I'd have thought the history of that place would make it unsellable. Or at least decrease its value dramatically. Would you want to live in a house where someone was murdered?'

'Ah, but she wasn't murdered, was she?' Joe points out. 'Not officially. Matthew Walsh was found not guilty, remember?'

'Hmm. Would you, though, mind living in a house with that sort of history?'

'Well, as long as I was living with you, not the murderer, and the place wasn't haunted, I wouldn't rule it out.'

'What about a house where a body was found in the garden? Would that put you off?"

'No. I don't think so. Why? Is Rose Cottage on the market, too?'

'Oh, no. Not as far as I know. I was just wondering. Not exactly the right area for us anyway, is it?'

'No, somewhere between Barnstaple and Saunton Sands would be better.' Joe turns to Gabi. 'Why do you suppose Walsh sold Rose Cottage? He'd buried a body in the garden. Wasn't he afraid it might be found?'

'He told me he didn't want to sell it, but he didn't have a choice, financially.'

'But he could have sold Blackmoor Manor instead.'

Gabi shrugs. 'Blackmoor Manor was their home – Scarlett and Trixie's; it was near their schools. And Rose Cottage is tiny. Plus, I imagine from Matt's point of view, his wife's body was at Rose Cottage, but his memories of her were at Blackmoor Manor.'

'Maybe.' Joe sounds dubious. 'I think it was arrogant of him to think his secret would stay buried along with his wife's body once he sold his mother's home.'

'Hmm. But if the Martins hadn't decided to put in a kitchen extension, the body might never have been found. It's ironic he wound up selling both houses, isn't it?'

'Even more ironic that the solution to his financial problems was also buried in the grounds of Rose Garden.'

'The Roman coin. I know! Matt said the same thing, actually. The irony wasn't lost on him. Imagine if he'd found the coin when he was burying Leona. His story would have had a completely different ending. Ooh, look, there's a nice semi in Braunton.' Gabi angles her computer so Joe can see the screen better. 'Take a look at this.'

'It does look good,' he agrees. 'Mark it as favourite.'

Gabi clicks on the heart, then flips down the lid of her laptop and stands up. 'Speaking of Matthew Walsh …' she says.

'Time to go?' Joe asks.

'Yep. 'Fraid so.'

'Good luck.'

Against her better judgement, Gabi has finally given in. She hasn't seen Matt since the trial, three months ago, but in that time, he must have written her a dozen emails and letters, telling her about prison life, asking if she's seen Trixie or Scarlett, neither of whom has been to see him in jail, and begging Gabi to come and visit him. She feels sorry for him and he has finally worn her down. Plus, she's thinking about doing a feature on prison life.

After his trial, Matt was transferred to His Majesty's Prison Channings Wood, a Category C men's prison near Newton Abbot in South Devon. Gabi's car has finally given up the ghost, so she's borrowing Joe's wheels. She feels self-conscious in the bright orange car, but she's thankful for the satnav. It's an hour and a quarter's drive and she has no sense of direction whatsoever.

HMP Channings Wood is about two miles down a narrow road just outside the village of Denbury. Gabi parks in the visitors' car park and remembers to leave her mobile phone in the glove box. She takes her handbag with her and heads for the Visitors' Centre, outside the prison gates, where she has to show her ID and the Visiting Order, and fill in and sign a declaration form.

'Is it your first visit to HMP Channings Wood?' the receptionist asks. She has short, mousy hair and earrings that dangle almost to her shoulders.

'Yes,' Gabi says. She has a feeling it won't be her last.

The receptionist patiently takes her through what to expect, her earrings swinging hypnotically every time she moves her head. Gabi wonders how many times she has reeled off this speech. This might not even be her first time going through the instructions today – Gabi has arrived early, but there are already a handful of visitors waiting to see prisoners. When she has finished her spiel, the receptionist hands Gabi a card with a number on it.

Before she can enter the main visits room inside the prison itself, Gabi has to put her handbag in a locker. She is told to pocket the key. Then a female guard gives her a rub down search and asks her to stand still for the drugs dog. The Alsatian must smell Gabi's dogs on her clothes because it gets a little excited, but it eventually gives her the green light.

Gabi hands her card to a uniformed guard who points her to

the corresponding table in a large hall with about fifty identical tables, each with four plastic chairs – three grey and one blue. The blue one is for Matt. She takes a seat and scans the large room while she waits for him. The room is quiet for the moment, but more women have entered since Gabi came in. Her attention is drawn to a table in the corner, where a man wearing a prison uniform is sitting in the blue seat next to a young boy and opposite a woman and a girl. Their table is next to the play area. It must be hard for families when a member – in this case, the father – is in prison. Do Scarlett and Trixie find the idea of coming here too daunting? Or do they both blame their father for killing their mother?

Matt enters the visits room with a slight spring in his step and a broad smile on his face. She's surprised to see he's wearing jeans. She thought he'd be in a prison uniform, like the man in the corner. She stands up and he hugs her. She almost expects someone to tell them off, but it appears to be allowed.

'Would you like a tea or coffee?' she asks.

'Whatever you're having,' Matt replies. 'Apparently, they do good bacon baps if you're hungry.'

Minutes later, they're sitting opposite each other at their allocated table. Gabi sips her coffee while Matt tucks in to his bacon roll.

'I don't have much to complain about here,' Matt says, his mouth full, 'apart from the prison food. It's utterly gross.' He smiles sadly. 'Gross. That used to be one of Scarlett's words. I don't know if it still is.'

Gabi could have guessed the food wasn't good. Matt's as scrawny as the last time she saw him – in the dock at Exeter Law Courts.

'This, though' – Matt waves his roll at her – 'is every bit as delicious as everyone says.'

'Am I the first visitor you've had?' Gabi asks.

'Oh no. Adam has been a couple of times, although Roxanne

doesn't know. But he never has any cash on him.'

If Adam has to come here in secret, that might explain why Trixie has never visited Matt in prison. As a minor, she has to be accompanied by an adult. Scarlett has refused to come and perhaps Roxanne won't allow Trixie to visit. Funny how Roxanne never trusted her brother-in-law, but Adam always believed in Matt's innocence.

'So, what's it like in here?' Gabi asks. 'How are you managing?'

'It's not too bad. You should write an article about life inside.'

Gabi chuckles. 'That's what I was thinking,' she says. 'Great minds.'

'It's probably not quite what people on the outside imagine. I mean, there are a few violent prisoners and there's a bit of a drugs problem, which is no doubt the case in most UK prisons, but it's nowhere near as bad as I anticipated.'

Is that true? Or is Matt putting on a brave face?

'The guards are short-staffed,' he continues, 'but most of them are OK. I've worked my way up to enhanced prisoner status, so I've gained some privileges.'

'Oh?'

'Yeah. I can receive more visits – in theory. I also have a TV in my room. And I can spend more time outside my cell and wear my own clothes.' So that's why he's wearing jeans. 'As I told you in my emails and letters, I'm taking horticultural classes. I'm not at all green-fingered – Leona was the gardener – but, well …'

He breaks off. Gabi's mind fills in the part Matt has left unsaid with Rose's words, which come back to her. *Matthew has many talents, but gardening is not one of them.* The last time Matt did anything in the garden was probably when he dug a shallow grave at Rose Cottage to bury his wife. *He was doing the gardening, at night, in the winter.* Is that what's going through Matt's mind, too?

'It's a shame they don't let you cook,' Gabi says, remembering that was one of Matt's hobbies. She instantly cringes as an image of a kitchen knife bursts into her head.

'Oh, the sex offenders do the cooking,' Matt says.

Gabi doesn't know what to say to that.

'My writing mojo has come back,' Matt says, changing the subject. 'I'm writing my memoir. I have a lot of time on my hands in here, so I'm going to make the most of that.'

'That's a good idea,' Gabi says with as much enthusiasm as she can muster.

For a while, neither of them speaks. Their time isn't up, but Gabi wonders if she should get going.

'Listen, Matt,' she says. 'I'll offer to bring Trixie next time I come, if you like.'

Before Gabi can get to her feet, Matt sits up straighter in his chair and leans towards her, a strange glint in his eyes. 'Have you seen Trixie lately?' he asks.

'No, I haven't. I'm sorry. I've been meaning to pop in and see your mum, but I'm afraid I haven't got round to it. I can take Trixie with me when I go to the care home, too. Has she written to you?'

'Yes, she has. She sends emails.' Matt lowers his voice conspiratorially. 'I'm very worried about her, Gabi.'

Instinctively, Gabi leans across the table towards him, too. 'Why's that?' she asks.

'According to Adam, Roxanne is taking her to see a doctor – a shrink. He specialises in hypnosis, apparently. Can I ask you a favour, Gabi?'

'Yes, of course.'

'Could you please go and see Roxanne and talk her out of taking Trixie to see this … this quack.'

'What makes you think he's a quack? Have you considered it might be therapeutic for Trixie, Matt? She's had a hard time.'

Matt shakes his head emphatically. 'No. Your mind represses trauma for a reason.' The volume and pitch of his voice have both cranked up a notch. 'There are things that are best left forgotten, some memories that are better left blanked out.'

Gabi is suddenly on full alert. 'Memories of the night Leona died?'

Matt doesn't answer.

'You can tell me, Matt. It's over. You can tell me now.'

'I'm just worried about Trixie. That's all. Please?'

'You don't think that she might need—?'

'After that night, Trixie regressed, you know, went back to sucking her thumb. She also had night terrors and regularly wet the bed. That has all stopped. I'm not saying she's no longer messed up. I'm just anxious about someone poking at wounds that are still raw. She has a therapist – someone I trust – that she has been seeing for a while to help her with her difficulties. Don't get me wrong, I'm grateful that Roxanne is looking after my daughters. But I don't want her to interfere in this matter. Can you help me? Please?'

'Listen, I'll have a chat with Roxanne,' Gabi says. 'And I'll look out for Trixie.'

'She was too young to know ...' He lowers his head. His voice is almost inaudible, as if he's talking to himself.

Gabi hardly dares to breathe. Is he finally going to tell her the truth? Will she believe him if he does? She wants to shake it out of him, but waits. She reaches across the table and takes his hands in hers. How does that sentence finish? She was too young to know what was happening?

'What were you and Leona arguing about, Matt?' Gabi asks gently. She has always been convinced this is the key.

'Leona let Trixie watch things on TV that weren't suitable for her age. Sex, swearing, violence. She watched *Scream*, for Christ's sake. She was seven years old.'

'That's what you were arguing about?'

'No.'

'So what were you arguing about, Matt?' Gabi tries – and fails – to keep the impatience out of her voice. 'I know you remember.'

He sighs. 'It was because Leona hit ...'

'Because she hit you?'

'Not *me*.'

Gabi's not sure she's heard correctly. 'You mean she hit the girls? You said you could handle it as long as she never laid a finger on the girls. You said she'd never hit them.'

'That evening Trixie had bruises on her arms. She told me it wasn't the first time, but her mummy had always been very sorry afterwards. Leona had made Trixie promise not to tell me, but Trixie has never been good at lying.' He gives a tight smile. 'Not like her father.'

'Go on.'

'Trixie told me Leona had hit Scarlett, too. On several occasions. Beat her. I had no idea. Look, Gabi, you're the only person who knows Leona was violent towards me and now you're the only person, apart from Scarlett, Trixie and me, who knows she … abused the girls. You have to promise me.'

'I promise,' Gabi says. 'Matt, why didn't you say in court that Leona had been physically abusive towards you? It would have strengthened your argument for self-defence.'

Matt scoffs. 'I would never blemish Leona's memory like that. I had no proof anyway. And I didn't want my daughters to have to defend their father by bad-mouthing their mother.'

Gabi senses he's close to cracking. She needs to tread carefully. What is it that Matt doesn't want Trixie to remember? Did she see her father kill her mother? Is that it?

'Where was Trixie that night?' Gabi asks gently. 'Did she go to her bedroom, like you said?' The blood drains from Matt's face and she knows she has hit the nail on the head. 'Trixie was in the kitchen, wasn't she?'

'Yes,' he whispers.

'So she saw everything?'

For a long time, Matt says nothing. He doesn't move. He won't look Gabi in the eye. Then he releases his hands from hers and cradles his head, shaking it once, almost imperceptibly, from behind his fingers.

Gabi's mind goes into overdrive. Trixie witnessed everything, but she doesn't remember all of it. She has blanked out the most traumatic part – the stabbing. Very convenient for Matt. Unless …

With sudden clarity, as if she witnessed the scene that night herself, it comes to her. *She mustn't remember. She was too young to know …*

'She was too young to know what she was doing,' Gabi says aloud. 'Is that it, Matt? That's it, isn't it? Oh my God. Trixie's the one who stabbed Leona.'

For several seconds, Matt remains immobile, his face still hidden behind his hands. Then, with a sigh, he finally looks up and his eyes, glistening with tears, lock on to Gabi's. 'Please don't ever repeat that,' he says.

'I won't,' Gabi says, although she knows she'll share this with Joe. She can't keep something this big to herself.

Gabi sits in the car. She's shaking, her heart pummelling her ribcage. She wants more than anything else to get away from this place, but she doesn't trust herself to drive. Not just yet. She should try to think about something else, but the last few minutes of her conversation with Matt echo in her head, again and again, getting louder instead of softer. She can't quite process all this. She needs to work through it, see the full picture. She sifts through the details she has amassed over the past five years – from Matt himself, from his daughters and sister-in-law, from witnesses who saw or knew Leona, from the court case. She visualises what happened in the kitchen that fateful night, the scene playing out in front of her as if she's watching a film.

While Leona was out running with the dog, Matt spotted bruising on Trixie's arm. Trixie admitted that her mum had been physically abusing both her and Scarlett. Matt has just told her this. She can only imagine how livid Matt must have felt. He must have been spoiling for a fight, so as soon as Leona got home, they had a row. The row got out of hand. Perhaps Leona started to hit Matt, beating her fists against his chest and screaming at him. The din would have been unbearable to Trixie, who can't stand too much noise or commotion. Her instinct would probably have been to fly to her father's aid. Was it Trixie who grabbed the knife? Maybe. She might not even have registered what she was doing. She simply re-enacted a scene she'd seen in a horror film. She certainly didn't intend for things to end the way they did. Gabi feels sure she didn't see her mum die. Matt would have ordered her to go to her room at this point.

The next bit, Matt explained in court. Leona clung to him, begging him not to call for help, as she lay, dying, on the kitchen floor and he knelt by her side, holding her, until she took her last breath. Did Leona want to protect Trixie, too? Did she know it was too late for her, but not for her family? She loved her daughters, although she failed to show it when she lost her temper.

Matt covered up the incident. He admitted this in court, too. He pleaded guilty to preventing a lawful and decent burial. To shield his daughters – both of them. And to preserve his wife's reputation. What was left of it, in the immediate aftermath of the embezzlement scandal. And, more importantly, to preserve her memory. Their family unit. Team Walsh, as Matt liked to think of them. So he threw Leona's rucksack into the reservoir to make it look like she'd drowned; planted a red herring – the shoe – in the woodland around the lake in order to buy himself some time and muddy the waters, so to speak; reported his wife missing the following morning and then buried her body in the garden of his mother's cottage a few days later. And his story could almost have ended there, the investigation petering out as the nation skidded into lockdown, if only Leona's remains hadn't been discovered a few years later.

Matt could have taken the blame, claimed it was self-defence or an accident, but it was too risky. His wife's death looked suspicious. It looked like murder. Especially now they had a body.

And he would be the obvious suspect. If he'd gone to prison, he would have left his children without a father as well as without a mother. No doubt he intended to swear Trixie to secrecy, keep the whole thing between the two of them. It must have come as a massive relief when he realised she'd repressed the memory of the shocking climax to that evening. No wonder he doesn't want Trixie to see a hypnotist! He's trying to shelter her from the truth. It will be devastating for Trixie if the memory comes back to her. It could destroy her.

Gabi doesn't know how long she sits there, staring into space through the windscreen with blurred eyes, digesting what she has just found out. At last, she puts on some music – Dizzee Rascal, Joe's music is growing on her – and starts up the car. She's still in shock, but she feels strangely liberated as she drives away from HMP Channings Wood, as if she can finally turn the page and put this chapter of her life behind her.

Epilogue

April 2025

Gabi has been backwards and forwards on this with Joe, and she's still in two minds about it. She's no expert and from what she can see online, there's controversy between the experts themselves about the benefits and drawbacks of recovering repressed memories. Perhaps it's too soon for Trixie to try to remember what happened that night. On the other hand, maybe she needs to recall the events in order to process what happened. But the bottom line is that Matt is Trixie's father. It should be his call. Not Roxanne's. Gabi doesn't really want to get involved, but a promise is a promise. So she resolves to keep her word and try to discourage Roxanne from taking Trixie to see a hypnotist. Or at least make her think twice about it.

Gabi has been very busy with work and getting ready to move house – the offer they put in for the semi-detached house in Braunton was accepted – and it's a full month after her visit with Matt at HMP Channings Wood when Gabi drives out to Combe Cottage to pick up Trixie. They're going to see Rose at the care home. Roxanne opens the door before Gabi can knock and offers her tea. Gabi asks for coffee, but regrets it. It's instant and it tastes foul. She drinks it, though. She knows she's way too fussy about her coffee. Gabi takes a seat on a chair covered in cat hair and tells Roxanne a true story – one she reported on ages ago – about a young girl who had memory distortions under hypnosis. The girl 'remembered' being molested by her older brother, only to realise years later that these were in fact false memories. But not before it tore their whole family apart and the brother was sent to jail. Gabi has printed out the piece she wrote for Roxanne.

She also persuades Roxanne – with Adam's help – to allow her to take Trixie to HMP Channings Wood. Scarlett has recently scheduled a visit. She'll probably never know the whole story and perhaps she'll never believe in her dad's innocence, but at least she's willing to see him. That's a start.

Trixie is unusually talkative on the way to Swimbridge to see her grandmother. She has had her hair cut and unless Gabi's mistaken, she's wearing just a hint of make-up. Every now and then, out of the corner of her eye, Gabi sees her smile as she chats away.

Rose is delighted to see them. Gabi vows to come more often. Just as the last time they came here together, Trixie makes tea for Gabi and Rose, then helps her grandmother to drink hers.

'I-I've read your articles on the p-prison sit … situation,' Rose tells Gabi.

Gabi is hoping to talk to some of Matt's fellow inmates at HMP Channings Wood about life inside and is waiting for an answer to her request from the prison governor. In the meantime, she has published an article about rehabilitation. She found it interesting to compare the UK – notorious for its overcrowded and understaffed prisons – with the Netherlands and Norway, both of which have fewer prisons with fewer prisoners, better mental health treatment, less cell time for the inmates and lower recidivism rates. She was lucky enough to interview James Timpson, the UK Minister of State for Prisons, Probation and Reducing

Reoffending, in person, about the work he has been doing since his appointment.

Rose waits until Trixie goes to the loo to ask Gabi about Matt. Her speech seems clearer and less hesitant today. Or perhaps Gabi is getting used to it.

'He's doing OK, Rose,' Gabi says.

'Do you think I'll ... see him again?'

'Oh, yes. He'll be out in no time,' Gabi says. 'You'll see.'

Could she take Rose to see her son in prison? She'll ask the care home staff if it's possible and whether it's a good idea. It might be upsetting for Rose, or too strenuous. At the very least, Gabi could help Rose arrange a video call with him. She should have thought of that before.

'I l-loved my daughter-in-law, dear, but M-Matthew was too good for her,' Rose says, her tone conspiratorial. 'He d-doesn't deserve to pay for what happened.'

How much does Rose know? Did she follow the court case? Does she suspect Trixie's the one who killed Leona, not Matt? But Gabi doesn't want to ask her. It doesn't matter now what Rose does or doesn't know. Plus, Trixie will be back any second.

'It broke his heart, you know, w-when he found out,' Rose says.

'When he found out what, Rose?'

Rose points an unsteady finger at Gabi, as if accusing her of something. 'W-when he found out he was a c-cuck-old.'

Gabi's heart stops, then races. 'What did you say?'

'He con-confronted Leona. She d-didn't deny it. She promised to end the ... affair.'

'He knew Leona was cheating on him with Toby Wigmore?'

'Matthew d-didn't know his name,' Rose says. 'Not until the p-police told him.'

'When did he find out?' Gabi asks.

'Um ... a-bout a year ... before she d-died.'

Gabi can't quite get her head around this. Matt had known Leona was cheating on him all along?

'She ... p-promised to end it w-with her l-lover,' Rose continues, 'but I think Matthew knew she was still seeing him. You know, d-deep d-down. He p-pretended everything was O-OK. But he c-can't fool me. I'm his m-mother. He didn't want to lose Lee-Leona. So he t-turned a blind eye.'

Matt might not be able to fool his mother, but he certainly fooled everyone else.

'Or maybe he was ... wh-what's the expression? ... in d-denial. I think he wanted to b-believe she was being f-faithful again.'

'How did Matt – Matthew find out?' Gabi's voice has ratcheted up a notch. Rose recoils. She's pushing the elderly woman too hard. 'How did he find out, Rose?' she asks, forcing herself to speak softly.

'He overheard a ph-phone ...'

'Matt overheard Leona on the phone?'

Rose nods. 'I loved my d-daughter-in-law, b-but I will never forgive her f-for ... that. Matthew d-doesn't d-deserve to pay ... for what h-happened.'

'What do you mean by that, Rose?'

But before Rose can answer, they hear the toilet flush from Rose's en-suite bathroom and Trixie comes back into the room.

Gabi fixes a smile on her face, although it feels more like a rictus, and does her best to act as if she isn't reeling from the bombshell Rose has just delivered. But her head is spinning with thoughts and questions. Another lie. Why is she so shocked? Matt's incapable of telling the truth. A pathological liar. Does this change anything? So he pretended he didn't know Leona was cheating on him. It doesn't mean he killed her, does it? Only that he knew about the affair. It would have given him a motive if he'd admitted he knew.

As Trixie chatters away to her grandmother, Gabi ponders the conversation she had with Matt when she went to visit him in prison. He didn't actually say Trixie had killed Leona. Not in so many words. He just let her think it. He neither confirmed nor denied it. She was the one who made that assumption. He implied Trixie was influenced by the violence she'd seen on TV, in particular, the slasher film *Scream*. Or was that just what Gabi inferred?

But Matt would have to be a monster to let Gabi believe Trixie had killed Leona, if all along he was the one who had murdered his wife. And Gabi doesn't believe he's a monster. She knows Matt. Doesn't she? A liar, yes. A monster, no. And, as Joe said, a liar does not a murderer make.

'Gabi, shall we go and walk the babies?' Trixie's question snaps Gabi back to the present.

Rose raises an eyebrow.

'That's what she calls her dogs,' Trixie explains to her grandmother. 'Their real names are Snoopy and Scooby.'

It's true. They were already named when Gabi and Joe adopted them, their previous owners showing no more imagination than interest in their respective dogs.

'Good idea,' Gabi says. 'Let's go.'

Trixie smiles. Gabi has always been struck by how much she looks like Leona did at her age. But there's something mischievous in that smile and for the first time she can see a resemblance to Matt, too, a paler version of his deviousness in his daughter. Then it's gone. Blink and you miss it. Trixie's smile widens and Gabi is reminded of the ubiquitous photo of Leona, the one that was used in the media when she first went missing, that soon became etched permanently in everyone's minds. Leona with her white grin, coppery curls cascading to her shoulders and piercing green eyes looking straight at the camera. Trixie is still the spitting image of her mother. Beautiful, mesmerising. The picture of innocence.

Acknowledgements

While writing a novel can be quite a solitary process, publishing that novel is a team effort and I'm indebted to a number of people for getting my seventh psychological thriller out into the world. First and foremost, a massive thank you to my new editor, Kate Mills, for your invaluable feedback and insightful edits. I'm so happy to be working with you! I'd also like to thank the incredible team at HQ, in particular Lisa Milton, Rachael Nazarko and Anna Sikorska.

As ever, I'd like to thank my family: my husband, Florent, and our wonderful children, Benjamin, Amélie and Elise; my parents; my aunts, uncles, cousins, second cousins and in-laws in England, Scotland, Northern Ireland, Australia and France for reading my books and for your praise and support.

A huge thank you to my writing buddies: Sarah Clarke, author of *The Night She Dies*, and Louise Mangos, author of *Five Fatal Flaws*, for your friendship, help and advice every step of the writing process.

A massive thank you to my friends and fellow HQ authors Tina Orr Munro, author of the *CSI Ally Dymond* series, also set in North Devon, and to Neil Lancaster, author of the *DS Max Craigie* series, for helping me out with police procedure. Thank you, also, to fellow HQ author Nadine Matheson, author of the *Inspector Anjelica Henley* series, for your invaluable help with my courtroom chapters. Any mistakes in this book with police procedure or the justice system are mine and I hope my readers will allow me to put them down to artistic licence!

A big thank you to Lionel François, my French friend. You were a great help with the information and inspiration I needed for the police divers in this book. *Un grand merci à toi, Yo.*

Heartfelt thanks to Poppy and the team at Waterstones, Barnstaple, for your energy and support. Thanks to everyone in North Devon, especially my friends from West Buckland School. Your support for my books has been overwhelming.

Many thanks to everyone who has bought / borrowed / blogged about / read / recommended / reviewed / raved about my books.

A special mention for book bloggers Mark Fearn and Stu Cummins.

And, finally, thank YOU for reading this book. I hope you enjoyed it as much as I enjoyed writing it. If you did, please consider leaving an online review, choosing it for your book club or recommending it to a friend, or reading another of my novels.

I love hearing from readers, so please get in touch, or follow me on social media:

X: @dianefjeffrey

Instagram: @dianefjeffrey

Facebook: Diane Jeffrey Author

Alternatively, (or better still, additionally,) you can sign up to my newsletter via my website. I don't often send out newsletters, so I won't spam your inbox, but you will be the first to know about new releases and promos.

THANK YOU!

xxx

Gripped by *The Crime Writer*?
Don't miss *The Other Couple*...

**THEY RUINED YOUR LIFE.
IT'S TIME TO GET REVENGE.**

'Tense, twisty and unpredictable'
T.M. LOGAN

'Dark, gripping and suspenseful'
LESLEY KARA

DIANE JEFFREY

**Two couples. A fatal accident.
And a decision that changes everything...**

The Other Couple is out now!

The Guilty Mother

She says she's innocent.

DO YOU BELIEVE HER?

2013

Melissa Slade had it all: beauty, money, a successful husband and beautiful twin babies. But, in the blink of an eye, her perfect life became a nightmare – when she found herself on trial for the murder of her little girls.

PRESENT DAY

Jonathan Hunt covered the original Slade Babies case for the local newspaper. Now that new evidence has come to light, Jon's boss wants him back on the story to uncover the truth.

With Melissa's appeal date looming, time is running out. And, as Jon gets drawn deeper into a case he'd wanted to forget, he starts to question Melissa's guilt.

Is Melissa manipulating Jon or telling him the truth? Is she a murderer, or the victim of a miscarriage of justice?

And if Melissa Slade is innocent, what really happened to Ellie and Amber Slade?

Dear Reader,
We hope you enjoyed reading this book. If you did, we'd be so appreciative if you left a review. It really helps us and the author to bring more books like this to you.

Here at HQ Digital we are dedicated to publishing fiction that will keep you turning the pages into the early hours. Don't want to miss a thing? To find out more about our books, promotions, discover exclusive content and enter competitions you can keep in touch in the following ways:

JOIN OUR COMMUNITY:
Sign up to our new email newsletter: http://smarturl.it/SignUpHQ
Read our new blog www.hqstories.co.uk

https://twitter.com/HQStories
www.facebook.com/HQStories

BUDDING WRITER?
We're also looking for authors to join the HQ Digital family!
Find out more here:

https://www.hqstories.co.uk/want-to-write-for-us/

Thanks for reading, from the HQ Digital team

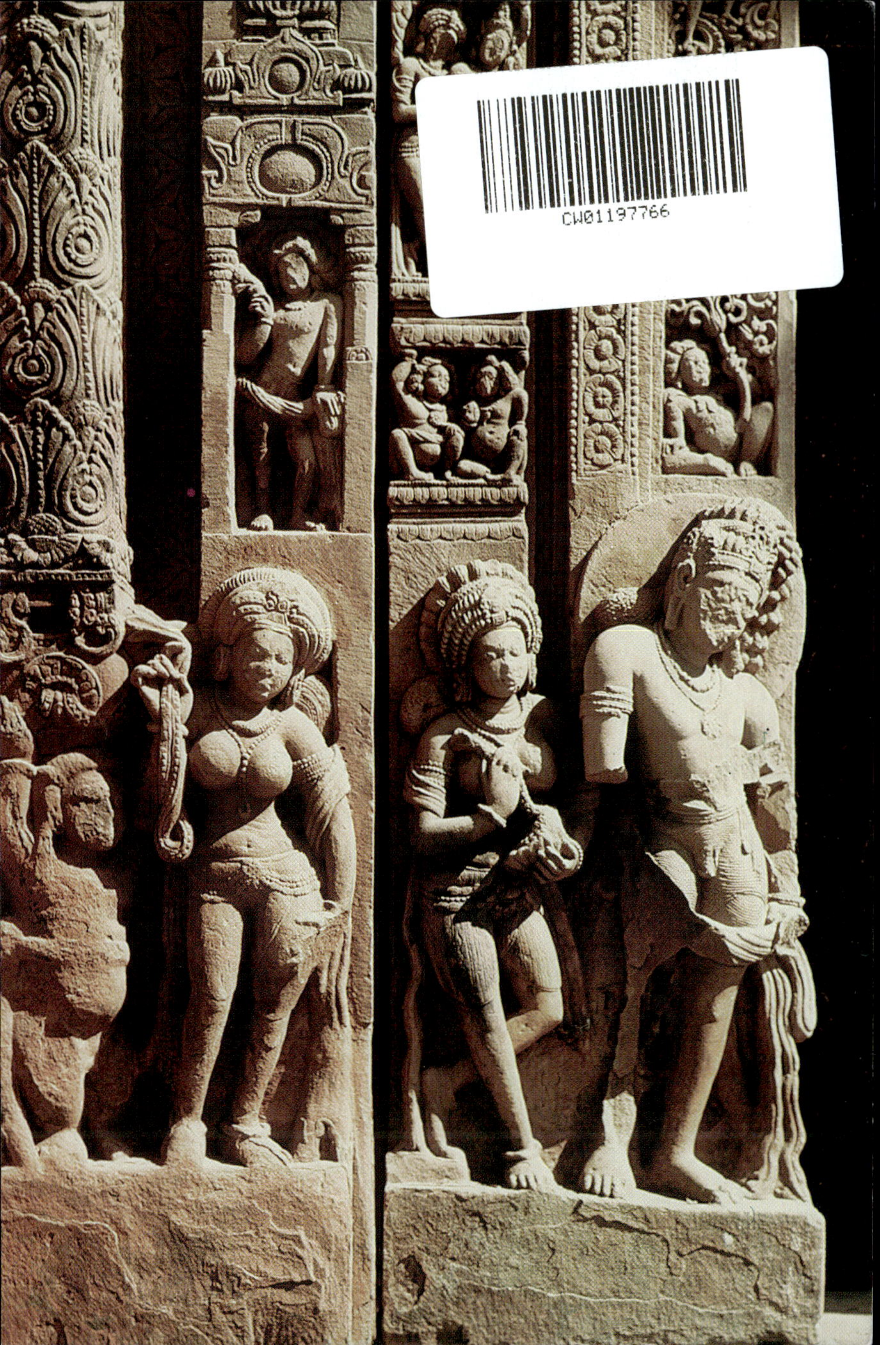

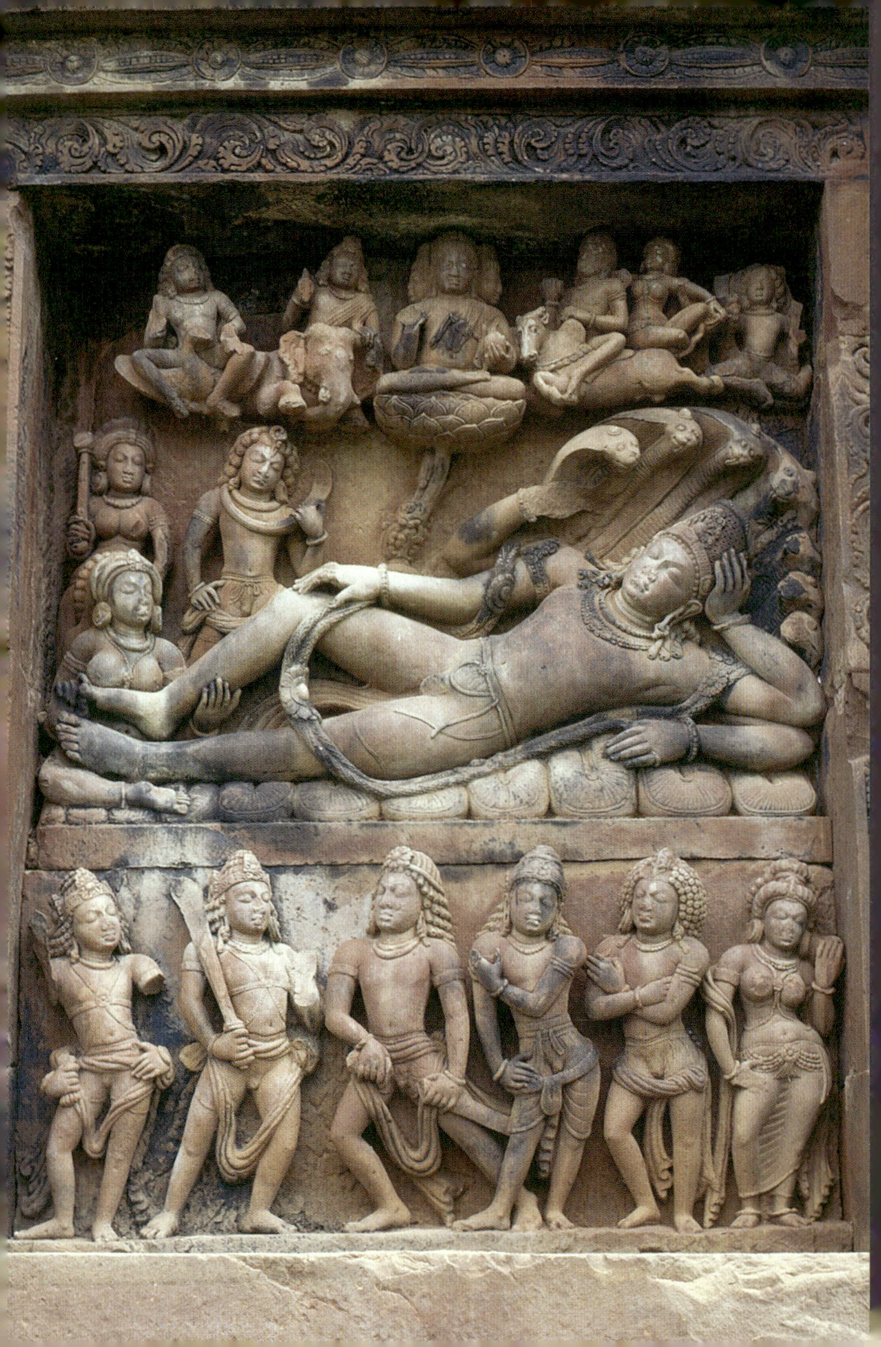

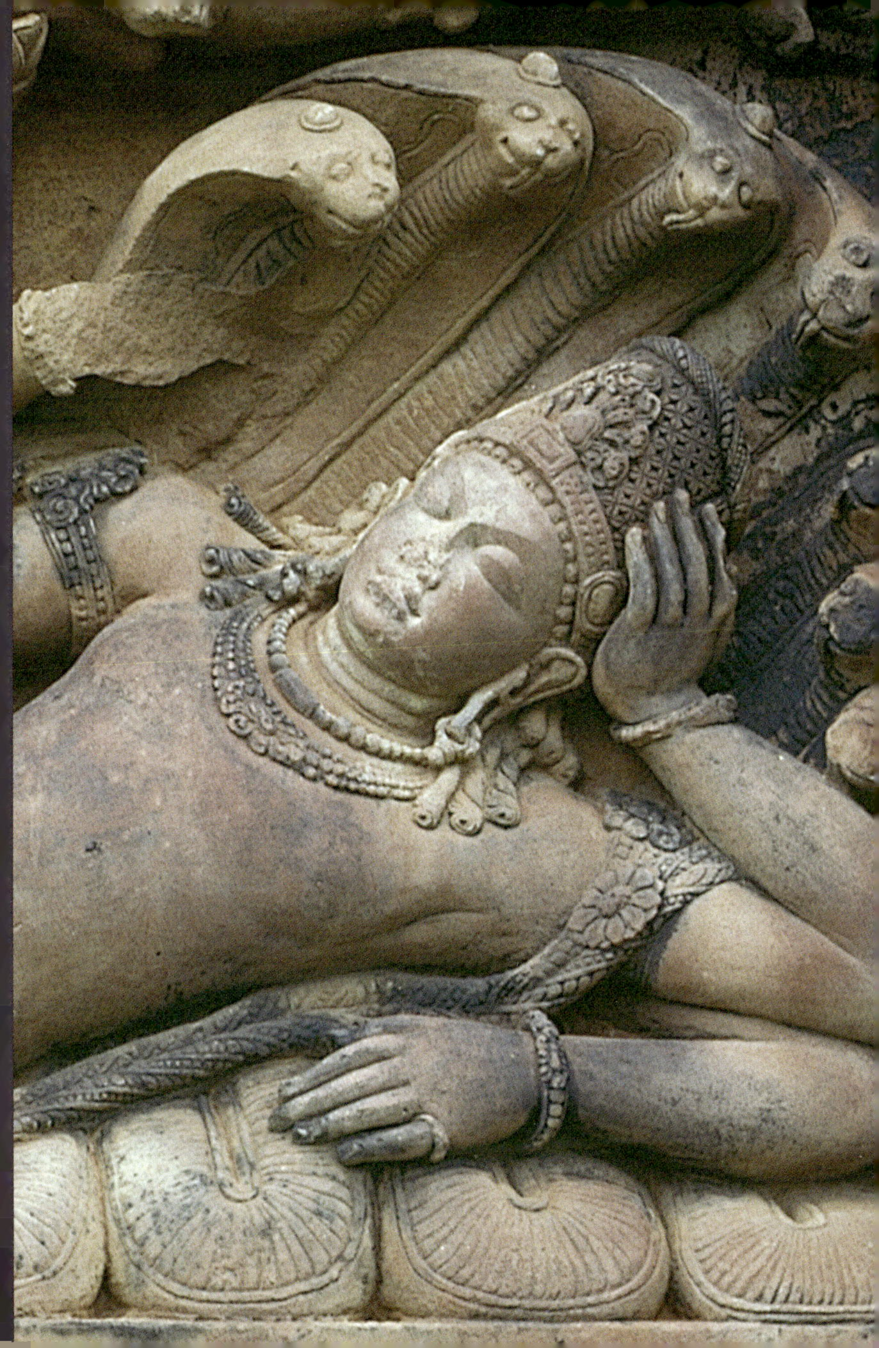

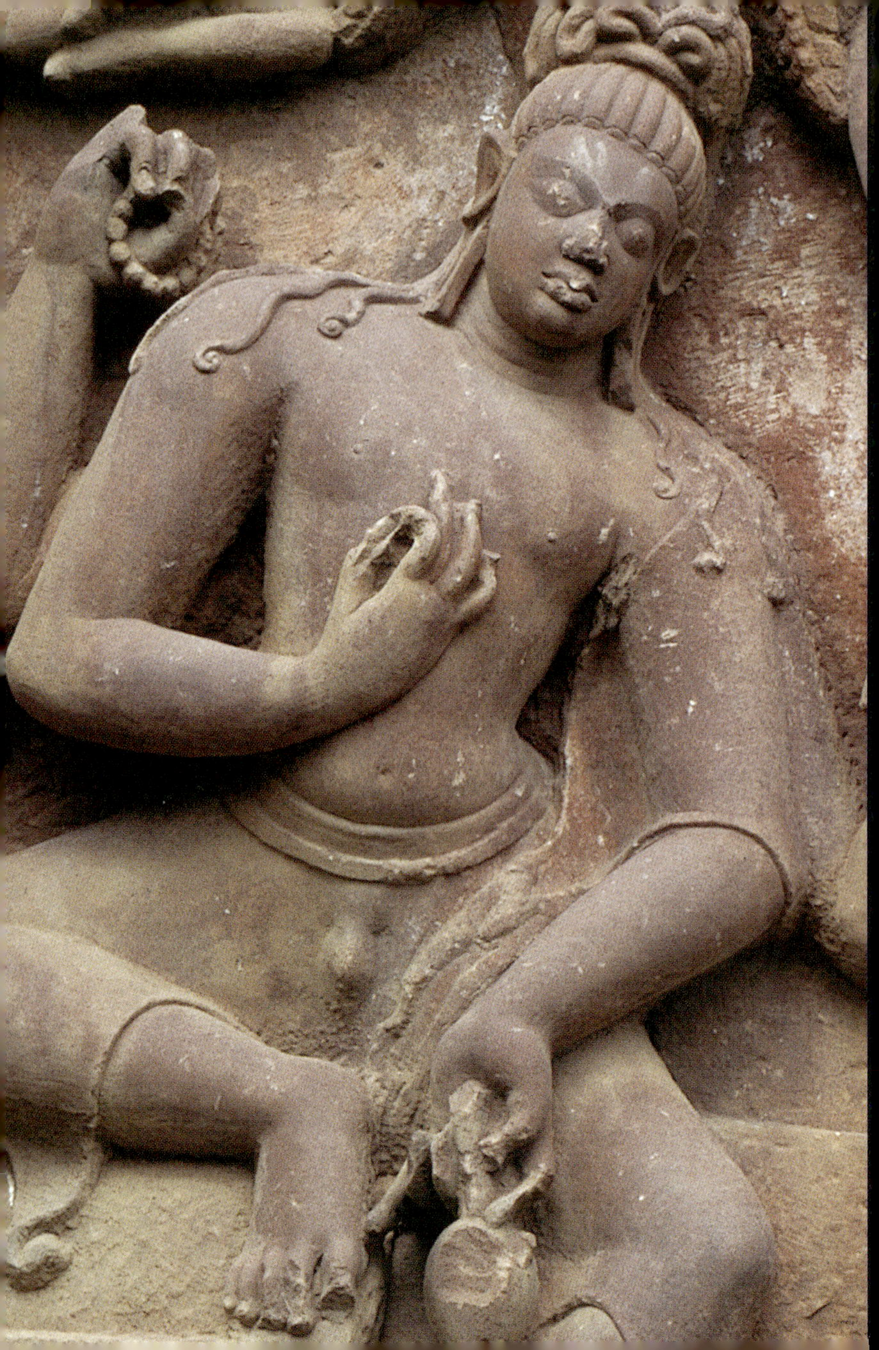

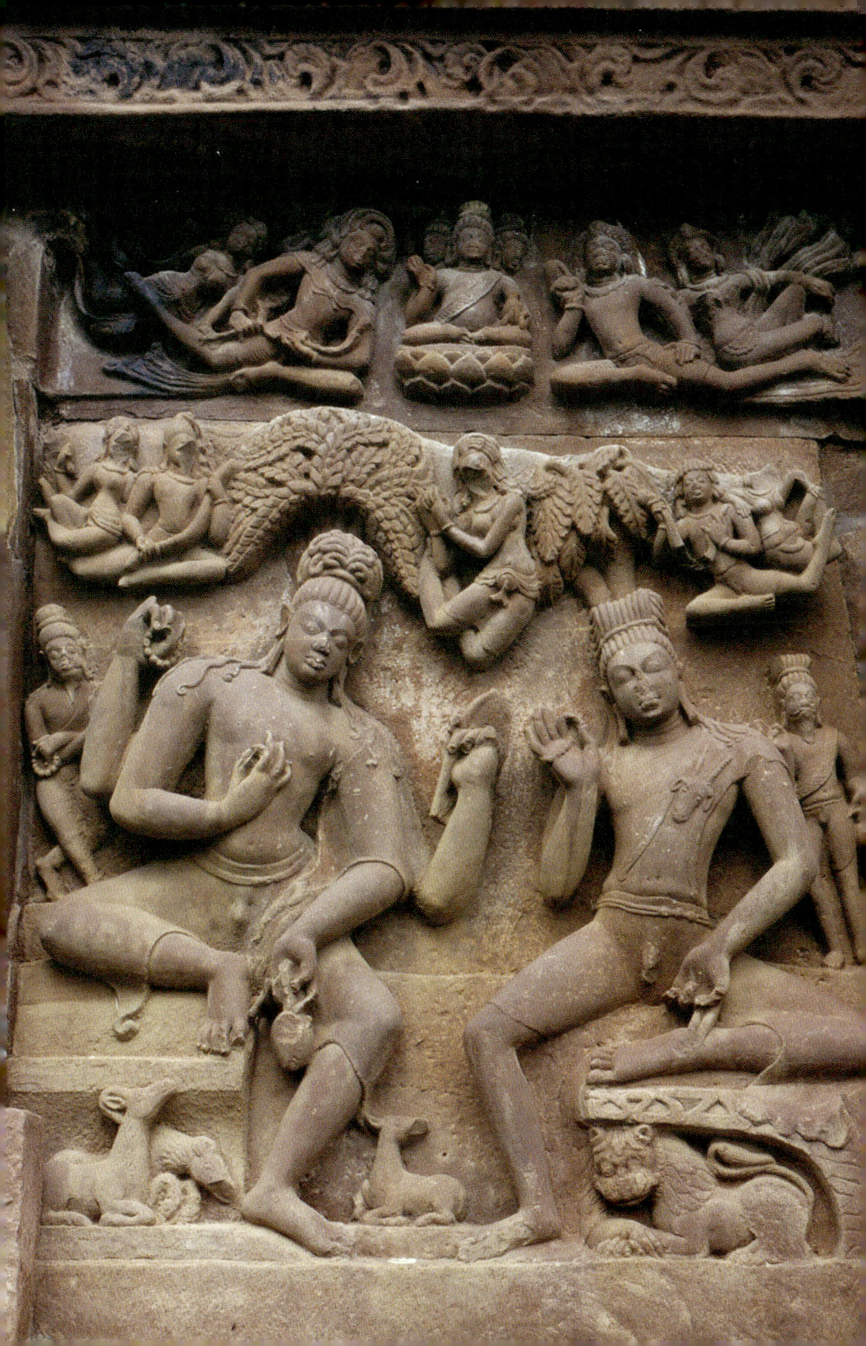

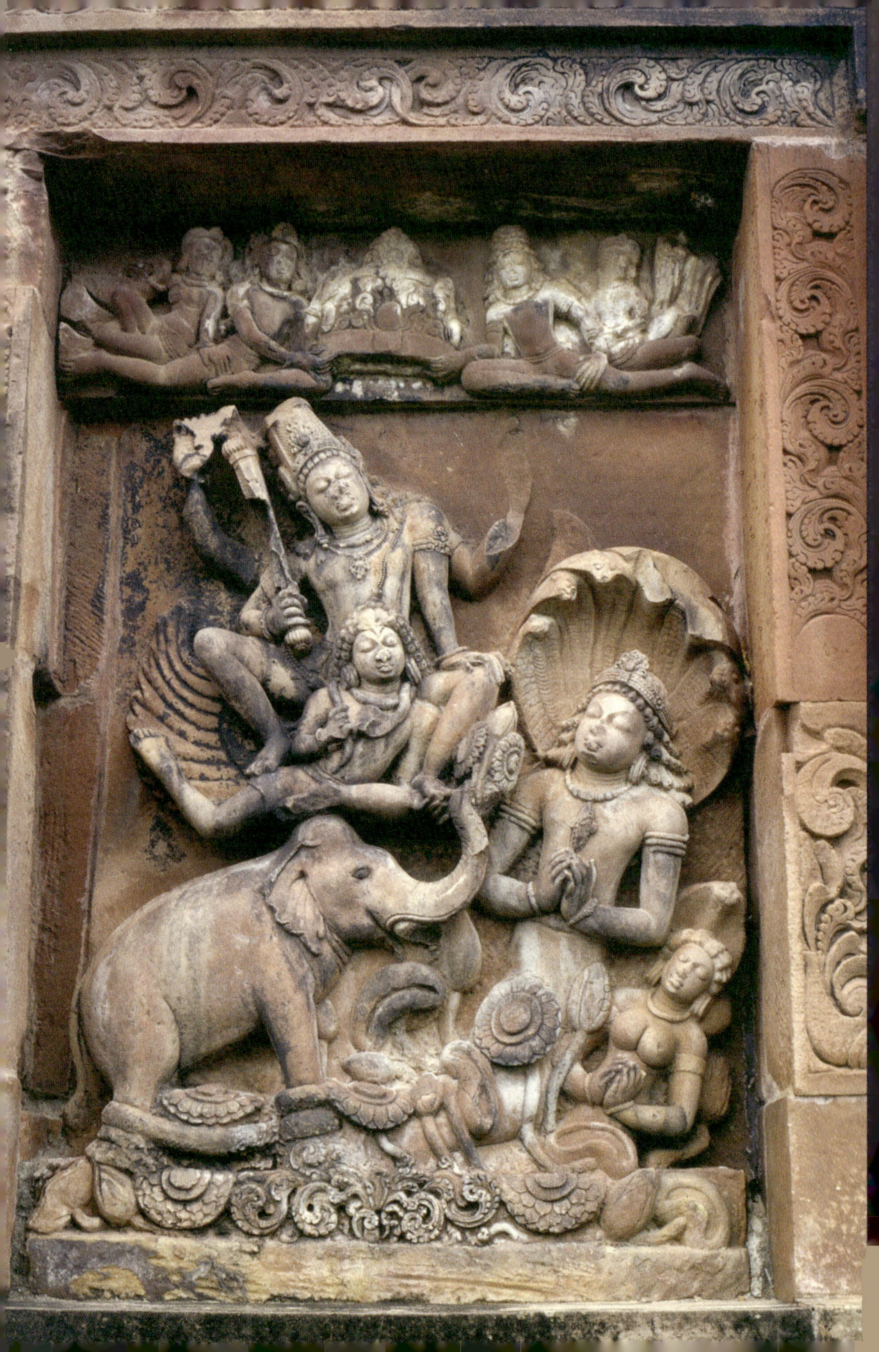

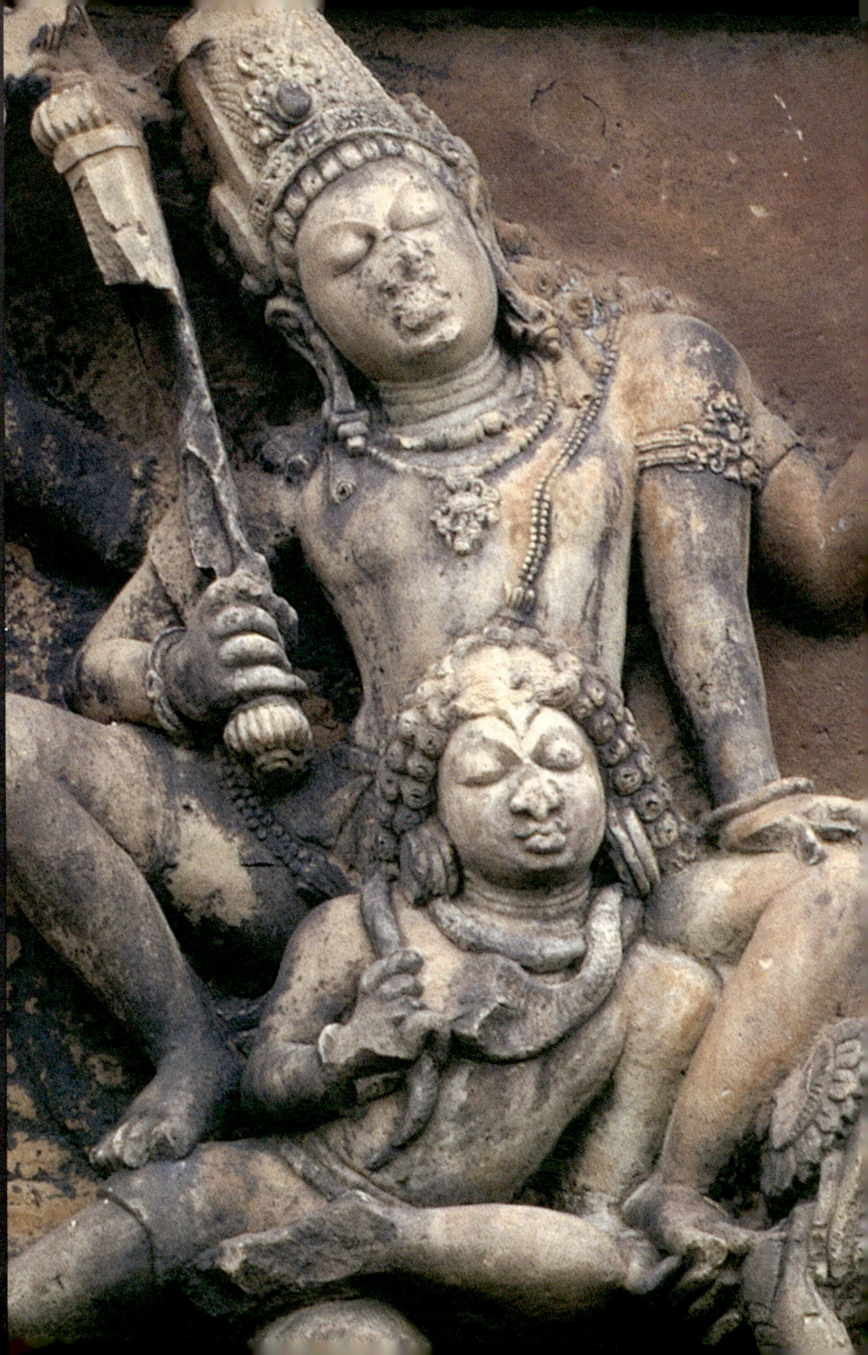

SOMMAIRE

10
Chapitre 1
L'INDE AVANT LES GUPTA
Les villes de l'Indus. Civilisation âryenne et védisme. L'émergence du jaïnisme et du bouddhisme. Alexandre le Grand aux portes de l'Orient. L'empire des Maurya.

28
Chapitre 2
DES KUSHÂNA AUX GRANDS GUPTA
Du Ier au IIIe siècle, les dynasties d'origine étrangères des Shaka et des Kushâna ; l'empire des Sâtavâhana. Du IVe au VIe siècle, la brillante dynastie des Gupta : Samudragupta et Chandragupta II.

42
Chapitre 3
UNE POLITIQUE DE TOLÉRANCE RELIGIEUSE
Des souverains d'obédience vishnuite. Les autres courants sectaires au sein du brahmanisme : shivaïsme, culte au dieu Soleil ou à la Grande Déesse. Le développement du bouddhisme et du jaïnisme.

58
Chapitre 4
BELLES-LETTRES ET CULTURE SAVANTE
Un rayonnement sans précédent de la langue et de la littérature sanskrites. Le développement des sciences : astronomie, médecine, mathématiques. L'épanouissement des belles-lettres : Kâlidâsa, chantre inégalé de cet âge d'or.

68
Chapitre 5
L'ART DE L'INDE CLASSIQUE
Un art religieux. Les temples et leur décor. La statuaire gupta. Mathurâ et Sârnâth. Apogée de la sculpture et de la peinture.

82
Chapitre 6
LE RAYONNEMENT DU CLASSICISME INDIEN
Une influence culturelle majeure. Les grottes d'Ajantâ. L'empreinte gupta en Asie.

97
Témoignages et documents
Échos d'un âge d'or ; Kâlidâsa et les lettres sanskrites ; L'engouement pour *Shakuntalâ* ; Ajantâ, un haut lieu de l'art indien ; L'art gupta et son rayonnement.

L'ÂGE D'OR
DE L'INDE CLASSIQUE

Amina Okada et Thierry Zéphir

DÉCOUVERTES GALLIMARD
RÉUNION DES MUSÉES NATIONAUX
HISTOIRE

10

Lors de la fondation du premier grand empire de son histoire vers 320 av. J.-C., l'Inde est déjà riche de millénaires d'évolution culturelle. De la civilisation de l'Indus à l'arrivée des Âryens, du ritualisme védique aux spéculations philosophiques des *Upanishad*, de l'émergence du bouddhisme et du jaïnisme à la conquête d'Alexandre le Grand, l'Inde antique se modèle au rythme des invasions et d'un bouillonnement intellectuel et spirituel incessant.

CHAPITRE 1

L'INDE AVANT LES GUPTA

Les antiques cités de la vallée du Gange ne sont plus connues que par certains bas-reliefs, (à gauche, les murailles de Râjagriha, détail du grand *stûpa* de Sânchî, début de l'ère chrétienne). Le chapiteau aux Lions de Sârnâth (IIIe siècle av. J.-C., ci-contre), vestige du pilier d'Ashoka, est le témoin de la gloire de cet empereur maurya et le plus grand chef-d'œuvre de la statuaire ancienne.

Du néolithique aux villes de l'Indus

Dès 7000 av. J.-C. le nord-ouest du sous-continent indien a été le théâtre de la révolution néolithique, ainsi que l'ont montré les fouilles de Mehrgârh au Bâlûchistan. Ce site, aujourd'hui détruit, a permis de suivre l'évolution d'une communauté villageoise, de sa sédentarisation à la veille de l'émergence des grandes cités de la civilisation de l'Indus, autour de 2500 av. J.-C. Jusqu'au début de leur lente extinction, dès 1900/1850 av. J.-C., ces villes, au premier rang desquelles figurent les sites de Mohenjo-Daro et Harappâ, ont été d'importants foyers culturels, disposant d'une écriture qui n'est pas encore déchiffrée à ce jour. Prospérant grâce à la maîtrise de techniques d'irrigation savantes, les cités de l'Indus étaient aussi de grands centres artisanaux où une partie non négligeable de la population vivait du commerce. Situées au sein d'un réseau de voies de communication très développé, elles avaient établi un système d'échanges avec des régions parfois fort éloignées du bassin de l'Indus et de ses affluents, depuis les

Les sceaux en stéatite découverts en grand nombre dans les villes de l'Indus sont souvent gravés d'animaux réels ou imaginaires, tel cet unicorne figuré derrière une sorte de brûle-parfum (ci-dessous). Leur empreinte se retrouve parfois sur des récipients en céramique, mais leur usage reste encore énigmatique.

L'INDE AVANT LES GUPTA 13

confins orientaux de l'Iran jusqu'à la région de Delhi (actuel Haryâna), d'est en ouest, et de l'antique Bactriane (nord-est de l'Afghanistan) à la presqu'île du Kâthiâwâr (actuel Gujarat), du nord au sud. La découverte d'objets harappéens dans certaines tombes royales d'Ur, en Mésopotamie, a permis d'assimiler la vaste zone d'influence de la civilisation urbaine de l'Indus avec le royaume de Meluhha dont parlent divers textes mésopotamiens et qui, par le golfe Persique, commerçait avec les villes des cours inférieurs du Tigre et de l'Euphrate.

La fin des grandes cités de l'Indus relève d'un ensemble de facteurs complexes : changements climatiques, crise économique et perte de certains débouchés commerciaux, notamment vers l'ouest. Ces problèmes s'accompagnent d'une notable modification du système agraire autour de 2000 av. J.-C. : au blé et à l'orge, connus depuis longtemps, viennent en effet s'ajouter le millet et surtout le riz, deux céréales plus caractéristiques des économies vivrières d'Asie du Sud que de celles du Proche-Orient, auxquelles se rattachait plus particulièrement l'agriculture indusienne. On observe alors une nette ouverture des régions nord-occidentales du sous-continent vers la moyenne vallée du Gange, à l'est, et vers le plateau du Deccan, au sud.

Les cités de l'Indus étaient construites en brique. La ville haute ou « citadelle » regroupait les édifices communautaires, tels le « grand bain », l'« entrepôt » ou le « collège sacerdotal » (page de gauche, Mohenjo-Daro). La population résidait principalement dans la ville basse (ci-contre), dont les rues étaient parcourues de canaux collecteurs permettant l'évacuation des eaux usées.

La statuaire de l'Indus présente des affinités stylistiques avec le monde sumérien, comme en témoigne le célèbre buste dit du *Roi-prêtre* (2400-2000 av. J.-C., ci-dessous).

La civilisation âryenne et le védisme

À l'échelle de la culture indienne, l'arrivée des Âryens (ou Ârya en sanskrit) s'est révélée de plus profonde et plus durable portée que les apports de la civilisation de l'Indus. Ces populations nomades, originaires des rivages de la mer Caspienne et des zones méridionales de l'Asie centrale, ont en effet joué un rôle fondateur dans maints domaines de la culture classique.

Arrivant par vagues successives dès avant le milieu du IIe millénaire av. J.-C., les Âryens se sont dotés d'un type d'organisation sociale dans lequel on a pu reconnaître un système préfigurant celui des castes. Au sommet de la hiérarchie, les *brâhmana* (prêtres) et les *kshatriya* (nobles guerriers) dominaient la société ; au-dessous, les *vaishya* (hommes du commun) composaient un ensemble dans lequel se recrutaient les éleveurs et les agriculteurs, mais aussi les commerçants et certains artisans. Ces trois groupes représentaient la société âryenne, claire de peau – d'où la désignation ultérieure des castes par le terme sanskrit *varna*, signifiant couleur –, par opposition aux populations locales, les Dâsa, de carnation plus sombre ; ces derniers, bientôt désignés sous le nom de *shûdra* (serfs), étaient au service des trois autres groupes et ne jouissaient apparemment d'aucun statut social particulier.

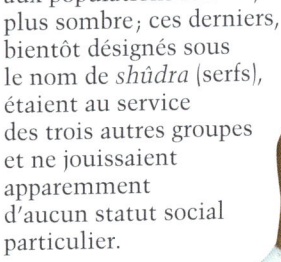

Le dieu Brahmâ possède quatre têtes censées avoir révélé les *Veda*. Personnification du *brahman*, il tient ici (à gauche) la cuiller servant aux oblations de beurre clarifié dans le feu sacrificiel, et (à droite) le livre symbolisant le Savoir. Les prêtres chargés des sacrifices sont issus de la caste des brahmanes (ci-dessous, assemblée de brahmanes).

Les Âryens parlaient une forme archaïque du sanskrit, cette langue « apprêtée ou formée » (selon les règles des grammairiens), appelée à devenir le vecteur par excellence de toute forme élevée de culture dans le monde indien ; plus important encore, ils disposaient d'une religion, le védisme, portant en germe de multiples aspects des spiritualités ultérieures de l'Inde, tout particulièrement l'hindouisme. Le *Veda*, littéralement le « Savoir », ce corpus de textes sacrés sur lequel se fonde la religion védique, s'est d'abord transmis oralement, avant d'être compilé à une date qui reste d'ailleurs indéterminée. Il se compose de quatre recueils (*samhitâ*) dont le plus important, le *Rigveda*, comprend 1 028 hymnes répartis en 10 livres. Les divinités auxquelles ces textes font référence représentaient des forces de la nature, tels l'orage, les vents, les eaux, le feu ; certaines plantes, comme le *soma*, la plante sacrificielle dont l'essence immortelle se manifestait au cours des opérations de pressurage qui participaient de nombre de rituels ; le soleil ; la lune ; ou encore des concepts abstraits comme le contrat unissant les hommes aux dieux et par quoi l'Univers se développe harmonieusement.

À la suite du *Veda*, d'autres textes, commentant et précisant certains points des *samhitâ*, introduisent des notions spirituelles d'importance : la croyance en la réincarnation des âmes (*samsâra*) se fait jour dans les *Brâhmana* (à partir de 1000 av. J.-C.),

Près de deux cents hymnes védiques sont consacrés à Agni, le Feu, vénéré sous ses diverses formes, notamment le Feu sacrificiel, porteur de l'oblation aux dieux et « messager » entre le ciel et la terre. Ses cheveux sont de flammes, ses langues ardentes et son sillage de cendres (ci-dessus, sculpture du dieu avec sa monture, datant du XIe siècle et située dans le temple de Râjarânî à Bhubaneshvar).

et plus pleinement dans les *Upanishad* (à partir des VIIe-VIe siècles av. J.-C.), où apparaît également la notion de *karman* : la sujétion aux actes et à leurs conséquences. Ce *karman* détermine notamment le cheminement de l'âme individuelle d'un être (*âtman*) au cours de sa progression vers le salut (*moksha*) où elle s'unit à l'âme universelle du créateur (*brahman*), dont elle n'est qu'une parcelle.

L'émergence des spéculations métaphysiques propres aux *Upanishad* et la mise en forme d'une mythologie dans laquelle les grands dieux védiques s'effacent peu à peu devant des divinités tels Shiva, Vishnu ou Devî, qui détermineront bientôt les courants majeurs de la pensée religieuse classique, marquent le passage du védisme proprement dit au brahmanisme ou hindouisme. Les épopées du *Mahâbhârata* et du *Râmâyana*, sans doute élaborées sur de longs siècles, procèdent également des importants changements survenus dans la spiritualité indienne au cours de la seconde moitié du Ier millénaire av. J.-C.

Sur le champ de bataille du Kurukshetra, les Pândava affrontèrent leurs rivaux, les Kaurava, au cours d'une bataille titanesque qui fit rage durant dix-huit jours et s'acheva par la victoire chèrement acquise des Pândava. D'innombrables combats singuliers (ci-dessus, sur une miniature du XIXe siècle) jalonnent la grande épopée du *Mahâbhârata*, dont la composition est attribuée à l'ascète mythique Vyâsa.

Poèmes épiques et réalité historique

Selon certains historiens, les guerres du *Mahâbhârata* (ou *Grande Geste des Bhâratides*, entendons des habitants de l'Inde) – le plus long poème épique de la littérature universelle, probablement compilé entre le IVe siècle av. J.-C. et le IVe siècle apr. J.-C. – pourraient revêtir un caractère historique et refléter certains événements survenus au cours de la période védique tardive, dans la première moitié du Ier millénaire av. J.-C. L'archéologie tend à confirmer une telle interprétation ; divers sites mentionnés dans l'Épopée, en effet, ont livré une poterie grise à motifs peints en noir caractéristique de cette époque. Le *Mahâbhârata* a pour sujet l'affrontement de deux clans cousins mais néanmoins ennemis, les Pândava et les Kaurava. Les premiers règnent à Indraprastha, l'actuelle Delhi, les seconds, à Hastinâpura, à une centaine de kilomètres plus au nord. Au terme d'une partie de dés, les cinq frères Pândava perdent leur royaume au profit de leurs rivaux. Exilés pour une période de douze ans, ils errent dans les forêts pour finalement revenir chez eux et reconquérir leur pouvoir. Dans le combat qui les oppose aux Kaurava, les Pândava reçoivent l'aide de Krishna, le « Noir », héros divin perçu ultérieurement comme un aspect du dieu Vishnu. L'Épopée évoquerait ici un changement d'ordre social où, à l'âryanité pure des débuts de l'époque védique succéderait une âryanité mixte prenant mieux en compte les populations locales.

Poème mystique inséré dans le *Mahâbhârata*, la *Bhagavad-Gîtâ* ou « Chant du Bienheureux » est conçue comme un dialogue entre Arjuna, l'un des Pândava, et son conducteur de char, Krishna. Exhortant au courage et au combat le guerrier qui se sent défaillir à l'idée de mettre à mort des ennemis issus de sa propre race, le divin Krishna (à droite sur l'image) choisit alors de dévoiler à Arjuna émerveillé sa forme cosmique – infinie, incommensurable, immanente et omnisciente –, dans laquelle est inclus l'ensemble de la création.

Le triomphe des Pândava représenterait celui d'une coalition d'Âryens et de tribus autochtones dont Krishna, régnant sur un royaume méridional par rapport à ceux des belligérants et, surtout, de couleur sombre, serait l'expression métaphorique. Si cette interprétation n'est pas retenue par tous, elle offre néanmoins divers points d'ancrage de la somme culturelle considérable que représente le *Mahâbhârata* dans l'époque censée l'avoir vu naître.

L'émergence de nouvelles religions : jaïnisme et bouddhisme

En réaction à la domination sociale exercée par les brahmanes, seuls détenteurs des clefs des rituels extrêmement complexes qui régissaient la vie religieuse de l'époque védique, divers mouvements de pensée, au premier rang desquels figurent le jaïnisme et le bouddhisme, apparaissent autour du Ve siècle av. J.-C. La doctrine jaïne s'est développée sur des bases morales très strictes prônant la non-violence (*ahimsâ*) et un mode de vie ascétique poussé à l'extrême. Vers le Ier siècle av. J.-C., ce courant de pensée, dans lequel le salut consiste à laver son âme du *karman* par la pénitence afin d'échapper à la transmigration, se scinde en deux groupes : les Digambara (ceux qui sont « vêtus d'espace », ils ne portent donc aucun vêtement) et les Shvetâmbara (ceux qui sont « vêtus de blanc »).
Le bouddhisme prône également la non-violence, mais avec une rigueur moindre ; le salut consiste de même à se libérer

Les tîrthankara, – « faiseurs de gué » – jaïns sont souvent figurés debout et figés dans une nudité absolue. Cette posture dite de l'« abandon du corps » (*kâyotsarga*) traduit un parfait détachement et une intense méditation, comme le montre ce bronze du début du IVe siècle représentant Rishabhanâtha ou Adinâtha, premier des vingt-quatre tîrthankara (à gauche). Les dates de Vardhamâna (également appelé Mahâvîra, le « Grand Héros »), le fondateur historique du jaïnisme, comme d'ailleurs celles du Buddha, fondateur du bouddhisme, restent l'objet de nombreuses incertitudes. Vardhamâna serait mort à la fin du VIe siècle av. J.-C., à l'âge de 72 ans. Le Buddha – « l'Éveillé » – serait mort à 80 ans en 544-543 av. J.-C. selon le comput des bouddhistes cinghalais. Pour les scientifiques, cette date est erronée. Un consensus s'était établi autour de 484-483, mais de récentes recherches tendent à considérer une date autour de 400 comme plus vraisemblable.

Dans l'iconographie bouddhique ancienne, le Buddha n'est pas représenté concrètement. Lors de sa naissance, le nouveau-né est censé se trouver sur le lange tenu par les dieux, au centre du panneau (ci-contre, dans l'art d'Amarâvatî, au IIe siècle). En Inde du Nord, l'image du Buddha apparaît au Ier siècle, dans les écoles du Gandhâra (ci-dessous) et de Mathurâ.

du cycle infernal des réincarnations qui enchaînent l'âme dans la souffrance. Les trois principales formes du bouddhisme – le theravâda (« opinion des anciens »), également appelé hînayâna, ou bouddhisme du petit véhicule, le mahâyâna, ou bouddhisme du grand véhicule, et le vajrayâna, ou bouddhisme du véhicule de diamant –, en principe nullement exclusives l'une de l'autre, sont apparues au fil de l'histoire indienne pour se développer plus encore, en dehors de cette histoire, dans l'ensemble de l'Asie.

L'Occident aux portes de l'Orient

La région de l'Indus, frontalière de la Perse ancienne, est soumise par le grand roi Cyrus à la fin du VIe siècle av. J.-C. L'établissement de satrapies achéménides et, bientôt, l'épopée militaire d'Alexandre le Grand (356-323 av. J.-C.) ont joué un rôle considérable dans l'apparition d'une véritable conscience politique au sein des différents royaumes gangétiques. L'un des plus importants, le royaume de Magadha, correspondant plus ou moins aux régions centrales et méridionales de l'actuel État du Bihâr, allait être le berceau de l'extraordinaire Empire maurya.

La puissance du Magadha, dont la capitale était la ville de Râjagriha (moderne Râjgir), trouve son origine durant le règne de quelque cinquante ans du roi Bimbisâra, cinquième des dix rois de la dynastie des Shaishunâga, au tournant des VIe et Ve siècles av. J.-C. Ces dates, si l'on s'en tient à la chronologie traditionnelle, font du monarque un contemporain du Buddha et de Vardhamâna. Bimbisâra se serait d'ailleurs converti au bouddhisme et, après une vie de conquêtes brillantes, aurait trouvé une mort misérable, emprisonné par son propre fils Ajâtashatru. Sous la conduite de ce dernier, le Magadha entre en guerre contre les puissants clans confédérés des Vriji et le royaume de Koshala, tous situés dans le nord du Bihâr. Au cours de ces conflits, un ministre du roi Ajâtashatru, Varshakara, fait édifier un fort à Pâtaligrâma, la future Pâtaliputra (moderne Patna), appelée à un brillant avenir, notamment à l'époque maurya. Dès lors, l'hégémonie du Magadha ne cesse de croître.

En mai 327 av. J.-C., Alexandre le Grand traverse avec sa formidable armée les passes montagneuses de l'Hindû Kûch, en Afghanistan oriental, pour parachever sa conquête de l'empire achéménide et avec l'espoir de repousser ses frontières plus loin vers l'est que ne l'avait fait Cyrus le Grand. Débute alors une campagne militaire (327-325 av. J.-C.) particulièrement riche en péripéties, dont les sources grecques font état avec force détails alors qu'elle est à peine mentionnée dans les sources indiennes.

En février 326, Alexandre franchit l'Indus et parvient bientôt à Takshashilâ (Taxilâ), dont le roi lui est tout acquis. Lorsqu'il atteint l'Hydaspès (actuel Jelham), la résistance se fait plus farouche :

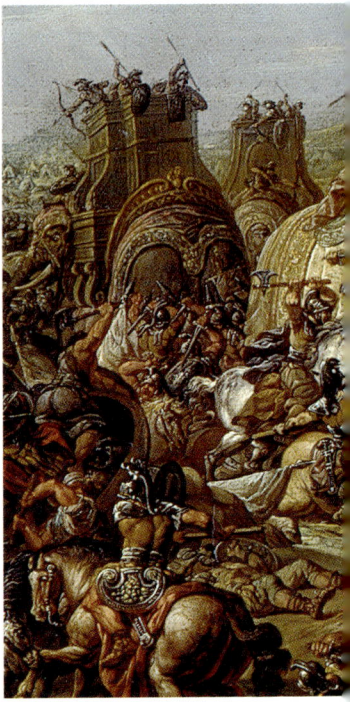

"Les éléphants étaient maintenant pris dans un espace étroit, et ils créaient autant de ravages dans leur propre camp que dans le camp ennemi, piétinant tout dans leurs volte-face et leurs charges. La cavalerie indienne, bloquée autour d'eux, fut massacrée. La plupart des cornacs avaient été tués à coup de javelots, et les éléphants [...] ne pouvaient plus être maintenus à leur poste de bataille.**"**

Arrien, *Anabase*, livre V

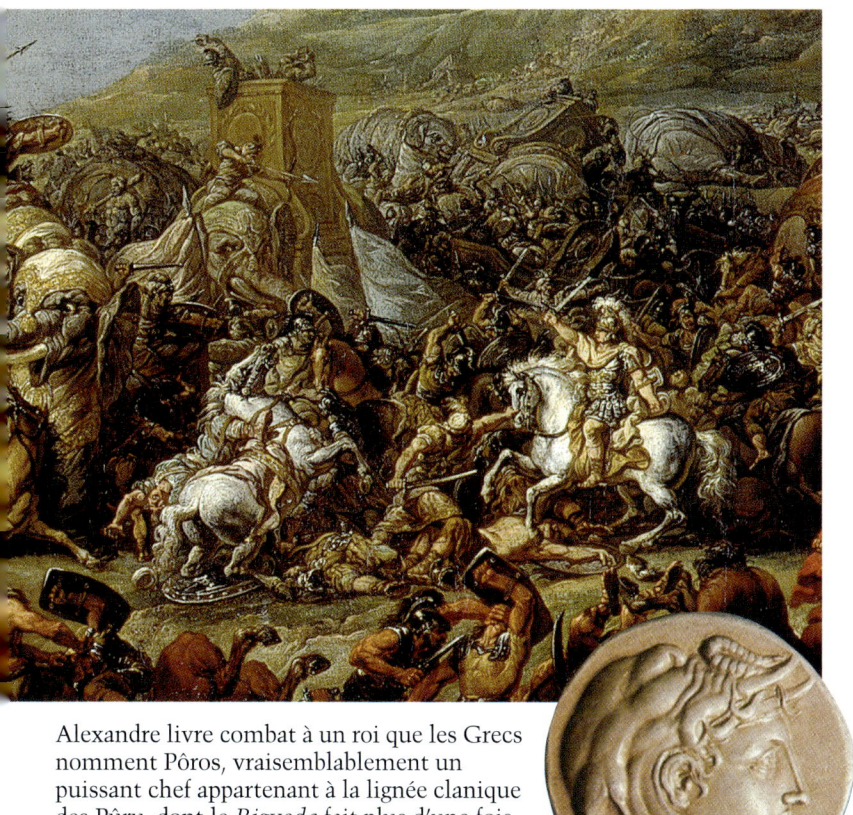

Alexandre livre combat à un roi que les Grecs nomment Pôros, vraisemblablement un puissant chef appartenant à la lignée clanique des Pûru, dont le *Rigveda* fait plus d'une fois mention. Les Macédoniens sortent vainqueurs de la bataille et, plutôt que de mettre à mort son courageux adversaire, Alexandre lui fait grâce et le maintient sur son trône pour mieux s'assurer de sa loyauté dans la suite de la conquête. Cette dernière s'avère particulièrement difficile, et se révélera même impossible, en raison de la résistance d'un roi puissant, Sandrakottos, dont on ne sait avec précision s'il s'agit du dernier souverain de la lignée des Nanda, éphémère mais puissante dynastie de l'Inde septentrionale (fin V^e- IVe siècle av. J.-C.), ou du fondateur de l'Empire maurya, le célèbre Chandragupta.

Après sa victoire sur l'Indien Pôros (ci-dessus, à gauche), certaines monnaies grecques montrent Alexandre le Grand coiffé d'une dépouille d'éléphant (ci-dessus), à l'instar d'Héraclès arborant la dépouille du lion de Némée.

La première Inde : l'empire des Maurya

Les débuts de la carrière de Chandragupta, tout comme ses origines, sont obscurs. On retient traditionnellement la date de 320 av. J.-C. pour son accession au trône du royaume de Magadha. Avant cela, il participe, semble-t-il, à la résistance indienne lors des ultimes combats contre les Grecs, peu de temps avant le retrait des généraux d'Alexandre restés sur place après son retour en Perse, à la fin de l'année 325 av. J.-C. Les sources grecques et romaines laissent entendre que son action est décisive lorsque, vers 312 av. J.-C., Séleucos Nikatôr, l'un des généraux

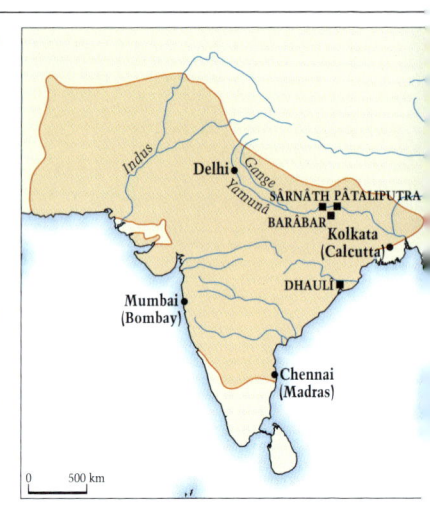

Débordant sur les actuels Pakistan et Afghanistan, l'Empire maurya couvrait la quasi-totalité de l'Inde. Seul l'extrême sud a été tenu à l'écart des conquêtes de Chandragupta et de son illustre successeur, Ashoka.

La tradition architecturale indienne s'oriente dès l'origine dans deux voies distinctes : l'architecture construite, dont rien ne nous est parvenu pour les époques reculées, et l'architecture excavée, dont divers exemples anciens survivent. Les grottes de Barâbar (ci-contre, la façade de la grotte de Lomas Rishi) ont été offertes par les Maurya à la secte des Âjîvika, aujourd'hui disparue.

L'INDE AVANT LES GUPTA 23

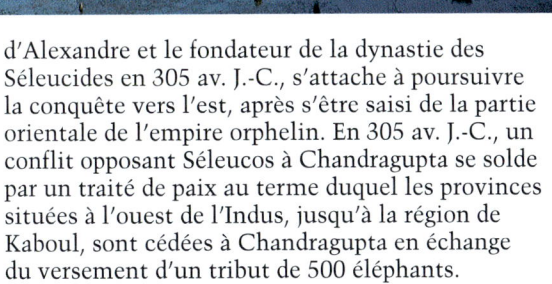

d'Alexandre et le fondateur de la dynastie des
Séleucides en 305 av. J.-C., s'attache à poursuivre
la conquête vers l'est, après s'être saisi de la partie
orientale de l'empire orphelin. En 305 av. J.-C., un
conflit opposant Séleucos à Chandragupta se solde
par un traité de paix au terme duquel les provinces
situées à l'ouest de l'Indus, jusqu'à la région de
Kaboul, sont cédées à Chandragupta en échange
du versement d'un tribut de 500 éléphants.

Une grande partie des connaissances de l'Occident
sur l'Inde de ce temps repose sur le
témoignage de Mégasthène, l'ambassadeur
de Séleucos à la cour maurya de Pâtaliputra,
alors capitale de l'immense empire sur
lequel régnait Chandragupta. Bien que
l'original du rapport de Mégasthène soit
perdu, divers historiens en citent de
longs passages dans lesquels la richesse
et la puissance de l'empire apparaissent
sans équivoque. La capitale était une
vaste et opulente cité fortifiée,
et la société, fortement hiérarchisée,
vivait sous la férule du monarque
et de son administration, laquelle incluait
une armée de métier entretenue

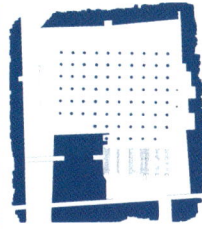

De la splendide
Pâtaliputra rien ne
demeure aujourd'hui.
La salle hypostyle de
Kumrahâr, un faubourg
de l'actuelle Patna,
est le seul ensemble
qui puisse être mis en
rapport avec la capitale
maurya (ci-contre,
le site; ci-dessus, le
plan). Ses 80 colonnes
d'environ 10 m de haut
étaient en grès poli,
selon une technique
héritée de la Perse
achéménide. Leur
agencement en rangées
régulières évoque les
salles d'audience de
Persépolis. Cette tête
d'homme (ci-dessous)
est l'un des rares
exemples de la statuaire
raffinée des Maurya.

par l'État et un corps d'informateurs essentiels à son bon fonctionnement.

Les sources indiennes, notamment l'*Arthashâstra* («*Science des intérêts*»), ce célèbre traité de politique dû au principal ministre de Chandragupta, le brahmane Kautilya, s'accordent bien avec le témoignage de Mégasthène, qui donne de l'Inde maurya l'image d'un État très centralisé dans lequel la prospérité du souverain et de son royaume dépend de l'interventionnisme accusé de l'administration, dont l'efficacité repose sur les qualités propres du monarque et de ses ministres, la richesse, la force militaire et la pertinence des alliances politiques. Selon certains textes jaïns, Chandragupta, dont toutes les sources s'accordent à dire qu'il a régné 24 ans, aurait fini sa vie vers 296 av. J.-C., en se laissant périr de faim, selon la forme d'accomplissement suprême du saint homme prescrite par la tradition jaïne.

Ashoka, le « Bien-aimé des dieux »

On sait peu de chose du règne du fils de Chandragupta, Bindusâra qui, selon toute vraisemblance, maintient l'empire dans sa prospérité pendant un règne de 25 ou 28 ans. À sa mort, deux de ses enfants, Sumana et Ashoka, se disputent le pouvoir ; le second l'emporte

Couronnée d'un chapiteau campaniforme surmonté d'un lion, la colonne de Lauriyâ Nandangarh (Bihâr) porte, gravés sur son fût de grès poli, six édits d'Ashoka. Inscrits sur le roc ou sur de hautes colonnes commémoratives (*lât*), ces textes fournissent de précieux renseignements sur le règne et le mode de gouvernement du grand empereur.

L'INDE AVANT LES GUPTA 25

en faisant assassiner son frère. Malgré cela et en dépit des conquêtes sanglantes auxquelles il s'est livré par la suite, Ashoka reste dans l'histoire indienne l'archétype du monarque vertueux et magnanime, celui que ses épithètes décrivent comme le « Bien-aimé des dieux » ou le souverain « au Regard propice ».

Les 36 ou 37 ans qu'ont duré son règne ont été marqués par sa conversion au bouddhisme, 11 ans après son sacre. Cette conversion lui aurait d'ailleurs été inspirée par le remords d'avoir causé de grandes souffrances et la perte de nombreuses vies lors de la conquête de l'État du Kalinga, après 9 années de pouvoir. Sa piété, dès lors, le conduit à mener une politique d'équanimité dans tous les domaines et selon les lois du *dharma*, l'Ordre par excellence dans la tradition culturelle de l'Inde : une sorte d'idéal de nature politique, sociale et religieuse, un *dharma* dont il expose la teneur dans les nombreuses inscriptions qu'il fait graver sur roc ou sur colonne au cours de son règne. Sous sa conduite, l'administration devient plus complexe avec la

À Dhaulî (Bihâr), un puissant avant-corps d'éléphant, taillé dans la roche vive, se dresse à proximité des édits gravés par Ashoka durant la douzième année de son règne (ci-contre). La pratique de graver des édits sur le roc fut sans doute héritée de la Perse achéménide.
Les inscriptions sont en écriture *brâhmî* ou en *kharoshtî* – cette dernière dérivant de l'araméen, l'écriture officielle de l'Empire achéménide. Selon la littérature bouddhique, Ashoka aurait élevé près d'une quarantaine de *lât* à proximité des lieux saints du bouddhisme, notamment à Sârnâth (ci-dessous).

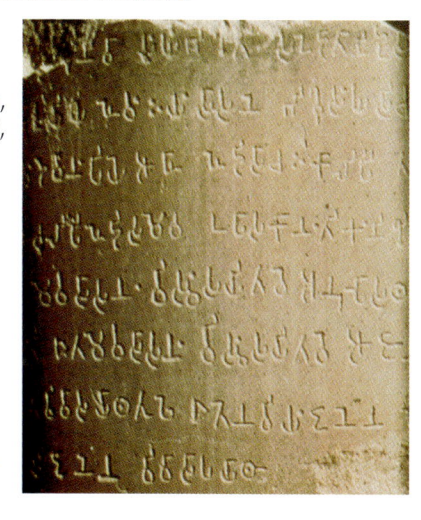

création de nouveaux postes de fonctionnaires ayant pour charge de veiller dans tous les domaines à cet ordre auquel il aspire et qui doit garantir le bien-être matériel et spirituel de son peuple. La tradition bouddhique met au compte d'Ashoka la fondation d'innombrables monuments et une activité missionnaire forcenée par laquelle la Loi du Buddha aurait trouvé son chemin dans un grand nombre de pays asiatiques.

La fin de l'Inde ancienne

La fin de la dynastie maurya est moins brillante. Les successeurs d'Ashoka se révèlent incapables de maintenir la cohésion d'un empire peut-être déjà partagé entre les différents héritiers du grand souverain et dans lequel diverses régions, relativement autonomes en raison de leur éloignement des centres du pouvoir, ne demandaient qu'à faire sécession.

Vers 176 av. J.-C., Pushyamitra, l'un des généraux du dernier empereur maurya, assassine son souverain et prend le pouvoir en fondant la dynastie des Shunga sur un territoire en pleine effervescence et où émergent diverses dynasties obscures dont l'activité conduira rapidement le pouvoir central à renoncer à toute prétention d'hégémonie territoriale. L'État shunga, en effet, doit être perçu comme une sorte de conglomérat de royaumes entretenant entre eux des liens de suzeraineté ou de vassalité. Au terme de 112 années de règne, autour de 64 av. J.-C., les Shunga cèdent la place aux Kânva,

Construit en brique par Ashoka et agrandi sous les Shunga, le grand *stûpa* de Sânchî (ci-dessus) fut complété sous les Sâtavâhana, qui élevèrent sa longue balustrade circulaire et les quatre portes monumentales qui l'accompagnent. Ces dernières offrent un riche répertoire de scènes de la vie du Buddha et de ses vies antérieures (*Jâtaka*).

qui ne se maintiennent à la tête de leur royaume que pendant 45 ans. L'empire brillant fondé par les Maurya redevient alors ce royaume de Magadha dont il était issu et dont la puissance sera revivifiée par les Gupta au IVe siècle.

Dans la première moitié du Ier siècle av. J.-C., au Kalinga (actuel Orissa), la région même dont la conquête avait poussé Ashoka à se convertir au bouddhisme, un roi de l'éphémère dynastie des Chedi, Khâravela, se taille un important domaine indépendant des pouvoirs shunga et kânva. Cette région connaît alors une brillante période : les documents épigraphiques concernant les fondations religieuses ou d'intérêt public du souverain abondent et témoignent de la prospérité politique et économique du royaume qui, pourtant, s'étiole rapidement sous les règnes des deux successeurs de Khâravela, incapables de faire fructifier leur héritage. Le royaume peut toutefois avoir conservé une partie de son prestige, car il est mentionné comme relativement puissant par Pline l'Ancien (23-79) dans son *Histoire naturelle*, cette grande encyclopédie de la science dans l'Antiquité.

Offrant un abri aux moines pendant la saison des pluies, les premiers monastères bouddhiques étaient établis à l'écart des centres urbains, mais suffisamment proches pour que les fidèles puissent en assurer l'entretien et subvenir aux besoins de la communauté religieuse. Les ensembles excavés (ici Bhâjâ, au Mahârâshtra, IIe siècle av. J.-C.) faisaient exception, alors que les édifices construits en matériaux légers étaient plus nombreux. Divers éléments en bois (façades, cerces soulignant la voûte en berceau des *chaitya*) entraient en jeu dans ces grandioses réalisations.

28

L'histoire de l'Inde classique est marquée par l'œuvre de quelques souverains remarquables. À la charnière des Ier et IIe siècles, Kanishka, le grand empereur kushâna, tente, sans lendemain, une audacieuse synthèse des cultures grecque, iranienne, indienne et centrasiatique. Dans la seconde moitié du IVe siècle et au début du Ve siècle, les rois Samudragupta et Chandragupta II, champions de l'indianité la plus pure, portent la culture de l'Inde au faîte de sa gloire.

CHAPITRE 2

DES KUSHÂNA AUX GRANDS GUPTA

L'Inde ancienne a bénéficié d'apports culturels divers comme le montre, à droite, cette tête gandhârienne (IIe siècle), dont la chevelure nouée sur le crâne évoque le *crobylos* des Grecs. Certaines monnaies gupta (à gauche) retiennent aussi une thématique étrangère, ici d'origine sassanide : celle du roi-chasseur.

Le temps des invasions : l'Empire kushâna

Dès le milieu du IIe siècle av. J.-C., les nomades scythes, connus en Inde sous le nom de Shaka, commencent à descendre des confins iraniens vers la Bactriane occidentale et la vallée de l'Indus. Au début du Ier siècle av. J.-C., le grand roi shaka Mauès règne sur un domaine s'étendant du Gandhâra, dans le nord de l'actuel Pakistan, aux régions de Mathurâ (en Uttar Pradesh) et Ujjayinî (au Madhya Pradesh). Le pouvoir des Shaka se substitue à celui des rois gréco-bactriens, bientôt battu en brèche par l'arrivée des nomades yuezhi, originaires de la province chinoise du Gansu. Au cours du Ier siècle de l'ère chrétienne, sous le nom de Kushâna, les Yuezhi fondent un grand empire allant de l'Oxus aux plaines fertiles du cours moyen du Gange.

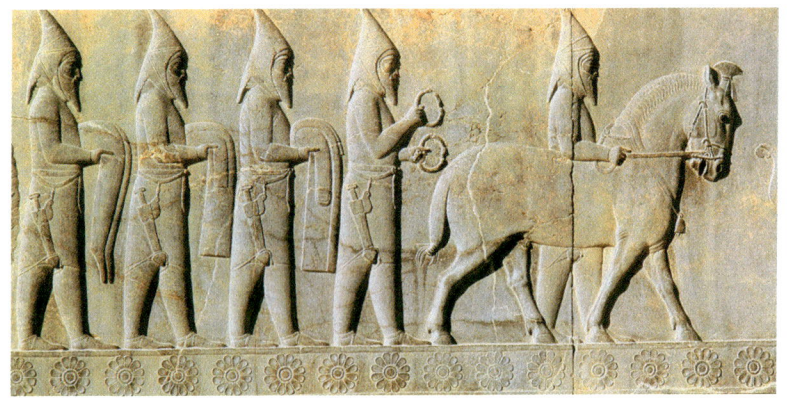

Kujulakadphisès, mort octogénaire à la fin du Ier siècle, va asseoir cet empire sur des bases territoriales fermes : il conquiert notamment le Kapishâ autour de 50 et le Gandhâra une quinzaine d'années plus tard, et pénètre ensuite assez profondément dans le nord de l'Inde, dont la conquête sera achevée par son fils, Vimakadphisès.

De tous les empereurs kushâna, Kanishka reste le plus célèbre et le plus énigmatique. Si l'on ignore quelle était sa foi personnelle, le bouddhisme s'est

Parmi les peuples payant tribut à l'empereur achéménide Darius qui figurent sur les bas-reliefs de Persépolis (VIe-Ve siècle av. J.-C.), les Scythes (Shaka) se reconnaissent à leur coiffe pointue, en feutre ou en cuir (ci-dessus). On les représentera de la même manière en Inde, au début de l'ère chrétienne (en haut).

Fondé sous Ashoka et agrandi par la suite (ci-contre, dans son état du Ve siècle), le *stûpa* Dharmarâjika de Taxilâ rappelle les premiers *stûpa* indiens. Avec d'autres portraits royaux, le sanctuaire de Mât (Mathurâ) a livré cette statue de Kanishka (ci-dessous), représenté dans le costume traditionnel des nomades d'Asie centrale. Les dates du souverain restent controversées : il pourrait avoir accédé au trône en 78 ou entre 120 et 144.

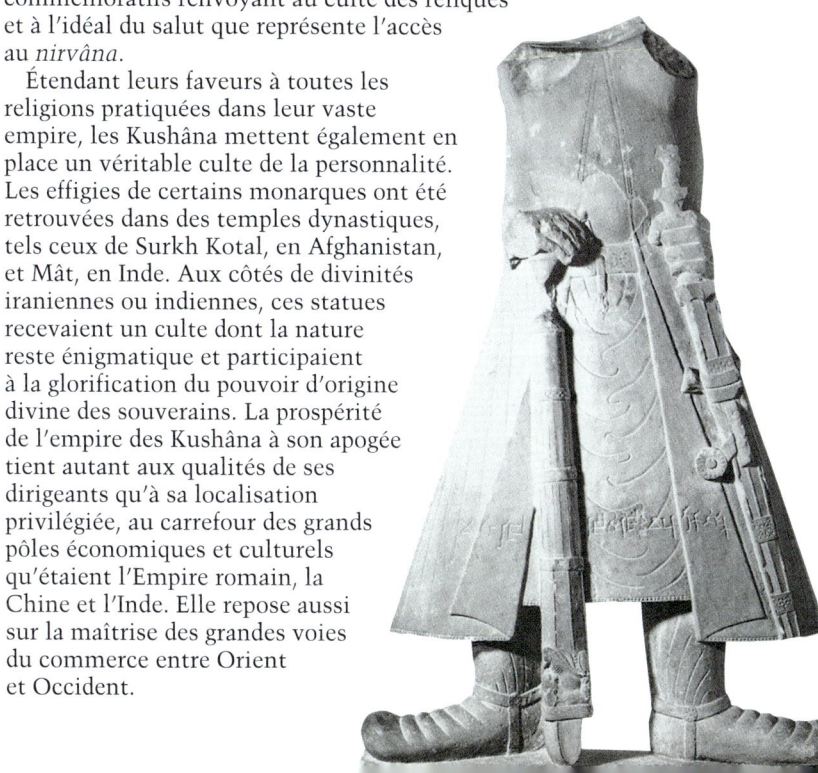

considérablement développé sous son règne. Le souverain est considéré comme un « ardent adorateur de reliques » – dont le culte était devenu fondamental au lendemain même de la mort du Buddha – et un grand fondateur de monuments, notamment de *stûpa*, ces édifices reliquaires et commémoratifs renvoyant au culte des reliques et à l'idéal du salut que représente l'accès au *nirvâna*.

Étendant leurs faveurs à toutes les religions pratiquées dans leur vaste empire, les Kushâna mettent également en place un véritable culte de la personnalité. Les effigies de certains monarques ont été retrouvées dans des temples dynastiques, tels ceux de Surkh Kotal, en Afghanistan, et Mât, en Inde. Aux côtés de divinités iraniennes ou indiennes, ces statues recevaient un culte dont la nature reste énigmatique et participaient à la glorification du pouvoir d'origine divine des souverains. La prospérité de l'empire des Kushâna à son apogée tient autant aux qualités de ses dirigeants qu'à sa localisation privilégiée, au carrefour des grands pôles économiques et culturels qu'étaient l'Empire romain, la Chine et l'Inde. Elle repose aussi sur la maîtrise des grandes voies du commerce entre Orient et Occident.

Les contre-pouvoirs shaka

Alors que les Kushâna sont au faîte de leur puissance dans la vallée du Gange, une lignée de satrapes (*kshatrapa*) shaka, connue sous le nom de Kshaharâta, occupe l'actuel Gujarât, le sud du Râjasthân, l'ouest du Madhya Pradesh et la partie septentrionale du Mahârâshtra. Largement ouvert sur la mer d'Oman, le royaume des Kshaharâta, probablement vassal de l'Empire kushâna, contrôle une grande partie du commerce maritime de l'Inde. À ce titre, il est mentionné dans le *Périple de la mer Érythrée*, ouvrage rédigé dans la seconde moitié du Ier siècle qui décrit des villes côtières avec lesquelles il était possible de commercer. La richesse du roi Nahapâna (c. 78-125), le plus connu des Kshaharâta, est restée légendaire.

Une seconde lignée shaka, celle des *kshatrapa* d'Ujjayinî (actuelle Ujjain), est attestée dans l'épigraphie indienne vers 130. À peu près à la même époque, dans sa célèbre *Géographie*, l'astronome grec Claude Ptolémée (IIe siècle) mentionne sous le nom de Tiastanès le premier de ces *kshatrapa*, Chashtana. Dans une inscription datée de 150, son petit-fils, Rudradâman, affirme régner sur un vaste domaine

DES KUSHÂNA AUX GRANDS GUPTA 33

et avoir vaincu ses ennemis à diverses reprises. Au terme du développement chaotique de leur lignée, les riches et puissants *kshatrapa* d'Ujjayinî sont renversés par les Gupta, vers 400.

Les premiers grands royaumes d'Inde du Sud

Pendant les trois premiers siècles de l'ère chrétienne, la situation politique du Deccan et du sud de la péninsule indienne est particulièrement complexe. Le royaume des Ândhra, ou Ândhrabhritya, couvre de manière lâche et irrégulière l'ensemble du Deccan mais demeure centré sur la région comprise entre les cours moyens et inférieurs de la Godâvarî et de la Krishnâ (l'actuel Ândhra Pradesh). Les territoires ândhra semblent avoir été dirigés par plusieurs souverains appartenant à deux familles, les Sâtakani et les Sâtavâhana. Au Ier siècle, Pline l'Ancien précise que les « *Andarae* » disposaient de nombreuses cités fortifiées et d'une très importante armée qui en faisait le plus puissant pouvoir en Inde du Sud.

À la fin du Ier siècle et au début du IIe, la partie occidentale de leur domaine est sans doute sous la domination des Kshaharâta, mais très vite, dès 125, le roi Gotamîputa réinstaure dans sa plénitude la puissance ândhra, qui se confond désormais avec le destin de la lignée des Sâtavâhana.

Fouillé entre 1937 et 1939, le site de Begrâm, en Afghanistan, a livré un ensemble d'objets de luxe chinois (laques), indiens (ivoires, os gravés), méditerranéens (bronzes, verrerie syro-alexandrine) : ci-dessus, un verre peint avec la scène de l'enlèvement d'Europe par Jupiter. Retrouvée à Pompéi, cette statuette en ivoire (ci-contre) originaire d'Inde centrale, témoigne aussi des liens commerciaux unissant Orient et Occident au début de l'ère chrétienne.

Provenant du sanctuaire de Mât, cette statue (page de gauche) représente Chashtana. Le premier souverain de la lignée des *kshatrapa* d'Ujjayinî, vêtu de la tunique et du pantalon des nomades, arbore une ceinture ornée de cavaliers, dont l'un porte la coiffe pointue des Scythes (détail en haut).

Le royaume sâtavâhana s'étend d'une côte à l'autre, et son rôle dans le commerce maritime entre les différents pays d'Asie et, au-delà, avec la Rome impériale, lui a assuré une grande prospérité ainsi qu'une ouverture féconde sur le monde méditerranéen, notamment dans le domaine artistique. Le royaume ne semble pas avoir été particulièrement centralisé, à l'inverse des grands empires maurya et kushâna. Un réseau dense de potentats gérait ponctuellement les intérêts généraux. Leur tendance naturelle à l'indépendance aurait pu conduire le royaume à l'éclatement, mais il semble que les établissements religieux, tant hindous que bouddhiques, principaux bénéficiaires des largesses royales, ont grandement contribué à la cohésion d'un domaine aussi vaste que structurellement distendu. Dès le IIIe siècle, pourtant, le royaume se disloque.

Dans l'extrême sud, le pays tamoul, qui deviendra si important à l'époque médiévale, est le domaine de trois lignées : les Pândya, les Chera et les Chola, déjà mentionnées dans les inscriptions d'Ashoka au IIIe siècle av. J.-C. Ces royaumes se livrent à d'incessantes guerres pendant les premiers siècles de l'ère chrétienne, mais leurs rapports avec le reste de l'Inde demeurent mal connus, cependant qu'ils commercent activement eux aussi avec l'Occident. Ptolémée, en effet, cite un grand nombre d'*emporia* dans la région, dont Podoukè, qui correspond sans doute à la moderne Pondichéry.

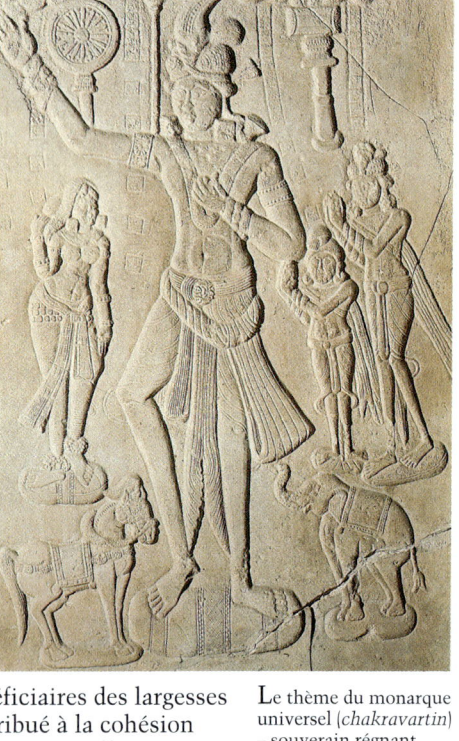

Le thème du monarque universel (*chakravartin*) – souverain régnant selon les règles du *dharma* – est l'un des sujets privilégiés de l'iconographie bouddhique ancienne. Cette plaque de revêtement de *stûpa* (art ândhra, Ier siècle av. J.-C.) le représente avec les sept trésors qui lui sont associés : épouse, ministre, général, cheval, éléphant, richesse (évoquée par le coffret sur le pilier en haut, à droite) et roue représentant le *dharma*.

DES KUSHÂNA AUX GRANDS GUPTA 35

La fondation d'un brillant empire : les premiers Gupta

Les origines de la dynastie gupta sont mal connues. La généalogie fournie par l'inscription d'Allahabad, due à Harishena, un ministre du roi Samudragupta (c. 335-375), révèle les noms de Shrîgupta et Ghatotkacha, son fils, tous deux *mahârâja* (« grands rois »), mais dont on ne sait rien par ailleurs, si ce n'est qu'ils régnaient à la fin du IIIe siècle, sans doute sur un petit royaume de l'est de l'Uttar Pradesh ou du Bihâr occidental. La dynastie apparaît vraiment en pleine lumière avec celui que les historiens considèrent réellement comme son fondateur : Chandragupta Ier (c. 320-335). L'accession au trône de Chandragupta, vers 320, marque à la fois le début de la lignée des Gupta impériaux et la fondation d'une nouvelle ère.

La partie orientale de l'empire des Sâtavâhana tombe sous la tutelle des Ikshvâku à la fin du IIIe siècle. D'affiliation hindoue, ces rois perpétuent la tradition de tolérance à l'égard de toutes les religions menée par leurs prédécesseurs. Ils fondent ou participent au développement de nombreux sites bouddhiques, tel Nâgârjunakonda, d'où provient ce bas-relief figurant un prince entouré de courtisanes (ci-dessus).

Héritier d'un petit royaume, Chandragupta se maria à une princesse du nom de Kumâradevî. Elle était issue de l'antique lignée des Licchavi, une ancienne famille royale qui, au temps du Buddha, régnait à Vaishâlî, dans le nord du Bihâr, et appartenait à la confédération des Vriji. Les descendants de Chandragupta suivront cette stratégie politique en épousant les héritiers des royaumes dont ils pouvaient craindre l'opposition ou dont, à l'inverse, ils recherchaient l'appui.

Comme tout grand monarque indien, Chandragupta chercha à agrandir son domaine et effectua un certain nombre de conquêtes, notamment au Bihâr. L'accroissement des territoires sur lesquels Chandragupta étendait son autorité et le développement de son pouvoir se traduisent par son titre de *mahârâjâdhirâja*, « roi suprême des grands rois », plus important et pompeux que le simple titre de *mahârâja* porté par son père et son grand-père. Sa capitale était probablement Prayâga (actuelle Allahabad), où de très importantes inscriptions ont été retrouvées et dont les environs comportent divers monuments d'époque gupta.

Les conquêtes de Samudragupta

Parmi les nombreux titres de gloire dont peut se prévaloir Samudragupta (c. 335-375) figure celui de grand conquérant. Dans le panégyrique qu'il

Considéré comme d'habile politique, le mariage de Chandragupta Ier avec Kumâradevî lui a probablement conféré un statut auquel sa propre ascendance ne lui donnait pas accès. Cette alliance permit peut-être à son fils, Samudragupta, d'affirmer certaines prétentions au trône de son grand-père maternel. En haut à gauche, Chandragupta Ier et son épouse, à l'avers d'une monnaie frappée peu après 320.

DES KUSHÂNA AUX GRANDS GUPTA 37

a fait graver sur une antique colonne d'Ashoka, à Allahabad, la célèbre *prashasti* de Prayâga, sont énumérées ses diverses conquêtes et le degré de vassalité ou de dépendance qu'elles ont induit pour les vaincus. L'inscription offre un tableau assez précis des pouvoirs en présence autour du domaine de l'ambitieux monarque. « Dans l'Aryâvarta » (le pays des Ârya), ce « dieu qui habiterait ce monde », entendons le roi, « déracina » de nombreux souverains afin de s'attribuer un très vaste territoire s'étendant du Bengale occidental, à l'est, jusqu'aux régions de Mathurâ (Uttar Pradesh), à l'ouest, et Vidishâ (Madhya Pradesh), au sud-ouest. Parmi les rois soumis par Samudragupta, certains ont été purement et simplement éliminés, leurs possessions entrant alors de manière organique dans l'Empire gupta. D'autres, faits prisonniers, ont été graciés puis replacés sur leur trône au rang peu glorieux d'administrateurs de leurs propres États : Samudragupta jugeait sans doute plus avantageux de laisser en place ces rois vaincus, pour s'attirer leur gratitude. D'autres encore, sans avoir été à proprement parler soumis, ont dû reconnaître la suprématie du monarque et s'engager à lui verser un tribut, sans doute afin d'éviter une possible

Le monnayage gupta offre un vivant écho aux données historiques de l'épigraphie. Sur certaines monnaies, le roi est debout, appuyé sur une hache de combat, auprès d'un étendard à l'effigie de Garuda, l'emblème de la dynastie (page de gauche, monnaie de droite). Sur d'autres, il apparaît faisant l'oblation au feu rituel (ci-dessus, à gauche) ou assis et jouant du luth, en tant que poète et musicien (ci-dessus, à droite, monnaie à l'effigie de Samudragupta).

Sur la foi d'une inscription aujourd'hui illisible, ce cheval très stylisé provenant de Khairigarh (à la frontière indo-népalaise) a pu être associé à l'époque de Samudragupta et au Sacrifice du cheval, si important à l'époque gupta (au centre).

agression ; d'autres enfin, sont restés indépendants tout en entretenant des relations diplomatiques avec l'Empire gupta. Samudragupta était devenu *de facto* suzerain de l'ensemble de l'Inde septentrionale.

Il se lança alors dans une campagne dirigée vers des régions situées hors du champ naturel de ses prétentions territoriales, dans le sud du sous-continent, parachevant son œuvre de conquête impériale par l'antique Sacrifice du cheval, qui le consacrait *chakravartin* (monarque universel).

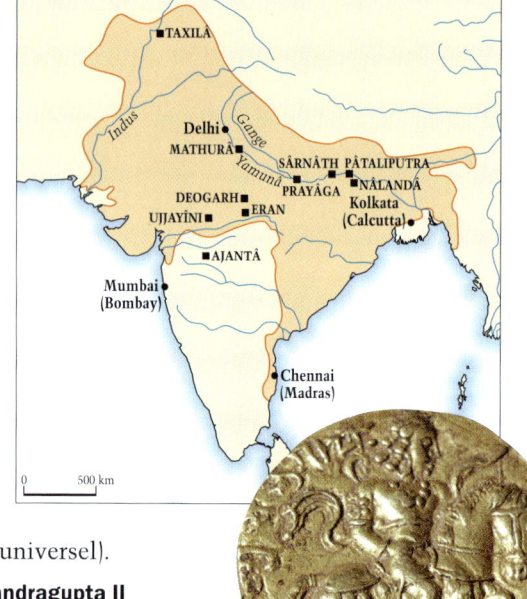

Le temps de l'apogée : Chandragupta II

La période qui suit la mort de Samudragupta voit l'affrontement de Chandragupta II (c. 375-415), et de son frère Râmagupta (c. 375), l'héritier légitime. Selon une légende, Râmagupta, afin d'assurer sa sauvegarde et celle de son peuple, aurait démérité en cédant, lors d'un conflit, son épouse Dhruvadevî à un *kshatrapa* shaka d'Inde occidentale, Rudrasimha III. Devant cette ignominie, Chandragupta, déguisé en femme, se serait rendu chez le Shaka et l'aurait tué, gagnant du même coup l'estime de son peuple et celle de la reine. Redoutant que Râmagupta ne cherchât à se débarrasser d'un frère devenu trop puissant, Chandragupta feignit un temps la folie ; une fois la défiance de son aîné endormie, il le tua, épousa la reine outragée et se saisit du trône.

Chandragupta II semble avoir hérité des qualités politiques et diplomatiques de son grand-père et de la valeur militaire de son père. Son plus grand succès fut de soumettre les *kshatrapa* d'Ujjayinî au tournant

Disposant du pouvoir sur l'ensemble des terres qui s'étendaient de la mer de l'Est à la mer de l'Ouest, les souverains gupta ont régné sur un immense territoire (ci-dessus). Chandragupta II (ici, monnaie attribuée à ce souverain) – parfois désigné sous le titre glorieux de Vikramâditya, « Soleil d'héroïsme » – et son fils, Kumâragupta, furent aussi de grands mécènes qui accueillaient artistes et poètes à leur cour.

des IVe et Ve siècles, mettant un terme au pouvoir des Shaka en Inde et élevant Ujjain au rang de ville impériale. L'inscription du pilier de Fer à Delhi évoque ses hauts faits, rappelant qu'il aurait aussi poussé ses armées loin vers le nord-ouest, jusqu'en Bactriane, et conquis divers territoires situés à l'est de son empire. Sous sa tutelle, le domaine gupta atteignit sa plus grande extension. Perpétuant la politique d'alliances matrimoniales de son grand-père, il épousa Kuveranâgâ, une princesse de la dynastie des Nâga que son père avait précédemment « déracinée » et dont la capitale était la ville de Padmâvatî (Pawâyâ). De même, il donna sa fille Prabhavatî en mariage au roi Rudrasena II des Vâkâtaka, faisant entrer ce puissant royaume du Deccan dans le giron de l'empire.

Le pèlerin chinois Faxian, qui visita l'Inde durant le règne de Chandragupta II, évoque un royaume cosmopolite, prospère et d'une grande tolérance religieuse. Ce détail d'une peinture murale figurant une scène de prédication bouddhique, dans la grotte n° 17 du site d'Ajantâ (Mahârâshtra), restitue bien l'ouverture d'esprit de l'époque : divers personnages y sont vêtus et coiffés selon des modes non indiennes.

Certains historiens font intervenir un hypothétique roi Govindagupta (c. 415) à la mort de Chandragupta II, mais son véritable successeur fut son fils, Kumâragupta Ier (c. 415-455). Sous son long règne, l'empire conserva son intégrité, mais aucune nouvelle conquête n'eut lieu. Le Sacrifice du cheval fut une nouvelle fois célébré. Dans les dernières années d'un règne pacifique, le souverain s'est sans doute adonné à la vie érémitique, tout en conservant un regard sur la conduite des affaires. Dans le même temps, des troubles militaires éclatent dans le sud-ouest de l'empire. Le règne de Skandagupta (455-467) inaugure une période difficile. Le roi doit répondre à l'agression des Pushyamitra, au sud-ouest, et aux premières attaques de tribus nomades d'Asie centrale, les Shvetahûna (Huns blancs), au nord-ouest. Il parvient à rétablir l'ordre et maintient l'intégrité des territoires et le prestige de la dynastie.

Les œuvres d'Eran représentent Vishnu ou ses *avatâra*. La plus impressionnante figure Varâha, le « Sanglier », sous sa forme zoomorphe (ci-dessous). Elle fut érigée, peu après 485, la première année du règne du roi hun Toramâna, par le prince Dhanyavishnu, dont le frère aîné avait été vassal des Gupta. Outre la déesse Terre, suspendue à l'une de ses défenses, le Sanglier porte sur son corps la multitude des sages et des divinités, qui ne sont qu'une infime partie de lui-même.

Une fin annoncée

L'ordre de succession des monarques ultérieurs n'est pas connu avec précision. Plusieurs souverains ont d'ailleurs pu régner ensemble sur un empire à la veille de s'effondrer et qui se fissure autant de l'extérieur que de l'intérieur. À Skandagupta pourrait avoir brièvement succédé son frère, Purugupta (c. 467 ?). Puis, d'une liste peu explicite se détache le nom de Budhagupta, qui était sur le trône en 476, mais qui pourrait tout aussi bien y avoir accédé une dizaine d'années plus tôt. Régnant jusque dans les années 495, Budhagupta est le dernier des grands Gupta.

Miné par l'émergence de nouvelles dynasties au sein même de ses territoires, affaibli par les attaques répétées des Huns et très probablement déstabilisé par des troubles intérieurs, l'Empire gupta vacille et voit se succéder plusieurs souverains de faible personnalité : Narasimhagupta, Vainyagupta, attesté en 507, Bhânugupta, dont le nom est mentionné dans une inscription d'Eran datée de 510, etc. L'empire s'effondre. Quelques souverains se maintiennent localement au Magadha jusqu'au VIIe siècle, mais ils n'ont plus rien à voir avec leurs illustres prédécesseurs. Les destinées de l'Inde passent alors en d'autres mains.

L'émergence de nouveaux pouvoirs

Malgré leur arrivée tumultueuse dans la seconde moitié du Ve siècle, les nomades huns établissent un pouvoir fort dans la partie nord-occidentale de l'Empire gupta. De la fin du Ve siècle au milieu du VIe, l'action de la dynastie hûna est brutale. Au début du VIe siècle, l'un de ses plus grands souverains, Mihirakula, converti à l'hindouisme, se livre à de nombreuses exactions et persécute particulièrement les bouddhistes.

À la faveur de la prise de pouvoir des Hûna, les Maitraka établissent leur puissance sur la partie occidentale du domaine gupta (l'actuel Gujarât), où elle se maintient jusqu'au milieu du VIIIe siècle. Durant la première moitié du VIe siècle, les Maukhari s'affranchissent du pouvoir gupta dans les régions centrales de l'empire, dominant les zones situées le long des cours moyens du Gange et de la Yamunâ jusqu'aux premières décennies du VIIe siècle. À la veille de l'époque médiévale, certains monarques, tel Harsha de Kanauj (606-647), de la dynastie des Pushyabhûti, tenteront de raviver la splendeur et la puissance perdues du grand empire, sans réellement y parvenir.

Depuis l'époque maurya, les hauts piliers-étendards inscrits (*dhvajastambha*) jouent un rôle politique et religieux. Sous les Gupta, ils supportent souvent quelque emblème vishnuite. Daté de 485, le pilier d'Eran (ci-dessous) fut commandité par le *mahârâja* Mâtrivishnu et son frère cadet Dhanyavishnu, vassaux du dernier des grands Gupta, le roi Budhagupta.

42

Le règne des empereurs gupta fut marqué par une grande tolérance religieuse, un œcuménisme pragmatique et serein dont la littérature, l'épigraphie et les arts offrent de nombreux et éloquents témoignages. Souverains de confession vishnuite, les Gupta n'en eurent pas moins à cœur de favoriser également les autres religions ou courants sectaires attestés dans leur empire. Si le jaïnisme accusa un relatif déclin, le shivaïsme et le bouddhisme en revanche s'épanouirent sans contrainte.

CHAPITRE 3

UNE POLITIQUE DE TOLÉRANCE RELIGIEUSE

Dans l'Empire gupta, les dieux coexistent en bonne intelligence : ici (à gauche), sculptée dans la caverne n° 5 à Udayagiri, une effigie colossale de Vishnu, dans son *avatâra* de Varâha, le « Sanglier ». Ci-contre, Shiva, sous l'aspect de Natarâja (« Seigneur de la danse »), exécute la danse cosmique qui détruit et recrée les mondes.

Dans le climat de tolérance religieuse qui prévalait à l'époque gupta, les anciennes prescriptions védiques n'étaient pas lettre morte. Le premier acte politique de deux souverains gupta, Samudragupta et son petit-fils Kumâragupta Ier, fut notamment de célébrer le prestigieux Sacrifice du cheval, l'*ashvamedha*, restaurant un rite ancestral et primordial qui, depuis plusieurs siècles, était quelque peu tombé en désuétude.

Mais les temps avaient changé. Désormais, la célébration de sacrifices védiques n'était plus considérée comme le meilleur moyen de se concilier la faveur divine ou de progresser sur le plan spirituel. Sous l'influence de textes sectaires comme la *Bhagavad-Gîtâ* et de la montée en puissance des grandes divinités purâniques – la triade (*trimûrti*) Brahmâ, Vishnu et Shiva –, la dévotion (*bhakti*) à une divinité d'élection (*ishtadevatâ*) avait commencé de supplanter le culte des anciens dieux védiques et leurs rituels séculaires.

Une dynastie d'obédience vishnuite

Les empereurs gupta furent de fidèles et constants dévots du dieu Vishnu. Leur affiliation au vishnuisme remonte au règne du fondateur de la dynastie, mais c'est l'empereur Chandragupta II qui, le premier, adopta le titre explicite de *parama-bhâgavata*, « ardent dévot du dieu Vishnu », que la plupart de ses successeurs reprirent à leur compte. Les sceaux royaux et

Des divers sacrifices védiques participant à la consécration royale, le plus important était le Sacrifice du cheval (ci-contre, symbolisé sur une monnaie gupta). Avant d'être immolé, l'animal était laissé libre de déambuler une année durant : les territoires traversés étaient alors considérés comme appartenant au roi et, le cas échéant, conquis par ses armées.

les monnaies témoignent ostensiblement de cette obédience sectaire : les sceaux portent souvent l'effigie de la déesse Shrî-Lakshmî, l'épouse de Vishnu, ou encore de l'aigle solaire Garuda, la monture du dieu. Les monnaies d'or et d'argent, qui comptent au nombre des plus beaux exemples de numismatique indienne, s'ornent presque toujours au revers de l'image de Shrî-Lakshmî, dont la présence est justifiée du fait de son statut de déesse de la Fortune, mais aussi en vertu de son rôle de protectrice de la royauté (*râjyalakhsmî*) et des cités (*nagaralakshmî*).

Marquée par la renaissance de l'hindouisme, l'époque gupta vit la rédaction, la compilation ou le remodelage des principaux *Purâna* ou « récits antiques », recueils de textes mêlant cosmologie, mythologie et liturgie, dont beaucoup exaltent la gloire de Vishnu, vénéré comme divinité suprême. Dès la fin du IVe siècle, et notamment sous l'impulsion des Gupta, le vishnuisme se développa considérablement et la théorie des *avatâra*, les « descentes » ou « incarnations » du dieu Vishnu – déjà en germe dans la littérature védique tardive –, connut une grande popularité.

Ce sceau royal, gravé d'un texte sanskrit, fournit de précieux renseignements sur la succession dynastique des empereurs gupta après Kumâragupta Ier. On y voit Garuda, monture de Vishnu et emblème des Gupta. Les ailes déployées, un serpent autour du cou, l'oiseau doté d'une face humaine porte la coiffure en boucles de l'époque gupta.

Les *avatâra* de Vishnu

Des différents *avatâra* de Vishnu, celui du Sanglier (Varâha) qui sauve la déesse Terre des eaux menaçant de l'engloutir fut l'objet d'un véritable culte. Le monumental relief de la caverne n° 5 d'Udayagiri, où un Varâha semi-thériomorphe à corps de géant et à hure de sanglier semble jaillir de la paroi sculptée, témoigne de l'importance religieuse dévolue à cet *avatâra* en particulier, et à un épisode mythologique

Sculptée à Mathurâ, cette effigie de Vishnu est un chef-d'œuvre de l'art gupta (au centre). Elle conserve, à la saignée des bras, des fragments de la guirlande de fleurs forestières traditionnellement dévolue à ce dieu.

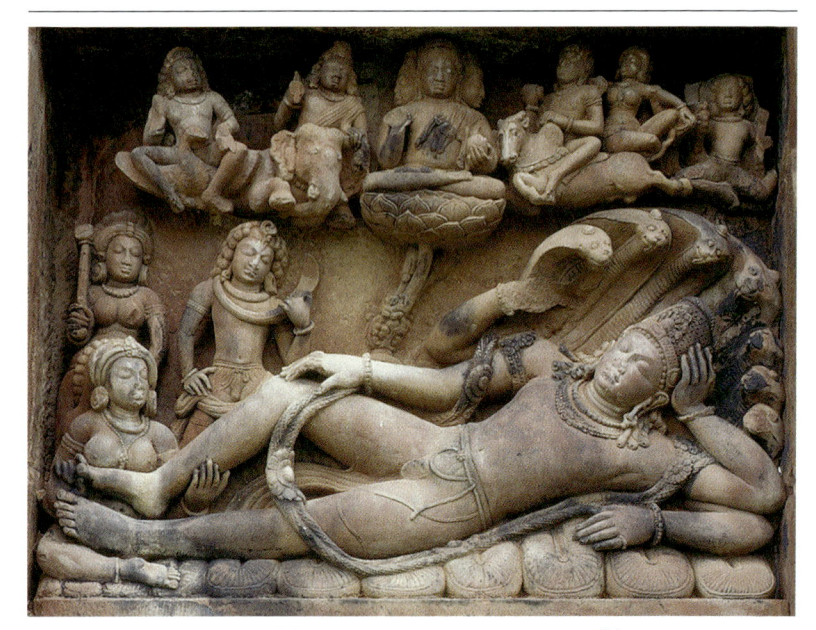

qui, selon toute vraisemblance, revêtait une dimension politique. Certains croient reconnaître, dans le gigantisme et l'exaltation du Sanglier salvateur de la Terre submergée sous les eaux, une manière d'allégorie commémorant les victoires militaires du roi Chandragupta II sur les ennemis de l'empire que furent les Scythes ou Shaka occidentaux. À Eran et à Aphsad, de colossaux sangliers en ronde bosse – figurés pour l'un sous une forme semi-thériomorphe, pour les deux autres sous une forme zoomorphe – attestent aussi le culte dont Varâha faisait l'objet jusque dans les confins de l'empire et sous le règne de monarques contemporains ou feudataires des Gupta.

La protection accordée au vishnuisme par la dynastie régnante a favorisé les aspects et les manifestations les plus divers de cette dévotion. L'un des plus beaux temples de l'époque gupta tardive, le temple de Deogarh, est consacré à Vishnu, qui y est notamment représenté reposant sur le serpent d'Éternité, Ananta. Cette iconographie

L'un des plus remarquables reliefs du temple gupta de Deogarh figure Vishnu couché sur le serpent d'Éternité, Ananta ou Shesha, et flottant sur les eaux primordiales. Dans cet état de sommeil mystique (*yoganidrâ*), le dieu médite le monde entre deux ères cosmiques (*kalpa*). À son réveil, il émettra de son nombril un lotus doré d'où surgira Brahmâ, qui créera un nouvel Univers. Au-dessus de lui, chevauchant leurs montures, Skanda (ou Varuna ?), Indra, Shiva et Pârvatî entourent Brahmâ trônant sur le lotus.

UNE POLITIQUE DE TOLÉRANCE RELIGIEUSE 47

particulière illustrant le sommeil cosmique du dieu se retrouve à Udayagiri. Au chant X du *Raghuvamsha* (*La Lignée de Raghu*), le grand poète Kâlidâsa évoque aussi le dieu reposant sur Ananta avec, à ses pieds, la déesse Lakshmî. Comme l'attestent plusieurs inscriptions, la conception de Shrî-Lakshmî en tant qu'épouse de Vishnu est également l'un des traits du vishnuisme à l'époque gupta.

De nouvelles formes iconographiques du dieu se font jour, se fixent ou se précisent. Il est notamment figuré sous sa forme cosmique (Vishvarûpa). Jusque-là de modestes dimensions, les images de Vishnu, volontiers monumentales désormais, reflètent la vitalité et la prééminence religieuse du vishnuisme. Ainsi, l'une des œuvres les plus impressionnantes de la statuaire gupta figure Krishna – *avatâra* majeur de Vishnu – soulevant le mont Govardhana ; une impression de majesté et de puissance surhumaine émane de cette ronde-bosse haute de plus de deux mètres.

Krishna est ici figuré soulevant le mont Govardhana, afin d'abriter les habitants du pays de Braj d'un violent orage déchaîné par le dieu Indra. Conformément aux conventions plastiques en vigueur dans l'art de l'Inde ancienne, le mont Govardhana, que le dieu maintient à bout de bras au-dessus de sa tête, est évoqué de manière abstraite et symbolique par un amoncellement géométrique de rochers cubiques.

Destinées à exalter la prééminence de Vishnu au sein du panthéon brahmanique, des images du dieu figuré sous sa forme cosmique de Vishvarûpa apparaissent (ci-contre).

L'épanouissement du shivaïsme

Si l'essor du shivaïsme fut moindre à l'époque gupta, il fut loin cependant d'être insignifiant, comme l'attestent divers temples shivaïtes (aujourd'hui ruinés) qui furent élevés en diverses régions de l'empire : Bhumârâ, Nâchnâ Kûthârâ, Ahicchattrâ. Certains feudataires des Gupta, comme les puissants Vâkâtaka, étaient pour nombre d'entre eux d'obédience shivaïte. C'est à l'époque gupta qu'est traditionnellement assignée la rédaction de certains des grands *Purâna* shivaïtes, tel le *Shiva* (ou *Vâyu*) *Purâna*. Et le chantre de l'époque gupta, le poète Kâlidâsa, était lui-même un dévot de Shiva, auquel il a consacré l'une de ses œuvres majeures, *La Naissance de Kumâra*.

L'art témoigne également de cet épanouissement du shivaïsme. Quelques-uns parmi les plus beaux *linga* à un visage (*ekamukhalinga*) – plus rarement à quatre visages (*caturmukhalinga*) – furent sculptés à l'époque gupta, et étaient vénérés dans la pénombre des cellas des temples de Bhumârâ ou de Khoh. L'épigraphie nous apprend qu'un sanctuaire rupestre d'Udayagiri (caverne n° 7) fut consacré à Shiva par Shâba Vîrasena, ministre de l'empereur Chandragupta II ; ou encore qu'en 117 de l'ère gupta (437), Prithivîsena, ministre et commandant en chef du roi Kumâragupta Ier, consacra lui aussi un *linga*.

La secte shivaïte des Pâshupata était particulièrement florissante dans la ville de Mathurâ, où s'élevaient alors de nombreux temples. C'est en effet à Mathurâ qu'au IIe siècle se serait établi Kushika, l'un des quatre principaux disciples du fondateur de cette secte, Lakulîsha – lequel est considéré, dans la tradition shivaïte, comme une manifestation de Shiva enseignant.

Comme pour le vishnuisme, cet essor du shivaïsme entraîna un renouvellement de son iconographie et vit l'apparition de formes nouvelles du dieu, appelées à connaître une fortune durable. Les premières représentations de Shiva Natarâja, le « Seigneur de la Danse », d'Ardhanârîshvara, Shiva

Symbole phallique de Shiva, dont il incarne la force vitale et l'énergie créatrice, le *linga* est le « signe » du dieu destructeur et créateur de la *trimûrti* brahmanique (ci-contre dans le sanctuaire shivaïte de Bhumârâ ; ci-dessous, à Khoh). Signe de la présence des Pâshupata, ce pilier en grès rouge de Mathurâ (page de gauche) est sculpté d'un trident shivaïte. Il montre un ascète tenant dans sa main droite un bâton ou un gourdin, attribut traditionnel de la secte.

Androgyne, ou encore du dieu figuré aux côtés de son épouse Pârvatî (Umâmaheshvaramûrti) font leur apparition.

La vitalité des cultes sectaires

Le culte dévolu à Kumâra, fils de Shiva et chef des armées divines, n'était pas moins important. Comme l'indiquent les monnaies qu'il fit frapper – où figurent le dieu Kumâra chevauchant sa monture, le paon Parâvani, ou encore le souverain lui-même nourrissant un paon –, le roi Kumâragupta Ier, tout en préservant les allégeances vishnuites de sa famille, semble avoir fait preuve d'une prédilection marquée pour le dieu de la Guerre, dont il portait le nom. Il appellera d'ailleurs son propre fils Skanda, un autre nom du dieu Kumâra. Sous la plume de Kâlidâsa, on trouve, dans *Le Nuage messager*, une allusion poétique à un temple voué au dieu de la Guerre, à Devagiri. Une inscription lapidaire atteste pour sa part qu'un important temple consacré à Kumâra s'élevait alors à Bilsadh. Et de nombreuses sculptures, émanant de diverses régions de l'empire, témoignent de la vigueur du culte dont le chef des armées divines faisait alors l'objet.

Le culte de Kumâra était souvent associé à celui des Mâtrikâ, les « Mères », comme le montre un ensemble de sculptures exhumées sur le site de Tanesara-Mahâdeva au Râjasthân. Une inscription sur le pilier de Bihâr mentionne l'édification – peut-être sur ordre de l'empereur Kumâragupta Ier – d'un groupe de temples voués au culte de Kumâra et des « Mères ». C'est précisément à l'époque gupta que se développe le culte des déesses-mères, et surtout de la Grande Déesse, adorée sous des noms divers et vénérée en tant que *shakti*, la contrepartie féminine et l'énergie personnifiée des grands dieux védiques et purâniques. Intégré au *Mârkandeya Purâna* antérieurement au VIIe siècle, le *Devî-Mâhâtmya* ou *Célébration de la Grande Déesse* exalte la grandeur et la gloire de la déesse Chandî-Durgâ et

Kumâra, « le Jeune », a pour attribut la lance, que lui forgea, à partir d'un rayon de soleil, l'architecte des dieux, Vishvakarman, et pour monture le paon Parâvani, que le dieu du Feu, Agni, lui offrit à sa naissance. Sur cette sculpture du Ve siècle, le dieu de la Guerre porte les attributs distinctifs des jeunes garçons : la coiffure à trois mèches et le collier orné de griffes de tigre qui soulignent sa nature éternellement juvénile.

UNE POLITIQUE DE TOLÉRANCE RELIGIEUSE 51

relate son combat victorieux contre le démon-buffle Mahishâsura, ennemi des dieux – un épisode que l'art gupta figura à maintes reprises, notamment dans la caverne n° 6 d'Udayagiri.

Le culte voué au dieu Soleil, Sûrya, était également florissant, comme l'attestent plusieurs inscriptions mentionnant tour à tour l'édification ou la restauration de divers temples solaires. La plus célèbre et la plus complète est celle de Mandasor, l'ancienne Dashapura, qui relate la construction en 437, par une guilde d'artisans soyeux originaires de la ville de Lâta dans le Gujarât, d'un temple dédié à Sûrya, ainsi que la restauration du même édifice quelque trente-six années plus tard, en 473 – sans doute à la suite des dévastations qui accompagnèrent le passage des Huns Hephtalites. De nombreux sceaux portant l'image d'un disque solaire ou d'un autel du feu (*agnikunda*), possessions des zélateurs du dieu Soleil, les Saura, attestent l'existence d'un culte au Soleil, tout comme les nombreuses effigies d'époque gupta qui figurent le dieu Sûrya invariablement vêtu du costume scythe ou shaka – tunique évasée et bottes de feutre –, celui-là même qu'arborent les monarques sur certaines de leurs monnaies d'or.

La déesse Durgâ est ici figurée chevauchant sa monture, le lion, un trident dans la main gauche. Dès les premiers siècles de notre ère, Durgâ fut représentée mettant à mort le démon-buffle Mahishâsura, épisode souvent illustré à l'époque gupta.

" Rien ne se peut comparer à ta vaillance, rien non plus à ta forme qui inspire à la fois le charme et la terreur; et pourtant, ô Déesse qui distribue les grâces, on T'a vue dans les trois mondes être à la fois impitoyable au combat et pleine de compassion dans ton cœur ! **"**
Devî-Mâhâtmya

Le jaïnisme

Le petit nombre de monuments, de vestiges et de témoignages épigraphiques semble indiquer la moindre popularité du jaïnisme à l'époque gupta. Seules de rares inscriptions font état de l'installation d'images de tîrthankara à Kahaum,

Udayagiri (caverne n° 20) ou encore Mathurâ, cette
dernière ville demeurant, tout comme Valabhî,
un bastion de la secte jaïne des Shvetâmbara.
C'est toutefois durant cette époque intellectuellement
féconde que furent rédigés de nombreux
commentaires des textes sacrés du jaïnisme et que
le théologien et philosophe Siddhasena Divâkara
composa ses célèbres traités de logique.

Le statut paradoxal du bouddhisme

S'il n'eut jamais à souffrir de l'hostilité déclarée
de la dynastie régnante, le bouddhisme ne bénéficia
de son patronage que de façon modérée. Seuls
trois empereurs, Kumâragupta Ier, Budhagupta
et Narasimhagupta Bâlâditya, furent associés
à la fondation de monastères bouddhiques à
Nâlandâ (Bihâr).

Toutefois, si l'on en croit le pèlerin chinois Yijing,
le premier souverain gupta, Shrîgupta, aurait fait
bâtir à Mrigashikhâvana, à l'est de Nâlandâ,
un temple doté des revenus de quarante villages
et destiné aux pèlerins bouddhistes venant de
Chine. Selon une autre source chinoise, l'empereur
Samudragupta aurait accordé au roi du Shri Lankâ,
Meghavanna, l'autorisation de bâtir un monastère

ainsi qu'une « maison pour les pèlerins » à Bodh Gayâ – à proximité de l'arbre de la Bodhi, sur le lieu même où le Buddha Shâkyamuni avait obtenu l'Éveil –, destinée aux moines et visiteurs venant de Ceylan. Et, semble-t-il, le vishnuite Samudragupta confia l'éducation de son fils au grand érudit bouddhiste Vasubandhu, illustrant ainsi tout l'esprit de tolérance d'une lignée de dynastes éclairés.

En revanche, le bouddhisme a indéniablement pâti de l'essor croissant de l'hindouisme, qui était mieux structuré et plus organisé que durant les siècles précédents. Dans nombre de *Purâna* compilés à l'époque gupta par une orthodoxie brahmanique soucieuse de réformer l'hindouisme, longtemps menacé par le bouddhisme et le jaïnisme, les tenants de la doctrine du Buddha sont stigmatisés comme de dangereux hérétiques (*pârhanda*), dont les croyances perverties constituent une menace pour la société.

Haut lieu du bouddhisme, le site de Nâlandâ fut très prospère dès l'époque des Gupta et, plus encore, sous le règne de leurs successeurs. Des ruines impressionnantes (temples, monastères (*vihâra*), sanctuaires, *stûpa* votifs) témoignent de l'importance de cette cité monastique et universitaire, qui accueillait par milliers des maîtres et des étudiants venus de tout le monde bouddhique (ci-dessous, détail du site ; à gauche, buddha et bodhisattva dans les niches du grand *stûpa*).

La littérature profane ne se montre guère plus charitable et se complaît volontiers à caricaturer moines et nonnes bouddhistes, mais aussi jaïns, les confinant souvent à des rôles d'intermédiaires amoraux, voire débauchés.

Le rayonnement de la pensée et de l'art bouddhiques

Pourtant, en dépit de ce contexte trouble, le bouddhisme se développa de façon notable à l'époque gupta, et quelques-uns de ses plus grands érudits et maîtres à penser, tels Asanga, Vasubandhu ou Dignâga, y produisirent leurs travaux les plus célèbres. Loin des spéculations métaphysiques qui agitaient les adeptes du mahâyâna – Mâdhyamika ou Yogâchâra –, les tenants du courant hînayâniste, représenté par les sectes des Sarvâstivâdin, des Sâmmitiya ou des Sthaviravâdin, s'employaient de leur côté à fonder d'importants centres monastiques et académiques. Dans la seule ville de Mathurâ, le pèlerin chinois Faxian ne dénombra pas moins d'une vingtaine de monastères bouddhiques en activité ; il nota qu'il s'y élevaient de nombreux *stûpa* et qu'un culte y était rendu aux bodhisattva Avalokiteshvara et Manjushrî. À Pâtaliputra, qui fut l'une des capitales de l'empire, le moine pèlerin signale également la présence de deux monastères, l'un d'obédience hînayâna, l'autre mahâyâna, fréquentés par 600 à 700 moines, et il mentionne l'enseignement de deux grands maîtres du mahâyâna, Râdhasvâmin et Manjushrî. L'épigraphie nous éclaire également sur les développements doctrinaux du bouddhisme aux Ve-VIe siècles – essor du mahâyâna, développement de l'image de culte, culte des bodhisattva – ainsi que sur les liens pour le moins ténus que la religion du Bienheureux entretenait avec la dynastie régnante.

Avalokiteshvara fut l'un des bodhisattva les plus vénérés. On le reconnaît dans cette sculpture de Sârnâth grâce à l'image d'un buddha assis en méditation à l'avant de la coiffure et à la fleur de lotus rose (*padma*), dont seule la tige subsiste dans sa main gauche.

UNE POLITIQUE DE TOLÉRANCE RELIGIEUSE 55

C'est aussi durant l'époque gupta que les monastères bouddhiques commencèrent à se transformer en grands centres d'éducation religieuse. À Nâlandâ, à Sârnâth, et jusqu'à Ajantâ, divers vestiges – *stûpa* votifs, monastères, sanctuaires rupestres, innombrables sculptures – témoignent d'une intense activité monastique et de la vigueur du bouddhisme sous l'égide des Gupta comme des Vâkâtaka.

C'est dans le parc aux Gazelles de Sârnâth que le Buddha prêcha pour la première fois les « nobles vérités » à cinq anciens compagnons d'ascèse, devenus ses premiers disciples. Datant de l'époque gupta tardive, le *stûpa* Dhamekh de Sârnâth (ci-dessus) domine de sa masse imposante les vestiges des monastères et des bâtiments conventuels qui abritaient jadis près de quinze cents religieux. D'inestimables sculptures bouddhiques furent exhumées sur le site de Sârnâth.

C'est d'ailleurs surtout le bouddhisme qui inspira de façon magistrale les artistes gupta, qui sculptèrent dans le grès rouge de Mathurâ et le grès beige de Sârnâth quelques-unes des plus belles et des plus nobles images de buddha et de bodhisattva de tous les temps. Fleurons de l'art gupta, ces effigies altières et épurées constituent un impressionnant chant du cygne du bouddhisme – avant que, sous la poussée triomphale du brahmanisme, la religion du Bienheureux ne s'éteigne à jamais dans la contrée même qui l'avait vue naître.

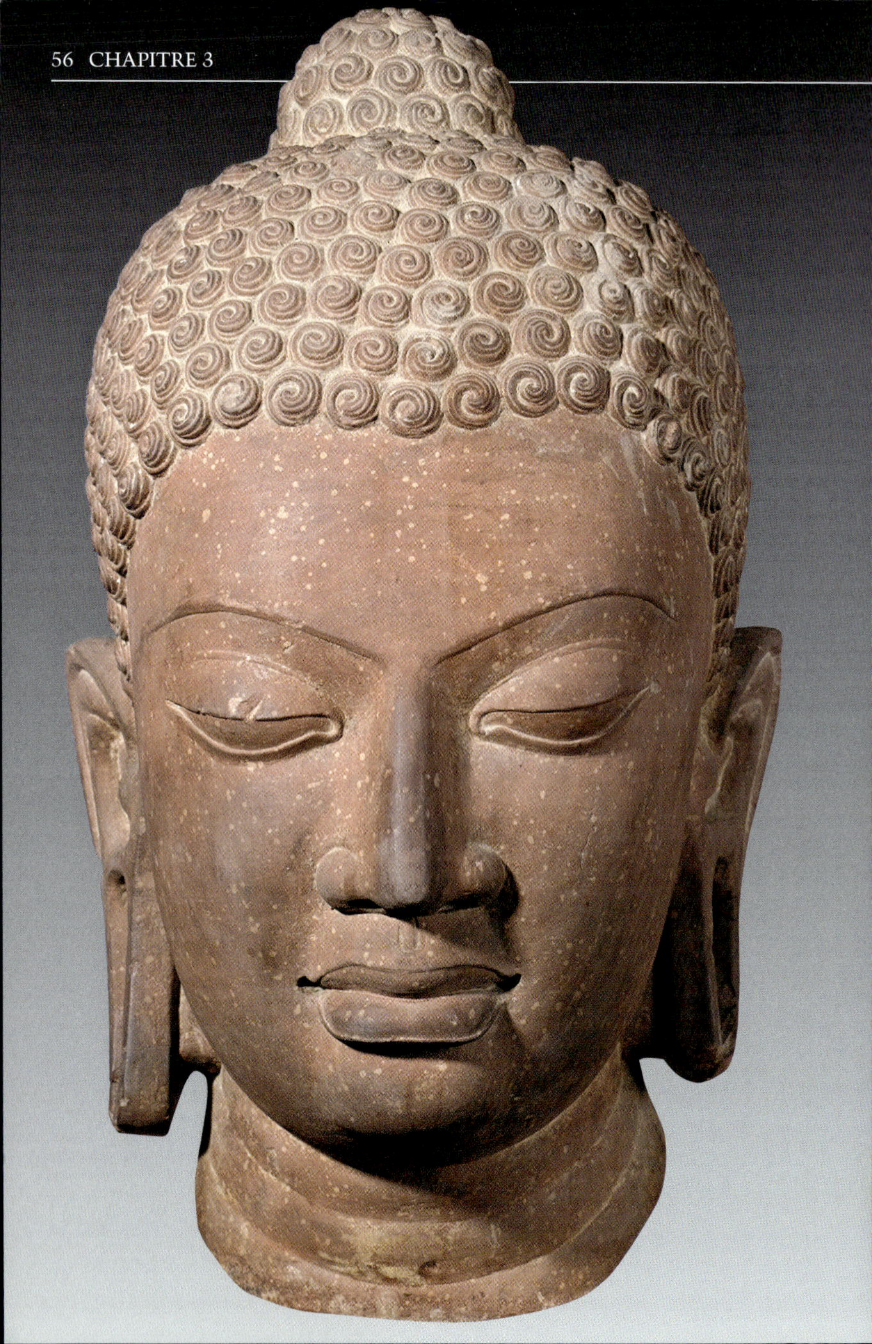

Empreintes d'une sereine grandeur et d'une altière noblesse, les images du Buddha des écoles de Sârnâth (ci-contre et ci-dessus) et de Mathurâ (page de gauche) comptent au nombre des plus grands chefs-d'œuvre de l'art gupta et de l'art universel. L'arête aiguë des sourcils, les yeux mi-clos aux lourdes paupières, la bouche au tracé sinueux et aux lèvres charnues confèrent à ces effigies épurées et idéalisées une expression méditative faite d'intense intériorité et de parfait détachement.

58

L'époque gupta est à juste titre considérée comme un véritable âge d'or, une époque féconde où, sous l'égide d'une lignée d'empereurs tolérants et éclairés enclins à promouvoir un œcuménisme religieux de bon aloi, les sciences, les lettres et les arts s'épanouirent et brillèrent d'un éclat jusqu'alors inégalé.

CHAPITRE 4

BELLES-LETTRES ET CULTURE SAVANTE

Conçu comme un art total au service duquel entrent la danse, le chant, la mimique et la récitation, le théâtre est considéré dans le *Nâtyashâstra* comme un cinquième *Veda* créé par Brahmâ. Dépeintes avec une grâce exquise, danseuses et musiciennes furent souvent figurées dans l'art gupta (à gauche, sur un linteau de Pawâyâ; ci-contre, à Ajantâ, grotte n° 1).

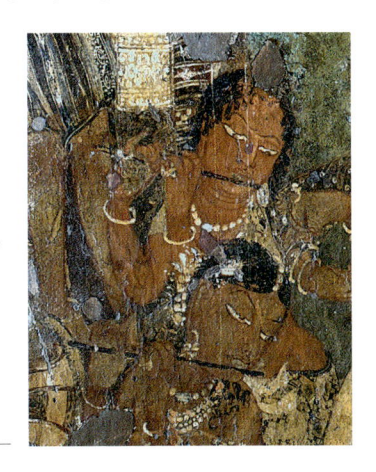

La prééminence du sanskrit

Si l'époque gupta s'accompagna de facto d'une renaissance du brahmanisme, comme l'atteste entre autres le développement de la littérature purânique, elle fut également marquée par le rayonnement sans précédent de la langue et de la littérature sanskrites. Le sanskrit est la langue par excellence de la civilisation indienne classique, mais aussi et surtout la langue du *Veda* et d'un immense corpus de textes irriguant tous les champs de la religion, de la pensée et du savoir. Issu d'antiques parlers indo-âryens, il est considéré dans la tradition indienne comme la « langue des dieux » (*devabhâshâ*), transmise aux hommes par une révélation et tenue pour être à l'origine de toutes les langues du monde – lesquelles n'en seraient que des formes corrompues. Vers le Vᵉ siècle avant notre ère, un grammairien de génie, Pânini, décrivit de façon magistrale la structure du sanskrit dans le plus ancien traité de grammaire sanskrite qui soit conservé, l'*Ashtâdhyâyî* (« *Les Huit sections* »). Langue idéale et sublimée, conçue comme un modèle éternel et universel et investie d'un statut métaphysique, le sanskrit acquiert à l'époque gupta une situation dominante. Les empereurs gupta lui vouaient, dit-on, une telle admiration qu'ils en préconisaient l'usage et la pratique jusque dans l'intimité des gynécées royaux !

Sous l'égide des Gupta, le sanskrit est consacré langue de l'épigraphie. Sceaux (tel celui de Bhitari : détail ci-dessus), chartes de fondation ou de donation, inscriptions votives ou panégyriques royaux (à droite, sur le pilier de Fer de Mehrauli) sont désormais rédigés dans la « langue des dieux ».

Dans l'Inde classique, la grammaire fut l'instrument privilégié de l'interprétation. Analyse grammaticale, exégèse des textes et art du raisonnement constituaient les trois grandes disciplines du savoir classique (ci-dessous, enfant étudiant).

Invariablement rédigés en sanskrit, les *Purâna*, livres sacrés de l'hindouisme compilés à des fins religieuses et sectaires, furent pour la plupart définitivement fixés à l'époque gupta. Avec de nombreux traités techniques (*shâstra*) compilés vers la même époque, ils témoignent de l'essor magistral de la « langue des dieux », tout comme les mathématiques, l'astronomie et la médecine dont les textes de base, versifiés car souvent destinés à être appris par cœur, et augmentés d'abondants commentaires, étaient également rédigés en sanskrit.

L'essor des sciences

D'immenses talents scientifiques purent s'épanouir à l'époque gupta, au premier rang desquels figure le plus illustre des mathématiciens et des astronomes indiens, Âryabhata, auteur en 499 – à l'âge de 23 ans ! – d'un magistral traité de mathématiques, l'*Âryabhatîya*. Né à Pâtaliputra en 476, Âryabhata détermina la valeur de « pi » comme étant 3,1416 et établit que les éclipses, loin d'être l'œuvre du démon Râhu comme on le croyait alors, avaient une origine naturelle et résultaient

Le célèbre pilier de Fer de Mehrauli – qui se dresse aujourd'hui dans l'enceinte du Qutb Minâr et de la mosquée Quwwatu'l-Islâm à Delhi – est un impressionnant témoignage des connaissances métallurgiques à l'époque gupta. Exposée depuis 1 500 ans aux intempéries et à la chaleur humide du climat indien, cette élégante colonne de fer haute de plus de 7 mètres (ci-contre) ne présente nulle trace de rouille, ni de corrosion. L'inscription gravée sur son fût (détail au centre) est généralement associée au règne de Chandragupta II. Dans sa vaste compilation encyclopédique, la *Brihatsamhitâ* – la « *Grande Collection* » –, le mathématicien et astronome Varâhamihira fournit quelques données parcimonieuses sur les connaissances métallurgiques de son temps. Mais l'ouvrage aborde les sujets les plus variés, de l'astrologie à l'étude des pierres précieuses, de la construction de maisons et de temples à la fabrication des images, de la description de la terre aux présages pouvant être tirés de l'observation des cieux, des animaux et des objets les plus divers.

Avec le développement de l'astronomie et de l'astrologie au VIe siècle, les images de Sûrya, le dieu Soleil, se font plus nombreuses (ci-dessous). Les planètes aussi sont représentées : ci-contre, Jupiter, Vénus et Saturne aux côtés de Râhu dépourvu de corps. Pour le châtier d'avoir dérobé l'ambroisie lors du Barattage de l'océan de Lait, Vishnu trancha le corps du démon en deux tronçons.

de la projection de l'ombre de la Terre sur la Lune. Il développa la théorie des épicycles afin d'expliquer les inégalités observées dans le mouvement des planètes. Surtout, il fut le premier à affirmer – à l'encontre des astronomes indiens qui la décrivaient jusqu'alors comme un globe immobile – que la Terre était ronde et tournait sur son axe, ainsi que l'exprime un vers célèbre de l'*Âryabhatîya* : « Tout comme d'un bateau en mouvement on voit la montagne se déplacer dans le sens contraire, ainsi vont plein ouest, sous l'équateur, les étoiles tout aussi immobiles. » Âryabhata, toutefois, ne fut pas suivi dans cette opinion. Mais sa contribution majeure à l'histoire des sciences demeure son système de notation numérique abstraite fondée sur le système décimal et établie par le truchement de l'alphabet sanskrit, où les voyelles déterminent la valeur de la position décimale des chiffres notés par les consonnes.

Astronomie, médecine, mathématiques

Varâhamihira (seconde moitié du Ve siècle), bien que réfutant la théorie d'Âryabhata sur la sphéricité de la Terre, fit œuvre d'astronome, mais plus encore de compilateur encyclopédique. Outre des ouvrages d'astronomie pure comme la *Panchasiddhântikâ*, compilation des enseignements des astronomes antérieurs, son œuvre maîtresse est la *Brihatsamhitâ*, une vaste somme à caractère encyclopédique recensant l'état des sciences et des connaissances de son époque.

Dans le domaine de la médecine, Vâgbhata, qui passait pour être bouddhiste, condensa au VIᵉ siècle les textes fondamentaux de la médecine ayurvédique, telles la *Sushrutasamhitâ* ou la *Charakasamhitâ* datant des premiers siècles de notre ère, en un traité majeur de près de dix mille vers sanskrits : l'*Ashtângahridayasamhitâ* ou « *Corpus de l'essence de la science en huit articles* ». Traduit en tibétain et connu jusqu'en Perse, le traité de médecine de Vâgbhata aborde des domaines aussi variés que la chirurgie, l'ophtalmologie, l'oto-rhino-laryngologie, la médecine interne, l'exorcisme, la puériculture, la toxicologie, les cures de rajeunissement et les aphrodisiaques. Les sciences vétérinaires n'étaient pas en reste, et des traités consacrés aux maladies des chevaux et des éléphants et à leurs traitements, tel l'*Hastyâyurveda* de Pâlakâpya, furent produits vers la fin de l'époque gupta. L'étude de la médecine était du reste enseignée dans les grandes institutions bouddhiques, comme à l'université de Nâlandâ, et l'on sait, grâce au témoignage des pèlerins chinois, que la ville de Pâtaliputra comptait de nombreux hôpitaux, remarquablement tenus et dirigés.

Les mathématiques se développèrent hautement sous les Gupta. Un système de notation numérique à l'aide de mots-symboles (feu = 3, etc.), supposant la connaissance du système décimal, apparaît dans le *Sûryasiddhânta*. Dès le VIᵉ siècle, la numération par position et l'usage du zéro sont acquis (ci-dessus, manuscrit indien du XIIᵉ siècle avec le nombre 109.305 et chiffres sanskrits de 1 à 0). C'est aussi en Inde, dans l'*Âryabhatîya* et le *Sûryasiddhânta*, qu'apparaissent la trigonométrie et les notions de sinus et de cosinus.

Kâlidâsa, le « Prince des poètes »

L'époque gupta vit surtout l'épanouissement des belles-lettres et de la littérature profane et le seul nom du poète et dramaturge Kâlidâsa suffit à incarner l'âme et le génie de cet âge d'or où la culture de cour mariait raffinement, élégance et beauté. On sait paradoxalement peu de chose de la vie et de la personnalité de celui qui est unanimement considéré comme le plus prestigieux des poètes indiens, le *Mahâkavi* ou « Grand Poète » par excellence. Il semble que ce brahmane dévot de Shiva ait vécu à Ujjayinî, sous le règne de l'empereur Chandragupta II (c. 375-415). Ses œuvres empreintes de sensibilité, de noblesse et d'élégance morale dessinent, entre les lignes, l'image d'un observateur attentif et subtil de l'âme humaine – et, tout particulièrement, de la psyché féminine –, d'un admirateur inspiré de la nature saisie et dépeinte sous ses multiples formes et dans toute son éblouissante beauté, ainsi que d'un connaisseur averti des usages et de l'étiquette de la vie de cour. Kâlidâsa est l'auteur de poèmes épiques

L'Europe lettrée et savante du XIXe siècle manifesta un véritable engouement pour le chef-d'œuvre de Kâlidâsa, *Shakuntalâ* – auquel Goethe, Herder, Michelet, Chateaubriand, Lamartine, Cazalis et bien d'autres rendirent de vibrants hommages. *Shakuntalâ* nourrit également l'inspiration littéraire de Théophile Gautier qui en entreprit l'adaptation en 1858, et produisit un livret d'opéra, *L'Anneau de Shakuntalâ*, sur une musique de L. E. Reyer. Le ballet-pantomime de Gautier fut créé à l'Opéra de Paris le 14 juillet 1858 (ci-dessus, un des décors de la création).

(*La Naissance de Kumâra*, *La Lignée de Raghu*), de poèmes lyriques et élégiaques (*Le Nuage messager*, chef-d'œuvre de grâce et de virtuosité), de drames et de pièces de théâtre (*Mâlavikâ et Agnimitra*, *Urvâshî conquise par la vaillance*, et surtout *Shakuntalâ au signe de reconnaissance*). Considérée comme le chef-d'œuvre du théâtre indien, *Shakuntalâ* est aussi la plus achevée et la plus émouvante des trois pièces de Kâlidâsa et un pur joyau de la littérature sanskrite. Ce fut aussi l'un des tout premiers ouvrages sanskrits à être traduits, et ce dès 1789 en anglais par le grand sanskritiste William Jones, avant de l'être en allemand en 1791 et enfin en français en 1830 par A. L. de Chézy.

Maître inégalé d'une langue souveraine, orfèvre ciselant avec une confondante virtuosité des vers d'une précieuse simplicité et d'une limpide élégance, maître des métaphores les plus subtiles et interprète des sentiments les plus délicats, Kâlidâsa incarne à lui seul et domine de sa prestigieuse stature les lettres sanskrites de son temps. Pourtant, d'autres talents fleurirent à ses côtés ou dans son sillage. Tels Shudraka (IVe siècle), auteur d'une charmante comédie, *Le Chariot de terre cuite*, Bhâravî (VIe siècle), réputé pour ses poèmes épiques comme *Le Combat de Shiva et d'Arjuna*, ou Dandin (fin VIe-début VIIe siècle), auteur de fables

Le caractère facétieux des personnages de cette terre cuite (ci-contre) évoque les conventions du théâtre sanskrit, où figurent maints personnages hauts en couleur, tel le *vidûshaka*, sorte de « bouffon » dévoué au roi.

Le thème de la jeune femme se balançant sur une escarpolette fut souvent évoqué par les poètes – notamment par Kâlidâsa dans *Mâlavikâ et Agnimitra*. Il fut également traité par les artistes, en peinture à Ajantâ, ou en terre cuite (ci-dessous).

et d'histoires romancées, dont le fameux *Dashakumâracharita, L'Histoire des dix princes*. Ou encore, au VIIe siècle, Mâgha, Bhartrihari et Bâna, poète de cour du roi Harsha de Kanauj, lui-même poète de talent et auteur de trois drames, où l'on décèle maintes réminiscences de Kâlidâsa.

Traités théoriques et littérature technique

La littérature technique atteint également son plein développement dans les domaines de la grammaire et de la lexicographie. L'*Amarakosha*, ou « *Lexique d'Amara* », sans doute composé au IVe siècle, est le modèle de ces prolixes traités lexicographiques qui constituaient un élément essentiel de l'érudition indienne et fournissaient d'inestimables instruments de travail à l'usage des poètes, qu'ils pourvoyaient en synonymes, homonymes et autres termes rares ou techniques.

Traditionnellement attribué à Bharata et sans doute fixé à l'époque gupta, le *Nâtyashâstra*, ou « *Traité d'art dramatique* », envisage l'art dramatique sous ses aspects les plus divers : théâtre, danse et mimique, « saveurs » (*rasa*) et « états intérieurs » (*bhâva*), figures

Qualifié de *rasarâja* (« roi des *rasa* ») ou de *rasapati* (« seigneur des *rasa* »), le Sentiment Érotique (*shringâra*) est le plus important des neuf *rasa* reconnus traditionnellement par les théoriciens indiens. Prééminent, dès les VIe-VIIe siècles, dans une abondante production littéraire d'expression sanskrite, il s'exprime également dans l'art indien, qui figure volontiers des couples d'amoureux (*mithuna*) – chastes ou dépeints dans des poses lascives, voire résolument érotiques – dont la présence était tenue pour bénéfique (ci-dessus, à Ajantâ : couples d'amoureux en bas relief et en peinture). Page de droite, en bas, détail du visage d'une danseuse.

et qualités, genres et compositions dramatiques, costumes et fards, distribution et acteurs, musique et chant.

C'est également à l'époque gupta qu'est assignée la composition du traité d'érotique indien le plus connu, le *Kâmasûtra*, ou « *Recueil d'aphorismes sur l'amour* », attribué à Vâtsyâyana. Rédigé, affirme son auteur, « en extrême chasteté et concentration spirituelle », il est conçu à l'usage du *nâgaraka* – l'« homme de la ville » –, c'est-à-dire du citadin élégant, cultivé et enclin aux plaisirs, mais aussi à l'usage des femmes en général, et plus particulièrement des courtisanes et autres hétaïres (*ganikâ*). Mais le fameux manuel était, peut-être et surtout, destiné aux dramaturges et aux poètes de l'époque classique, dont la production littéraire témoigne d'une indéniable familiarité avec la science érotique – laquelle est, en Inde, une science quasi encyclopédique touchant à une masse de disciplines des plus variées.

Le *Nâtyashâstra* traite de l'art de la représentation ou mimique de scène, où mouvements de la tête, de la nuque, des yeux, des mains, attitudes et postures du corps contribuent à susciter chez le spectateur le *rasa*, la « saveur » appropriée.

68

Expression parmi les plus abouties du génie esthétique humain, l'art gupta décline cette sujétion de la forme à l'esprit qui marque tous les classicismes, de la Grèce de Périclès à la Florence des Médicis. La profonde introspection, la capacité de traduire les émotions d'ordre spirituel en termes plastiques, l'élégance, le raffinement et la mesure expressive dont les sculpteurs gupta ont su faire preuve témoignent d'une civilisation aussi brillante que sophistiquée.

CHAPITRE 5

L'ART DE L'INDE CLASSIQUE

Les plus anciens monuments construits bien conservés remontent à l'époque gupta. À gauche, le temple n° 17 de Sânchî est attribué au début du Ve siècle en raison de la forme particulière de ses piliers. Ci-contre, extrémité de linteau de Sârnâth, ornée d'un lion cornu (*vyâla*) et de deux guerriers célestes.

L'étude de l'art à l'époque gupta donne lieu à deux constats : c'est d'abord la difficulté à définir sa spécificité ou son caractère novateur pendant les quelque cinquante ans suivant l'accession au trône de Chandragupta Ier, en 320. C'est ensuite le fait que, dès les dernières années du Ve siècle, la dynastie entre dans une période de rapide déclin et n'apparaît plus à même de soutenir ou d'orienter la création artistique.

Tradition et innovation : de timides débuts

Le domaine le plus révélateur des innovations de l'époque gupta au IVe siècle est celui de la numismatique. Une grande originalité s'y fait jour, avec l'apparition de nouveaux types de monnaies, notamment en or, dont la facture délicate témoigne d'une parfaite maîtrise technique. Comme souvent dans l'art monétaire, les monarques gupta ont su faire inscrire leurs aspirations politiques et religieuses dans quelques grammes d'or avec, certes, l'économie de moyens inhérente au genre, mais aussi presque autant de précision que lorsqu'ils commanditaient de longs panégyriques gravés dans la pierre ou le métal.

La rareté des œuvres attribuables aux règnes de Chandragupta Ier et de son successeur Samudragupta ne s'accorde pas avec l'importance politique

Intemporelle dans sa perfection physique idéalisée, cette *apsaras* (nymphe céleste), dont la personnalité s'affirme dans un regard à la fois doux et perçant, incarne l'extrême raffinement de la civilisation gupta. La liberté de touche des motifs de passementerie du turban le dispute au caractère arachnéen des pendeloques du collier.

L'ART DE L'INDE CLASSIQUE 71

de l'empire naissant et les prétentions de ses dirigeants. Jusque vers 375, la plupart des manifestations artistiques sont la prolongation de l'art vivant et éclectique de l'époque kushâna (Ier-IIIe siècles). La statuaire a livré des témoignages dans lesquels de nouvelles tendances semblent se dessiner ; l'architecture, en revanche, n'est représentée que par quelques fragments d'éléments décoratifs n'évoquant guère la naissance et l'originalité de l'esthétique classique appelée à se manifester dans les dernières décennies du IVe siècle. De hauts piliers-étendards (*dhvaja stambha*), généralement dressés sur des sites religieux, figurent parmi les rares commandes impériales parvenues jusqu'à nous.

Peu d'œuvres, parmi le nombre relativement important conservé à cette époque, peuvent être reliées directement au mécénat de l'un ou l'autre des souverains gupta. Certes, leurs noms apparaissent dans diverses inscriptions dédicatoires, mais la commande elle-même n'émane généralement pas d'eux : un fait sans doute lié aux aléas de la conservation et aux vicissitudes de l'Histoire.

Rien, malheureusement ne subsiste de l'art profane ni des arts dits mineurs (textiles, orfèvrerie, et autres), et tous ces trésors, aussi fragiles que convoités, sont à jamais perdus. Il reste malgré tout possible de s'en faire une idée assez précise grâce à la sculpture ou à la peinture, dans lesquelles costumes et bijoux sont figurés avec un luxe de détails inouï.

L'importance accordée aux bijoux et à la parure en général ne s'est jamais démentie au fil des siècles. Selon les époques, le nombre et la complexité des colliers, bracelets et autres ornements a pu varier. Sous les Gupta, une certaine sobriété était de mise et l'on faisait grand usage de rangs de perles torsadés ou de délicates pendeloques en métal repoussé auxquelles étaient suspendues de fines chaînettes (ci-dessous et à gauche).

L'architecture gupta : le passé recomposé

C'est dans les domaines de l'architecture et de la sculpture religieuses, que l'époque gupta se révèle particulièrement novatrice. La tradition de l'excavation, qui remonte au moins à l'époque maurya, se perpétue cependant. Au début du IVe siècle, le site hindou d'Udayagiri (Madhya Pradesh) donne à voir un ensemble de grottes sans grande prétention mais abritant de magnifiques hauts-reliefs. L'écho magnifié de tels ensembles se retrouvera dans les grottes d'Elephanta (VIe siècle) ou d'Ellora (VIe-VIIIe siècle).

Outre de célèbres panneaux en haut relief illustrant certains thèmes fondamentaux du vishnuisme, le site d'Udayagiri comporte diverses excavations plus modestes, comme la grotte n° 4. Un *ekamukhalinga* en occupe la cella, attestant sa destination shivaïte et la coexistence harmonieuse d'adeptes de Vishnu

Dans le registre, très ancien aussi, de l'architecture des *stûpa* bouddhiques, un affinement progressif des lignes se met en place, comme le montrent les vestiges de Devnîmorî (IVe siècle), au Gujarât, ou ceux de Mirpur Khas (Ve siècle), au Sind, dans l'actuel Pakistan. Cette évolution est sensible dans le *stûpa* Dhamekh de Sârnâth (VIe siècle), en Uttar Pradesh, dont le décor s'inscrit dans la continuité logique, et presque organique, des plus belles réalisations gupta du Ve siècle, telles les magnifiques auréoles des statues de Buddha provenant de ce site.

et de Shiva en ce lieu. L'encadrement de porte affecte la forme d'un T, caractéristique du décor architectural à l'époque gupta. Un porche en bois aujourd'hui disparu complétait cette façade (ci-dessus).

Les temples les plus anciens, reflets du monde des dieux

Pour la première fois, sous les Gupta, des monuments dans lesquels se fait jour une vraie science de la construction sont édifiés en matériaux pérennes, brique ou pierre. Certains remontent bien à l'époque de l'hégémonie des principaux monarques de la dynastie; d'autres, et non des moindres, peuvent sans doute être inscrits à l'actif de commanditaires dépendant de princes issus des familles royales moins prestigieuses, qui, dès la seconde moitié du Ve siècle, dominent certaines régions périphériques de l'empire en déclin. Ces temples, modestes à l'échelle des réalisations architecturales ultérieures, n'en sont pas moins les modèles à partir desquels s'élaborent les monuments si spectaculaires de l'époque médiévale. Le plan, l'élévation et le décor de ces édifices se révèlent variés et riches de symboles.

En Inde, l'architecture religieuse se veut la transcription dans le monde des hommes des palais célestes dans lesquels sont censés résider les dieux. Le sanctuaire est conçu comme la demeure terrestre de la divinité, une demeure d'autant mieux adaptée à son rôle qu'elle reproduit fidèlement les descriptions littéraires des traités normatifs de l'architecture (*Shilpashâstra*, ou « *Science de l'architecture* », et *Vâstuvidyâ*, ou « *Science du site et de l'édification* »).

Développant la formule élaborée dans les siècles précédant le début de l'ère chrétienne, le *stûpa* Dhamekh de Sârnâth (restitution, ci-dessus, et vue actuelle, ci-dessous) possédait un dôme surhaussé, orné de quatre niches orientées selon les points cardinaux, en accord avec certaines innovations iconographiques propres au bouddhisme mahâyâna. Sa base élevée (ci-contre) conserve d'élégants bas-reliefs où fleurs et rinceaux de feuillage alternent avec un motif typique de l'art gupta : la grecque.

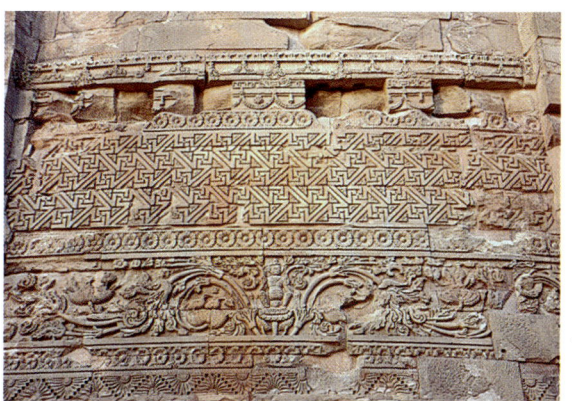

Le petit temple bouddhique n° 17 du site de Sânchî (début du Ve siècle), au Madhya Pradesh, fait un peu figure d'archétype par sa composition simple. Ce monument présente, en effet, les deux parties principales de toute architecture sacrée dans le sous-continent : une cella (*garbha griha*) précédée d'un petit porche à piliers dans lequel on peut reconnaître l'embryon des futures salles réservées aux fidèles (*mandapa*). Par exception, ou simplement parce que les architectes cherchent encore leur voie, la toiture de ce monument est plate – particularité qu'il partage avec quelques temples légèrement plus tardifs (temples hindous de Kunda et de Tigowa, au Madhya Pradesh, troisième quart du Ve siècle).

Au Ve siècle, et sans doute dans la première moitié du VIe, divers monuments présentent des partis architecturaux différents qui, tous, se perpétueront par la suite.

Le temple de Deogarh, avec ses templions aux angles de la terrasse et sa tour sanctuaire principale, évoque le mont Meru de la cosmographie indienne – cette montagne cosmique, véritable *axis mundi*, si élevée qu'on dut l'entourer de quatre montagnes contreforts plus petites pour assurer sa stabilité. Dédié au dieu Vishnu et datant du VIe siècle, le temple de Deogarh est orné de reliefs monumentaux, magistralement sculptés, qui comptent parmi les plus grands chefs-d'œuvre de l'art gupta. Ci-dessus, vue actuelle du temple et à gauche, son plan.

Des toits sur des temples

Le temple hindou de Bhitargaon (seconde moitié du Ve siècle), en Uttar Pradesh, est l'un des rares exemples d'édifices en brique relativement bien préservés. Outre un décor en terre cuite de grande qualité et plein de verve, ce monument possède une toiture élevée, formule la plus constamment attestée par la suite dans l'architecture indienne. Son état de conservation et les restaurations importantes dont elle a été l'objet ne permettent cependant pas de préciser s'il s'agit déjà de la toiture à arêtes curvilignes (*shikhara*) typique de l'Inde septentrionale, par opposition aux toitures pyramidales à faux étages décroissants du monde dravidien (Inde du Sud). Ces deux formules ne seront d'ailleurs clairement identifiables que dans des monuments plus tardifs, à partir du VIIe siècle, à Sirpur (Madhya Pradesh) ou à Bhubaneshvar (Orissa), pour la première, et sur le site de Mahâbalipuram (Tamil Nâdu), pour la seconde.

Le temple dit de Pârvatî (fin du Ve siècle) – en fait un temple de Shiva – à Nâchnâ (Madhya Pradesh) et celui de Vishnu (première moitié du VIe siècle,) à Deogarh (Uttar Pradesh) présentent un plan et une élévation très différents les uns des autres, soulignant la richesse d'inspiration de l'architecture religieuse indienne. Dans son état d'origine, le temple de Nâchnâ comprenait un déambulatoire (*pradakshinapatha*), dont on retrouvera maints exemples à l'époque médiévale. Le temple de Deogarh, quant à lui, présentait quatre templions aux angles de la terrasse sur laquelle se dresse encore sa tour sanctuaire principale.

Frappé par la foudre dans la première moitié du XIXe siècle et aujourd'hui amplement restauré, le temple de Bhitargaon est surtout renommé pour la foisonnante variété de son ornementation – moulures et pilastres soigneusement décorés, panneaux de terre cuite d'une éblouissante richesse iconographique. Le style de ces reliefs, vigoureux et empreints de spontanéité et de verve, offre un subtil contrepoint aux formes plus hiératiques attestées dans la sculpture en pierre. Ci-dessus, vue actuelle du temple et à gauche, son plan.

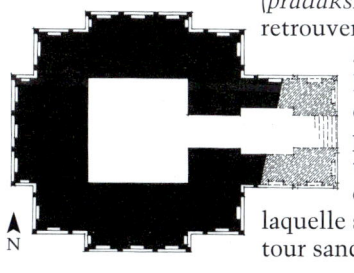

Mais c'est surtout par leur décor, dont divers éléments sont aujourd'hui conservés dans les musées indiens, que ces temples sont réputés. C'est le cas du temple shivaïte de Bhumârâ (première moitié du VIe siècle), au Madhya Pradesh, dont les magnifiques *chandrashâlâ* – ces arcatures entrant dans la décoration des parties hautes des édifices – sont habitées par les dieux les plus importants du panthéon hindou. Le nombre exceptionnel d'éléments décoratifs, en pierre ou en terre cuite, retrouvés lors des fouilles menées sur la plupart des sites importants de l'époque classique, de Mathurâ à Sârnâth, souligne, mieux peut-être que les monuments encore debout, l'extraordinaire sève créatrice qui sous-tend le domaine architectural.

Les jambes repliées dans l'attitude du vol, une guirlande de fleurs dans les mains, cet être céleste ou *vidyâdhara* s'inscrit dans une arcature en forme de *chandrashâlâ* (ci-dessus). Ces panneaux de terre cuite ornaient les niches et les murs extérieurs de temples en brique bâtis dans la vallée du Gange.

Deux grandes effigies en terre cuite des déesses fluviales Gangâ (ci-contre) et Yamunâ, aujourd'hui conservées au National Museum de New Delhi, se dressaient autrefois à l'entrée du temple de Shiva à Ahicchattrâ. C'est à l'époque gupta que les déesses fluviales commencèrent à être figurées à l'entrée des temples et des sanctuaires, dont elles gardaient le seuil afin que les fidèles y pénètrent symboliquement purifiés par la vision des deux fleuves sacrés.

Les plus hauts sommets de l'art : la statuaire gupta

D'une extrême diversité, la statuaire de l'époque gupta donne à voir les plus beaux chefs-d'œuvre de tout l'art indien qui, pourtant, n'est guère avare de trésors. L'ampleur du domaine des Gupta à son apogée explique le caractère unitaire de la statuaire aux Ve et VIe siècles ainsi que le fort régionalisme qui la marque dans le même temps. La nature centralisée de l'État gupta – devant lequel tout cédait, par la force ou la diplomatie – explique en grande partie la cohérence des différentes formes artistiques en présence. Au nombre des forces unificatrices de l'art, outre la politique d'hégémonie des souverains, l'iconographie, qui se fixe de manière canonique autour des IVe-Ve siècles, a également joué un rôle important. À l'inverse, sur un territoire presque aussi vaste que celui de l'Europe occidentale, il est logique de voir s'exprimer des traditions plastiques multiples. Ces facteurs semblent pouvoir justifier et expliquer l'existence d'un « style gupta » unitaire, toujours aisément identifiable malgré les différences de détail marquant nombre de ses réalisations. Ils permettent aussi de comprendre la rémanence du style et sa pérennité, longtemps après que les Gupta ont quitté la scène politique.

Au sein d'une production foisonnante, deux grandes écoles d'art se distinguent tout de même : celle de Mathurâ, largement inspirée par le passé kushâna du site qui lui a donné son nom, et celle de Sârnâth, où l'excellence des artistes se manifeste dès le IIIe siècle av. J.-C. avec le célèbre chapiteau aux Lions d'Ashoka. Si la première a laissé un nombre considérable d'images tant hindoues que jaïnes ou bouddhiques, la seconde est surtout célèbre pour les superbes buddha qu'elle a produits en abondance.

Les effigies de Shiva Androgyne (*Ardhanârîshvara*) montrent la fusion, en un seul et même être, du dieu et de son épouse Pârvatî – « pétris ensemble comme le mot et le sens », selon l'expression de Kâlidâsa. Coiffures différenciées, pendants d'oreilles distincts et présence du troisième œil sur le front distinguent le côté droit de l'effigie dévolu à Shiva de celui de son épouse – ou *shakti* – à gauche.

78 CHAPITRE 5

L'ART DE L'INDE CLASSIQUE 79

Cette sculpture, l'un des plus grands chefs-d'œuvre de l'école de Sârnâth et de l'art indien en général, illustre le premier sermon du Buddha dans le parc aux Gazelles de Sârnâth.

Le Buddha esquisse de ses mains réunies sur la poitrine le geste de prédication ou de « mise en mouvement de la roue de la Loi » (*dharmachakramudrâ*). De part et d'autre de la roue symbolisant l'enseignement du Bienheureux et de deux gazelles rappelant le lieu du premier sermon, de petits personnages aux mains jointes figurent les anciens compagnons d'ascèse du Buddha, qui devinrent ses premiers disciples. Taillée dans le grès beige pâle de Chunâr, cette sculpture incarne, par ses lignes pures et comme éthérées, l'intense et néanmoins sereine spiritualité des œuvres issues du classicisme gupta. Parfait exemple des canons esthétiques de l'école de Sârnâth, elle traduit en termes plastiques la perfection spirituelle du Bienheureux, ainsi que ses formes canoniquement parfaites qui, conformément aux prescriptions énoncées dans les textes bouddhiques, s'expriment en termes métaphoriques et esthétiques.

L'art de Mathurâ

Travaillant le grès rouge qui affleure partout dans leur région, les sculpteurs de Mathurâ ont élaboré un style imposant dont les caractéristiques procèdent directement de l'art des Kushâna, que ce soit pour l'ampleur des formes ou le modelé des visages. La dépersonnalisation des expressions, en revanche, est à mettre au compte d'une recherche orientée, à l'aune de la mentalité religieuse du temps, vers la traduction la meilleure de la spiritualité la plus élevée : celle que se doivent d'incarner des divinités hindoues, des tîrthankara jaïns et, a fortiori, le Buddha. C'est par les moyens les plus mesurés, mais aussi les plus efficaces dans leur sobriété, que les artistes de Mathurâ ont choisi de rendre sensible cette spiritualité ; ainsi se dévoile-t-elle dans des corps idéaux et longilignes, aussi éloignés que possible de la plus pure perfection physique de l'humaine nature, et dans des visages pleins, éclairés d'un discret sourire et dont le regard lointain semble se perdre dans le plus profond détachement face aux choses de ce monde.

L'art de Sârnâth

À Sârnâth, dans le grès beige de Chunâr, l'expérience esthétique sera poussée plus loin encore. Aux considérations développées à Mathurâ viennent s'adjoindre une rigueur formelle plus marquée ainsi qu'une certaine austérité de l'expression, toutes caractéristiques tempérées par le caractère volontairement éthéré des œuvres, lesquelles figurent en grande majorité le Buddha, mais aussi quelques bodhisattva et de rares

Le traitement du vêtement monastique (*uttarâsanga*), aux plis concentriques et réguliers, caractérise les images de Buddha dans l'école de Mathurâ (ci-dessous). Sous la robe monastique se devine, comme en transparence, le vêtement de dessous (*antaravâsaka*), retenu à la taille par un cordon noué sur le flanc gauche.

Encore peu nombreux dans l'art gupta, les bodhisattva – ces entités spirituelles douées d'Éveil qui retardent leur accès au *nirvâna* pour venir en aide à tous les êtres – recueillent une part importante de la foi des fidèles dans le bouddhisme du grand véhicule. Leur iconographie, qui se met en place au cours de l'époque gupta, connaîtra d'importants développements dans tous les pays d'Asie où le mahâyâna s'implantera par la suite. À Mathurâ, mais aussi à Sârnâth d'où provient cette sculpture (ci-contre), elle est encore balbutiante.
Cette œuvre atypique figure Avalokiteshvara, identifiable au petit buddha assis en méditation au-dessus de sa tête. En accord avec les doctrines mahâyâniques, il ne s'agit pas ici de Shâkyamuni, le Buddha historique, mais d'Amitâbha, l'un des cinq jina (« vainqueur ») – ou buddha de méditation – siégeant au sommet du panthéon. Les deux personnages placés sur les épaules du bodhisattva sont plus délicats à identifier. La pureté du modelé des corps et les visages doux et souriants relèvent pleinement de l'esthétique de Sârnâth aux V{e}-VI{e} siècles.

divinités brahmaniques. La grandeur de nature souveraine qui caractérise les plus belles œuvres de Mathurâ fait place, à Sârnâth, à une esthétique noble et hautaine, encore plus proche de cette forme idéale du divin et du beau que les artistes indiens ont toujours recherchée et de laquelle ils ne se sont jamais mieux approchés que dans l'art brillant de l'époque gupta, aussi maître de ses moyens que conscient des buts qu'il tentait d'atteindre.

82

Au-delà de ses frontières géographiques et de son aire d'influence très directe, la culture gupta a rayonné sur l'ensemble de l'Asie, dans l'espace et dans le temps. Avec un décalage que les vicissitudes de l'Histoire et l'immensité des territoires permettent de comprendre, l'Inde gupta peut être tenue pour la mère patrie culturelle de l'Extrême-Orient classique.

CHAPITRE 6

LE RAYONNEMENT DU CLASSICISME INDIEN

À partir du Ve siècle, l'image du Buddha tend à se substituer à celle du *stûpa*, si importante dans l'imagerie religieuse de l'Inde antique (à gauche, le Buddha dans la grotte n° 19 d'Ajantâ). À la même époque, les peintures de Sigiriya, au Shri Lankâ (ci-contre), participent de l'élégance de l'art pictural indien.

Ajantâ, un site exemplaire

Bien que situé en territoire vâkâtaka, aux franges du vaste domaine sur lequel ont régné les souverains gupta, le site bouddhique d'Ajantâ (Mahârâshtra) est sans conteste l'un des plus représentatifs des qualités esthétiques de l'art de l'Inde classique. Dans le registre tout aussi éblouissant que rare de la peinture murale, Ajantâ constitue un accomplissement, tant par la richesse thématique qui s'y déploie que par la finesse du dessin, le caractère sophistiqué des compositions ou encore le chatoiement irréel des couleurs. Comme tous les ensembles monastiques excavés de l'Inde ancienne, Ajantâ comprend deux types principaux de monuments : les sanctuaires (*chaitya*), de plan absidal avec une nef centrale séparée des bas-côtés par une rangée de piliers, et les habitations mêmes des moines (*vihâra*), de plan carré et comportant diverses petites cellules qui constituent autant de chambres réservées aux membres de la communauté religieuse.

Le site d'Ajantâ se déploie le long d'une falaise rocheuse (en haut) dominant un cours d'eau d'où il était possible d'accéder aux quelque 30 grottes qui le constituent (ci-dessus, plan du site). Les façades austères, souvent dotées d'une colonnade, ne laissent guère imaginer l'opulence décorative et le foisonnement iconographique des intérieurs. Chaque *vihâra* (ci-contre, la grotte n° 1) est doté d'un petit sanctuaire abritant une triade composée d'une image du Buddha enseignant et de deux bodhisattva.

LE RAYONNEMENT DU CLASSICISME INDIEN

C'est au cours d'une chasse au tigre organisée par des militaires britanniques que le site d'Ajantā fut découvert fortuitement en 1819. L'intérêt suscité dès cette époque par les peintures qui ornent les grottes se révèle dans le labeur exceptionnel du capitaine Robert Gill – un artiste attaché à l'armée de Madras – qui, dès 1844, réalise dans des conditions très difficiles des copies grandeur nature de la plupart des scènes importantes. Peu de temps avant leur présentation au grand public londonien, ces précieuses copies disparaissent dans le dramatique incendie du Crystal Palace en 1866. Avec leur minutieuse précision et leur caractère romantique, les dessins et gravures du XIXe siècle (ci-dessus) restituent l'atmosphère d'Ajantā alors qu'aucun travail de dégagement ou de restauration n'avait encore eu lieu.

Le site a connu une longue période d'occupation, depuis sa fondation, vers les IIe-Ier siècles av. J.-C., jusqu'aux environs des VIIIe-IXe siècles, date après laquelle on ne dispose plus d'aucune information. La période d'activité artistique la plus intense se situe à l'apogée de l'époque classique, dans la seconde moitié du Ve siècle; à ce titre, elle participe pleinement du renouvellement esthétique suscité par les monarques gupta dans toute l'Inde septentrionale et une grande partie du Deccan.

Miraculeusement préservées malgré leur fragilité, les peintures d'Ajantā apparaissent comme autant d'instantanés vivants restituant l'image précise d'une Inde mythique dont bien des composantes nous demeurent inconnues. Dans un contexte culturel que le respect des normes associées à l'art religieux n'a pas pu scléroser, et avec une infinité de détails révélateurs des mœurs en vigueur aux Ve et VIe siècles, elles illustrent en majorité la vie du Buddha ou, plus encore, certaines de ses vies antérieures. Elles offrent nombre de scènes urbaines ou villageoises, des représentations de palais et de spectacles de cour, d'extraordinaires paysages à la magie desquels participent une flore exubérante et une faune à la fois réaliste et cocasse.

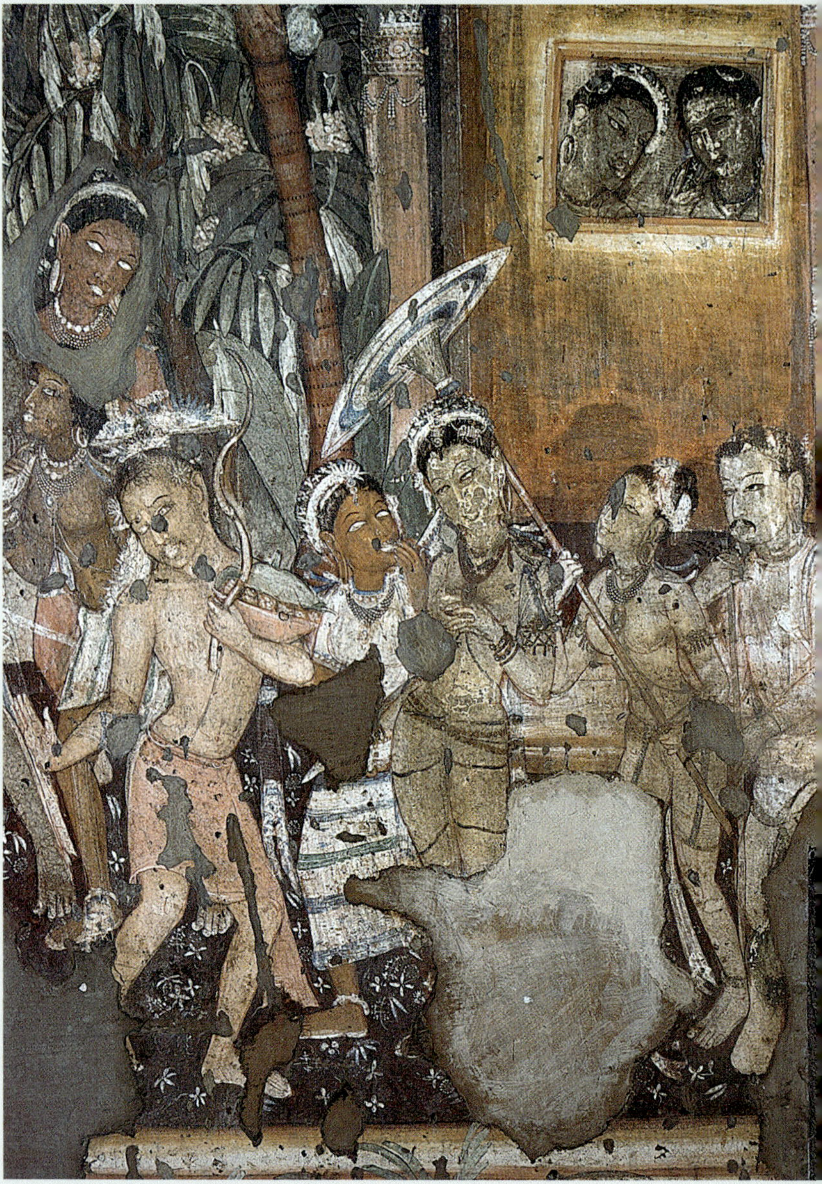

Sur les parois rocheuses irrégulières des grottes, un enduit – constitué de sable, de terre, de chaux, de résine et de divers matériaux de renfort (paille, crin de cheval) – était appliqué en couches successives, puis recouvert d'un lait de chaux destiné à lisser les surfaces à peindre. Après séchage, la composition était réalisée à main levée ou à l'aide de poncifs et de cartons. Considéré comme l'étape la plus importante, le dessin précédait l'application des couleurs, composées de pigments minéraux ou végétaux. Ce coloriage s'effectuait selon des techniques de modelé dans lesquelles les effets de volume étaient obtenus par juxtaposition de plages monochromes de tonalités différentes faisant saillir telle ou telle partie d'un visage, d'un corps ou d'un objet. Certains détails pouvaient enfin être repassés en noir avant l'application éventuelle d'une dorure là où elle semblait souhaitable. Ci-contre, deux détails d'une scène de *Jâtaka* dans la grotte n° 17 : à gauche, une princesse accompagnée de serviteurs sort de son palais ; à droite, un couple princier se délasse sous un pavillon de plaisance. Pages suivantes : deux bodhisattva dans la grotte n° 1.

88 CHAPITRE 6

LE RAYONNEMENT DU CLASSICISME INDIEN 89

Le Népal des Licchavi

L'art newâr de la vallée de Kâthmandu, au cœur de l'actuel Népal, est sans doute le surgeon artistique le plus proche du grand modèle gupta. Mal connues, les relations entre l'Empire gupta et le petit royaume des Licchavi (vers 350-750) devaient être étroites si l'on en juge par la majorité des œuvres népalaises anciennes parvenues jusqu'à nous. L'iconographie et le style dérivent pleinement de ce que l'on peut observer dans les grands foyers artistiques de Mathurâ et Sârnâth.

Dans le domaine hindou, aux côtés de très belles œuvres shivaïtes, tel le *linga* à visage de Mrigasthalî (début du VIe siècle), l'accent semble mis sur le vishnuisme : Vishnu Varâha sauvant la déesse Terre des eaux, de Dhum Varâhî (VIe-VIIe siècle), Vishnu Trivikrama (le dieu aux Trois Pas) conquérant l'Univers en trois enjambées de Tilganga (467), Krishna Kâliyamardana (destructeur du démon serpent Kâliya) dans l'une des cours du palais royal de Kâthmandu (VIIe siècle), Vishnu Anantashâyin (étendu sur le serpent d'Éternité)

La célèbre image de Vishnu couché sur le serpent d'Éternité de Budhanîlakantha – un petit village situé au pied des pentes boisées du mont Shivapuri, à environ 8 km au nord de Kâthmandu – fut commanditée peu après 641 par le roi licchavi Vishnugupta. L'image monumentale mesure près de 7 m de long et se trouve au centre d'un bassin artificiel représentant l'océan primordial duquel procède toute vie. Reprenant l'un des thèmes les plus importants de l'art hindou à partir de l'époque gupta, l'artiste licchavi produit une œuvre originale, proche cependant de l'esthétique gupta et post-gupta.

LE RAYONNEMENT DU CLASSICISME INDIEN

de Budhanîlakantha (VIIe siècle). À l'harmonie des formes et à la mesure expressive chères aux artistes des Ve-VIe siècles, succède un art de tension dans lequel les contrastes formels renouvellent le discours esthétique. Le serpent lové sur lui-même sur lequel repose le grand Vishnu couché de Budhanîlakantha en est un bon exemple.

La statuaire bouddhique dérive aussi du grand modèle gupta. L'influence de l'art de Sârnâth se dévoile dans des œuvres comme le Buddha de Bangemura, à Kâthmandu (VIe siècle) ou le magnifique *stûpa* votif orné d'images de buddha et de bodhisattva de Dhvaka Bâhâ, à Kâthmandu également (VIIe siècle).

L'art pâla du Bengale et du Bihâr

Dans le nord-est de l'Inde, l'art du royaume pâla (VIIIe-XIIe siècle), dont la plupart des souverains furent d'actifs mécènes bouddhistes, dérive en grande partie des traditions esthétiques et iconographiques élaborées à Sârnâth dans la seconde moitié du Ve siècle. Les formes les plus complexes de la doctrine s'élaborent entre les murs de véritables cités monastiques (parmi lesquelles figure la célèbre université de Nâlandâ), comportant un grand nombre de *vihâra* (monastères) et d'imposants temples dont l'architecture de brique

Dans la partie sud des ruines de Nâlandâ, le temple n° 3 (VIe siècle) conserve de magnifiques stucs représentant le Buddha et divers bodhisattva (ci-dessus). Ces sculptures, modelées sur âme de brique et en partie moulées, étaient originellement peintes. Elles apparaissent comme les héritières directes de l'école de Sârnâth, dont elles conservent la pureté des formes, l'élégance des volumes et la fluidité des lignes.

Ce Buddha monumental en bronze (VIIe-VIIIe siècle ; à gauche) fut découvert à Sultanganj, faubourg de l'actuelle Patna. Le traitement du visage et les proportions allongées du corps, comme la position des mains et le vêtement monastique diaphane, renvoient aux modèles gupta de l'école de Sârnâth, dans un traitement plus géométrique et moins sensuel.

s'adapte aux nouvelles exigences du bouddhisme. Toutes les sciences religieuses, du védisme aux théories les plus novatrices du bouddhisme vajrayâna (véhicule de diamant), y étaient enseignées.

Dès le X⁰ siècle, à la faveur des liens tissés entre les universités du nord-est de l'Inde et nombre de pays bouddhistes, l'héritage gupta contribuera à modeler de manière significative l'art des pays himâlayens ou celui de certains pays d'Asie du Sud-Est, par exemple le royaume de Pagan, en Birmanie.

Les royaumes anciens d'Asie du Sud-Est : la transmutation des formes

Les terres ou îles de l'or, selon l'antique désignation appliquée en Inde aux riches pays d'Asie du Sud-Est avec lesquels le sous-continent entretenait un commerce lucratif, se composent de deux grands ensembles géographiques : l'Asie du Sud-Est continentale, comprenant les actuels Thaïlande, Vietnam et Cambodge, et l'Asie du Sud-Est insulaire, dont l'Indonésie constitue le pôle principal. Ces pays modernes se sont substitués à un ensemble de royaumes qui tous participaient de la culture indienne. La plupart ont aujourd'hui disparu, tels les royaumes de Dvâravatî (VI⁰-IX⁰ siècle), jadis situé dans le centre et le nord-est de la Thaïlande, ou du Champa (II⁰ siècle-1832), dans le centre et le sud du Vietnam.

L'art de Dvâravatî n'est guère connu que par sa statuaire, presque exclusivement bouddhique. Ses monuments, édifiés en brique, ont presque totalement disparu. Les œuvres les plus caractéristiques sont des images du Buddha, apparentées au style de Sârnâth mais présentant une remarquable originalité iconographique. Au Champa, c'est également dans la statuaire que les influences indiennes sont les plus sensibles.

LE RAYONNEMENT DU CLASSICISME INDIEN 93

Aux environs du VIe siècle, certaines formes classiques trouvent une traduction originale, source du développement ultérieur d'une plastique parmi les plus surprenantes de toute l'Asie.

Au Cambodge, l'époque dite pré-angkorienne (IIIe-VIIIe siècle) est celle au cours de laquelle les influences indiennes se font le plus fortement ressentir. Des œuvres aussi remarquables que le grand Vishnu à huit bras du Phnom Da (VIe siècle), conservé au musée national du Cambodge, à Phnom Penh, ne peuvent se concevoir qu'à la lumière des influences gupta, sans être toutefois de serviles copies. Le génie propre des Khmers a su tout autant transcender la sensualité subtile de l'Inde qu'en adapter les iconographies religieuses à ses besoins propres.

Sur la péninsule malaise et dans l'île de Java, en Indonésie, certaines œuvres anciennes, représentant principalement Vishnu, révèlent leur dette à l'égard de l'Inde dès le Ve siècle. Plus que dans d'autres régions du Sud-Est asiatique, ces sculptures renvoient à de multiples sources : art kushâna de Mathurâ, art de l'Ândhra Pradesh et, bien sûr, art gupta. Ces nombreuses influences s'expliquent par les conditions politiques et économiques de cette partie de l'Asie, largement ouverte au commerce : les marchands indiens qui écumaient les mers d'Asie du Sud-Est venaient de toutes les régions du sous-continent. Il est logique d'observer

Les premières œuvres khmères (ci-contre, une sculpture du VIIe siècle figurant la déesse Durgâ) présentent une souplesse et un sens du mouvement hérités de l'art classique du sous-continent indien.

Aux côtés de sculptures en bronze et d'œuvres en stuc ou en terre cuite participant au décor des monuments, l'art de Dvâravatî en Thaïlande a livré de remarquables images du Buddha en grès (page de gauche). Représenté debout, le Bienheureux possède les caractéristiques iconographiques qui le définissent dans l'art indien à partir du IVe siècle environ : expression méditative et souriante, paupières mi-closes, protubérance crânienne, chevelure composée de petites boucles, vêtement monastique lisse et traité dans l'esprit de l'art gupta de Sârnâth. Les mains esquissaient de manière symétrique le geste de l'argumentation (*vitarkamudrâ*), pouce et index joints, selon une iconographie spécifique des arts anciens de l'actuelle Thaïlande.

94 CHAPITRE 6

Représentant les 5 jina, 504 images de buddha occupent les multiples niches et les 72 *stûpa* campaniformes de Borobudur (VIIIe-IXe siècle), dans le centre de Java (ci-contre).

Ce reliquaire en bois provenant d'Asie centrale (ci-dessous) témoigne de la fusion d'une iconographie fréquente au Gandhâra et du style gupta de Sârnâth. Pour rendre hommage au buddha Dîpankara (premier des 24 prédécesseurs de Shâkyamuni), un étudiant brahmanique déploie sa chevelure sous ses pieds.

dans les arts naissants de la région une grande diversité de sources. Et il ne faut pas oublier l'apport essentiel de l'art cinghalais à la constitution des styles bouddhiques anciens. Pour Java, enfin, le célèbre Borobudur dévoile un type d'influences secondaires largement attestées dans l'ensemble de l'Asie. En fonction des iconographies propres au bouddhisme du grand véhicule qui s'y déploient, c'est par le biais de l'art pâla que l'esthétique gupta a marqué les innombrables statues de buddha dans ce monument et dans les temples qui lui sont associés (VIIIe-IXe siècle).

Les routes de l'Extrême-Orient

En Afghanistan, les stucs de Hadda (IVe-Ve siècle), certaines peintures murales et les grands Buddha rupestres de Bâmiyân (Ve-VIe siècle), de même que les terres cuites de Fondukistân (VIIe-VIIIe siècle), permettent de suivre le cheminement de divers modes d'expression artistique purement indiens vers le nord-ouest du sous-continent et les routes de la soie. Les formes y sont tout aussi dépendantes des traditions plastiques locales, notamment gandhâriennes, que du rayonnement de l'esthétique gupta. Les caractéristiques composites mais réellement originales de l'art bouddhique de l'Afghanistan ancien ont d'ailleurs conduit le classicisme indien à laisser une empreinte fugace, mais néanmoins réelle, dans l'art des oasis d'Asie centrale (par exemple à Duldur-Aqur, vers les VIe-VIIe siècle) et au-delà, dans les arts chinois d'époque Tang (618-907) et japonais d'époque Hakuhô (645-710).

Un accomplissement esthétique majeur

À l'image d'une plante qui meurt et renaît chaque année, les arts de l'Inde et des pays sur lesquels elle a étendu son influence n'ont cessé de se renouveler au cours de leur tumultueuse histoire. Il en ressort un tableau d'une extrême complexité mais aussi d'une richesse particulière. C'est finalement dans la remarquable diffusion de l'esprit de l'art gupta, sinon dans celle de ses formes, que l'Inde classique a donné au monde l'exemple d'un accomplissement esthétique majeur, dont l'écho s'est étendu à l'ensemble de l'Asie, des franges du sous-continent dans ses frontières historiques (Népal, Afghanistan) jusqu'à de plus lointaines contrées (Asie du Sud-Est, Chine et Japon).

Avant leur récente destruction, deux immenses Buddha rupestres scandaient la falaise constellée de grottes du site de Bâmiyân, étape importante sur les routes caravanières reliant l'Inde à l'Asie centrale. Le plus grand (V^e-VIe siècle environ) mesurait 55 m (ci-dessus) et offrait une synthèse harmonieuse de l'art du Gandhâra et de l'art gupta de Mathurâ.

96

TÉMOIGNAGES ET DOCUMENTS

Échos d'un âge d'or

Kâlidâsa et les lettres sanskrites

L'engouement pour *Shakuntalâ*

Ajantâ, un haut lieu de l'art indien

L'art gupta et son rayonnement

Les monnaies des empereurs gupta

Chronologie

Bibliographie

Table des illustrations

Échos d'un âge d'or

C'est sous l'Empire gupta que la civilisation indienne parvint à son apogée. Un âge d'or dont l'art et la littérature sont le reflet et dont l'épigraphie ou encore les relations de voyage laissées par les pèlerins chinois, venus sur la terre du Buddha afin de s'y procurer reliques et textes sacrés, se font également l'écho.

Le témoignage de Faxian

De retour à Nankin au terme d'un long périple dans les lieux saints du bouddhisme, le pèlerin chinois Faxian, qui parcourut l'Empire gupta pendant les premières années du Ve siècle, rédigea sa Relation des royaumes bouddhiques *– véritable guide à l'usage des pèlerins bouddhistes. Il y dresse un passionnant état de la religion du Bienheureux dans l'Inde des Gupta, où régnait alors une grande tolérance religieuse.*

En traversant le fleuve et en continuant vers le sud sur un yôjana, nous arrivons au Magadha et à la ville de Pa-lin-fou (Patna). C'est la ville dans laquelle régnait le roi Asôka.

[...] De tous les royaumes d'Inde centrale, les villes de ce pays sont particulièrement grandes. Les gens sont riches et prospères et vertueux. Chaque année, au huitième jour du deuxième mois, il y a une procession d'Images. À cette occasion, ils construisent un char à quatre roues, sur lequel ils érigent une tour de cinq étages, composée de bambous liés entre eux, le tout étant supporté par un mât central ressemblant à une grosse lance à trois pointes, de plus de 22 pieds de haut. Ainsi, cela ressemble à une Pagode. Ils couvrent alors l'ensemble avec une fine étoffe de lin blanc, sur laquelle ils peignent toutes sortes de dessins aux couleurs chatoyantes. Après avoir fabriqué des effigies de tous les Dêvas et les avoir décorées avec de l'or, de l'argent et de la verroterie colorée, ils les installent sous des dais de soie brodée. Puis ils construisent aux quatre coins du char des niches dans lesquelles ils disposent des effigies du Buddha assis avec un Bôdhisatwa se tenant à ses côtés. Il y a peut-être une vingtaine de chars préparés de la sorte, et chacun décoré de façon différente. Le jour de la procession, prêtres et laïcs se réunissent en grand nombre. Il y a toutes sortes de jeux et de réjouissances (pour ces derniers), tandis que les prêtres offrent fleurs et encens en guise d'offrandes religieuses. Les Bramachârîs (les fils ou disciples des Brâhmans) s'approchent pour rendre hommage à Buddha, et l'un après l'autre, les chars pénètrent dans la cité. Après avoir traversé la ville, ils gagnent leurs différents emplacements. Alors, durant toute la nuit, le peuple brûle des flambeaux, se livre à des jeux, et fait des offrandes religieuses. Telle est la coutume de tous ceux qui se réunissent à cette occasion depuis les contrées alentour. Les nobles et les propriétaires terriens de ce pays ont fondé des hôpitaux dans la ville, où les pauvres de tous pays, les indigents, les estropiés et les malades viennent chercher un abri. Ils y reçoivent toute l'aide requise à titre gracieux. Des médecins examinent leurs maladies, et selon les cas prescrivent boissons et nourritures, médicaments ou décoctions, tout ce qui peut en réalité contribuer à leur rétablissement. Une fois guéris, ils partent quand ils le souhaitent.

Faxian témoigne aussi du caractère magnanime du gouvernement impérial.

Les habitants sont nombreux et heureux. Ils n'ont pas à déclarer leurs biens, ou à se soumettre à des magistrats et à leurs règlements. Seuls ceux qui cultivent les terres royales doivent verser une part des gains qu'ils en retirent. S'ils veulent partir, ils partent; s'ils veulent rester, ils restent. Le Roi gouverne sans trancher les têtes ou recourir aux châtiments corporels. Les coupables reçoivent simplement une amende, plus ou moins lourde, selon la gravité de leurs délits. Et même s'ils sont convaincus de tentatives répétées de rébellion, on se borne à leur couper la main droite. Les gardes du corps et la suite du roi perçoivent tous un salaire.

Travels of Fah-Hian and Sung-Yun, Buddhist pilgrims from China to India, (400 A.D. and 518 A.D.), Traduit du chinois par Samuel Beal. Asian Educational Services, New Delhi, 1993

L'inscription de Mandasor

Témoin du haut degré de raffinement culturel de l'époque gupta, l'inscription de Mandasor a été réalisée par les tisserands de soie de Lâta. Elle relate la construction puis la restauration d'un temple au dieu Soleil sur les berges du fleuve. Ellle est rédigée dans le style Kâvya, le sanskrit poétique le plus classique et le plus abouti, utilisé pour les poèmes narratifs et pour les récits dramatiques, et dont Kâlidâsa fut le plus illustre représentant. Un mode poétique extrêmement sophistiqué, régi par une métrique complexe et dont l'expression est caractérisée par un recours constant à d'abondantes métaphores. Ici, le bien-être des tisserands à Lâta:

Et au fil du temps, cette cité devint le diadème de la terre, qui est ornée d'un millier de montagnes dont les rochers ruissellent de la sérosité suintant des tempes d'éléphants en rut, et dont les pendants d'oreilles sont semblables aux arbres alourdis de fleurs. Ici les lacs peuplés de canards *karandava* sont magnifiques et les eaux bordant le rivage, ornées de nymphéas éclos, luisent de toutes les fleurs tombées des arbres poussant sur la berge. Par endroits, des cygnes recouverts du pollen des nymphéas agités par l'onde frémissante; ailleurs des nénuphars ployant sous la lourde charge de leurs filaments ajoutent encore à la beauté des lacs. Ici les forêts sont parées d'arbres majestueux qui se courbent sous le poids de leurs fleurs, et elles résonnent du bourdonnement sonore des abeilles ivres du nectar des fleurs qu'elles butinent, et des chants incessants des femmes de la ville.

Ici les maisons ont des oriflammes qui flottent au vent et des femmes délicates les habitent, Ces demeures très blanches et très élevées ressemblent aux sommets des nuages blancs zébrés d'éclairs flamboyants. Et, sur les toits des maisons, d'autres bâtiments allongés sont splendides avec leurs charmilles; semblables aux fiers sommets du mont Kailasa; bruissants de chansons pareilles à celles des Gandharvas; et ornés d'images peintes et de bosquets de bananiers ondulants.

in J.C. Harle, *Gupta Sculpture, Indian Sculpture of the Fourth to the Sixth Centuries A.D.*, Clarendon Press, Oxford, 1974

Kâlidâsa et les lettres sanskrites

À la cour des Gupta se trouvèrent réunies toutes les conditions propices à l'éclosion d'une littérature d'expression sanskrite marquée au sceau d'une perfection et d'un raffinement jusqu'alors inégalés. Par sa beauté souveraine et son irréprochable élégance, l'œuvre de Kâlidâsa domine les lettres sanskrites de son temps. Le grand poète de l'Inde classique porta à son apogée l'art complexe et sophistiqué du kâvya – *la «poésie savante» ou «composition en style orné».*

La «langue des dieux» et le «Prince des poètes»

Le terme de sanskrit (*samskrta*), qui apparaît relativement tard dans l'usage littéraire (*Râmâyana*), signifie «formé selon les opérations prescrites par les grammairiens». Hors de son acception linguistique, le mot s'applique dès l'origine aussi bien à un mets «préparé» selon les recettes qu'à une œuvre littéraire «composée» selon les règles ; il se dit aussi, sur le plan religieux, du jeune Indien qui a reçu l'initiation brahmanique. Toutes ces résonances sont présentes dans l'emploi linguistique : une parole «sanskrite», un discours «sanskrit», cela a été d'abord une parole, un discours «équipés», pour être efficaces, par l'application des procédés de rhétorique, de rituel, de magie. Le terme s'oppose à *prâkrta*. Pour la tradition indienne le sanskrit, langue des dieux (*devabhâsâ*), existe de tout temps, est à l'origine de toutes langues et a été transmis aux hommes par une révélation.

Comme les premiers documents du sanskrit sont les textes du Veda, on appelle «védique» l'état de langue qu'ils représentent. Le «védique» n'est donc autre que du sanskrit archaïque. Les relations avec le sanskrit littéraire de date plus récente, dit «sanskrit classique», se laissent comparer à celles qui existent entre la langue homérique et la koinè.

[…] Certaines des conditions nécessaires à l'éclosion d'une poésie savante sont donc réunies dès les derniers siècles précédant notre ère. Un instrument linguistique tout prêt, susceptible de servir de grande langue de civilisation, un vaste trésor de récits légendaires ou mythiques, une tradition de lyrique religieuse. Il manquait sans doute encore ces disciplines qui doivent alimenter l'inspiration, et qui n'ont guère pu prendre naissance avant les débuts de notre ère : les «systèmes», philosophiques, la théorie du Plaisir condensée dans le *Kâmasâstra*, la théorie du Profit représentée par l'*Arthasâstra* (si toutefois l'on admet, comme une partie de l'opinion savante y incline, que ce domaine a pris sa forme littéraire vers la même époque que le

Kâmasâstra, soit peu avant l'ère gupta), enfin la *Smrti* elle-même, issue des *Dharmasûtra* védiques. Il manquait aussi l'élément le plus important, cet ambitieux enseignement des figures de style, des qualités, des défauts, des ressorts intimes de l'œuvre d'art, que nous voyons s'ébaucher dans le *Nâtyasâstra* pour aboutir vers le VIe-VIIe siècle, aux traités autonomes de poétique qui nous sont conservés.

Il manquait surtout les conditions extérieures favorables. Les progrès du bouddhisme, étranger à tout souci littéraire et axé sur des langues de propagande religieuse, ne pouvaient que retarder l'apparition, ou du moins le succès, d'une littérature d'inspiration brahmanique et de forme sanskrite. Les monarchies étrangères qui, à la suite des Maurya, se sont succédé presque sans interruption dans le nord de l'Inde jusqu'à la venue des Gupta n'étaient pas davantage en état de favoriser un instrument aussi profondément indien, indigène, qu'est le *kâvya* sanskrit. Il a fallu le déploiement de la vie de cour, les conditions privilégiées faites à la littérature (comme aux beaux-arts et à la science) sous les premiers Gupta, cette époque miraculeuse dans l'histoire de l'Inde ancienne, pour amener une surrection de grandes œuvres, dont le seul nom de Kâlidâsa permet de mesurer l'importance.

[…] Ils [les drames de Kâlidâsa] se signalent par les mêmes qualités que les poèmes lyriques : élégance souveraine de la forme, ressources d'un talent également apte au récit, à la description, auquel ne manquent ni la force dramatique, ni éventuellement l'humour et la malice. Pour peindre les joies et les peines d'amour Kâlidâsa a des touches délicates, comme pour esquisser des scènes de la nature, qu'il sait mettre en harmonie avec les passions du moment. On oublie la fiction, l'irrationnel de certaines données quand on voit, dans un épisode fameux, Sakuntalâ qui s'efforce en vain de rappeler au roi les instants heureux de leur amour tout proche ; elle lui parle du faon qu'elle avait adopté et qu'il se plaisait à caresser, mais qui n'osait par timidité venir boire dans sa main. Le charme, conventionnel certes, mais rafraîchi par le prestige des mots, de la nature indienne, la forêt, la vie paisible des ermites, sont l'arrière-plan d'une œuvre comme *Sakuntalâ*, qui baigne ainsi dans une sorte de primitivité concertée. Rien d'encombrant, de pédant dans cet art ductile, un peu menu. La prose du dialogue est d'une grande limpidité, et les strophes mêmes, cette parure du drame, n'ont en général que des images propres à exalter l'émotion du spectateur ; la tradition vante la beauté des *upamâ* (comparaisons) chez Kâlidâsa.

Il se peut que chaque scène ait été conçue pour illustrer les situations requises par les dramaturges, et que l'auteur ait trouvé chez ses devanciers des procédés : mais il a certainement un don d'animer et d'émouvoir qui n'appartient qu'à lui ; il est « la grâce de la poésie », disait déjà de lui l'auteur du *Prasannarâghava*.

Les caractères sont tracés avec soin, au moins dans *Mâlavikâ* et *Sakuntalâ* : ainsi les deux suivantes de la jeune ermite, l'une joviale et malicieuse, l'autre grave et réfléchie. Les gens du peuple sont bien saisis, ainsi les policiers avec leur lourde gaîté, leur orgueil brutal en face du pêcheur humble et tremblant. L'emploi du merveilleux, limité autant qu'il était possible dans les deux principaux drames, se voit à plein dans la féerie d'*Urvasî*, où pourtant l'art du poète lui ménage une sorte de lointaine crédibilité.

Louis Renou et Jean Filliozat,
*L'Inde classique, Manuel
des Études Indiennes*, t. I et II,
Payot, Paris, 1947

La Naissance de Kumâra

Dans le Kumârasambhava, *Kâlidâsa retrace les événements mythiques qui présidèrent à la naissance du dieu Kumâra, le fils de Shiva et d'Umâ-Pârvatî. Pour mieux séduire Shiva, absorbé dans une ascèse farouche et rigoureuse, la déesse entreprit tout d'abord de lui dévoiler sa beauté rayonnante et souveraine, avant de se livrer sous ses yeux aux mortifications les plus extrêmes.*

XVIII
Cependant, comme l'austérité et la concentration spirituelle, ainsi pratiquées, ne lui obtenaient pas le fruit souhaité, elle négligea la faiblesse de son corps et s'adonna à une vie de violente mortification.

XIX
Le jeu de la balle suffisait à l'épuiser, elle prit le mode d'existence réservé aux grands ascètes : en vérité son corps, créé pareil à un lotus d'or, était par nature, délicat, mais, aussi, résistant!

XX
Elle, au pur sourire, à la taille mince, s'en fut, au temps clair, entre les quatre feux sacrés flamboyants. Triomphant de l'éclat qui ruine le regard, elle contempla le soleil, la vue fixée sur lui seul.

XXI
Les rayons solaires enflammaient son visage; il eut la splendeur des lotus; cependant, les angles extérieurs, si allongés, de ses yeux se couvrirent, peu à peu, d'une teinte foncée.

XXII
Seuls rompaient son jeûne l'eau qu'elle obtenait sans la demander et les rayons du Maître des étoiles qui a pour essence l'ambroisie : son mode de vie, en vérité, ne différait pas des moyens d'existence de l'arbre!

XXIII
Brûlée à l'extrême par les feux de toutes sortes, par ceux qui errent dans le ciel et par ceux que le bois alimente, arrosée par les eaux nouvelles au départ du temps chaud, elle dégagea, avec la terre, une vapeur qui s'élevait:

XXIV
Un instant suspendues à ses cils, frappant ses lèvres, broyées dans leur chute par l'opulence des seins, glissant le long des plis du ventre, les premières gouttes de rosée, lentement, pénétrèrent dans l'ombilic.

XXV
Tandis qu'elle couchait sur le roc et demeurait, sans demeure, au milieu des pluies et des vents incessants, les nuits, qui la regardaient en ouvrant leurs yeux faits d'éclairs, étaient là comme pour témoigner de son extrême pénitence.

XXVI
Elle passa les nuits d'hiver, où les vents soulèvent une masse de neige, ferme à se tenir dans l'eau et fut pleine de pitié pour un couple de cakravâka qu'elle voyait devant elle: les oiseaux, séparés, s'appelaient l'un l'autre!

XXVII
Avec son visage odorant comme un lotus, ravissant, avec ses lèvres, tremblants pétales, la nuit, elle sembla donner aux eaux, dont la profusion de lotus était dévastée par les pluies glacées, de nouvelles fleurs.

XXVIII
Vivre uniquement de feuilles mortes est l'extrême limite de l'ascèse : elle dédaigna, cependant, cette nourriture et, voilà pourquoi ceux qui sont instruits des choses du passé, parlent, en la nommant «Sans feuilles», de celle au joli visage.

XXIX

Ainsi les nuits et les jours, au moyen de
toutes ces observances, usaient
son corps, mince comme une tige de
lotus : elle dépassa de beaucoup le
mérite acquis par les corps,
plus vigoureux, des ascètes.

XXX

Alors, couvert de la peau d'antilope
noire et muni du bâton en bois de Palâsa,
la voix hardie et comme étincelant
de l'éclat fait du Sacré, un étudiant
brâhmanique, semblant le premier stade
de la vie du Brâhmane personnifié,
pénétra dans le bois de pénitence.

Kâlidâsa
*La Naissance de Kumara
(Kumarasambhava)*, Traduit du sanskrit
par Bernadette Tubini, Gallimard, 1958

« Le Nuage messager »

Dans le Meghadûta, *Kâlidâsa évoque
en vers les tourments d'un* yaksha *banni
de sa terre natale et condamné à vivre un
an loin de son épouse bien-aimée. Avisant
à la saison des pluies un nuage voguant
vers le nord, le* yaksha *lui confie sa peine
et le charge d'un message destiné à la
bien-aimée lointaine.*

1. Séparé de sa bien-aimée par
la malédiction du Maître, en sévère
châtiment d'une négligence, déchu pour
un an de sa grandeur, un Yaksa habitait
les ermitages du Mont de Râma,
aux eaux sanctifiées par les ablutions
de la fille de Janaka, sous l'ombre
aimable des arbres de la forêt.

2. Après quelques mois passés sur la
montagne, loin de sa jeune épouse,
au premier jour du mois d'Âsâdha,
l'amant passionné, dont le poignet restait
à nu laissant glisser son bracelet d'or,
aperçut, embrassant le sommet, un nuage
magnifique comme l'éléphant qui, dans
ses ébats, s'attaque à la terre d'un talus.

3. Se levant à grand'peine devant
Celui qui fait naître la fleur du ketaka,
refoulant ses larmes, le serviteur
de Dhanapati rêva longuement :
à la vue des nuées la pensée de l'être
heureux lui-même se trouble ; que
dire de celui qui brûle de se jeter au cou
de l'amante lointaine ?

4. Le mois des Brumes étant donc
proche, afin de soutenir la vie de la bien-
aimée par de bonnes nouvelles, il conçut
le désir de les confier au nuage : offrant
d'abord à ce visiteur l'hommage
de fleurs fraîches du Jasmin des Sommets,
il lui adressa, gracieux, avec d'aimables
paroles, un salut de bienvenue.

5. Un nuage n'est qu'un amas
de vapeurs, de feu, d'eau et de vent.
Comment lui confier un message que
seuls pourraient porter des êtres qui
pensent ? Dans sa passion, le Yaksa n'y
prenait pas garde, il lui fit sa requête :
ceux que tourmente l'amour adressent,
lamentables, leur prière à tous les êtres,
animés ou non.

6. Je te sais né de la race fameuse
des Puskara et des Âvartaka ;
tu es le ministre aux formes changeantes
de Maghavan : éloigné donc par
la volonté du Destin de Celle qui m'est
chère, je viens t'implorer. Mieux vaut
prier en vain un être noble qu'être
exaucé par un vilain.

7. Tu es le secours de celui qu'un
tourment consume : prends donc,
ô Dispensateur de la pluie, un message
pour ma bien-aimée, dont me sépare
la colère de Dhanapati. Tu iras à la ville
d'Alakâ, séjour des princes des Yaksa ;
dans les jardins qui l'entourent se tient
Çiva, et les palais y ruissellent de la clarté
de la lune qui pare le front du dieu.

8. Quand tu passeras sur la route
des vents, les femmes des voyageurs,
relevant leurs boucles, te regarderont

confiantes et rassurées : qui donc,
lorsque tu es ainsi en marche, négligerait
son épouse que la séparation accable,
s'il n'est, comme moi, soumis à
une volonté étrangère ?

9. Embrasse, pour lui dire adieu,
ce mont élevé, ton ami très cher,
qui porte sur ses pentes la marque,
que les hommes vénèrent, des pieds
de Raghupati. Chaque fois que tu
le rejoins, son affection paraît aux larmes
brûlantes qu'il répand après la longue
séparation.

10. Tandis que le vent favorable
t'entraîne doucement, ce câtaka avide
d'eau fait entendre à ta gauche sa voix
agréable et les balâkâ dont tu charmes
les yeux, sûres maintenant d'être
fécondées, viendront former dans les airs
des guirlandes en ton honneur.

11. Ta route parcourue sans obstacle,
tu ne manqueras pas de trouver en vie,
occupée à compter les jours, l'épouse
fidèle de ton frère : dans l'absence,
d'ordinaire, le lien de l'espérance retient
le cœur des femmes prêt à défaillir,
telle une toile d'araignée la fleur qui va
tomber.

12. Les oreilles charmées par tes
grondements qui fécondent la terre et la
font se couvrir de çilindhra, les cygnes
royaux auront hâte de retrouver le lac
Mânasa. Emportant pour viatique
quelques fragments de lotus, ils te
rejoindront pour t'accompagner dans
les airs jusqu'au Mont Kailâsa.

13. Écoute maintenant, ô nuage, que
je t'explique le chemin qu'il te convient
de suivre ; tu prêteras ensuite à mon
message ton oreille attentive. Je vais
te dire les sommets où, brisé de fatigue,
tu iras te poser, les rivières dont,
amaigri, tu boiras l'eau légère. [...]

77. À ces signes, sage ami, gravés dans
ton esprit, à la vue aussi de la Conque et
du Lotus, dont l'image est tracée de part
et d'autre de la porte, tu pourras
reconnaître ma maison en mon absence,
à présent, certes déchue de sa splendeur :
quand le soleil a disparu, le lotus de jour
n'étale plus sa beauté.

78. Posé sur le monticule au gracieux
sommet que je t'ai dit, réduis aussitôt,
pour t'approcher plus rapide, ta taille
à celle d'un jeune éléphant ; tu pourras
alors, d'un de tes éclairs mais pâle,
bien pâle, telle la lueur d'un essaim
de lucioles, jeter un regard dans
l'intérieur du palais.

79. Une femme en pleine jeunesse
est là, svelte, aux dents aiguës, à la lèvre
telle une cerise mûre, à la taille mince,
aux yeux de gazelle inquiète, au nombril
profond ; le poids de sa croupe alanguit
sa démarche, ses seins l'obligent à
s'incliner un peu : entre toutes les jeunes
belles, c'est le chef-d'œuvre du Créateur.

80. Reconnais en elle celle qui est
ma vie ; ses paroles sont rares ; loin
de moi, son compagnon, elle reste
solitaire comme l'oiseau fidèle ;
la tristesse profonde de la séparation,
au cours de ces jours pesants déjà
écoulés, l'a, je le crains, bien changée,
tel l'hiver flétrit la fleur du lotus.

81. Les larmes abondantes ont sans
doute gonflé ses yeux, les continuels
soupirs brûlants décoloré sa lèvre, et
son visage, qu'elle appuie sur sa main,
à demi-caché par ses boucles pendantes,
a la tristesse de la Lune dont ta présence
offusque la clarté.

82. Elle s'offrira à tes regards occupée
à de pieuses offrandes, ou bien peignant
mon image qu'elle se représente
amaigrie par l'absence ; peut-être
interrogeant la merlette en cage, à la
douce voix : « Te souvient-il de notre
maître, mignonne ? Il t'aimait ! »

83. Peut-être, ami, posant son luth sur
ses genoux, couverts d'un vêtement sans
éclat, voudra-t-elle entonner un chant où

les mots s'ordonnent pour former
mon nom : attaquant à grand'peine
les cordes mouillées de ses larmes, elle
oublie et oublie encore la gamme
qu'elle-même a choisie.

84. Peut-être aussi, pour les calculer,
représentera-t-elle à terre, avec les fleurs
amassées sur le seuil, les mois qui restent
du temps fixé au jour de mon départ ;
ou encore goûtera-t-elle par avance
les plaisirs qu'elle se promet dans son
cœur pour le moment de notre réunion.
Ce sont là, d'ordinaire, les passe-temps
d'une belle éloignée de son amant.

85. Ces cheveux qu'au premier jour
de notre séparation elle a rassemblés,
rejetant son diadème, et que,
la malédiction prenant fin, je dois,
délivré de mes peines, défaire
moi-même, elle en écarte à présent
de ses joues la tresse unique, rude,
irrégulière, qu'elle froisse continuellement
d'une main aux ongles non coupés.

86. Parmi ses occupations, mon
absence, le jour, doit lui être moins dure ;
la nuit, je pense, son chagrin s'accroît par
l'oisiveté. Au milieu de la nuit, donc,
te tenant à la fenêtre proche de
sa couche sur le sol, vois à consoler
par mon message cette épouse fidèle
que fuit le sommeil.

87. Amaigrie, étendue de côté sur
sa couche solitaire, elle semble le corps
de l'astre aux froids rayons, dont il ne
reste qu'un mince croissant, à l'horizon
oriental ; elle voudrait évoquer le plaisir
de s'unir à moi, fût-ce en songe,
et cherche le sommeil que des torrents
de larmes bannissent de ses yeux.

88. Avec des soupirs qui flétrissent
les tendres boutons de ses lèvres
de fleur, elle rejette les boucles raidies
par l'eau toute pure, qui pendent sur
ses joues. Cette nuit qui, dans les plaisirs,
à mes côtés, s'écoulait en un instant,
elle en passe maintenant, dans les larmes
brûlantes, la durée que l'absence accroît.

89. Les rayons de la lune, frais comme
le nectar, pénètrent par le grillage
de la fenêtre : elle tourne vers eux,
tout d'abord avec joie, mais pour
le détourner aussitôt, un œil qu'elle
cache, fatiguée, sous des cils lourds
de ses larmes : elle ne dort ni ne veille,
telle la fleur de l'hibiscus par un jour
nuageux.

90. Je sais le cœur de la bien-aimée
plein d'amour pour moi et je la crois,
dans cette première séparation, telle que
je viens de te la montrer. La fatuité ne
grandit pas mes paroles, ô mon frère ;
tu verras bientôt toi-même tout ce que
je te dis.

91. Sans force, dans l'excès de sa
douleur, elle laisse à tout instant tomber
au fond de sa couche son corps délicat
privé de toute parure. À coup sûr,
elle te fera verser même à toi des pleurs
qui seront faits de ton eau nouvelle :
d'ordinaire sont pitoyables ceux dont
le cœur est tendre.

92. Son œil de gazelle voile sous
les boucles ses regards de côté, le fard
n'y brille plus et, maintenant qu'elle
repousse le vin, il a oublié la manœuvre
des sourcils. À ton approche, sans doute,
il frémira tout à coup, gracieux comme
le lotus nocturne qui s'agite, heurté par
un poisson.

93. Sa cuisse gauche peut-être aussi
palpitera, dorée comme le tronc plein
de sève du bananier ; mes ongles,
à présent, n'y impriment plus leur trace ;
elle a, par la volonté du destin, perdu
l'habituelle parure de ses réseaux
de perles et ne sent plus, comme jadis
à la fin de notre union, la caresse
accoutumée de ma main.

Kâlidâsa,
Meghadûta (Le Nuage Messager),
Traduit par R. H. Assier de Pompignan,
Les Belles Lettres, Paris, 1938

L'engouement pour *Shakuntalâ*

De toutes les œuvres fraîchement traduites du sanskrit qui révélèrent l'Inde à l'Europe à l'aube du XIXe siècle, Shakuntalâ *brilla d'un éclat sans pareil. La pièce la plus subtile du grand Kâlidâsa,* Shakuntalâ au signe de reconnaissance, *allait envoûter durablement les esprits les plus éclairés de l'époque.*

Lors d'une partie de chasse, le roi Dushyanta s'éprend d'une jeune ermite, Shakuntalâ. Celle-ci, perdue dans sa rêverie amoureuse, s'attire par inadvertance la malédiction de l'irascible ascète Durvâsas, qui lui prédit que le roi l'oubliera. Ému toutefois par le désespoir de la jeune fille, Durvâsas tempère sa malédiction : un signe de reconnaissance – l'anneau royal découvert dans le ventre d'un poisson – permettra à Dushyanta de recouvrer la mémoire et de retrouver Shakuntalâ.

ACTE II

LE ROI, regardant sa suite.
Emportez mon équipage de chasse. Quant à toi, Raivataka, remplis les devoirs de ta charge.

LA SUITE
Aux ordres du roi!

Ils sortent.

LE BOUFFON
Voilà, grâce à vous, la place nette de mouches! Maintenant, à l'ombre des arbres que rend délicieuse un dais fait de lianes, prenez place sur ce banc. Moi-même, je m'y assiérai.

LE ROI
Va devant.

LE BOUFFON
Venez, Sire.

Ils se déplacent autour de la scène et s'assoient.

LE ROI
Mâthavya, tes yeux ignorent encore la récompense ultime, puisque tu n'as pas vu l'objet qu'il fallait voir.

LE BOUFFON
Comment! N'êtes-vous pas devant moi?

LE ROI
Certes, chacun se voit aimable, mais c'est de l'ornement de l'ermitage, c'est de Sakuntalâ que je parle.

LE BOUFFON, en aparté.
Nous y voilà! Je ne lui donnerai pas l'occasion de la peindre. (Haut.) Ah ça, ami, il semble que tu désires la fille d'un ascète!

LE ROI
Ami, les descendants de Puru ne tournent pas leur cœur vers un objet qu'on leur défend.

*La fille de l'ascète,
Au vrai l'enfant d'une jeune déesse,
Fut de lui recueillie quand on*

l'abandonna.
Ainsi la fleur, au jasmin échappée,
Tombe sur l'arbre arka .

LE BOUFFON, éclatant de rire.
Ce désir que vous affichez, dédaigneux des femmes les plus exquises, est pareil à l'envie de tamarin chez un homme fatigué des dattes!

LE ROI
Tu ne l'as pas vue pour en parler ainsi!

LE BOUFFON
Sans doute, ce dont Sa Majesté elle-même s'émerveille doit être ravissant!

LE ROI
Ami, qu'ajouter encore?

> *Que l'eût douée de vie le créateur,*
> *Quand il l'eut peinte, ou qu'il l'eût faite en son esprit*
> *La somme des beautés,*
> *Elle apparaît, joyau parmi les femmes,*
> *L'unique création, quand je contemple*
> *Et les pouvoirs de son auteur et sa beauté.*

LE BOUFFON
S'il en est ainsi, voilà répudiées toutes les belles.

LE ROI
C'est bien ce que ressent mon cœur :

> *Fleur jamais respirée,*
> *Bourgeon que n'a coupé nul ongle,*
> *Perle jamais percée,*
> *Nectar nouveau dont nul n'a goûté la saveur,*
> *Fruit préservé des mérites passés,*
> *Telle est sa beauté sans défaut.*
> *J'ignore qui sera l'élu du créateur*
> *Pour en jouir en ce monde.*

LE BOUFFON
En ce cas, hâtez-vous de la prendre sous votre protection avant qu'elle ne tombe aux mains de quelque ermite aux cheveux luisants de l'huile d'i*ngudî*.

LE ROI
L'adorable enfant ne peut disposer d'elle-même, et son père est absent.

LE BOUFFON
Quel amour ses yeux ont-ils fait paraître pour Votre Majesté?

LE ROI
Les filles des ermites sont naturellement timides. Cependant,

> *Sous mon regard, elle baissait les yeux,*
> *Donnant une autre cause au sourire naissant.*
> *Tandis que la pudeur entravait son essor,*
> *L'amour n'était ainsi ni celé ni montré.*

LE BOUFFON
Certes, elle ne pouvait pas monter sur ton genou dès la première rencontre!

LE ROI
À nouveau, au moment de se séparer, la belle, malgré sa réserve, trahit assez son sentiment. En effet,

> *Prétextant la blessure infligée à son pied*
> *Par la pointe d'une herbe,*
> *La svelte enfant interrompit sa marche,*
> *Après à peine quelques pas,*
> *Et demeura le visage tourné,*
> *À libérer son vêtement d'écorce*
> *Que nul arbre pourtant n'accrochait de ses branches.*

LE BOUFFON
Prends en ce cas des provisions de route. Car, à ce que je vois, tu as changé la forêt d'ascèse en un bois de plaisance.

ACTE V

Paraissent le Roi, sur son trône, et le Bouffon.

LE BOUFFON, prêtant l'oreille.
Ami, écoute attentivement. On entend, venant de l'intérieur du théâtre, le prélude d'un chant doux et très pur. Ah! je sais! C'est la reine Haṃsapadikâ qui travaille sa voix.

LE ROI
Fais silence, que j'écoute!

UNE VOIX, dans les airs. (On chante.)

> Quand, dans ton désir d'un nectar nouveau,
> Ardent, tu baisais la fleur du manguier,
> Bourdon, se peut-il qu'ici tu l'oublies,
> Heureux d'habiter le simple lotus?

LE ROI
Ah! Quel charme en ce chant!

LE BOUFFON
Et, dans ce chant, as-tu vraiment saisi le sens des mots?

LE ROI, souriant.
Cette femme fut un jour aimée de moi. Je comprends qu'elle me fait ainsi grief de la reine Vasumatî. Mâthavya, mon ami, va dire de ma part à Haṃsapadikâ que son blâme est habile.

LE BOUFFON
J'obéis. (Se levant.) Cependant, ami, quand elle m'aura livré aux mains d'autrui, je n'aurai pas plus de salut, saisi par la mèche et battu, que l'ascète victime d'une Apsaras!

LE ROI
Va, et, en bon courtisan, trouve les paroles qui l'apaisent.

LE BOUFFON
Quelle issue?

Il sort.

LE ROI, en aparté.
À présent que j'ai compris le sens de ce chant, pourquoi cette mélancolie profonde quand je ne suis séparé d'aucun être chéri? Cependant,

> *Quand, à la vue d'objets charmants,*
> *À l'écoute de sons suaves,*
> *Un être, heureux pourtant, est saisi de tristesse,*
> *Il faut qu'à son insu son esprit se souvienne,*
> *Arrêtées en son cœur,*
> *Des tendres passions de ses vies antérieures.*

Il demeure troublé. Entre le chambellan.

LE CHAMBELLAN
Hélas! En quel état suis-je réduit!

> *Ce bambou que, veillant au gynécée royal,*
> *J'avais en main selon l'usage,*
> *Après tant d'années écoulées,*
> *S'est changé en soutien de mes pas chancelants.*

Allons! Assurément le roi ne saurait négliger ses devoirs. Toutefois, comme il vient de quitter le tribunal, je n'ose lui annoncer, nouvelle entrave, l'arrivée des disciples de Kaṇva. Il n'est pourtant pas de repos pour qui reçoit le gouvernement du monde. En effet,

> *Le soleil, une fois, attelle ses coursiers,*
> *Et le vent odorant s'ébranle jour et nuit.*
> *Seṣa toujours soutient le fardeau de la terre;*
> *Et le prince qui jouit de la sixième part*
> *A le même devoir.*

Je vais donc remplir mon office.

ACTE VII

SAKUNTALÂ
On me dit que l'herbe de Sarvadamana a conservé sa forme quand elle aurait dû se métamorphoser. Mais je n'espère plus le bonheur. À moins peut-être qu'il n'en soit comme me l'a rapporté Sânumatî.

LE ROI, regardant Sakuntalâ.
C'est elle! Voici la noble Sakuntalâ:

En ces deux vêtements assombris de poussière,
Le visage émacié par les austérités,
Elle a noué sa tresse, et chaste en son maintien,
Observe le long vœu de la séparation
Que je lui imposai, impitoyablement.

SAKUNTALÂ, regardant le roi que le remords pâlit.
Non! Ce n'est pas là mon époux! Mais alors, qui est cet homme qui souille de son contact le corps de mon enfant, quand l'amulette le protège?

L'ENFANT, s'approchant de sa mère.
Maman, quel est cet homme qui m'embrasse en m'appelant son fils?

LE ROI
Bien-aimée, même ma cruauté à ton égard s'achève heureusement, puisque je te vois aujourd'hui me reconnaître.

SAKUNTALÂ, en aparté.
Respire, ô mon cœur, respire enfin! Dépouillant son hostilité, le destin a pitié de moi. C'est bien mon époux.

LE ROI
Bien-aimée,
   Une heureuse mémoire a déchiré la nuit
   De mon égarement,
   Et, femme au beau visage, à mes yeux tu parais,
   Ainsi que Rohinî s'offre à l'astre nocturne,
   Quand s'achève l'éclipse.

SAKUNTALÂ
Victoire! Victoire à mon époux!

Elle s'interrompt, la voix étouffée par les larmes.

LE ROI
Belle,

   Quand tes pleurs font obstacle à ce cri de victoire,
   Je suis pourtant vainqueur,
   Car j'ai vu ton visage où reste sans apprêt
   Ta lèvre au pli pâli.

L'ENFANT
Maman, qui est-ce?

SAKUNTALÂ
Mon fils, interroge ton destin.

LE ROI, se prosternant aux pieds de Sakuntalâ.
   Que la douleur de mon dédain,
   Belle, s'efface de ton cœur.
   Mon faible esprit cédait alors
   À un puissant égarement.
   Qui est des ténèbres la proie
   Souvent traite ainsi le bonheur,
   Et l'aveugle veut rejeter
   Même la guirlande à son front,
   La soupçonnant d'être un serpent.

SAKUNTALÂ
Relevez-vous, mon cher Seigneur! En ces jours-là sans doute, un acte commis autrefois, obstacle à mes mérites, était près de porter son fruit, puisque mon époux, si compatissant, me refusa sa tendresse.

Le roi se relève.

Mais comment mon cher Seigneur s'est-il souvenu d'une infortunée?

LE ROI
Je te le dirai quand j'aurai arraché le dard de l'affliction.

> *En ma nuit autrefois, belle, j'ai dédaigné*
> *Tes larmes épanchées qui harcelaient ta lèvre.*
> *Quand j'aurai essuyé cette larme aujourd'hui*
> *Qui se prend à la courbe infime de tes cils,*
> *Du repentir alors je serai délivré.*

Il le fait.

SAKUNTALÂ, *voyant le sceau au nom du roi.*
Mon cher Seigneur, c'est là ton anneau!

LE ROI
En retrouvant cet anneau, j'ai recouvré la mémoire.

SAKUNTALÂ
Il a causé bien du malheur en disparaissant au moment où je devais convaincre mon cher Seigneur.

LE ROI
Alors, que la liane retrouve sa fleur, signe de son union avec le printemps.

SAKUNTALÂ
Je ne me fie plus à lui. Portez-le, mon cher Seigneur!

Le Théâtre de Kâlidâsa
Sakuntalâ au signe de reconnaissance,
traduit du sanskrit et du prâkrit
par Lyne Bansat-Boudon,
Gallimard, 1996

L'Europe apprend le sanskrit

« *Une époque Sacountalâ* » : Raymond Schwab intitule ainsi l'un des chapitres de La Renaissance orientale, *afin de rendre compte de l'extraordinaire engouement de l'Europe pour le drame de Kâlidâsa.*

C'était *Sacountalâ* qui, en France, décidait en 1800 la vocation de Chézy; l'angélique jeune philologue aux boucles blondes voulait vérifier de ses propres yeux si vraiment une littérature récemment encore ignorée cachait de tels trésors. Quand, en 1830, il donna sa version française, la première faite sur l'original, il reproduisit en épigraphe les vers célèbres de Goethe, et le poète l'en remercia par une lettre où il mettait *Sacountalâ* au nombre des étoiles qui lui rendaient la nuit plus agréable que le jour : quarante années n'avaient donc pas éteint sa passion. *Sacountalâ* a été un événement littéraire, l'un de ceux qui concouraient à préparer un XIXe siècle tel qu'il fut; non par influence directe, mais en introduisant une compétition inattendue dans le répertoire universel. Lamartine va y apercevoir « réuni dans un seul poème le triple génie d'Homère, de Théocrite et du Tasse » (*Cours familier*, III, 338). Chateaubriand, à son ordinaire, a lancé le signal; dans les notes du *Génie du Christianisme*, il la cite sous la rubrique « Poésies sanskrites » en la rapprochant d'Ossian, après Jones. La référence indiquée est « Robertson's Indie »; en effet, Robertson traitait de *Sacountalâ* dans *An Historical Disquisition*, publié en 1791, traduit aussitôt en allemand et en français (*Recherches historiques sur l'Inde*), ouvrage remarquable pour sa date.

Raymond Schwab, *La Renaissance orientale,* Préface de Louis Renou, Payot, Paris, 1950

Shakuntalâ et l'Occident

Les artistes se laisseront aussi séduire par l'héroïne de Kâlidâsa. Les amours contrariées de Shakuntalâ et de Dushyanta fournirent à Camille Claudel le thème du plus célèbre et du plus émouvant de ses groupes sculptés, Sakuntala ou L'Abandon. *Et Goethe aura même le projet d'adapter* Shakuntalâ *à la scène allemande.*

D'autres, préférant s'en tenir aux traductions ou aux adaptations, se sont tout spécialement intéressés à l'histoire de Çakuntalâ, déjà répandue par Jones, Forster et Chézy. [...]

Bruguières, Fauche, Foucaux, Bergaigne et Lehugeur, Pottecher, Hérold s'exerceront au long du siècle à traduire l'œuvre la plus célèbre de la littérature hindoue, dont le succès s'altérera trop vite en mode. Tous l'ont fait avec conscience, – ce qui n'exclut pas les platitudes et les belles infidèles ; – mais tous l'ont fait en philologues beaucoup plus qu'en poètes.

Seul, Gautier figure parmi eux, pour ne s'en tenir d'ailleurs qu'au livret d'un opéra, *L'Anneau de Cakuntala*, dont Louis Étienne Reyer compose la musique, et qui sera représenté en 1858. Il faut dire que Kâlidâsa inspire surtout les musiciens ; et l'on n'a point de peine à citer ballets, opéras, ouvertures, poèmes symphoniques, qui se succéderont de Schubert à Zimmermann et Kaan Albest, d'Alfano à Weingartner, en n'oubliant pas Bachrich, Foulds, Goldmark, Scharwencka, Bertelin, Perfall et Bréville.

Jean Biès,
*Littérature française
et pensée hindoue,
Des origines à 1950,*
Klincksieck, 1974

Camille Claudel, deuxième étude pour *Sacountala*, vers 1886-1888, terre cuite.

La Sacontale d'Apollinaire

*C'est naturellement l'héroïne de Kâlidâsa qu'il convient de reconnaître dans la « Sacontale » qu'évoque Guillaume Apollinaire dans « La Chanson du Mal-Aimé » (*Alcools*). Dans ses* Poèmes inédits*, l'auteur consacre également deux strophes à Shakuntalâ.*

« L'époux royal de Sacontale,
Las de vaincre, se réjouit
Quand il la retrouva plus pâle
D'attente et d'amour yeux pâlis
Caressant sa gazelle mâle. »

Apollinaire,
« La Chanson du Mal-Aimé »,
Alcools, Gallimard, 1920

Ajantâ, un haut lieu de l'art indien

Miraculeusement préservées – depuis 1500 ans ! – des outrages du temps, les peintures bouddhiques d'Ajantâ constituent l'un des sommets de l'art indien. Les conventions esthétiques et les canons plastiques du classicisme gupta s'y révèlent dans toute la perfection d'un art hautement idéalisé.

« Une fragile éternité »

Depuis sa découverte à l'aube du XIXe siècle, le site d'Ajantâ n'a cessé de retenir l'attention des historiens de l'art, soucieux de préciser les séquences chronologiques successives des cavernes et d'identifier plus précisément les sujets des peintures endommagées ou en partie détruites.

Redécouvertes fortuitement en 1819, les grottes d'Ajantâ ne cessèrent, tout au long du XIXe siècle, de susciter l'intérêt émerveillé des voyageurs, des savants, des artistes et des peintres qui les visitèrent et, parfois, s'efforcèrent d'exécuter de leurs célèbres peintures de fidèles copies. En 1844, un Conseil chargé de la conservation des sanctuaires et de la copie des peintures était constitué par les autorités britanniques de l'Empire des Indes et le peintre Robert Gill arrivait à Ajantâ – où il devait séjourner quelque vingt-sept années ! –, résolu à veiller à la conservation des peintures murales et à effectuer de ces dernières d'exemplaires reproductions. Le voyageur français Alfred Grandidier, qu'un long périple avait conduit aux Indes dans les années 1862-1864, eut la bonne fortune de rencontrer Robert Gill, de visiter Ajantâ en sa compagnie et de découvrir, en outre, dans l'atelier du peintre, certaines des copies que Gill avait alors exécutées.

Dans *Le Tour du Monde* de 1869, Grandidier relate brièvement sa rencontre avec le maître des lieux : « C'est sous les auspices du major Gill que j'ai visité les temples souterrains d'Adjountah. Cet officier anglais a été préposé par le gouvernement de l'Inde à la conservation de ces monuments, et il s'est occupé activement depuis plusieurs années de reproduire sur toile les fresques qui se détériorent chaque année. J'ai visité avec plaisir l'atelier de cet artiste, où plusieurs tableaux étaient en voie d'exécution.

Le major Gill était un des sportsmen les plus connus de l'Inde ; chasseur intrépide et audacieux, il ne comptait pas moins d'une centaine de tigres ou panthères et d'une vingtaine d'éléphants et rhinocéros parmi les victimes sacrifiées à sa passion dominante. Je lui promis de venir le prendre au mois de mars de l'année suivante pour aller nous joindre aux officiers de Mhaou qui chaque année entreprennent une croisade contre les bêtes féroces. La maladie et la pente de mes études, qui m'entraînèrent vers la côte orientale d'Afrique peu de temps après ma visite aux grottes d'Adjountah, m'ont malheureusement fait manquer à cet engagement. »

Pourtant, les copies fidèles de Gill, qui devaient préserver pour la postérité la beauté des peintures murales d'Ajantâ, périrent dans l'incendie du Crystal Palace de Sydenham survenu en 1866, où elles se trouvaient provisoirement exposées. Malgré une tristesse et une amertume légitimes, Gill continua, jusqu'à sa mort, à reproduire inlassablement les chefs-d'œuvre des imagiers d'Ajantâ, afin de les arracher à l'oubli et de les soustraire – fût-ce par copies interposées! – aux déprédations inévitables et aux ravages du temps. Quelques années plus tard, John Griffiths reprenait le flambeau et, avec un groupe d'étudiants de la Bombay School of Arts, s'attachait à son tour à copier les peintures d'Ajantâ. Mais l'histoire, parfois, semble se répéter et, en 1885, plus de la moitié des reproductions dues au pinceau de Griffiths et de ses élèves disparaissait dans l'incendie du musée de South Kensington à Londres où, là encore, les œuvres se trouvaient passagèrement exposées. Les élèves de Griffiths se remirent vaillamment à l'ouvrage et, en 1896-1897, paraissaient, sous le titre *The Paintings in the Buddhist Cave-Temples of Ajanta*, les deux premiers volumes de reproductions des peintures d'Ajantâ.

Dans le sillage des contributions initiales de Gill et de Griffiths, d'autres séries d'aquarelles et d'autres recueils de planches illustrées devaient voir le jour dans les premières décennies du XXe siècle – telles les délicates aquarelles dues au pinceau subtil de Lady Herringham. Enfin, dans les années 1920-1921, la première campagne de restauration des peintures d'Ajantâ était confiée aux spécialistes italiens Orsini et Cecconi, campagne qui allait ouvrir la voie à une concertation nationale et internationale visant à la sauvegarde des sanctuaires rupestres d'Ajantâ et de leurs inestimables peintures.

Amina Okada, *Ajantâ*,
Préface d'André Bareau,
Imprimerie Nationale, Paris, 1991

Ajantâ et le théâtre sanskrit

Un jeu de « correspondances » plastiques subtiles et d'affinités formelles avec les arts du théâtre et de la danse est parfois perceptible dans la composition complexe des peintures murales d'Ajantâ. Les scènes peintes préservent une saveur profane, en dépit de leur inspiration bouddhique.

Plus caractéristiques encore que ces attitudes sont les actes eux-mêmes qui, dans le théâtre sanskrit, sont très souvent de véritables *actes plastiques*.

À Ajantâ, devant les murs des cavernes couverts de peintures, impression de confusion, tout d'abord, de surcharge, d'extrême multiplication de personnages, presque de grouillement. Opposition avec l'Occident. Dans les églises d'Italie, les scènes rectangulaires, exactement délimitées et découpées – au début du XIVe siècle à la chapelle des Scrovegni ou Arena de Padoue par exemple – se présentent comme un quadrillage d'aspect assez fâcheux dans son ensemble. Dans l'Inde, rien de tel. Le mur est entièrement couvert sans séparation et les scènes, à Ajantâ, dans les cavernes habitations de moines (vihâra), se poursuivent tout le long des parois entourant les entrées de cellules et donnent cette impression de pullulement.

Analogie peut-être avec le sanscrit classique où les mots s'unissent par les règles d'assonance et rencontres entre voyelles formant de longs composés, de longues phrases étirées assurant continuité et fluidité sans heurt, cependant que rythmes et rebondissements permettent de s'orienter dans la phrase et que la formation des mots (suffixes et préfixes) reste précise.

De même dans les peintures murales. Continuité sans coupure mais rythme. Surcharge et confusion s'évanouissent quand on sait regarder. Dans cette suite souple sans division, des scènes s'organisent, se composent, la direction des regards en indique souvent le centre où se détache le groupe important; des personnages de dos ou hanchés en triple flexion (porteuse de chasse-mouches) ou simplement courbés en assurent les limites sans aucun découpage. Ailleurs c'est un couple d'amoureux entre des colonnes qui isole deux épisodes. Ainsi, cette nécessité même de distinguer des scènes non séparées amène à un groupement de personnages harmonieux, balancé, immobile. Plutôt qu'action ou récit rebondissant, nous sommes ici devant des scènes plastiques.

Or, le théâtre, lui aussi, s'organise autour d'actes plastiques. Tout ce qui est action, mouvement, explication nécessaire pour comprendre est ramassé dans de courts prologues, avant-scènes ou intermèdes laissant à l'acte (ou grande partie de l'acte) son unité et son immobilité dans un groupement heureux déterminé, *sorte de tableau vivant dont les personnages s'entretiendraient entre eux.*

Philippe Stern,
«Aspects plastiques de l'ancien théâtre indien et peintures murales d'Ajantâ», *Les Théâtres d'Asie,* CNRS, Paris, 1961

Composition et narration dans les peintures d'Ajantâ

L'enchaînement narratif des thèmes illustrés à Ajantâ peut paraître dense, confus et indéchiffrable. Pourtant, une composition savante, procédant de règles précises, détermine l'agencement des scènes entre les divers groupes de personnages.

Les sujets représentés sont tous bouddhiques, empruntés aux *jâtaka* (une trentaine) et à la dernière vie humaine du Buddha (une quarantaine). Ils se déroulent sur les murs des halls, des chapelles et des vérandas selon une conception assez curieuse: la succession narrative ne s'établit pas, comme dans les autres sites anciens, selon le développement chronologique des épisodes, mais d'après un ordre géographique ou topographique; quel que soit l'intervalle de temps qui les sépare, tous les événements qui se sont passés dans un même lieu sont groupés dans une même fresque, ce qui en a rendu le déchiffrement assez difficile.

La composition des fresques narratives occupe toute la surface murale disponible, sans délimitation linéaire ni solution de continuité. C'est pourquoi l'identification de leurs thèmes a été si ardue: on n'en voit ni le commencement ni la fin et l'on ne peut séparer un épisode d'un autre qu'en isolant un groupe précis donnant la clef du reste. C'est l'exemple le plus parfait peut-être de la composition «d'enchaînement». On y voit de longs cortèges savamment ordonnés qui se déroulent à la sortie des villes, dont les portes figurées en diagonale sont comme les ponctuations d'un récit et qui jouaient un rôle semblable dans les écoles plus anciennes, notamment celle d'Amarâvatî. Piétons, éléphants, cavaliers se mêlent dans une cohue tout orientale mais rythmée, d'où émergent des parasols et des emblèmes brandis au bout de hampes. Parmi les bruns assourdis des chairs et le scintillement des bijoux d'or, la bigarrure des costumes semble mouvante. Des pavillons de bois aux colonnes laquées de bleu ou de rouge, aux chapiteaux dorés, servent de cadre à des scènes entières ou d'abri à des couples amoureux. Des orchestres accompagnant des danseuses distraient des princes languissamment assis sur des sièges ouvragés; ceux-ci donnent audience ou reçoivent des présents, jouent aux dés, rendent un jugement. Des théories de femmes, à peine vêtues d'un pagne de mousseline ou d'étoffes rayées, couvertes de fines parures d'or, s'avancent sur un sol émaillé de fleurs; quelques-unes se mêlent aux conversations princières, certaines s'appuient gracieusement à des colonnes, d'autres apportent des plateaux de fleurs, pilent le grain, préparent des pâtes odorantes, veillent au bien-être de leurs maîtres en agitant des éventails et des chasse-mouches. Plus haut, volent des génies semblables à des hommes, parmi de curieux nuages et des rochers cubiques aux couleurs heurtées. Çà et là, une plante délicatement observée déploie son arabesque; rarement (caverne XVII, mur de droite), une indication sommaire d'un paysage montagneux sert de fond.

Dans ces amas de personnages et de détails, le spectateur distingue mal, à première vue, une ordonnance voulue, une ligne conductrice. Pourtant l'œil s'accoutume peu à peu à y discerner des groupes. Conduit de l'un à l'autre par des gestes ou des plans assez subtils, il finit par les dénombrer et passer de l'un à l'autre sans effort. La liaison entre des groupes voisins est obtenue par des personnages secondaires; ils servent de «passages», de «fondu enchaîné» (comme on pourrait dire en termes de cinéma), comme dans le relief d'un objet les demi-teintes forment la transition entre les zones d'ombre et de lumière. Une attitude, l'orientation d'un geste, la flexion d'un déhanchement, la direction d'un visage tourné vers l'extérieur de la scène, tout cela rattache ces personnages d'une part à l'action du groupe auquel ils appartiennent et d'autre part au groupe contigu. C'est un procédé bien connu dans la majorité des compositions asiatiques, notamment dans l'art de l'Asie centrale, mais nulle part ailleurs qu'à Ajantâ il ne fut employé avec une telle délicatesse ni une telle aisance.

Or si l'on y regarde de plus près, on s'aperçoit que beaucoup des groupes principaux sont construits d'après un schéma circulaire ou ovale; mais seuls la disposition des personnages, la direction de leurs membres et de leurs regards, le sens des courbes et des lignes font deviner la figure géométrique sous-jacente. Chaque groupe se replie vers un centre, comme les pétales d'une fleur se referment en calice. Cette disposition (qui est fort bien illustrée à Bâgh également) est l'aboutissement d'un type traditionnel de composition dont on peut suivre l'évolution depuis l'époque de Bhârhut dans les reliefs en médaillon et dont l'école d'Amarâvatî a produit les plus belles réalisations. À ses qualités esthétiques, supérieurement développées à Ajantâ, ce mode de groupement ajoute une valeur mystique pleine de signification : celle du *mandala* dont on a vu l'importance à propos de l'architecture. Dans celui-ci comme dans les compositions narratives circulaires, il y a une même idée : pénétrer vers un centre; dans le *mandala*, pour que l'initié y rencontre le divin; dans les groupements plastiques, pour y découvrir le personnage principal de la scène. Dans les deux cas, il s'agit d'un mouvement, physique ou mental. [...] L'incomparable adresse des peintres d'Ajantâ leur a permis d'assouplir à l'extrême et de nuancer habilement la figure initiale dont ils se sont inspirés visiblement. Il est juste d'ajouter qu'ils n'ont pas utilisé ce procédé à tout coup, mais seulement de temps à autre, construisant d'autres scènes sur des diagonales ou d'après des schémas moins systématiques.

Jeannine Auboyer,
«Introduction à l'étude de l'art en Inde»,
Serie Orientale Roma, XXXI,
Istituto italiano per il medio ed estremo Oriente, Rome, 1965

L'art gupta et son rayonnement

Né au IVe siècle dans la vallée du Gange, l'art gupta marqua d'une empreinte durable les styles ultérieurs qui fleurirent en diverses régions de l'Inde. Mais son influence novatrice et féconde se fit également sentir dans les arts de maintes contrées de l'Asie des moussons.

Le classicisme gupta

Élégant, épuré, empreint d'une grâce ineffable et d'une subtile spiritualité, l'art gupta fut également le creuset et le ferment de formes et d'iconographies renouvelées, appelées à connaître une féconde pérennité.

L'époque gupta est caractérisée par l'éclosion d'un style nouveau qui, tout en se rattachant aux styles antérieurs, traduit des préoccupations différentes. Jamais peut-être une telle importance ne fut accordée dans l'Inde à la pureté des formes et de la ligne, à l'équilibre des masses et des valeurs, à la mesure harmonieuse des proportions. Comme l'école d'Amarâvatî qui le précède, l'art gupta choisit le corps humain pour thème principal ; il l'observe cependant d'une manière moins spontanée et l'idéalise davantage, cherchant avec une sorte d'application à atteindre une certaine perfection, un raffinement et une élégance aimable, sans tomber pour autant dans la mièvrerie et le maniérisme auxquels céderont les époques décadentes. On a souvent attribué au style gupta le qualificatif de classique ; il vaudrait mieux sans doute le considérer comme une forme de «purisme», car il conserve – malgré une grâce un peu froide – une robustesse et une simplicité de stylisation à travers lesquelles on sent jaillir une rigueur créatrice et une richesse d'invention bien différentes de l'académisme propre aux époques classiques.

L'impulsion donnée sur l'ensemble du territoire indien par l'art gupta, du IVe au VIe siècle environ, fut si forte et si pleine d'unité que les thèmes fixés par lui se perpétuèrent longtemps après la chute de la dynastie, où que ses qualités plastiques engendrèrent d'autres éclosions artistiques. Cependant, tout en reprenant les thèmes gupta et en les transformant selon les lois de mutation qui caractérisent l'art indien, les styles «locaux» qui s'élaborèrent tant au Mahârâsh*t*ra (style châ*l*ukya, VIe-VIIIe siècles environ) qu'au Dekkan oriental (style pallava, VIe-VIIe siècles) trahirent un esprit bien différent, dû peut-être au développement de plus en plus important de l'art brâhmanique. Seul le style pâla du Bengale (VIIIe-XIIe siècles) peut être considéré comme le conservatoire véritable du style gupta bien qu'il ne sût pas en renouveler la puissance de création.

Progressivement, la distinction entre l'art bouddhique et l'art brâhmanique s'amplifie, non pas dans le détail mais dans la conception esthétique. Cette différence est naturellement plus visible dans les compositions narratives que dans les icônes isolées et la décoration. Ainsi, les formes et les motifs décoratifs sont à ce point identiques qu'il est difficile, sans le secours de données iconographiques précises, d'attribuer à l'une ou à l'autre de ces religions la plupart des œuvres gupta, post-gupta et pâla-sena, tandis que l'on ne peut confondre les hauts-reliefs entre eux, même si l'on ignore leur identification, car le dynamisme brâhmanique leur imprime un rythme particulier rarement utilisé dans les œuvres bouddhiques, généralement plus statiques et plus symétriques.

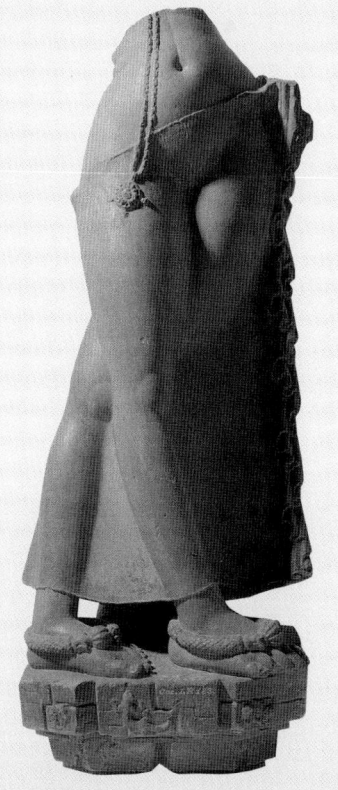

Jeune femme au scorpion, grès rose de Mathurâ, VIe siècle.

Parallèlement à ces caractéristiques, l'époque gupta et post-gupta révèle un remarquable sens du monumental, qui se développa surtout dans le haut-relief hindouiste du Mahârâsh*t*ra vers les VIIe-VIIIe siècles.

Les arts gupta et post-gupta constituent donc une des étapes les plus importantes de l'évolution esthétique indienne. Riches de véritables chefs-d'œuvre comme les buddha de Sârnâth et de Mathurâ (IVe-Ve siècles), les fresques d'Ajantâ (VIe siècle) et les hauts-reliefs de Mahâbalipuram (VIIe siècle) et d'Ellorâ (VIIe-VIIIe siècles), ils illustrent particulièrement bien le système évolutif propre à l'Inde, masquant une grande diversité d'inspiration derrière la pérennité d'un même répertoire décoratif.

Le prolongement de ces formules dans le style pâla-sena du Bengale traduit à la fois un désir de préserver l'héritage gupta sans y apporter de changements fondamentaux. Pendant les quelque trois cent cinquante ans que dura sa production, l'évolution s'effectua sur place, presque en vase clos, et sans qu'une inspiration vivifiante soit venue ranimer les formes toutes conventionnelles de l'art pâla, qui dérivent directement de celles de l'art post-gupta.

De même que les styles gupta et post-gupta ont profondément marqué l'art des pays où l'influence de l'Inde a pénétré, de même le style pâla a imprimé sa marque sur l'art des contrées soumises à l'influence du Bengale, et plus particulièrement à la Birmanie et au Népal, ce dernier ayant, à son tour, transmis au Tibet méridional l'essentiel de son esthétique.

Jeannine Auboyer,
Les Arts de l'Inde et des pays indianisés
Presses Universitaires de France,
Paris, 1968

LES MONNAIES DES EMPEREURS GUPTA

Les souverains gupta sont connus à travers leurs superbes monnaies d'or et d'argent, qui constituent autant de portraits impériaux. Le monnayage gupta témoigne de l'obédience religieuse et des affiliations sectaires des monarques qui les firent frapper. En 1946, un exceptionnel trésor comprenant de remarquables monnaies gupta fut découvert à Bayana (Bharatpur), au Râjasthân. Les particularités de ces monnaies nous sont données par Louis Renou et Jean Filliozat, auteurs de L'Inde classique, Manuel des Études Indiennes *(Payot, Paris, 1947).*

Les plus brillantes suites monétaires indigènes de l'Inde sont celles des Gupta. Les premiers types héritent de ceux des Kusâna. Le roi est représenté en pied dans un costume à deux pans rappelant un peu celui des Kusâna mais plus court. Jusqu'à Skandagupta, l'étalon romain du denarius est employé pour l'or, mais sous Skandagupta, il est remplacé par celui du *suvarna* (9 gr., 2 donc un peu inférieur au poids moyen du *suvarna* selon Manu) peut-être déjà introduit depuis quelque temps. Dans une même inscription, probablement de Kumâragupta Ier, antérieur à Skandagupta, les termes de *dinâra* et de *suvarna* sont employés l'un et l'autre. Mais il existe de grandes variations.

Les monnaies d'argent sont imitées de celles des Ksatrapa d'Ujjayinî correspondant à l'hémidrachme mais avec au revers un paon au lieu d'un caitya.

Le monnayage de cuivre est rare, celui des Kusâna, très abondant au contraire, restait largement en usage et rendait inutiles des frappes en grandes quantités. Les spécimens existants montrent une assez grande originalité. Ils portent généralement une représentation de Garuda. Les principaux types de monnaies d'or sont les suivants. Un premier type représente Candragupta Ier et Kumâradevî en pied avec mention de la vieille famille des Licchavi. D'autres types sont distingués selon les attributs que le roi porte, l'attitude qui lui est donnée ou les représentations qui l'accompagnent ; type à l'étendard, à l'arc, à la hache, au tigre, à la *vînâ*, au parasol, au cavalier, au tueur de tigre. Un type spécial commémore un sacrifice du cheval fait par Samudragupta et a été frappé probablement pour la distribution de la daksinâ aux brahmanes. Au revers Laksmî est fréquemment représentée assise sur un lotus *(kamalanilayanâ)* car cette Laksmî, la Fortune, demeure éternellement chez le vainqueur par excellence, Visnu (inscr. de Skandagupta à Junagar). Or Visnu est le plus grand des Aditya et les Gupta par leurs surnoms sont des Aditya. Les légendes sont en sanskrit, en caractères gupta. Elles sont souvent très longues, versifiées (mètre *upagîti*) et écrites en abrégé, les signes vocalisants sont en partie omis. Un bon nombre peuvent être restituées, par exemple : *samaraçatavitatavijayo jitaripur ajito divam jayati* (« vainqueur dans plus de cent combats, ses ennemis vaincus, invaincu (lui-même), il vainc le ciel ». Le titre royal habituel est *mahârâjâdhirâja* « empereur », littéralement « grand roi suprême des rois ».

La déesse Shrî-Lakshmî, monnaie en or, revers, IVe-Ve siècle.

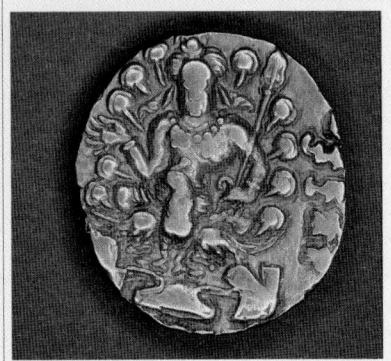

Skanda sur le paon, monnaie en or, revers, Ve siècle.

CHRONOLOGIE

Les dates de l'histoire indienne sont très souvent approximatives et varient d'un historien à l'autre en raison de la diversité des sources.

Vers -7000 – vers -5000 Néolithique.
Vers -5000 – vers -2500 Chalcolithique.
Vers -2500 – vers -1800 Civilisation de l'Indus.
À partir d'environ -1500 Arrivée progressive des Ârya par le nord-ouest de l'Inde.
-543 *Nirvâna* du Buddha d'après les sources cinghalaises.
Vers -527 ou vers -477 *Nirvâna* de Mahâvîra, fondateur du jaïnisme.
Vers -518 Établissement de satrapies achéménides dans le nord-ouest de l'Inde.
-327-325 Campagne militaire d'Alexandre le Grand dans la région de l'Indus.
Vers -324 ou -313 – vers -185 ou -176 Dynastie des Maurya qui règne sur toute l'Inde à l'exception de l'extrême sud.
Vers -324 ou -313 Accession au trône de Chandragupta Maurya, fondateur de la dynastie.
Vers -305 Traité de paix entre Chandragupta Maurya et Séleucos Nikatôr (dynastie séleucide).
Vers -302 – vers 297 Séjours de Mégasthène, ambassadeur de Séleucos Nikatôr, à la cour maurya.
Vers -264 ou -261 – vers -227 ou -226 Règne d'Ashoka, le plus célèbre monarque maurya.
Vers -176 – vers -64 Dynastie des Shunga.
Vers -64 – vers -19 Dynastie des Kânva.
1re moitié du Ier siècle Fondation de la dynastie des Sâtavâhana dans le Deccan.
Arrivée des nomades Shaka (Scythes), originaires d'Asie centrale, dans le nord-ouest et le nord de l'Inde.
2e moitié du Ier siècle Règne du roi Khâravela de la dynastie des Chedi.
Fin du Ier siècle Dynastie des Sâtavâhana dans le Deccan.

APRÈS JÉSUS-CHRIST

1re moitié du Ier siècle Fondation de la dynastie des Kushâna dans le nord-ouest et le nord de l'Inde.
78 Début de l'ère shaka.
78 ou entre 120 et 144 Couronnement de Kanishka, le plus célèbre monarque kushâna.
Vers 78 – vers 125 Règne du roi Nahapâna, monarque shaka du nord-ouest de l'Inde.
226 Établissement de la dynastie sassanide en Perse.
Milieu du IIIe siècle Fin de l'hégémonie de la dynastie kushâna sur le nord-ouest de l'Inde. Démembrement de l'empire des Sâtavâhana.
320 Début de l'ère gupta.
Vers 320 – vers 335 Règne de Chandragupta Ier, fondateur de la dynastie gupta.
Vers 335 – vers 375 Règne de Samudragupta.
Vers 375 – vers 415 Règne de Chandragupta II.
401 – 411 Voyage en Inde du pèlerin chinois Faxian.
Vers 415 – vers 455 Règne de Kumâragupta.
Vers le milieu du Ve siècle Début des invasions des Huns hephtalites (Huns blancs) en Inde du Nord.
Vers 455 – vers 467 Règne de Skandagupta.
Vers 475 – vers 500 Règne du roi Harishena de la dynastie des Vâkâtaka.
606 – 647 Règne de Harsha de Kanauj dans le nord de l'Inde.

PRINCIPALES DYNASTIES APRÈS LES GUPTA

Milieu VIe siècle – milieu VIIIe siècle Dynastie des Châlukya au Karnâtaka.
Milieu VIe siècle – fin VIIIe siècle Dynastie des Pallava au Tamil Nâdu.
Milieu VIIIe siècle – milieu XIe siècle Dynastie des Gurjâra-Pratîhâra au Râjasthân.
Milieu VIIIe siècle – milieu XIIe siècle Dynastie des Pâla au Bengale et au Bihâr.
Milieu VIIIe siècle – fin Xe siècle Dynastie des Râshtrakûta au Mahârâshtra.
Milieu IXe siècle – milieu XIIIe siècle Dynastie des Chola au Tamil Nâdu.
Début Xe siècle – milieu XIIe siècle Dynastie des Chandella au Madhya Pradesh.
Milieu XIe siècle – fin XIIIe siècle Dynastie des Ganga en Orissa.
Début XIe siècle – milieu XIVe siècle Dynastie des Hoysala au Karnâtaka.
Milieu XIVe siècle – 1565 Empire de Vijayanagara dans le sud de l'Inde.

Kumâragupta avec un paon, monnaie en or, avers, Ve siècle.

BIBLIOGRAPHIE

- Arrien, *Le Voyage en Inde d'Alexandre le Grand* (Traduit du grec par P. Charvet, Commentaires P. Charvet, F. Baldissera, K. Karttunen), Nil éditions, Paris, 2002.
- *L'Art de l'Asie du Sud-Est*, «L'art et les grandes civilisations», Citadelles et Mazenod, Paris, 1994.
- J. Auboyer et coll., *La Vie publique et privée dans l'Inde ancienne*, PUF, Paris, depuis 1955.
- J. Auboyer, *Le Trône et son symbolisme dans l'Inde ancienne*, PUF, Paris, 1949.
- A. L. Basham, *La Civilisation de l'Inde ancienne*, Arthaud, Paris, 1976.
- G. Béguin, *Les Arts du Népal et du Tibet*, École du Louvre, Les grandes étapes de l'art, Desclée de Brouwer, Paris, 1990.
- N. R. Bhatt, *La Religion de Siva d'après les sources sanskrites*, Éditions Agamat, Palaiseau, 2000.
- M. Biardeau, *L'Hindouisme, Anthropologie d'une civilisation*, «Champ Histoire», Flammarion, Paris, 1981.
- M. Biardeau et M.-C. Porcher, *Le Râmâyana de Vâlmîki*, «Bibliothèque de la Pléiade», Gallimard, Paris, 1999.
- R. Billard, *Astronomie indienne*, publication de l'École française d'Extrême-Orient, Paris, 1971.
- J. Bloch, *Les Inscriptions d'Açoka*, Les Belles-Lettres, Paris, 1950.
- J. Boisselier, *La Sagesse du Bouddha*, Découvertes-Gallimard, Paris, 1981.
- *Choix de Jataka extraits des Vies antérieures du Bouddha* (traduit du pâli par G. Terral), «Connaissance de l'Orient», Gallimard, Paris, 1958.
- G. Cœdès, *Les États hindouisés d'Indochine et d'Indonésie*, Éditions E. de Boccard, Paris, 1964.
- M. Cohen et J. Giès, *Sérinde, Terre de Bouddha. Dix siècles d'art sur la Route de la soie*, Exposition au Grand Palais, 24 oct. 1995 - 19 fév. 1996, Réunion des musées nationaux, Paris, 1995.
- J. Dupuis, *Histoire de l'Inde des origines à la fin du XXe siècle*, «Civilisations & sociétés», Kailash, Paris, 2005.
- J. Filliozat, *Les Philosophies de l'Inde*, «Que sais-je?», PUF, Paris, 1987.
- J. Filliozat, *La Doctrine classique de la médecine indienne*, École française d'Extrême-Orient, Paris, 1949.
- J. Gonda, *Les Religions de l'Inde, védisme et hindouisme ancien*, t. I, Payot, Paris, 1979.
- J. Harle, *Gupta Sculpture*, Munshiram Manoharlal Publishers, New Delhi, 1996.
- S. L. et J. C. Huntington, *The Art of Ancient India, Buddhist, Hindu, Jain*, John Weatherhill, New York et Tokyo, 1985.
- J.-F. et C. Jarrige, *Les Cités oubliées de l'Indus. Archéologie du Pakistan*, Exposition au musée national des Arts asiatiques-Guimet, 16 nov. 1988 - 30 janv. 1989, Association française d'action artistique, Paris, 1988.
- M. C. Joshi, *L'Âge d'or de l'Inde classique, L'Empire des Gupta*, catalogue de l'exposition (Grand Palais, printemps 2007), Éditions de la RMN, avril 2007.
- *Le Kamasoutra de Vatsyâyana* (traduit du sanskrit par F. Lamairesse), Georges Carré éd., Paris, 1891.
- E. Lamotte, *Histoire du bouddhisme indien*, Publications de l'Institut Orientaliste de Louvain, 1958.
- A. M. Loth, *Védisme et hindouisme, Images du divin et des dieux*, Éditions Chapitre Douze, Bruxelles/Paris, 2003.
- *Le Mahâbhârata*, (traduit du sanskrit par J. M. Péterfalvi), 2 vol., GF/Flammarion, Paris, 1986.
- R. C. Majumdar, *The History and Culture of the Indian People*, 11 vol., Bombay, 1952-1965.
- J. Naudou, *Le Bouddha*, Les fondateurs des grandes religions, Aimery Somogy, Paris, 1973.
- A. Okada, *Sculptures indiennes du musée Guimet*, Trésors d'art du musée Guimet, ARAA et RMN, Paris, 2000.
- P. Pal, *The Ideal Image*, Asia House Gallery, New York, 1978.
- R. Régnier, *L'Arbre et le lotus, L'art bouddhique en Inde à Sanchi et à Bharhut*, «Patrimoines d'Orient», Findakly, Paris, 1998.
- L. Renou, *Hymnes spéculatifs du Véda*, «Connaissance de l'Orient», Gallimard/UNESCO, Paris, 1956.
- J. M. Rosenfield, *The Dynastic Arts of the Kushans*, University of California Press, Berkeley and Los Angeles, 1967.
- C. Sivaramamurti, A. Okada et T. Zéphir, *L'Art en Inde*, Citadelles et Mazenod, Paris, 1999.
- P. Stern, *Colonnes indiennes d'Ajantâ et d'Ellora*, Publications du musée Guimet, PUF, Paris, 1972.
- F. Tissot, *Les Arts anciens du Pakistan et de l'Afghanistan*, École du Louvre, «Les grandes étapes de l'art», Desclée de Brouwer, Paris, 1987.
- J. Varenne, *Mythes et légendes extraits des Brâhmana*, «Connaissance de l'Orient», Gallimard/UNESCO, Paris, 1967.
- J. G. Williams, *The Art of Gupta India, Empire and Province*, Princeton University Press, Princeton, 1982.
- G. Yazdani, *Ajanta, The Colour and Monochrome Reproductions of the Ajanta Frescoes Based on Photography*, 4 vol., Londres, 1930-1955.

TABLE DES ILLUSTRATIONS

COUVERTURE

1er plat *Apsaras* (nymphe céleste), détail d'une peinture murale d'Ajantâ, grotte n° 17, Ve-VIe siècle.
Dos Gardien de porte, sculpture en grès de Sârnâth, Ve siècle. Archaeological Museum, Sârnâth.
2e plat Temple de Vishnu à Deogarh (Uttar Pradesh), VIe siècle.

OUVERTURE

1 Bas-relief du temple de Vishnu à Deogarh (Uttar Pradesh), VIe siècle.
2-3 Vishnu couché sur le serpent Ananta entre deux ères cosmiques (ensemble et détail), bas-relief du temple de Vishnu à Deogarh (Uttar Pradesh), VIe siècle.
4-5 Nara-Nârâyana (Vishnu enseignant), (ensemble et détail), bas-relief du temple de Vishnu à Deogarh (Uttar Pradesh), VIe siècle.
6-7 Gajendramoksha (La délivrance du roi des éléphants; ensemble et détail), bas-relief du temple de Vishnu à Deogarh (Uttar Pradesh), VIe siècle.
9 Scène de lustration extraite du *Mahâjanaka Jâtaka*, peinture d'Ajantâ, grotte n° 1, Ve-VIe siècle.

CHAPITRE 1

10 Murailles de Râjagriha, bas-relief du grand *stûpa* de Sânchî, Ier siècle av. J.-C.-Ier siècle apr. J.-C.
11 Chapiteau aux Lions de Sârnâth édifié par l'empereur Ashoka, IIIe siècle av. J.-C.
12h Vue des vestiges de la cité de Mohenjo-Daro, civilisation de l'Indus, 2500-1850 av. J.-C.
12b Sceau en stéatite orné d'un unicorne, cité de Mohenjo-Daro, civilisation de l'Indus, 2500-1850 av. J.-C..
13h Rue dans la ville basse de Mohenjo-Daro, civilisation de l'Indus, 2500-1850 av. J.-C.
13b Buste dit du Roi-prêtre, civilisation de l'Indus, 2400-2000 av. J.-C.
14h Brahmâ, sculpture en schiste provenant de Gwâlior, XIe-XIIe siècle. Musée des arts asiatiques-Guimet, Paris.
14-15b Assemblée de brahmanes, miniature de Trichinopoly (Inde du Sud), vers 1820. British Library, Londres.
15h Dieu védique Agni, sculpture du temple de Râjarânî à Bhubaneshvar, XIe siècle.
16 Scène de combat extraite du *Mahâbhârata*, peinture de Païthan, XIXe siècle. Musée des arts asiatiques-Guimet, Paris.
17 Forme cosmique de Vishnu révélée à Arjuna, miniature de Bikaner, 2e quart du XVIIIe siècle. Jagdish and Kamala Mittal Museum, Hyderabad.
18 Tîrthankara jaïn, sculpture en bronze, IVe siècle. Musée de Patna.
19h Naissance du Buddha, bas-relief provenant du grand *stûpa* d'Amarâvatî, IIe siècle. British Museum, Londres.
19b Buddha, école du Gandhâra, Ier siècle apr. J.-C. British Museum, Londres.
20-21h *La Défaite de Porus par Alexandre*, peinture de Watteau, 1802. Musée des Beaux-Arts, Lille.
21b Alexandre le Grand coiffé de la dépouille d'un éléphant, monnaie de Ptolémée Ier.
22h Carte de l'Empire maurya, infographie d'Édigraphie.
22b Grotte de Lomas Rishi à Barâbar, IIIe siècle av. J.-C.
23hg Vestiges de la salle hypostyle de Pâtaliputra.
23hd Reconstitution de la salle hypostyle de Pâtaliputra.
23b Tête d'homme, sculpture provenant de Sârnâth, IIIe siècle av. J.-C., époque maurya. National Museum of India, New Delhi.
24 Colonne de Lauiyâ Nandangarh avec des édits d'Ashoka, IIIe siècle av. J.-C.
25h Éléphant sculpté et édits d'Ashoka gravés dans le roc à Dhaulî, IIIe siècle av. J.-C.
25b Édit d'Ashoka, détail d'un pilier de pierre à Sârnâth, IIIe siècle av. J.-C.
26 Grand *stûpa* de Sânchî, Ier siècle av. J.-C.-Ie siècle apr. J.-C.
27 Grottes bouddhiques de Bhâjâ, IIe-Ier siècle av. J.-C.

CHAPITRE 2

28h Roi chassant le lion, monnaie gupta en or, IVe-Ve siècle. National Museum, New Delhi.
28b Roi chassant le rhinocéros, *idem*.
29 Bodhisattva, sculpture du Gandhâra, II-IIIe siècle apr. J.-C. Philadelphia Museum of Art.
30h Tête d'homme scythe provenant de Mathurâ, Ier siècle apr. J.-C. National Museum, New Delhi.
30b Scythes, détail des bas-reliefs de Persépolis, Empire achéménide, VI-Ve siècle av. J.-C.
31h *Stûpa* Dharmarâjika, IIIe siècle av. J.-C.-Ve siècle apr. J.-C., Taxilâ (Pakistan).
31b Statue de Kanishka, provenant du temple de Mât (Mathurâ), début IIe siècle. Government Museum, Mathurâ.
32h et b Statue de Chashtana, provenant du temple de Mât (ensemble et détail de la ceinture), 1re moitié du IIe siècle. *Idem*.

33h Gobelet, verre provenant de Begrâm (Afghanistan), Ier siècle apr. J.-C. Musée des arts asiatiques-Guimet, Paris.
33b Statuette en ivoire provenant de Pompéi, Ier siècle apr. J.-C. Musée archéologique, Naples.
34 Le Monarque universel, bas-relief provenant d'un *stûpa* de Jaggayyapeta, Ier siècle av. J.-C. Government Museum, Madras.
35 Prince entouré de courtisanes, bas-relief provenant de Nâgârjunakonda, IIIe siècle apr. J.-C. National Museum, New Delhi.
36hg Chandragupta Ier et Kumâradevî, monnaie en or, vers 320. National Museum, New Delhi.
36hd Empereur gupta appuyé sur une hache de combat, monnaie en or, IVe siècle apr. J.-C. National Museum, New Delhi.
36-37b Cheval de Khairigarh, IVe siècle. State Museum, Lucknow.
37hg Empereur gupta faisant l'oblation au feu rituel, monnaie en or, IVe-Ve siècle. National Museum, New Delhi.
37hd Samudragupta jouant du luth, monnaie en or, IVe siècle. National Museum, New Delhi.
38h Carte de l'Empire gupta, infographie d'Edigraphie.
38b Empereur gupta à cheval, monnaie en or, IVe-Ve siècle. National Museum, New Delhi.
39 Assemblée écoutant une prédication bouddhique, détail d'une peinture murale d'Ajantâ, Ve-VIe siècle.
40 Varâha (Sanglier), site d'Eran, Ve siècle.
41 Pilier-étendard, Eran, 485 apr. J.-C.

CHAPITRE 3

42 Varâha (Sanglier), *avatâra* de Vishnu, bas-relief d'Udayagiri (Madhya Pradesh), fin du IVe siècle.
43 Shiva Natarâja provenant de Nâchnâ (Madhya Pradesh), sculpture en grès, Ve siècle. National Museum, New Delhi.
44h Sacrifice du cheval, monnaie en or, époque de Kumâragupta Ier, Ve siècle. British Museum, Londres.
44b Vishnu provenant de Mathurâ, sculpture en grès, Ve siècle. National Museum, New Delhi.
45 Sceau royal de Bhitari portant l'effigie de Garuda, monture de Vishnu, métal, Ve siècle. State Museum, Lucknow.
46 Vishnu couché sur le serpent d'Éternité entre deux ères cosmiques, détail d'un bas-relief du temple de Vishnu à Deogarh (Uttar Pradesh), VIe siècle.
47h Krishna soulevant le mont Govardhana, sculpture, Ve-VIe siècle. Bharat Kala Bhavan, Bénarès.
47b Vishnu sous sa forme cosmique (Vishvarûpa), sculpture en grès rouge de Mathurâ, Ve siècle. Government Museum, Mathurâ.
48 Pilier sculpté d'un trident shivaïte provenant de Mathurâ, IVe siècle. Government Museum, Mathurâ.
49g *Linga* dans le sanctuaire du temple de Bhumarâ, Ve siècle.
49d *Linga* à un visage, sculpture en grès, Ve siècle. National Museum, New Delhi.
50 Kumâra, dieu de la Guerre, avec son paon, sculpture en grès, Ve siècle. Bharat Kala Bhavan, Bénarès.
51 La déesse Durgâ chevauchant le lion, terre cuite de Shrâvasti, Ve siècle. State Museum, Lucknow.
52 Buddha et bodhisattva, détail de bas-relief du grand *stûpa* de Nâlandâ (Bihâr), fin du VIe siècle.
53 Site bouddhique de Nâlandâ (Bihâr).
54 Le bodhisattva Avalokiteshvara, sculpture en grès de Sârnâth, Ve siècle. Indian Museum, Calcutta.
55 *Stûpa* Dhamekh de Sârnâth, vers 500.
56 Tête de Buddha, sculpture en grès rouge de Mathurâ, Ve siècle. Government Museum, Mathurâ.
57g Tête de Buddha, sculpture en grès de Sârnâth, Ve siècle. Archaeological Museum, Sârnâth.
57d Tête de Buddha, sculpture en grès de Sârnâth, Ve siècle. Archaeological Museum, Sârnâth.

CHAPITRE 4

58 Danseuse et musiciennes, détail d'un linteau de porte provenant de Pawâyâ, Ve siècle. Gujari Mahal Museum, Gwâlior.
59 Joueuses de flûte, détail d'une peinture murale d'Ajantâ, Ve-VIe siècle.
60h Inscription sanskrite, détail du sceau royal de Bhitari, métal, Ve siècle. State Museum, Lucknow.
60b Enfant mémorisant l'alphabet, terre cuite, époque shunga, IIe siècle av. J.-C. National Museum, New Delhi.
61g Inscription du pilier de Fer de Mehrauli à Delhi (détail), IVe-Ve siècle.
61d Le pilier de Fer de Mehrauli à Delhi.
62h Représentation de quatre planètes, fragment de linteau provenant de Sârnâth, Ve-VIe siècle. Indian Museum, Calcutta.
62b Le dieu Soleil Sûrya, sculpture provenant de la région de Sârnâth, Ve siècle. Bharat Kala Bhavan, Bénarès.
63h Manuscrit dit Bakshali avec la figuration du zéro, XIIe siècle. Bodleian Library, Oxford.
63b Chiffres de 1 à 0 dans diverses graphies indiennes.
64 Maquette de décor pour l'opéra *L'Anneau de Shakuntalâ* de L. E. Reyer créé à l'Opéra de Paris, le 14 juillet 1858. BnF, Paris.
65h Scène de genre, terre cuite provenant

TABLE DES ILLUSTRATIONS 123

de Mathurâ, Ve siècle. Government Museum, Mathurâ.

65b Jeune femme sur une balançoire, terre cuite provenant de Râjghat (Sârnâth), Ve siècle. Bharat Kala Bhavan, Bénarès.

66 Couple d'amoureux, relief d'Ajantâ, grotte n° 16, V[e]-VIe siècle.

67h Couples d'amoureux, détail d'une peinture murale d'Ajantâ, grotte n° 17, V[e]-VIe siècle.

67b Expression de visage, détail d'une peinture murale d'Ajantâ, grotte n° 1, V[e]-VIe siècle.

CHAPITRE 5

68 Temple n° 17 de Sânchî, début du Ve siècle.

69 Lion cornu, fragment de linteau provenant de Sârnâth, Ve siècle. Archaeological Museum, Sârnâth.

70 *Apsaras* (nymphe céleste) richement parée, détail d'une peinture murale d'Ajantâ, grotte n° 17, V[e]-VIe siècle.

71h Parure, détail du Vishnu provenant de Mathurâ, sculpture en grès, Ve siècle. National Museum, New Delhi.

71b Torse de Vishnu ou d'un bodhisattva, sculpture provenant de Jaisinhapura (Mathurâ), Ve siècle. Government Museum, Mathurâ.

72 Grotte n° 4 d'Udayagiri (Madhya Pradesh), Ve siècle.

73h Restitution du *stûpa* Dhamekh de Sârnâth.

73bg Décor de la base du *stûpa* Dhamekh de Sârnâth, vers 500 apr. J.-C.

73bd État actuel du *stûpa* Dhamekh de Sârnâth, vers 500 apr. J.-C.

74h Temple de Vishnu à Deogarh (Uttar Pradesh), VIe siècle.

74b Plan du temple de Vishnu à Deogarh, *idem*.

75h Temple de Bhitargaon, seconde moitié du Ve siècle.

75b Plan du temple de Bhitargaon, seconde moitié du Ve siècle.

76h Être céleste (*vidyâdhara*), panneau de terre cuite provenant d'un temple gupta de la vallée du Gange, Ve siècle. Musée des arts asiatiques-Guimet, Paris.

76b Gangâ, déesse du Gange, sculpture en terre cuite provenant de Ahicchattrâ, Ve siècle. National Museum, New Delhi.

77 Shiva Androgyne (Ardhanârîshvara), sculpture en grès rouge de Mathurâ, Ve siècle. Government Museum, Mathurâ.

78-79 Buddha prêchant (détail et ensemble), sculpture en grès de Sârnâth, Ve siècle. Archaeological Museum, Sârnâth.

80 Torse de Buddha, sculpture en grès rouge provenant de Jamalpur (Mathurâ), Ve siècle. Government Museum, Mathurâ.

81 Avalokiteshvara, sculpture en grès de Sârnâth, VIe siècle. Archaeological Museum, Sârnâth.

CHAPITRE 6

82 Grotte n° 19 d'Ajantâ, V[e]- VIe siècle.

83 Nymphe céleste, détail d'une peinture rupestre de Sigiriya, Shri Lankâ, 2e moitié du Ve siècle.

84g *Vihâra* de la grotte n° 19 d'Ajantâ, V[e]- VIe siècle.

84d Plan des grottes d'Ajantâ (Mahârâshtra), V[e]- VIe siècle.

85h Vue générale actuelle des grottes d'Ajantâ (Mahârâshtra), V[e]- VIe siècle.

85b Entrée de la grotte n° 19 d'Ajantâ, gravure de Thomas Colman Dibdin, vers 1830-1893.

86 Princesse sortant d'un palais, peinture murale d'Ajantâ, grotte n° 17, V[e]-VIe siècle.

87 Couple princier sous un pavillon, *idem*.

88 Bodhisattva, peinture murale d'Ajantâ, grotte n° 1, V[e]-VIe siècles.

89 Bodhisattva, *idem*.

90 Vishnu couché sur le serpent d'Éternité de Budhanîlakantha (Népal), art licchavi, VIIe siècle.

91g Buddha debout, sculpture en bronze provenant de Patna, VIIe siècle. Birmingham Museum of Art.

91d Bodhisattva, temple n° 3 de Nâlandâ (Bihâr), VIe siècle environ.

92 Buddha debout, sculpture en grès de Dvâravatî (Thaïlande), VIIIe siècle. Musée national de Bangkok.

93 Durgâ, sculpture de Sambor Prei Kuk (Cambodge), VIIe siècle. Musée national du Cambodge, Phnom-Penh.

94h Buddha de Borobudur (Java), VIIIe-IXe siècles.

94b Buddha Dîpankara, reliquaire en bois de Duldur Aqur, région de Kucha, VIIe siècle. Musée des arts asiatiques-Guimet, Paris.

95 Buddha monumental de Bâmiyân (Afghanistan), V[e]-VIe siècle.

96 Couple de *nâga* (cobra) anthropomorphes, bas-relief, grotte n° 19 d'Ajantâ, V[e]- VIe siècle.

TÉMOIGNAGES ET DOCUMENTS

97 Tête masculine provenant de Sârnâth, Ve siècle. Bharat Kala Bhavan, Bénarès.

111 Camille Claudel, 2e étude pour *Sacountala*, vers 1886-1888, terre cuite. Coll. part.

117 *Femme au scorpion*, sculpture de Mathurâ, V[e]-VIe siècle. Indian Museum, Calcutta.

118g La déesse Shrî-Lakshmî (revers), monnaie en or, IVe-Ve siècle. National Museum, New Delhi.

118d et 119 Skanda sur le paon (revers), Kumâragupta avec un paon (avers), monnaie en or, Ve siècle, *idem*.

126. Bas-relief, terre cuite provenant de Râjghat (Sârnâth), Ve siècle. Bharat Kala Bhavan, Bénarès.

INDEX

A

Achéménide, empire 19, 20, *23*, 25, 30.
Afghanistan 13, 20, *22, 33*, 94, 95.
Agni, dieu *15, 50*.
Ahicchattrâ, temple de 48, 76.
Ajantâ (Mahârâshtra) *39*, 55, *65, 66, 83*, 84-87.
Ajâtashatru 20.
Âjîvika, secte des 22.
Alexandre le Grand 11, 19, 20-21, 22.
Allahabad, inscription d' 35.
Amarakosha ou *« Lexique d'Amara »* 66.
Amarâvatî, art d' 19.
Ândhra, art et royaume des 33, *34*, 93.
Anneau de Shakuntalâ, L' (Louis Ernest Reyer et Théophile Gautier) *64*.
Apsaras 70.
Araméen 25.
Arrien *20*.
Arthashâstra, ou « Science des intérêts » (Kautilya) 24.
Âryabhatîya (Âryabhata) 61, 62, *63*.
Âryens 14, 15, 17, 18.
Asanga 54.
Ashoka 24-25, 26, *26, 27, 31*, 34, 37.
Ashoka, pilier d' *11*, 77.
Ashtâdhyâyî (« Les Huit sections ») 60.
Ashtângahridayasamhitâ ou « Corpus de l'essence de la science en huit articles » 63.
Avalokiteshvara, bodhisattva 54, *54*.
Avatâra, théorie des 45.
Ayurvédique, médecine 63.

B

Bactriane 13, 30, 39.
Bâmiyân, Buddha de 94, *95*.
Bâna 66.
Bangemura, Buddha de (Kâthmandu) 91.
Barâbar, grottes de 22.
Barattage de l'océan de Lait *62*.
Begrâm (Afghanistan) *33*.
Bengale 37, 90.
Bhagavad-Gîtâ 17, 44.
Bhâjâ, grottes (Mahârâshtra) 27.
Bhânugupta 41.
Bharata 66.
Bhâravî 65.
Bhartrihari 66.
Bhitargaon, temple de (Uttar Pradesh) 75, *75*.
Bhitari, sceau de 45, *60*.
Bhubaneshvar (Orissa) *15*, 75.
Bhumârâ, temple de (Madhya Pradesh) 48, *49*, 76.
Bihâr 20, 35, 36, 90.
Bihâr, pilier de 50.
Bilsadh 59.
Bimbisâra 20.
Bindusâra 24.
Bodh Gayâ 53.
Bodhisattva 54, *54*, 55, 80, *81, 84, 87, 91*.
Bodhisattva Manjushrî 54.
Borobudur (Java) 94.
Bouddhisme 18-19, 25, *25, 27, 27*, 30, 34, *34, 35, 39*, 41, 43, 52-57, 63, 72, *73, 79, 83*, 84-87, 91, *91*, 92, *93*, 94.
Bouddhisme hînayâna, 54.
Bouddhisme mahâyâna 54, 73, 81.
Brahmâ, dieu *14*, 44, *46*, 59.

Brâhmana (textes) 15.
Brahmanes *(Brâhmana)* (prêtres) 14, *14*, 18.
Brâhmî, écriture 25.
Brihatsamhitâ (la « Grande Collection ») (Varâhamihira) *61*, 62.
Buddha Amitâbha *81*.
Buddha Dîpankara 94.
Buddha Shâkyamuni, vie du *18, 19*, 20, *26*, 36, 53.
Budhagupta 40, 41, *41*, 52.
Budhanîlakantha (Népal) *90*.

C

Chakravartin (monarque universel) *34*.
Cambodge 92, 93.
Cazalis *64*.
Chedi, dynastie des 27.
Champa, royaume du 92.
Chandî-Durgâ *voir* Durgâ.
Chandragupta (empereur maurya) 21, 22, 23, 24.
Chandragupta Ier 35, 36, *36*, 70.
Chandragupta II 29, 38-39, 44, 46, 48, *61*, 64.
Charakasamhitâ 63.
Chariot de terre cuite, Le (Shudraka) 65.
Chashtana (Tiastanès) 32, *33*.
Chateaubriand, François René de *64*.
Chera, lignée des 34.
Chézy, A. L. de 65.
Chine 30, 31, 52, 95.
Chunâr, grès de *79*, 80.
Combat de Shiva et d'Arjuna, Le (Bhâravî) 65.

Crystal Palace, incendie du *85*.
Cyrus le Grand 19, 20.

D

Dandin 65.
Darius Ier *30*.
Dashakumâracharita (L'Histoire des dix princes) (Dandin) 66.
Deccan, royaume du 39.
Delhi 13, 17, *61*.
Deogarh, temple de (Uttar Pradesh) 46, *46, 74*, 75.
Devagiri 50.
Devî 16 (*voir aussi* Durgâ).
Devî-Mâhâtmya ou *Célébration de la Grande Déesse* 50, *51*.
Devnîmorî (Gujarât) 72.
Dhamekh (Sârnâth), *stûpa* 55, 72, *73*.
Dhaulî (Bihar) *25*.
Dhruvadevî 38.
Dhum Varâhî 90.
Dhvaka Bâhâ, *stûpa* votif de (Kâthmandu) 91.
Digambara, secte des 18.
Dignâga 54.
Duldur-Aqur 95.
Durgâ, déesse 50, 51, *51, 93* (*voir aussi* Pârvatî).
Dvâravatî, art de 92, 93.

E - F

Elephanta, grottes d' 72.
Ellora, grottes d' 72.
Eran (Madhya Pradesh) *40*, 41, *41*, 46.
Faxian *39*, 54.
Fer, pilier de Mehrauli (Delhi) 39, 60, 61.
Fondukistân 94.

INDEX

G
Gandhâra 30.
Gandhâra, art du *19*, 29, *94*, 95.
Gangâ, déesse 76.
Gange, vallée du *11*, 13, 32, 41, 76.
Garuda *37*, 45, *45*.
Gautier, Théophile 64.
Géographie (Claude Ptolémée) 32.
Ghatotkacha 35.
Gill, Robert *85*.
Goethe 64.
Gotamîputa 33.
Govindagupta 39.

H
Hadda (Afghanistan) 94.
Hakuhô, époque 95.
Harappâ 12.
Harishena 35.
Harsha de Kanauj 41, 66.
Hastinâpura 17.
Hastyâyurveda (Pâlakâpya) 63.
Herder 64.
Hindû Kûch 20.
Histoire naturelle (Pline l'Ancien) 27.
Huns (Hûna) 40, *40*, 41.
Huns Hephtalites 51.

I
Ikshvâku, lignée des 35.
Indonésie 92, 93.
Indra, dieu *46*, 47.
Indraprastha (Delhi) 17.
Indus, civilisation de l' 11, 12-13.
Indus, vallée de l' 30.
Iran *voir* Perse 13.

J
Jaïnisme 43, 18, *18*, 52, 53.
Japon 95.
Jâtaka (vies antérieures du Buddha) *26*, *87*.

Java, île de 93.
Jones, William 65.
Jupiter *62*.
Kahaum 51.

K
Kâlidâsa 47, 48, 50, 64-65, 77.
Kalinga (actuel Orissa) 27.
Kâmasûtra, ou « Recueil d'aphorismes sur l'amour » (Vâtsyâyana) 67.
Kanishka 29, 30, *31*.
Kânva, royaume 27.
Kapishâ 30.
Kâthiâwâr, presqu'île du (actuel Gujarat) 13.
Kâthmandu, vallée de 90, *90*, 91.
Kautilya 24.
Khairigarh *37*.
Khâravela 27.
Kharoshtî, écriture *25*.
Khmers 93, *93*.
Khoh, temple de 48, 49.
Koshala, royaume de 20.
Krishna 17, *17*, 18, *47*.
Krishna Kâliyamardana (destructeur du démon serpent Kâliya) 91.
Kshaharâta, royaume des 32, 33.
Kshatriya (nobles guerriers) 14.
Kujulakadphisès 30.
Kumâra, dieu *46*, 49, 50, *50*.
Kumâradevî 36, *36*.
Kumâragupta Ier *38*, 40, 44, *45*, 48, 49, 50, 52.
Kunda, temple de (Madhya Pradesh) 74.
Kushâna, empire 29, 30-31, 32, 34, 71, 77, 80, 93.
Kushika 48.
Kuveranâgâ 39.

L
Lakshmî *voir* Shrî-Lakshmî.
Lakulîsha 48.
Lamartine, Alphonse de *64*.
Lâta (Gujarât)
Licchavi, royaume des 36, 90.
Lignée de Raghu, La (Kâlidâsa) 65.
Linga 48, *49*, 90.

M
Magadha, royaume de 20, 22, 27, 41.
Mâgha 66.
Mahâbalipuram (Tamil Nâdu) 75.
Mahâbhârata, épopée du 16, *16*, 18.
Maitraka 41.
Mâlavikâ et Agnimitra (Kâlidâsa) 65, *65*.
Mandasor (ancienne Dashapura) 51.
Mârkandeya Purâna 50.
Mât (Mathurâ), temple de 31, *31*.
Mathurâ (Uttar Pradesh) *19*, 30, 37, 45, 48, *49*, 52, 54, 55, *57*, 76, 77, 80-81, 90, 93, *95*.
Mâtrikâ (« Mères ») 50.
Mauès 30.
Maukhari 41.
Maurya, empire *11*, 20, 21, 22-25, 26, 27, 34, *41*, 72.
Mégasthène 23, 24.
Meghavanna, roi 52.
Mehrgârh, fouilles de (Bâlûchistan) 12.
Meluhha, royaume de 13.
Michelet *64*.
Mihirakula 41.
Mirpur Khas (Sind) 72.
Mohenjo-Daro 12, *13*.
Mrigashikhâvana 52.
Mrigasthalî 90.

N
Nâchnâ, temple de (Madhya Pradesh) 48, 75.
Nâga, dynastie des 39.
Nâgârjunakonda 35.
Nahapâna 32.
Naissance de Kumâra, La (Kâlidâsa) 48, 65.
Nâlandâ (Bihâr) 52, *53*, 55, 63, 91, *91*.
Nanda, lignée des 21.
Narasimhagupta 41, 52.
Nâtyashâstra ou « Traité d'art dramatique » (Bharata) *59*, 66, *67*.
Népal 90, *90*, 91, 95.
Newâr, art de 90.
Nuage messager, Le (Kâlidâsa) 50, 65.

P
Padmâvatî (Pawâyâ) 39.
Pakistan 22.
Pâla, art 90, 94.
Pâlakâpya 63.
Panchasiddhântikâ (Varâhamihira) 62.
Pândya, lignée des 34.
Pânini 60.
Parâvani, paon 49, *50*.
Pârvatî *46*, 49, 75, *77* *voir aussi* Durgâ.
Pâshupata, secte des 48, *49*.
Pâtaliputra 20, 23, *23*, 54, 61, 63.
Périple de la mer Érythrée 32.
Perse 19, 22, 63.
Persépolis *23*, *30*.
Phnom Da 93.
Phnom Penh 93.
Pilier-étendard *(dhvaja stambha)* *41*, 71.
Pline l'Ancien 27, 33.
Pompéi *33*.
Pondichéry 34.
Pôros 21, *21*.
Prabhavatî 39.

126 ANNEXES

Prayâga (Allahabad) 36.
Prithivîsena 48.
Ptolémée, Claude 32, 34.
Purâna 45, *48*, 50, *53*, *60*, *61*.
Purugupta 40.
Pushyabhûti, dynastie des 41.
Pushyamitra 26, 40.

Q - R

Qutb Minâr *61*.

Râdhasvâmin 54.
Raghuvamsha (*La Lignée de Raghu*) (Kâlidâsa) 47.
Râhu, démon 61, *62*.
Râjagriha (Râjgir) *11*, 20.
Râmagupta 38.
Râmâyana, épopée du 16-17, 18.
Rasa (« saveurs ») 66, *66*, 67.
Rigveda 21.
Roi-prêtre, buste du (civilisation de l'Indus) *13*.
Rome impériale 34.
Rudradâman 32.
Rudrasena II 39.
Rudrasimha III 38.

S

Sacrifice du cheval (*ashvamedha*) 37, 38, 40, 44, *44*.
Samudragupta 29, 35, 36-37, 38, 44, 52, 53, 70.
Sânchî *11*, 26, *69*, 74.
Sandrakottos 21.
Sanskrit 14, 15, *45*, 60, *60*, 61, 62, 63, 65, *65*, *66*.
Sârnâth *25*, 55, *55*, 57, *69*, 72, *73*, 76, 77, *79*, 80, 81, *81*, 90, 91, *91*, *94*.
Sârnâth, chapiteau aux Lions de *11*, 77.
Sassanides, dynastie des *29*.

Sâtakani, lignée des 33.
Sâtavâhana, dynastie des *26*, 33, 34, *35*.
Saturne *62*.
Saura, les 51.
Scythes (Shaka) 30, *30*, 32, 33, *33*, 38. 46, 51.
Séleucides, dynastie des 23.
Séleucos Nikatôr 22, 23.
Shâba Vîrasena 48.
Shaishunâga, dynastie des 20.
Shakuntalâ (Kâlidâsa) *64*, 65.
Shiva/shivaïsme 16, 43, *43*, 44, *46*, 48-49, 64, 72, 75, 90.
Shiva Ardhanârîshvara (« Androgyne ») 48, 49, 77.
Shiva Natarâja (« Seigneur de la danse ») *43*, 48.
Shiva Purâna 48.
Shrîgupta 35, 52.
Shri Lankâ 52, *83*, 94.
Shrî-Lakshmî 45, 47.
Shûdra (serfs) 14.

Shudraka 65.
Shunga, dynastie des 26, 27.
Shvetâmbara, secte des 18, 52.
Siddhasena Divâkara 52.
Sigiriya (Shri Lankâ) *83*.
Sirpur (Madhya Pradesh) 75.
Skanda, dieu (*voir* Kumâra).
Skandagupta 40.
Stûpa 31, 31, 34, *53*, 55, *55*, *72*, 73, *83*.
Sultanganj (Patna) *91*.
Vâtsyâyana 67.
Surkh Kotal, temple de (Afghanistan) 31.
Sûrya, dieu 51, *62*.
Sûryasiddhânta 63.
Sushrutasamhitâ 63.

T

Tanesara-Mahâdeva (Râjasthân) 50.
Tang, époque 95.
Taxilâ (Takshashilâ) 20, *31*.
Thaïlande 92, *93*.
Tibet 63.

Tigowa, temple de (Madhya Pradesh) 74.
Tilganga (Népal) 91.
Tîrthankara 18, 51, 80.
Triade *(trimûrti)* 44.

U

Udayagiri (Uttar Pradesh) *43*, 45, 47, 48, 51, 52, *72*, *72*.
Ujjayinî, *kshatrapa* d' 32, 33, *33*, 38.
Ujjayinî (Madhya Pradesh) 30, 64.
Upanishad 11, 016.
Ur, tombes royales d' (Mésopotamie) 13.
Urvâshî conquise par la vaillance (Kâlidâsa) 65.

V - Y

Vâgbhata 63.
Vainyagupta 41.
Vaishâlî 36.
Vaishya (hommes du commun) 14.
Vâkâtaka, lignée des 39, 48, 55, 84.
Valabhî 52.
Varâhamihira *61*, 62.

Vardhamâna
(Mahâvîra) 18, 20.
Varshakara 20.
Varuna *46*.
Vasubandhu 53, 54.
Vâtsyâyana 67.
Veda/védisme 14, 15, 15, 17, 18, 44, *44*, 45, 50, *59*, 60.

Vidishâ (Madhya Pradesh) 37.
Vietnam 92.
Vimakadphisès 30.
Vishnu/Vishnuisme 16, *41*, 43, *43*, 44, 45-47, *62*, 72, *74*, 75, 90, 91, 93.
Vishnu Anantashâyin (couché sur le serpent d'Éternité) *46*, 47, *90*, 91.
Vishnu Trivikrama (le dieu aux Trois Pas) 91.
Vishnu Varâha («Sanglier») *40*, *43*, 45, 46, 90.

Vishnu Vishvarûpa 47, *47*.
Vishnugupta *90*.
Vishvakarman *50*.
Vriji, clans des 20, 36.

Yamunâ, déesse 76.
Yijing, pèlerin 52.
Yuezhi, nomades 30.

CRÉDITS PHOTOGRAPHIQUES

Achilleus 23hg, 25h, 36-37b, 72, 73bg, 75h, 91d, 92, 93. Aditya Arya, New Delhi/Réunion des Musées nationaux dos, 37hd, 43, 44b, 45, 47b, 48, 49d, 54, 56, 57g, 57d, 58, 60h, 65h, 65b, 69, 71h, 71b, 77, 80, 97, 118g, 118d, 119, 126. AKG/British Library 14-15b. AKG/Nimatallah 12b. The Ancient Art and Architecture Collection Ltd, Pinner/ Bruce Norman 13h. The Ancient Art and Architecture Collection Ltd, Pinner/R. Sheridan 38b. Birmingham Art Museum 91g. BnF, Paris 64. Bodleian Library, Oxford 63. Bridgeman Giraudon 1. Bridgeman Giraudon/Ajanta, Maharashtra 66. Bridgeman Giraudon/National Museum of India, New Delhi 23b. Bridgeman Giraudon/Sarnath, Uttar Pradesh 25b. Peter Clayton 21b. La Collection/ Jean-Louis Nou 1er plat de couverture, 2, 3, 4, 5, 6, 7, 9, 10, 11, 17, 22b, 26, 27, 28h, 28b, 31b, 32h, 32b, 34, 35, 37hg, 39, 42, 46, 50, 51, 52, 53, 59, 60b, 61g, 61d, 62h, 62b, 67h, 67b, 68, 70, 73bd, 74h, 76b, 78h, 78b, 79, 81, 82, 83, 84b, 86, 87, 88, 89, 96, 117. Corbis/Christophe Boisvieux 55. Corbis/Burnstein Collection 29. Corbis/Historical Picture Archive 85(d). Corbis/Angelo Hornak 30h. Corbis/Wolfgang Kaehler 94h. Corbis/Charles et Josette Lenars 95.Digital South Asia Library/American Institute of Indian Studies 18, 49g. Archives Gallimard 22h, 38h. Leemage/Heritages Images/The British Museum 19h, 19b, 44h. Miranda MacQuitty International, Londres 12h. Antonio Martinelli pour Point de Vue/images du Monde 40, 41. Archives photographiques du musée des Arts asiatiques-Guimet, Paris 24, 47h, 90, 94b. Archives R. M. Paris/Denis Bernard 111. The Picture Desk/ Dagli-Orti 30b. The Picture Desk/Dagli-Orti/Musée national de Karachi 13b. Rapho/ Roland et Sabrina Michaud 15h. RMN/Richard Lambert 16, 33d. Réunion des Musées nationaux /Hervé Lewandowski 14h, 76h. RMN/René-Gabriel Ojéda 20-21h. Robert Harding Picture Library 31h. Scala, Florence 33g. Sipa/Dinodia 2e plat de couverture, 36hg, 36hd, 84-85h
© by ADAGP Paris 2007 111.

ÉDITION ET FABRICATION

DÉCOUVERTES GALLIMARD
COLLECTION CONÇUE PAR Pierre Marchand.
DIRECTION Elisabeth de Farcy.
COORDINATION ÉDITORIALE Anne Lemaire.
GRAPHISME Alain Gouessant.
COORDINATION ICONOGRAPHIQUE Isabelle de Latour.
SUIVI DE PRODUCTION Fabienne Brifault.
SUIVI DE PARTENARIAT Madeleine Giai-Levra.
RESPONSABLE COMMUNICATION ET PRESSE Valérie Tolstoï.
PRESSE David Ducreux et Alain Deroudilhe.

L'ÂGE D'OR DE L'INDE CLASSIQUE
ÉDITION Michèle Decré-Cyssau.
ICONOGRAPHIE Any-Claude Médioni.
MAQUETTE Valentina Leporé.
LECTURE-CORRECTION Jean-Paul Harris et Jocelyne Marziou.
PHOTOGRAVURE Nouveau CAP.

Amina Okada est conservateur en chef au musée des Arts asiatiques-Guimet, où elle est en charge des collections d'art indien. Elle a été commissaire de plusieurs expositions, en particulier « L'Âge d'or de l'Inde classique, L'Empire des Gupta » (Grand Palais, printemps 2007). Elle est aussi l'auteur d'ouvrages sur l'art et la civilisation de l'Inde : *Ajantâ* (Imprimerie nationale, 1991), *L'Inde du XIXe siècle, Voyage aux sources de l'imaginaire* (Agep Éditeur, 1991), *Le Grand Moghol et ses peintres, Miniaturistes de l'Inde au XVIe et XVIIe siècle* (Flammarion, 1992), *Tâj Mahal* (Imprimerie nationale, 1993), *Ganesh, la mémoire de l'Inde* (Findakly, 1995), *Râjasthân, vision de palais et de forteresses* (Hermé, 2000), *Un joyau de l'Inde moghole, le mausolée d'I'timâd ud-Daulah* (5 Continents, 2003). Elle a contribué à la remise à jour de *L'Art en Inde* (Citadelles et Mazenod, 1999).

Thierry Zéphir est ingénieur d'études au musée des Arts asiatiques-Guimet, où il est rattaché à la section des Arts de l'Asie du Sud-Est. Il enseigne les arts de l'Inde et du monde indianisé à l'École du Louvre et a été commissaire de plusieurs expositions : « Angkor et dix siècles d'art khmer » (Grand Palais, 1997), « Trésors d'art du Vietnam, La sculpture du Champa », en collaboration avec Pierre Baptiste (musée Guimet, 2005-2006), « L'Âge d'or de l'Inde classique, L'Empire des Gupta » (Grand Palais, printemps 2007). Il a collaboré à *L'Art de l'Asie du Sud-Est* (Citadelles et Mazenod, 1994) et à la réactualisation de *L'Art en Inde*, (Citadelles et Mazenod, 1999). Il a aussi publié *L'Empire des rois khmers* (Découvertes-Gallimard, 1997).

*Tous droits de traduction et d'adaptation réservés
pour tous pays © Gallimard/RMN 2007*

Dépôt légal : mars 2007
Numéro d'édition : 15752
ISBN Gallimard : 978-2-07-034161-0
ISBN RMN : 978-2-7118-5322-9
Imprimé en France par Pollina - L42597